GEOFFREY JENKINS

Southtrap

FONTANA/Collins

First published in 1979 by William Collins Sons & Co Ltd
First issued in Fontana Books 1980

© Geoffrey Jenkins 1979

Made and printed in Great Britain by
William Collins Sons & Co Ltd, Glasgow

SOUTHTRAP

GEOFFREY JENKINS was born in Port Elizabeth, South Africa and educated in the Transvaal, where he wrote his first book – a legal history – at the age of seventeen. After leaving school he worked as a sub-editor in Rhodesia, later becoming a newspaperman in both Britain and South Africa.

His first novel, *A Twist of Sand*, was published in 1959 and immediately became a bestseller; it was later filmed. Since then he has written eight more successful novels which sold over five million copies in twenty-three different languages.

Geoffrey Jenkins and his wife Eve Palmer, also an author, live near Pretoria.

Available in Fontana by the same author

A Twist of Sand
The Watering Place of Good Peace
The River of Diamonds
Hunter-Killer
Scend of the Sea
A Cleft of Stars
A Bridge of Magpies

On the frontier of Antarctica
triumph and death
are inseparable companions . . .

RICHARD S. LEWIS
A Continent for Science

FOREWORD

I have taken a liberty with the date when the Royal Navy visited Prince Edward Island during World War II. In fact, the cruiser HMS *Neptune* searched the remote islands of the Southern Ocean for secret U-boat bases in October 1940 and not a year later.

Likewise I have changed slightly the location of the German raiders' secret rendezvous area in the southern Indian Ocean code-named *Sibirien*. For the purposes of my story I have placed it to the south-west, near Prince Edward Island, and attributed it to the free Free Norwegian Navy.

GEOFFREY JENKINS

CHAPTER ONE

Erebus and Terror. The gates of hell. Darkness. Fear. That is what the words meant.

I shivered. The banner which bore these names bellied in the soggy, warm wind from the ship's gangway to which one end had been tied. Then it thumped against her plating, a dull sound like a boxer's punch that hasn't landed square.

'*Erebus-Terror Cruise to Prince Edward Island and the Sub-Antarctic Regions.*'

The banner had been a tourist winner all right, ever since Captain Prestrud had brought the *Quest* into the Cape Town docks ten days before. I wondered whose imaginative brain in Orbit Travels had conjured up the gimmick. We could have filled the *Quest*'s passenger accommodation three times over from the demand it had brought.

Nevertheless, it went against my seaman's grain to dredge up the names of two great ships from their graves – unknown graves in the frozen wastes of the North-West Passage – and exploit them the way the travel agency had done. When ships die, they die. True, HMS *Erebus* and *Terror* had sailed the way we were going to sail – first to Prince Edward and Marion Islands, 2300 kilometres from the Cape and a fifth of the way to Australia; then on eastwards to the Crozets Group, next Kerguelen, and finally New Zealand. That had been in the middle of the last century. They had been under the command of the great polar explorer, Sir James Clark Ross. They had broken open the way to the South Pole and Ross had put a ship's keel where none had ever dared before.

I was now thinking of the ultimate dreadful fate of *Erebus* and *Terror* as I stood on the quayside awaiting a taxi to take me to the hospital. The way the banner flapped kept drawing my attention to it. This warm, sunny, mid-January morning – a slight south-easter was raising an ensign of cloud on Table Mountain – seemed a strange time to be thinking of their fate. But anyone venturing into ice automatically challenges fate as did finally *Erebus* and *Terror*, despite their double oak hulls braced with massive beams, their water-tight compartments and reinforced decks. In the end nothing could have saved them from a fearful death in the ice.

Erebus, I seemed to recall, meant darkness. A name given to the icy regions through which the dead pass into hell. No wonder it was linked with terror.

Now the *Quest* had been linked with them. And the *Quest* wasn't even ice-strengthened.

I shivered.

'Captain!'

I had not noticed the man approach. He seemed to spring from nowhere out of the dockside clutter of cranes, bollards and hawsers. Except that you couldn't hide a man like that, as far as size was concerned.

The sullenness and intensity of the way he addressed me took me entirely by surprise. I guessed him to be in his fifties, but it was hard to tell his age. Weather exposure or possibly whaling could have chiselled his tough features at any stage of life and his looks were not enhanced by a stubbly beard. He wore a sailor's dark rig and a cap without a badge. His gear might have been stamped with the hallmark 'Southern Ocean'.

'Yes?'

He had been waiting for me to respond to the 'Captain', and when I did, a curious flash appeared in his light-blue Viking eyes. It was as out of place as a lightning-strike on a clear day – and as menacing. It was gone in a moment.

He raised his right hand in a kind of salute. If the first two fingers of the hand had not been missing, it might have been a V for Victory sign. As it was, the unnatural gap made a claw, an outsize crab's pincer, of the limb. The action and the hand were jerky and grotesque. They seemed to be activated by inner pressures.

'Captain . . .?' He left the question open-ended.

'Shotton,' I replied. 'John Shotton. And for the record . . .'

He crowded me before I could finish. For some reason he appeared desperately anxious about the captain bit.

'Captain Shotton – sir.'

His attempt at deference didn't come off. It sounded like something he'd worked at, trying to hold down his natural truculence. He wasn't a deck-hand. He'd been used to have men obey him – at the double.

'Wegger.'

He introduced himself in a formal Teutonic way. From his bearing and blue eyes, however, I would have put my head on a block that he was Norwegian, like most of *Quest*'s crew.

'Rolf Wegger. I'm looking for a berth. Your ship – ' he jerked his head in the direction of *Quest* – 'is going South. I know the ice. Whalerman. Know it well.'

I indicated the flapping banner while my mind tried to assess him. I temporized. I might well need the man. Half an hour ago an urgent call from the hospital had summoned me from the bridge: 'Come at once,' it had said. 'Casualty Department, Groote Schuur Hospital. Captain Prestrud is badly injured.'

'This isn't a whaling cruise,' I said to Wegger. 'It's . . .' I fumbled. What *was* the *Erebus-Terror* Cruise? *Quest* certainly was not the *Lindblad Explorer*; she was a converted freighter-cum-passenger vessel a quarter of a century old. That didn't mean to say she hadn't been beautifully built. She had first taken the water from a Bergen shipyard. She was one of the *Thor* type ships. You can always sell an ageing *Thor* ship anywhere. The thirty passengers and scientists the *Quest* would carry were not going to be cosseted behind air-conditioned promenade decks sipping gin and watching Antarctica slide by from a cosy capsule. They were a keen lot. They were going for adventure. The *Quest*'s other name in a safe, dreary world was *Adventure*.

'It's a special kind of cruise,' I told Wegger. 'Semi-scientific. No whales. Whaling is dead in the Southern Ocean anyway. It has been for years.'

'I should know.' He spoke with bitter vehemence. 'I should know.'

'Look here,' I went on. 'I'm not in a position to offer you anything now. I may know more in a couple of hours.'

He said, 'Captain Prestrud – I heard . . . I mean, him being hurt and all that – does that mean the cruise is off?'

There was a curious note in his voice, almost as if he feared to ask the question. He had a grudge against life in his eyes. The cruise – well, I couldn't answer that myself. It depended on how bad Captain Prestrud was.

'Maybe, maybe not. If not, then I may need an officer who knows the ice. What's your experience? Qualifications?'

The tone of his reply surprised me. It was over-eager, almost pleading.

'All the usual certificates. Also radio. I was in catchers — until the international convention killed whaling.'

I wondered for a moment at his mention of radio, an un-usual qualification for a catcher skipper. And at his age he must have been that. I would have to take his word for a lot of what he said; *Quest* was due to sail the next day and there would be no time to check. Yet he seemed competent enough. *Quest*'s second and third officers were young and inexperienced and Wegger could provide the sort of back-up I would like to see. I found myself thinking as though I were already in command of *Quest*, although nothing was more uncertain than that at the moment. Where in hell was that taxi?

'I'll see you aboard at eleven,' I told him. 'I'm on my way to the hospital now. I won't know any of the answers until I have seen Captain Prestrud.'

'He's bad?'

I eyed Wegger curiously, and couldn't help wondering how he'd heard. He was making a great effort to appear casual. I reasoned at the time that his probing about the injured skipper was due to anxiety about the job. He must have been badly on his uppers if it meant that much.

His inquisitiveness made me clam up. 'The hospital didn't say. I didn't speak to a doctor.'

'How come you go to Prince Edward Island?'

The unexpected question brought me up with a start. It was full of vehemence, as if he couldn't hold it back any longer. He took a half-step towards me, the sort of step a boxer makes before a punch.

'It's not my cruise, Wegger,' I retorted. 'I joined the *Quest* here only four days ago. I didn't plan it. Orbit Travels, the travel agency, master-minded it all. *Quest* is due to sail the route taken by Sir James Clark Ross. Prince Edward Island happened to be his first stop from the Cape. So the *Quest* stops there first, too.'

Wegger seemed undecided whether to go on or not.

I spotted a taxi. It slowed down, as if the driver were look-ing for a fare. I broke away from Wegger and flagged it.

A young man with cheeks bunkered by gingery sideburns lowered a rear window. 'The *Quest* . . .?'

'You're here,' I said, nodding towards the ship, 'and I'll take this cab. Dump your gear at the gangway and tell one of the crew to fetch it.'

'I'll see to it, Captain.'

Wegger was next to me again. Despite my hurry I could see that he was now falling over backwards to be obliging.

'You one of the meteorological team?' I asked the newcomer.

He opened the taxi door and got out carrying a couple of long cardboard cylinders.

'No. Volcanologist. I'm Eric Holdgate.'

'Look here, Mr Holdgate . . .'

'Doctor.'

'Sorry. I must get to the hospital – quick. There's been an accident. Captain Prestrud is injured.'

His sideburns champed unhappily. 'D'you mean we may not . . .?'

'I don't know what's happening yet.'

His voice was charged with feeling. 'But I've just *got* to go. It's the chance of a lifetime. How else can I get to Prince Edward Island?' Holdgate seemed more interested in volcanoes than in people. I don't think he noticed how Wegger looked. He said, as if giving a lecture, 'There are two distinct stages of volcanic activity discernible on Prince Edward Island. The old grey trachybasalt from the great cave definitely belongs to the first volcanic stage . . .'

The taxi driver laughed. 'Jeez! I've never driven one like this before!'

Wegger remained staring fixedly at Holdgate. The two remaining fingers of his damaged hand worked inwards towards his thumb as if they were searching for the missing bones.

I wasn't in the frame of mind for puzzling undercurrents. Turning to Holdgate, I snapped, 'We'd better shift your kit. Put it anywhere for now. If you want help from the ship, tell them I told you to ask.'

'Careful with those cylinders,' he replied. 'If those instruments get smashed I'm done for.'

The two of us humped the pile of luggage and parcels from the car. Wegger stood by, not doing a thing to help. When we had finished, Holdgate paid the driver and I got in.

Wegger seemed to snap out of his preoccupation. 'Eleven

11

sharp then, Captain?'

'Yes. Ask for me on the bridge.' Addressing Holdgate, I said, 'I'll let you know about Captain Prestrud as soon as I get back.'

He replied as if making an affirmation, 'That cave on Prince Edward is my whole life, you see.'

I didn't see. But what I did see, as the taxi pulled away, was Wegger staring at Holdgate and clenching and re-clenching his fists.

CHAPTER TWO

The driver brought the taxi round in a sharp right-hander so that we came close under *Quest*'s bows. She might not have been new, but her fine-raked bow with its triple blue stripes on the white hull – typical of the *Thor* class of ships – gave her a timeless beauty, a look of seeking faraway seas.

The taxi driver gestured at her figurehead – however often their names may be changed, *Thor* vessels are always distinguishable by the emblem depicting the god Thor with his right hand raised to cast his magic hammer.

'You running another sideshow, Cap'n?'

I was sitting next to him in the front seat – I never sit behind in a taxi – and he glanced at me in a slightly derisive way.

'Come again?'

'You're in the same place as that old sailing ship – I thought maybe they kept the same spot for the nut-ships.'

'*Quest* isn't a nut-ship. Or a fun-ship. The ice isn't for that type.'

He pulled a crushed packet of cigarettes from his shirt pocket and offered me one, as if approving of my attitude.

'You mean you didn't see that old sailer full of horrors?'

'No.'

A fortnight ago I'd been bringing the stout little store-ship *Captain Cook* in from a routine run from the Southern Ocean islands to Port Elizabeth, 700 kilometres to the east of Cape Town. I had had no idea then that soon I would be taking a ship-load of tourists and scientists the same way again. The *Quest* job was one of those things which come out of the blue, so easy that they seem pre-destined. Like a whirlwind romance. My comparison was spontaneous and bitter. Mine had finished in divorce.

'I thought everyone had seen it,' said the driver.

'I've only been here three or four days,' I replied. 'New job.'

'That explains it.' He shook his head and laughed. 'It was good for business. I taxied half Cape Town to the ship. But the show itself was enough to give anyone the shits.'

I remembered now. I'd seen the windjammer's picture in the paper carrying the advertisement which had brought me the *Quest* job. One long-distance call had practically clinched it. Captain Prestrud had told me to catch the next plane to Cape Town for a face-to-face interview. We had taken to one another at first sight. I had chucked my command of the *Captain Cook* and found myself first officer of the *Quest* in a matter of days. The windjammer the taxi driver was talking about was a modern replica of an old-time Australian convict hell-ship. She had called at the Cape on her way to Sydney.

'*Botany Bay*,' I said.

'Right, that was her name. I went for a look myself after a fare I'd brought to see her came back to the car and had hysterics.'

He chuckled and drew heavily on his cigarette without taking his hands off the wheel.

'My oath, you should have seen this doll! Well dressed, young – well, maybe not too young, but still making the running, if you know what I mean.' He leered at me. 'Comes back to this very car, flops down in the back, starts to gulp and sort of hiccup. Then she says, in a kind of high voice like I've never heard before. "They were cutting his balls off in there, that's what." "Pull yourself together, lady," I says. "They're only wax figures like Madame Tussaud's in London – they're not real."

'Then she looks at me and sort of gasps with the tears runnin' down her cheeks. "That's what's eating me," she kind of moans. "That it wasn't real." '

He took his eyes from the road. 'Women!'

He went on: 'So that's why I went and had a look-see myself. Of course, that doll was imagining things. What she saw was a kind of group – whadderyercallit?'

'Tableau?'

'That's it. Kind of tableau showing how the convicts were put in a salt bath when they first came aboard and were scrubbed with long brushes by the guards. The doll saw it her own way. My oath, she was carrying a load of sex!'

He shook his head again at the vagaries of the opposite sex.

'Was it as bad as that – the rest of the waxworks show, I mean?'

'I'll say. It really gave you the heebie-jeebies seeing what they did to those convicts down under in the early days – guys wearing neck-irons, guys locked in tiny cells where they couldn't sit, stand or kneel. Floggings, torture – you name it, they did it in those old hell-ships. You could see it all the way it was in *Botany Bay*.'

'Now she's on her way to Australia?'

'Left just before your ship came in. That's why I asked, are you another nut-show? The showbiz guy who owns *Botany Bay* must have coined a packet.'

We were approaching the dock entrance gates and he waved towards Cape Town's main street running in the direction of Table Mountain.

'The guide who showed us round the hell-ship said Cape Town just escaped being made a convict settlement and they named Adderley Street after the guy who had it stopped. Maybe that's why all the locals went to see what they'd escaped. Jeez, when I think what they did to those poor sods!'

I was interested in *Botany Bay*. I've sailed in all types of modern yachts and schooners, but never in a square-rigger.

'The owner – did he intend to *sail* her to Australia?'

'Not him. The show loaded him with dollars. He's still living it up at the Mount Nelson Hotel. He'll fly to Australia, and pick up another packet when *Botany Bay* goes on show there. He's got a crew do the dirty work of shifting the ship. Young guys. A dozen or so.

'That day I went to see for myself I heard one of 'em talking to the skipper. "Tom," he says, "the sooner we get to sea, the better. I can't take this circus much longer." "Nor me," the skipper tells him. "But it'll all be different in the Roaring Forties. You'll get all the sailing you want there." Nice guy, I thought.'

I said, 'They'll get all the sailing they want in the Roaring Forties, all right.'

'Know those parts, Cap'n?'

Know them! I've seen the gale-gusts come through the channel between Prince Edward and Marion hitting one hundred and twenty knots, the sea a tormented hell of corrugated water with waves fifteen metres from trough to crest, and the ice spicules spraying like automatic fire on the wind.

'Yes, I know them.'

He glanced sharply at me, and slowed for the dock checkpoint.

'Something wrong, Cap'n?'

'I was thinking of *Botany Bay* down those parts. A sailer. It's a bastard. You have to be tough to survive.'

We halted at the entrance to have our papers cleared. Then the driver pulled away into the open street beyond, making for the big roundabout on the foreshore which would lead us to the hospital on the mountain slope dominating the city.

'That guy was – the one you were speaking to by the ship.'

The driver was not unobservant, for all his blabbermouth.

'You know him?'

'Not to say know exactly. But he's been hanging around ever since *Quest* came in – he must sleep on the docks.'

I had a sudden flash of insight. 'Do you always do the dock run?'

He was cautious. 'What makes you ask?'

'I wondered if you took Captain Prestrud anywhere last night. He finished up in hospital.'

The man's chumminess froze. I could have kicked myself for having mentioned it.

He lied sullenly. 'It was my night off last night.'

We drove on in silence.

I glanced up at the bulk of Table Mountain. A streamer or horn of cloud was starting to work its way round one side preliminary to forming the famous 'tablecloth'. It reminded me of Prince Edward Island. I'd seen the same thing happen there a score of times. A cloud horn suddenly appears against the windward quarter of the mountain peaks of the great western escarpment. Then it works round to the north, shrouding the black summits. I hoped *Botany Bay* would steer clear of Prince Edward. Too many fine ships have gone missing without trace in its wild waters. Some last century and some this. Well-found vessels too, like the Danish training ship *Kobenhavn* perhaps.

Prince Edward Island. I'd be back there again within the week if the cruise was still on. But in what capacity? That depended on what I was going to find at the hospital. 'Severe head injuries but not a car accident.' That's all the hospital had said. He wasn't the right type, nor the right age to have gone on a pre-sailing bender ashore and got mixed up in a brawl in some sleazy joint. Could he have been mugged?

I pulled upright in my seat as the thought struck me. How had Wegger known about Captain Prestrud? He'd seemed very anxious to address me as captain, to feel that I was authorized to take him on in *Quest*. He'd also been hanging around the *Quest* ever since she docked . . .

I slammed on my mental brakes. I was being suspicious without reason. Maybe it was because the intensity of the man was still with me. I had made no secret of Captain Prestrud's injury around the ship – everyone had known within minutes of the hospital's telephone call. If Wegger had been anywhere close on the dockside, he could have heard it from one of the crew. There was nothing to connect Wegger with Captain Prestrud. Nonetheless, I decided to ask Captain Prestrud about him if he were fit enough.

The taxi turned on to the De Waal Drive and picked up speed in the direction of Groote Schuur Hospital. The driver pretended he was too occupied with the road for any further talk.

If Captain Prestrud were too badly hurt to carry on with the cruise, what then? Had *Quest*'s voyage simply been a tourist trip, it could have been called off. Linn Prestrud, Captain Prestrud's daughter, was due with the main party of passengers by jet from Europe that afternoon. They would be disappointed, but it was the scientists who were the real problem. The *Quest* had given a hard-and-fast commitment – no, it was more than that: it was a contract involving a time factor.

Quest was a key cog in an international meteorological

project known as the Global Atmospheric Research Programme in which one hundred and forty-five nations were taking part. She had been commissioned to launch, in the seas of the Southern Ocean where ships hardly ever go, a sophisticated drifting instrumented buoy which would gather marine and weather information. This would be transmitted via satellite to the American National Center for Atmospheric Research at Boulder, Colorado.

Quest also had the task of releasing a special high-altitude stratosphere balloon which would supply similar automatic data. Captain Prestrud himself had informed me that this was the bread-and-butter which would finance the *Quest*'s cruise – the passengers were secondary contributors. An intricate web of international communications – satellites, radio, telexes, computers – were already in operation in anticipation of *Quest*'s lonely voyage.

I wondered for one brief moment if I should risk taking Captain Prestrud along, if he were not too seriously injured. I immediately discarded the idea. The Roaring Forties are no place for the unfit, let alone the injured. That meant I had to have another officer. *Quest* had got to sail tomorrow and that didn't leave much time to find one. But Wegger had turned up as if in answer to prayer. His papers had seemed in order. It looked as if I was going to have to take Wegger.

We turned into the hospital grounds.

CHAPTER THREE

It was like hearing a mummy speak from out of its wrappings. His voice was so distorted by pain and the bandages that I hardly recognized it.

'John – is that you, John?'

'Yes, sir. This is John Shotton.'

I stood in the hospital ward and looked down at the figure in the bed. My comparison with a mummy persisted – the bandages which swathed his head were white, what was visible of the tanned face was off-white, and the faintly pungent, acrid smell of the medicaments was throat-catching, faintly sickly, like the odour of a mummy. The gallows-like iron thing – for patients to haul themselves upright, if they could – might have doubled for the device ancient Egyptian embalmers used for handling corpses. I could have used a brandy, even at that time of the morning.

'Is the *Quest* ready for sea?'

I hesitated before answering. Captain Prestrud reached out a hand and gripped my arm. I was surprised at the strength in it. Then I realized there were no injuries except on his head and face. All the damage was concentrated there.

'*Is she?*'

Pain dimmed his eyes, sunk deep in their sockets. He tried to focus on me past the helmet of bandages. Five minutes only, the nurse had warned. Now I realized she was being generous.

'John,' he said more strongly. 'I liked you from the moment I clapped eyes on you. You were the sort of man I needed for the *Quest*. An officer who could take over from me, any time, any place. Almost my second self.'

The feeling had been mutual. I had never met anyone I came to admire so much in such a short time. That was what had induced me to throw up my own ship and sign on as his second-in-command. That, and the fact that *Quest* was going to those far Southern seas that I longed to explore.

Before I could stumble out a reply he went on, 'I want you to take the *Quest* to sea tomorrow.'

'That's what I've come about,' I said.

He tried to pull himself up into a sitting position. His face clouded with a spasm of agony. He fell back, eyes shut. I reached across him for the emergency bell.

He must have guessed what I was doing. He raised his arm and chopped weakly at mine.

'Leave it, John. Leave it. Give me a moment. I've got to say something to you. Alone. Quickly.'

I waited. His eyes came open again. He was breathing in sharp spurts.

'What's holding up *Quest*?' he gasped. 'Is Linn delayed? The buoy . . .?'

'Linn is due with the bulk of the passengers this afternoon,' I assured him. 'The first of the scientists came aboard just as I was leaving the ship. The Weather Bureau's buoy is due this afternoon by special trailer from up-country. I'll have everything ship-shape and Bristol-fashion and ready for sea by this evening.'

He said in a firmer voice, 'Then there's nothing to stop you sailing first thing tomorrow.'

Except – I thought, but I didn't say it – that *Quest* was his own ship. He had sweated and saved his whole life to buy her, and now someone else was to take over his dream.

I said gently, 'We can't sail without you.'

He lay silent with his eyes closed for so long that I thought he had passed out.

He spoke at last. 'Yes, I'll be missing, John. I think you know what *Quest* and this cruise mean to me, don't you?'

'Yes, I know.'

He went on so softly that I had to lean forward to hear. 'Sometimes a man does something which seems right at the time, seems justified by events. But it changes his whole life. It comes back and haunts him. And it snatches away what he wants most of all.'

It sounded to me as if his mind was wandering.

Suspected brain damage, the nurse had warned me outside. Could be a piece of smashed skull bone pressing on the brain. They'd have to operate. It was only his will that was keeping him conscious.

I remembered her words. I let his answer go.

He opened his eyes and fixed me. 'I want you to promise, John, that you'll take the *Quest* to sea tomorrow. And tell my daughter Linn that I want her to sail whatever happens to me.'

'If that's the way you want it.'

'It's the way I want it.'

'*Quest* will sail tomorrow morning,' I assured him.

He gave a couple of jerky little sighs and tried to smile. His pulped lips weren't meant for smiling. I saw they'd smashed some of his teeth, too.

He said, 'It was like a dream, John. You know the way the light is, far South in high latitudes, in the middle of the summer? The night was all blue and silver. The mist was on the water like ghostly icebergs – you couldn't tell which was which. There'd been snow a little while before – squalls coming in from the south-west. Then it cleared about two in the morn-

19

ing. The first we knew of her was her searchlight lighting up the two factory ships and the catchers all moored round her, like puppies drinking. We couldn't see her six-inch guns because the searchlight blinded us. We had a few oil lights strung in our rigging. I remember thinking how warm they looked, and how icy and deadly the searchlight was – just like the Germans.'

Brain damage. Bone pressing on the brain. Yes, I'd seen that blue mystic light in the middle of the short Antarctic summer's night. Like a dream. Captain Prestrud in his delirium had recaptured its beauty. I wondered whether I had just made a promise to a man so sick that I shouldn't hold myself to it.

I got up to go for help. The windows in front of me showed a great sunlit view of far mountains; on my left were the sea and shipping of Table Bay. It was beautiful – and real. But Captain Prestrud's scene had the haunting quality of unreality.

I moved to the door and his voice went on: '. . . I often wished I'd met *Pinguin*'s captain. Krüder was first of all a sailor and a man. Only secondly a Nazi. He went down with *HK-33* when the British caught up with her.'

Pinguin – HK-33! One of the great surface raiders of World War II! Kapitän zur See Krüder, the legend!

I turned back from the door. I simply *had* to hear what Captain Prestrud had to say, however incoherent it might be.

His eyes opened when he sensed me back at his side.

'Do you know what a quisling is, John?'

He looked very bad: I knew I ought to go for help.

'I've heard the word,' I said.

'The quislings were the Norwegians who betrayed us to the Nazis.' He tried to smile but winced instead.

'We got him, Torgersen, Jacobsen and I. He came strutting aboard us with the raider's boarding party. He didn't learn those manners from Krüder. But he'd done his traitor's job and he was feeling proud of himself.'

It was like trying to piece together the bits of a jigsaw when you didn't know what the master-pattern was.

'Who was *he*, Captain Prestrud?'

He replied, very wearily. 'Krüder had three radio operators aboard the *Pinguin*. Two were German. The third was Norwegian – he had a German mother. He was the only one who

understood the R/T chatter between us Norwegian catcher
skippers. It was he who homed *Pinguin* on us. We never
knew *Pinguin* was near until she broke through the mist with
her searchlight on and her guns trained on us. She snapped
up the lot – two factory ships and eleven catchers. The whole
whaling fleet. Not a shot fired. That was the way Krüder
planned it. No loss of life . . .'

'The quisling . . .?' I prompted.

He lay back, silent, and I was afraid that the nurse would
appear before he'd told me more. I'd been there a shade over
five minutes.

'He killed Torgersen for it later,' muttered Captain Prestrud.
'He got a life sentence for the murder. John, you must promise
me that the anniversary celebration will go on in *Quest* even
though I'm not there . . .'

'What *happened*?' I demanded in a low voice. I thought
I heard someone outside the door. 'What *happened*, Captain
Prestrud!'

He blinked in a dazed manner. 'Maybe I . . . we . . .
shouldn't have done it. But it seemed right at the time. It
was war.' He appeared to get a grip on himself. 'The quisling
came aboard at the head of the Nazi boarding party. Torgersen
knocked him down. We took him with us.'

'You were captured, Captain Prestrud. Remember? You
and the entire Norwegian whaling fleet.'

'I kept warning the others we weren't safe, even deep
down there in the ice,' he muttered. 'That's why we had the
torpedo ready, night and day. It came down the greasy whale
slip as easy as easy.'

I turned away. He was mouthing words that made no sense.
Then came a laugh so startling that I turned back to the
bed.

'We escaped, the three of us – Torgersen, Jacobsen and I.
In our catchers. We went right past *Pinguin*, under her guns.
Krüder didn't fire. He wasn't the sort to open up on little
catchers.' He laughed again. 'He ordered me on the R/T,
"Turn back or be sunk," I just said, "Can't. Engine stuck" –
and I went ahead. Torgersen and Jacobsen covered me on
both flanks so that *Pinguin* wouldn't spot the torpedo . . .'

The door opened and the nurse made an imperative gesture with her head. 'Out!'

Captain Prestrud opened his eyes. Perhaps he saw me, perhaps not. But he knew I was there, because he called out urgently, desperately: 'John! *Stay away from Dina's Island!'*

The nurse was advancing on me. I hurried through the doorway.

Two doctors, a younger and an older, gave way for me as they were entering.

I said to the older man, 'He's in a bad way. He's been mugged.'

He said, 'I know. I examined him earlier. He wasn't mugged. He was pistol-whipped.'

CHAPTER FOUR

Dina the island was a non-event.

Back aboard the *Quest* after my visit to the hospital, I spread open in front of me in the ship's chartroom a chart of the Southern Ocean.

It showed Prince Edward as one of a handful of remote uninhabited islands of the Sub-Antarctic, tiny specks in the vastness of the wildest ocean in the world. The area into which *Quest* was due to venture was roughly a triangle with equal legs measuring 2300 kilometres, having Cape Town as the starting-point, Prince Edward as the south-eastern terminal, and Bouvet Island as the southernmost terminal. This is a wind desert without a history. It has never known the keels of battle fleets and if it had the sound of guns would have been puny beside its own thundering. It is colder than outer space; there are no stars because they are hidden by its ceaseless storm-wracks.

I scanned the area on the chart for any annotation, any clue, which Captain Prestrud might have left to indicate Dina's Island.

There was nothing.

I stood there staring at the great blanks between the pinpoints of islands. The West Wind Drift, it is called. Into these hostile seas the *Quest* would launch the drifter buoy with its sensitive instruments which would automatically relay via the orbiting satellite the hitherto unknown facts about currents, temperature, wind and drift. The stratosphere balloon would supplement its readings. It would be the first time man had attempted to put an electronic girdle round the Southern Ocean. The method to be used would be similar to the one which had succeeded in the frozen wastes of outer space – the automatic instrumented probe.

I had had personal acquaintance with these waters; I knew more about them than anything Captain Prestrud's chart showed. I paged through some manuals which complemented the chart – the Admiralty's *Antarctic Pilot*, the American *Manual of Ice Seamanship*, and the US Navy's *Marine Climatic Atlas*. For anyone like myself who had actually stuck out a Southern Ocean blow they made nice safe academic reading. They contained no reference to Dina's Island.

I decided, categorically, that Dina's Island did not exist.

My attention strayed from the chart and books to the chartroom itself. It was a warm, friendly, dark-panelled place, more like a library than a chartroom. I had to carry out my search, but I felt as if I were intruding into someone else's home. Captain Prestrud had chosen the *Quest* for more than just her sea-going qualities. A *Thor* ship has that something extra. And *Quest* had it – the chartroom was an example. She was small – only 5000 tons – beautifully proportioned, with a fine raked bow. Despite nearly a quarter of a century at sea, her 5600 horse-power Sulzer engines were still in splendid shape. I did not intend to drive her, but I might need their full 15½ knots where we were bound. The original excellent passenger accommodation had been for twelve in two double and eight single cabins. Cabins for the extra eighteen who were booked on the cruise had been added aft in the former No. 3 'tween decks.

I began to put the chart away. As I did so, my eye was caught by some writing underneath the folio and serial numbers to be found on all charts. It was neatly printed in Indian ink.

It read: *Teddy. Atlantis-Pinguin-Sibirien. January 14th 1941.*

Pinguin – that was Krüder's raider! The name was still fresh in my mind. Why should it crop up again here? I stared at the other names. They meant as little to me as Dina's Island. The

23

chart was an old one. For close-approach work to Prince
Edward I'd been using a newer one, but if it was a typical day
I wouldn't see the island until it was under *Quest*'s bows.

My train of speculation was broken by a knock at the door.
'Come in!'

It was McKinley, *Quest*'s second officer. One of my reasons
for wanting to get South was to see a 50-knotter blow
McKinley's hair-style to rags. Had Captain Prestrud taken
him on merely to squire the lady passengers?

He said in a bored voice, 'There's a rough type here says
he wants to see you.'

'McKinley,' I said. 'This isn't the Royal Navy, but you'll
address me as sir in future. Understood?'

His limpid eyes flickered more with amusement than anger.
'Understood – sir.'

'Have you got that searchlight rigged for'ard in the bows?'

I'd saved my skin before at night among the growlers and
bergy bits – those chunks of ice smaller than an iceberg which
break away from the parent berg and litter the sea – by
spotting with a searchlight. Growlers float low in the water.
Radar is helpless. In a storm, which happens often, white-
tops look just like growlers anyway. I wasn't happy about
the *Quest* not being ice-strengthened. I'd never used a ship
before in the Southern Ocean that wasn't. I felt unprotected
– like an Antarctican in underpants.

'Well – you see, I was side-tracked by some problems with
the forepeak tank so I . . .' He exercised his winning smile.

'Listen, McKinley,' I said emphatically. 'When I give an
order, I mean it to be carried out. Not some time or never
but now. We're headed for dangerous waters. A man's life
– the ship's life – can depend on everyone being on the alert.
Understood?'

He got my message, this time.

'Aye, aye, sir.'

'Then get the bloody thing rigged. Now.' I snapped. 'And
send Mr Wegger in.'

'*Mister* Wegger?' he asked.

'You may be in for a surprise soon,' I retorted as he left.

Wegger had certainly willed himself on to *Quest*, and I
would have preferred some elbow-room in choosing a new
officer. But we sailed tomorrow. The McKinleys might have

their place entertaining passengers but the sort of man I wanted out there where the ice was, was Wegger's type.

He came in, looking as if he were frapped with steel wire, and asked right away, 'How is Captain Prestrud, sir?'

'He's bad. They're operating now. Skull fracture.'

'What chance has he got, sir?'

I shrugged for reply.

Wegger made a gesture of enquiry which took in the chart which I had still not put away, and the ship at large. He must have heard me giving orders to McKinley.

I answered his unspoken question. '*Quest* sails tomorrow. I've taken over.'

He gave a smile, if you could call it that. It was more a self-satisfied twitch of the lips.

'I'm glad, sir.'

'How do you mean, you're glad?'

'I mean, I'm glad *Quest* will be sailing after all, and I'd rather see you in command than anyone else. I know a sailor when I see one.'

Oddly enough, I felt that he wasn't trying to flatter me. It was a sizing-up, as if he were gauging the odds.

I had a sudden thought. 'What do you know about Dina's Island?'

His face and eyes remained blank. But the cords knotted in his neck as if he were trying to raise the anchor from the seabed all on his own.

'Never heard of it,' he said.

'Nor have I.'

He picked his next words. 'Then what makes you ask, sir?'

All of a sudden there was about him that intensity which I had noticed earlier in the day, as if the pressure inside him were mounting to bursting-point.

'Captain Prestrud mentioned it.'

I could see Wegger was holding something back. His next words were too casual. It was this that decided me to tell him nothing more of what Capain Prestrud had said.

'What did he say?'

'It doesn't matter,' I replied. 'There is no Dina's Island. He probably didn't know what he was saying.'

'If he was as bad as you say, that's probably it.'

Wegger ought really to have been asking me about the job,

not concerning himself with Captain Prestrud. I hadn't got to the bottom of this, but it didn't make me any less keen to have a first-class officer aboard.

I asked, 'What do you know about Prince Edward Island?'

'I've been there.'

'When?'

I couldn't read his eyes.

'Years ago. Not recently.'

'I was there only a couple of weeks ago,' I said. 'It's the *Quest*'s first port of call – if by any stretch of the imagination you could call it a port.'

He then said, 'Why is *Quest* going to Prince Edward? There's nothing there. The logical stop would be Marion – it's only twenty-two kilometres away. It's also inhabited – the permanent weather teams are stationed there. They'd be glad to have a big ship like this call. And to see the tourists – plus a bit of skirt, whatever shape might be inside. They do a year's stint on Marion without a sight of a woman.'

'I told you this morning,' I replied. 'This cruise is following the route taken by HMS *Erebus* and *Terror*. They called at Prince Edward – or tried to. In fact, they never landed at all. They hove to off the island for the night but a gale caught them and blew them sixty miles towards the Crozets. That's why the *Quest* is bound for Prince Edward.'

'You're prepared to risk a ship for that sort of lark?'

'It's not my decision. That's the way the cruise has been planned. Miss Prestrud will fly in with the tourists this afternoon. That's what they're paying to get – and we've got to give it to them.'

I realized that by saying 'we' I had included him.

He went on forcefully, 'If the wind shifts south-east when you're anchored off Cave Bay, you can say your prayers.'

'I know. But it's usually out of the west, or south-west.'

'What about the kelp barrier?' he demanded further. 'If it fouls *Quest*'s engine intakes, you'll never get clear.'

The more I heard of his expertise, the more I knew that Wegger was the sort of officer I wanted. McKinley probably thought kelp was a new hair-spray. Nonetheless, I wasn't having Wegger supply me with a lesson in seamanship.

'Just for the record, Wegger, I've done a milk-run through the islands for some years now – Marion, Gough – keeping the weather stations supplied. I know.'

He eyed me. Something was still nagging him.

But my mind was jumping ahead to the thousand and one jobs which still lay ahead in order to get the *Quest* ready for sea.

I said briefly, 'This ship's in a mess. Can you start now? Not this afternoon, or in an hour, but right now. The job's yours if you can.'

'What job?'

'First officer.'

He looked surprised, then replied after a short pause, 'Right now it is. I brought my gear aboard – just in case.'

'Good. Then . . .' I was about to start on technicalities when he pulled a pistol out of his pocket and threw it on to the chart that lay half-rolled upon the table in front of me.

It was an old 9mm Luger with a four-inch barrel, one of those early war-time guns collectors go crazy about. But this wasn't a collector's gun. It had a streak of rust from the muzzle to the safety-catch.

'Mind if I bring this along?'

'Why?'

'If we're going ashore at Prince Edward I want some protection against the skuas.' He rolled up his left sleeve. There was a long scar on the forearm in the place where a man might throw up his arm to protect his head.

He said venomously, 'One of 'em did that. I hate the bastards. There's only one thing for them – shoot them.'

I said, 'All the wild life is protected. Both Prince Edward and Marion are nature reserves. Don't forget.'

He gave an exaggerated laugh. 'Show me just one game ranger on those goddamned places! If we shoot a few birds, who's going to know?'

He was right of course. And those skuas have no fear of man. I'd been attacked by them on my own deck.

'How much ammunition have you got?'

He put two small boxes next to the pistol. One had been breached.

'About a hundred rounds.'

'That's a lot of shells.'

'There's a lot of skuas.'

'All right then. But take it easy, Wegger. I don't want any complaints. Only if it's absolutely necessary . . .'

He leaned forward to scoop up the shells with his sound left hand. As their weight came off the chart it rolled itself up an inch or two of its own accord so that the names which had been inked in were under his fingers.

He snapped the parchment down again so hard that it crackled. He stared at the names as if transfixed: *Teddy. Atlantis-Pinguin-Sibirien. January 14th 1941.*

'Where does this come from?'

His question came out like a pistol shot as he picked up the Luger. He was so stunned by what he had just read that I don't think he realized what he was doing nor where he was pointing the gun.

In fact he was pointing it straight at me.

CHAPTER FIVE

Several hours later after lunch, I was alone in the Captain's cabin. I felt even more of an intruder than in the chartroom earlier. Captain Prestrud had left his imprint upon the place, even in the short time he had owned *Quest*. A big roll-top desk, old-fashioned and friendly, contained a mixture of official and private papers and photographs. A smoked pipe and tobacco jar and an unfinished letter all pointed to a man who had gone out and meant to come back. But I couldn't help doubting Captain Prestrud would ever return.

I could still sense his warm presence. It was here that I had had my interview for the *Quest* job. The ship's documents were now my immediate concern. For the sorting and clearing of the desk with its personal possessions I decided to await Linn's arrival. Among his books I noted Captain Benjamin Morrell's autobiographical *Voyage to the Antarctic*, dating back a century and a half. After its publication Morrell had been dubbed a liar but in the course of time his accounts were confirmed by others. I made a mental note to check if he mentioned Dina's Island.

Dina's Island – the chart. Why had Wegger attached so

much importance to it?

It was a question I had asked myself a score of times while sorting out all the things that needed doing to get the *Quest* ready for sea. I had asked him point-blank as he stood there staring at the chart: What was it that had shaken him so?

It had got me really rattled. Wegger had come aboard trailing as much tension as a primed hijacker's grenade and then this business of the chart. I was on the point of revoking my offer of the job. He sensed this, and had explained quickly that he had been serving in *Teddy,* a supply tanker to the Norwegian Antarctic whaling fleet at the outbreak of World War II. It was just that the unexpected sight of a chart from his first ship had touched a nostalgic chord of memory.

It sounded phoney. I told him so.

He then said that the *Teddy* had been captured and burned early in the war by a German raider and that it had moved him to see this tangible relic of her all these years later.

Wegger looked to me as sensitive as those Antarctic fish which don't need haemoglobin in their blood, they are so tough.

'What raider?' I asked.

With the third finger of his wrecked right hand he had stabbed the name hand-printed on the chart. *Atlantis.*

But he couldn't – or wouldn't – offer an explanation for that last name, *Sibirien*, or the date, or any possible connection with the other German raider *Pinguin.*

He was saved from further cross-examination by McKinley bursting in to say that the clutch on a derrick winch loading Number 3 hatch, between the bridge and the stack, had stripped. With it out of action, we'd never get to sea in time.

If I had my doubts about Wegger in one respect, I had no reason to question my judgment of him as a seaman in the next few hours. He personally took on the job of repairing the clutch – which even I considered to be a shore workshop job – and laboured at it, stripped and sweating in the hot wind, driving his squad as mercilessly as an old-time bucko mate until the job was done. When I was sure loading had been resumed, I made my way for'ard along the deck past the lifeboats – painted red for emergency sighting in the ice – to check the Captain's cabin. As the *Quest*'s new captain the cabin was now mine.

I left the desk and opened the ship's safe with the combination numbers I had discovered in a drawer. The *Quest*'s documents were all there, together with the wages for the crew. I riffled through the papers. Everything was in order.

Under a ledger I found a folding leather case, the sort of frame which is intended to house portrait photographs. I opened it. One half was empty: the other revealed a picture of one of the most beautiful women I have ever seen. She was young, dark, and her eyes seemed a little heavy. There was about her a timeless loveliness, a heart-stopping quality, and at the same time an almost unnatural stillness, a curiously blank expression in the eyes. She wore a sealskin jerkin with a high Cossack-like collar. I couldn't make out any more details.

I knelt down to get more light on the picture, but it didn't help. The photograph itself was poor. It looked as if it had been shot through glass with an electric flash.

Could this enigmatic face possibly be that of Linn Prestrud, now our tour leader?

'What are you doing with my father's belongings?'

As I spun round to face her, my mental tumblers fell into place as surely as those of the safe's combination: it wasn't Linn Prestrud's portrait that I held. It was she who stood in the doorway. Hers was an animated face by contrast with the picture's – somewhat puzzled, a little angry, maybe. Jet-lag after her 6000-mile flight from Europe showed round her green-grey eyes; she held her head back in a way which I was always to associate with her. She looked about twenty-five. Blue slacks with a blue-and-white striped top enhanced her slim figure. Her top blouse button was undone.

I felt at a disadvantage down on the floor, like a kid caught stealing jam. I said nothing and got to my feet.

She pushed aside a drift of corn-gold hair which was falling across her right temple.

'Who are you?'

'John Shotton. You must be Linn Prestrud.'

Her glance went over my grubby uniform. 'What are you doing prying into my father's things?'

A line that ran from the right-hand corner of her mouth showed how tired and tense she was.

I said quietly, 'You've had a long flight. Sit down and I'll order some coffee. Then I'll explain what I'm doing here and we'll work out things together.' I dreaded the moment when I would have to break the news about her father.

'Together? I don't even know who you are.'

'Until this morning I was the first officer. Your father hired me.'

She gave me a long searching look which came to rest on the photograph in my hand.

'What is that photograph you're stashing away in the safe?'

I held it out without replying and she came close. She had the dry, closed-in smell of jet travellers – upholstery, deodorants, the sterile accoutrements of high altitudes.

'Lovely face,' she said. 'But something odd about it.'

'I've never seen her before,' I told her. 'I've just found it tucked away in your father's safe.'

'That makes two of us.' She held the photograph sideways to get more light, as I had done.

'It's out of focus, or something,' she said.

'Or something. It must be your father's. I'd say it was rather precious to him too, to keep it locked away in a safe.'

I went to the desk and rang the chief steward. 'I want two cups of coffee and some sandwiches. In the Captain's cabin. Right away.' I listened to his reply for a moment. 'I don't give a damn whether or not twenty passengers have just come aboard. I want that coffee here quick.'

Linn Prestrud said, 'Anyone would think you were captain of this ship.'

I took the photograph from her and put it back in the safe.

'They'd be right,' I said. 'That's just what I am. And it's just what I want to talk to you about.'

I sat her down in a well-worn leather easy-chair and took Captain Prestrud's revolving desk-chair myself.

'Cigarette?'

'Thanks. I don't smoke.'

I couldn't see anything of her father in her features but she had something of his controlled warmth. I found it very attractive.

I said slowly, 'Your father has been injured and he is in hospital . . .' I gave her a quick run-down on the situation. She listened in shocked silence; when I told her the extent of his head injuries her fingers went to the undone blouse button and subconsciously fastened it, as if trying to shut out the bad news. As I proceeded to tell her the whole story, her eyes misted. I was relieved when the steward arrived with the coffee and sandwiches. I poured her a cup of strong coffee. Her hand trembled as she took the cup. She refused a sandwich.

As soon as the man was gone she said, 'I must get to the hospital right away.'

'I'm afraid there's nothing you can do at the moment,' I said gently. 'I received a call from the hospital just before you arrived. He's in a deep coma now, and they don't expect him to come out of it – not at least until after the operation. He should be in the operating theatre at this moment.'

'I must go just the same. My God, he's my father!' she said, choking with emotion.

I put a hand on her shoulder and told her of my last conversation with him a couple of hours ago. I told her that her father had made me promise to sail on schedule whatever happened to him. I also told her of his last request and my promise to tell her she must sail on *Quest* as arranged.

Quietly, she picked up her bag, asked me to call a taxi, and said she would be back as soon as she could. She gulped the last of her coffee, and was gone.

When she returned, a couple of hours later, her eyes red with tears, she came straight to my cabin and sat down in the chair she'd occupied earlier. She gave a deep sigh, and a pathetic smile.

'I don't know what to call you,' she said. 'I can't really call you Captain . . .'

'John will do,' I said. 'It's because of your stake in what is basically your father's dream that I want to talk to you.'

'Meaning?'

I was grateful to be deflected from the emotional aspect. She was taking the crisis well.

'What worries me is that I may have promised your injured father something that I had no right to promise.'

'Meaning?' she said again in a voice as faraway as Prince Edward Island.

'I gave your father an assurance that I would take *Quest* to

32

sea tomorrow on schedule to launch the drifter buoy and balloon. You are as much part of this cruise as he was. I think the decision ought now to be yours.'

'He must have trusted you very much to have asked you that,' she said.

'For the record, I greatly admire and like your father. But I feel like an actor stepping into someone else's part. I haven't the same motivations.'

She once again fiddled with the top button of her blouse. 'You may think so, John. But when you mentioned the Southern Ocean just now you talked in quite a different voice. My father must have noticed it too. That's why he asked you to step into his shoes.'

'There's no glamour down there in the ice, Linn, whatever the Orbit Travels' sales talk might have been. It's an icy hell which breaks men's bodies as well as their spirits. Prince Edward Island is nothing but one twin of a volcanic peak which had the nerve to stick its head out into the storms. If you want to see what a mere few thousand years of gales can do to solid rock you want to take a look at the western cliffline of the island where it faces the winds. It's the windpipe of the world, down there. Your ship can lie off for a month waiting for one day calm enough to land – if her engines can take it. I've known a destroyer's turbines at full revs unable to make headway of one knot against the wind. I *know*. I've been there.'

'And you've always gone back.'

I looked into her eyes. Tiredness and grief had receded. They were alive. She had Captain Prestrud's Southern Ocean genes in her.

I went on: 'You must face the fact that your father could die. Today. Tomorrow. Any time. And *Quest* will belong to you. It's your decision.'

'No,' she said, 'it's not mine alone. It's your decision too. You made up your own mind – and promised my father. But before I make my own decision, there are things I want to know which you haven't yet told me.'

I said, somewhat defensively, 'I've given you all the facts.'

'Facts – but not your impressions. Or your mental reservations.'

I lit another cigarette. So intent had I been on our conversation that I had stubbed out my first, half-smoked, in the ashtray.

I said, 'In the Southern Ocean you can be making your way through seas where you know there shouldn't be ice. Where there *can't* be ice. But you get a *feel,* a hunch that it's around. It's often too late even if you can smell it. Your ship's on it before you can put your helm hard over. That's how I feel about this cruise. There's ice about – but I don't know where.'

She looked at me wonderingly. 'You're a strange sort of man for a ship's captain,' she said.

I tried to laugh it off. 'Fanciful, you mean? Let's forget it. For a cruise like this you need a strong ship and strong men and we've got both.'

'No,' she said. 'We can't forget it. You're so worried about the *Quest*'s cruise, and I want to know why.'

'You're going to laugh at this,' I said slowly. 'I'm superstitious. Doesn't fit in the space age, does it? But there it is. I don't like starting a voyage on a Friday.'

She leaned forward impulsively as if to touch my arm, and then withdrew.

'That's not the whole of it,' she said. 'A skipper like you wouldn't be put off by superstition alone.'

Still I tried to fence. I didn't want to voice my fears.

'*Quest*'s a fine ship but she's old, and above all she isn't ice-strengthened. The later *Thor* ships that went up the St Lawrence seaway were ice-strengthened. It's very important. Without it a bergy bit on a dark night could tear open the plating as if it were brown paper. Don't forget we've got the lives of thirty passengers and scientists at risk.'

'I don't forget. Go on.'

Rather to my own surprise I did go on. 'There's another thing that's worrying me. It's the man I hired today as first officer. His name's Rolf Wegger. He's the right type, he's got all the right qualifications and he's already proved what he can do. With your father out of action it's essential I should have the right kind of support. There's no doubt that he can give it, but there's something about him I don't understand and don't like.'

'What's the matter with him?'

'I wish I knew. Little inconsistencies – things that don't ring true. He's as tough as they come and yet the sight of some old tanker's name written on a chart threw him into a flat spin. He said it made him feel nostalgic. Then there's Prince Edward Island. He says he's not been there for years but he seems to have some sort of obsession about it.'

It sounded lame and I could see she wasn't impressed. She said, 'Aren't these pretty nebulous grounds for anxiety? Especially at this late stage of things?'

'All I know is, I smell ice. Dangerous ice.'

She stood up. 'Thanks for taking me into your confidence, John. As far as I'm concerned the decision's already been made. As you promised my father, the *Quest* sails tomorrow.'

I felt as if I had lost her. 'I also promised your father that the dinner he'd planned to mark the anniversary of some wartime escapade he was involved in would go ahead without him.'

Linn said, 'Oh yes, I'd forgotten Captain Jacobsen. He was with Dad at the time. The dinner's for him, too. He'll have to be told about this business. He was on the plane with me.'

'Do you know anything about your father's war-time adventures?' I asked.

'Not very much. He didn't talk about them. I only know he escaped with two other catchers when the Antarctic whaling fleet was captured by a German surface raider.'

'So you don't know any details? Nothing about something he did and later felt guilty about? Nothing about a torpedo?'

'Did he tell you this himself?' she asked quietly.

'Yes, but he may have been delirious. He was in and out of a coma,' I replied. 'That's why I hesitated about my promise to him.'

She came so close that I could see the tiny golden flecks in her eyes. 'He said something else that's eating you, didn't he? Something you haven't told me?'

'Not your father,' I answered, 'but the doctor. He said your father's injuries had been caused by being pistol-whipped.'

Before she could reply, there was a knock at the door and Wegger came in.

CHAPTER SIX

'Sorry to interrupt, sir, but the weather team has just arrived on the dockside with the drifter buoy. They want to see you. Got to have the captain. You'd think the thing was made of gold.'

'It's the star of our show,' I replied. 'In a way it's the most valuable thing we'll be carrying in the *Quest*.'

He looked curiously at Linn. 'This is Miss Prestrud,' I said. 'Our tour leader. Captain Prestrud's daughter.'

A moment before, Wegger's bearing had been no more than that of a busy, competent officer. His oil-stained overalls, open to reveal his hairy chest, added to the picture. But as I introduced Linn there came over him that strange intensity I had sensed at our first meeting.

'You don't look like your father.'

No polite formalities, no sign of sympathy or concern, just that jerky, out-of-context remark.

It produced a silence between the three of us. In that vacuum, the thought struck me – to be able to make the comparison, Wegger must have met Captain Prestrud. That meant he had been lobbying for the job before I appeared on the scene.

Wegger jounced his oil-stained cap between his hands. He asked curtly, 'The cruise – it's still on?'

'Captain Shotton and I have discussed it,' Linn replied coldly.

Her tone pulled Wegger up short. He said hastily, 'All I meant was that if it's not, there's no point in rushing things the way we're doing – there are hundreds of things still to be done . . .'

'Go ahead, Mr Wegger, the cruise is on,' I told him. 'We sail first thing tomorrow.'

'Good. The drifter buoy . . .?'

'All right. I'm coming. Join me, Linn?'

She nodded. I found my cap – its badge depicted a penguin, which I thought ridiculous, but Captain Prestrud had insisted it was part of the tour motif – and we went out on deck.

Wegger went quickly aft ahead of us towards a group on the quayside opposite one of the ship's main lifeboats. McKinley was at the foot of the ladder to the main deck chatting to a dark girl whose sultriness exploded into a constellation of acne on her left cheek.

When we had passed them, Linn said, 'That's Barbara. She's the head of the Knowledge Hounds.'

'She'll get knowledge from McKinley all right.' I grinned at her. 'What sort of hounds did you say you'd brought aboard my ship?'

She slowed, as if not wanting to reach the quayside group too soon.

Her smile was all the more attractive because of its slight irregularity. 'They're very important passengers, Captain Shotton. The Knowledge Hounds. Five of them. Four women and one man. Never heard of them?'

'Never?'

'It's a society in Britain which specializes in in-depth studies of faraway places. Very intense. Very knowledgeable. They first got in touch with me because they thought the *Quest* was making for the Diomede Islands.'

'Don't trouble to ask whether I've heard of them. I haven't.'

'They're frozen islands in the Bering Sea. Twins like Marion and Prince Edward, but the other side of the world.'

'What made them pick on Prince Edward, for Pete's sake?'

She halted. 'What do you think made me?'

The south-easter was blowing her fine hair into her eyes. I could not read what was in them. She was still smiling as she pushed the hair aside. I wished the deck were a mile long to walk.

'Your father, I suppose. The Southern Ocean meant a lot to him.'

She unzipped the bag on her arm and pulled out a piece of faded blue satin, which was overprinted with what looked like a newspaper article.

She held it out. 'This is a souvenir of a grand ball which HMS *Erebus* and *Terror* gave about a hundred and forty years ago in Tasmania. They'd been to Prince Edward Island and had broken through the ice near the South Pole. The printed part is from the *Hobart Town Courier*. It's an account of one of the greatest social occasions Tasmania has ever known. Strange, how something can act as a trigger. I got hold of this in London, and it made me feel I simply *had* to see Prince Edward for myself. It was like a catalyst. It started off a whole process in me. It had nothing to do with my father. His reasons for the cruise were entirely different.'

I didn't want to dampen her enthusiasm, seeing her standing there with her hair blowing, as if the world had been made for her, but I felt I had to speak.

I pointed at the flapping banner at the gangway. 'Listen,' I said, 'I can see how *Erebus* and *Terror* sparked off the idea for you but frankly I don't care for the way the names have been exploited for publicity. Presumably Orbit Travels are responsible. But I can't help remembering that only a few years after that ball in Tasmania, *Erebus* and *Terror* – and every man jack who sailed in them – perished looking for the North-West Passage. That's the sort of shadow the two names cast for me.'

She folded up the satin and put it back in her bag. I think she was a little disappointed by my reaction. 'Is that another of those non-facts that worries you about this cruise?' she asked.

'I can't forget how those two fine ships died. That's what. There aren't any decorations or champagne or beautiful women at a ball at Prince Edward. There's a wind which gets hold of your lungs so that you could scream with cold, and a sea which shakes your guts out so that you wish you'd been born without any. And sometimes you wish you'd not been born at all. That's the way I view the *Erebus* and *Terror* gimmick. We aren't going to have any blue satin mementoes after we've been there. We'll be lucky if we get away with a ship with only a few lengths of railing gone. And maybe a man or two overboard into the bargain.'

Her head came up the way it had done when she first entered the cabin. 'I still want to go.'

On the quayside a group of men had gathered round an object with an orange head and long body which was lashed to a trailer.

'That's the drifter buoy, Linn,' I said, 'and the reason why we're taking it is because ships give Prince Edward a miss.

Once in a blue moon a vessel does go there but it's as rare as a meteor flashing across an empty sky. The Southern Ocean covers four-fifths of the Southern Hemisphere. It's got less than a dozen weather stations, widely scattered on god-forsaken, remote islands. The only way to get the facts about the Southern Ocean and its weather is to use some kind of unmanned craft where human endurance isn't a factor. That buoy over there is a marvel of automatic instrumentation, but it's got to be conveyed there. So the *Quest* is a vital factor in the biggest attempt yet made by man to observe wind, weather and sea on a global basis. The findings could lead to radical new facts. They could affect the weather forecasting of all the nations of the world in the next decade. Data-void is the official jargon for the seas where we are bound.'

'You make it sound very formidable.'

'That's exactly what it is. Now let's go and look at our un-manned probe.'

Wegger, three other men, and some bystanders were grouped round the drifter buoy. We faced them from the deck. The buoy was shaped like a long thin top – about three times the height of a man in all. It looked rather like a skeleton fish the cat has stripped, except that the ribs were missing and the backbone was a thin, smooth, black tube. Covering the trailer was an envelope of plastic which looked like a shroud for an outsize corpse. There was also a big un-identifiable flat package and several gas cylinders.

I read aloud the white-painted wording. ' "Satellite buoy. Do not disturb. Weather Bureau. South Africa." ' Under an American eagle badge were the words 'National Oceano-graphic and Atmosphere Administration, USA.'

One of the men in the group – a short, stocky, sunburned man in shorts and a safari suit top – came to the ship's side when he saw me. He held out his hand.

'Smit,' he introduced himself. 'Weather Bureau.'

He put his left hand over his right knuckles and cracked them loudly. 'She's beautiful, isn't she, Captain?'

'Beauty is in the eye of the beholder, they say.'

He didn't get it. He laughed uncertainly and cracked his knuckles again.

'She's fragile, too,' he went on. 'She mustn't be hoisted

39

aboard. That instrument package mustn't get buggered up anyways at all. She must be *carried*. That's what I wanted to see you about.'

'She?' I looked sideways at Linn.

'We've got a name for her – Bokkie,' he rushed on. 'She must be *carried* . . .'

'What's in the orange part that looks like the nose-cone of a missile?' I asked.

Smit looked rather less enthusiastic. 'That's not the works, Captain. That's only the buoyancy element. Mostly plastic foam to keep her head above water. The works are *there*.' He pointed to a section of what looked like strong segmented plastic tubing jutting out above the top-like nose-cone.

'Those holes are the barometer ventilators,' he explained eagerly, 'and that's the transmitting antenna at the top. Bokkie emits signals with a specific frequency at short intervals – that's how they identify her after the satellite has picked 'em up . . .'

His enthusiasm seemed set fair to keep us there all day.

I interrupted him. 'What's inside the shaft below the head?'

'It houses the pressure sensor, the electronics package for converting the sensor readings into signals to the satellite, thermistor, battery unity . . .'

Linn was smiling at his eagerness, too.

Smit cracked his knuckles again and said, 'Bokkie must be carried, Captain!'

'How heavy is she?' I found myself also sexing the object on the trailer.

'She's not very heavy. Three men could do it. Two if they're very strong. When we launch her, we can't risk using a derrick. It'll have to be a burial-at-sea-type launch.'

Burial at sea! My mind took a backward leap at the sound of these words. The eager weatherman and the dockside with its cranes faded away. The long object on the trailer became a canvas coffin over which I had pronounced those sombre but wonderful words: 'We therefore commit his body to the deep . . .' It had been off Prince Edward. The *Captain Cook* had been smashed by a freak wave the previous night, like a lioness taking a clip at a wayward cub. There was one victim to be buried. The canvas containing the body had made a momentary white patch in the black sea, and at the same moment a rare shaft of sunlight had broken through the storm clouds, touching the central snow-clad peak of Prince Edward, so that it showed up pure white against the blackness around, and the brick-red volcanic cones had been grouped about it like cardinals in their vestments. The words of the committal service said, 'When the sea shall give up her dead' – but that sea never would.

Linn exclaimed, 'John . . .?'

I pulled myself back to the present. I remarked to Smit, 'That thing underneath looks like a shroud.'

'It's a drogue for the buoy and the other plastic is the high-altitude balloon,' he explained, oblivious of my lapse. 'You don't get proper drift if you let the buoy run free without a drogue. The current won't carry a thin hull like hers. We've tested the drogue – the optimum size is five square metres . . .'

I called out to Wegger, 'Number One! D'you think you can manage to carry that thing with some help?'

Wegger had already cast loose the lashings. You didn't need a derrick when you had Wegger around. He gripped the buoy round the head and heaved it clear of the trailer himself. But it was too long for him to manage alone.

'Jannie, give him a hand,' said Smit to one of his two fellow-technicians.

'Capt'n,' said Smit as they started to move off, 'it sounds odd-ball, I know, but can I have Bokkie in my cabin with me until she's launched?'

'Sorry. I haven't a cabin aboard that size. I've arranged a special place for Bokkie and you scientists in number four 'tween decks. The volcanologist, Holdgate, is there too.'

'Whereabouts is number four 'tween decks?'

I gestured sternward. 'My first officer will show you.'

'Is it safe? I mean, if a wave came and damaged Bokkie . . .'

'Safest place in the ship,' I assured him. 'It's an empty space like an outsize cabin with two doors that lock. You're sleeping in a new set of cabins in number three 'tween decks, just next door. You can pop in any time if Bokkie feels lonely.'

He nodded and gave his knuckles a final crack and then

followed Wegger and the second weatherman called Jannie who were carrying the buoy. Jannie was wearing sandals, jeans and a T-shirt emblazoned with the words: 'I ride the same waves as Bokkie'. I felt about a hundred.

Linn and I were watching the third member of the meteorological team unlash the balloon container and its inflating cylinders when a gruff voice behind me said, 'Captain!'

A short middle-aged woman in a crumpled brown tweed suit was pointing at my cap badge with a long holder containing a cigarillo. There were globules of sweat on hairs on her upper lip. Her eyes were a little bloodshot. Her voice burred like a wood sander striking a knot.

'Have you WAPP's permission to wear that?'

I looked her up and down. I hoped it made her sweat more.

'Have you?' she demanded.

'Who are you?' I asked. 'And who in hell is WAPP?'

'I must protest,' she said. The way she said it, I felt she'd protested before. She addressed Linn. 'It's just this sort of abuse of creatures that can't defend themselves that led to the founding of the World Association of Polar Penguins. I am happy to say I'm a founder member.'

I wondered how long ago that was.

She went on, 'I am Judy Auchinleck, regional chairman for South Georgia and the Lesser Antarctics.'

It sounded like a caliph's title. Caliphs have harems. Judy Auchinleck's proclaimed empire was frigid.

Linn came to my rescue. I admired her placatory tone. 'Miss Auchinleck booked on our cruise because her organization feels that the penguin populations of the Antarctic are being over-exploited for publicity, especially by television teams. She wants to make sure this doesn't happen during the *Quest*'s cruise.'

'Have you any television cameramen aboard?' demanded Judy Auchinleck.

I passed the question to Linn.

'One,' she replied. 'Only one man. Not a team.'

'Good,' she snapped. 'Then I can keep him under my eye all the time. I know all about penguins.' She took a drag at the cigarillo. She had a nicotine stain on her lower lip. 'Any circus catchers?'

'Any circus catchers?' Linn's left eyelid half-closed as I

42

passed the ball to her again. But she answered with deadly
seriousness.

'None, Miss Auchinleck. None at all. Most of the people
on this cruise are here either because they have special
knowledge of the Antarctic islands or are particularly interested in them.'

'Good.' She turned to go, and then pointed the holder at
my cap badge. 'The penguin motif copyright is vested in
WAPP under the terms of the Geneva Convention. Any
infringement lays the offender open to prosecution.'

I said, 'I'll remember that in the ice, Miss Auchinleck.'

She glanced at me uncertainly, and then waddled off.

Linn was eyeing me, her lips twitching. 'Did you say you
had never handled tricky passengers before, John?'

I grinned back at her. 'I think it's about time you put me
in the picture about our passengers, Linn. They're as faceless
to me as my own crew – anyone could come aboard and tell
me he belonged and I wouldn't have a clue whether it was
true or not. You've got the list?'

She tapped her bag. 'All thirty of them.'

'Then let's get back to the cabin and look it over. I've met
Doctor Holdgate, the volcanologist, Smit, the buoy man, and
Jannie, his mate. And seen the third weatherman. That's
about all.'

'You've forgotten Miss Auchinleck.'

'She's the only WAPP aboard, I hope?'

'Yes. Actually she's been in some very remote places.'

'She'd be quite safe.'

She looked at me searchingly for a moment as if she was
going to comment on my remark, but all she said was, 'Let's
go.'

As we made our way for'ard, I remembered the assignment I had given McKinley. 'I've got to check something,' I
said. 'We'll get up on to the flying bridge.'

We made our way past the red-painted lifeboats secured to
the steel superstructure and reached the high vantage-point
from where I could see the *Quest*'s bows. We halted alongside a large brown board with the name *Quest* painted on it
in gold. The D/F, radio and radar aerials hung over our heads
like lifeless stars.

McKinley seemed to have done his job. I pointed out the

searchlight to Linn.

'That's in case we run into floating ice. I want to see where I'm going.'

'But surely you'll be using radar?'

I laughed. 'Radar's a very over-rated thing when it comes to ice. It's all very fine if the sea's calm and the ice is the right shape to reflect the impulses, but if you run into trouble, give me the human eye and nose every time. Radar's no use when it's rough and the sea clutter extends beyond a mile. Even if you do get warning there's usually no time to do anything about it. A growler can knock a hole in your hull before you can get your helm hard over.'

'Is that why you're so anxious about the *Quest* not being ice-strengthened?'

'Yes. Every time a big wave smacks her hull in the Roaring Forties I'll be wondering if it's a growler or a bergy bit.'

'Growler. Bergy bit.' She turned the words over on her tongue. 'That's the way my father talks. I'd like to phone the hospital again, John, when we get back to the cabin.'

We did so and were informed that Captain Prestrud was as well as could be expected but was still unconscious. If there was any change in his condition they would let us know.

'If you feel you'd like to go to the hospital again,' I began.

'Later,' she said. 'Let's finish our business.'

She sat down at the desk in the captain's cabin, which still felt so much more like Captain Prestrud's than like my own, and took the passenger list out of her bag.

'I've never had to shepherd passengers before,' I said. 'I don't even know the breakdown of men and women and how they're going to fit into the cabin space.'

'You don't need to worry about that,' she said. '*Quest* originally had two double cabins and eight singles, but my father had three of the singles converted into doubles. We've got five married couples. I'm using one of the original singles, and the new accommodation built in number three 'tween decks is all singles.'

'How many men and women?'

'Eighteen women and twelve men.'

'Which just proves that women are the tougher sex,' I

said, and we smiled at each other.

Then she looked down at her list. 'We've got the three met. men who are handling the buoy and the balloon. Then there's Doctor Holdgate who's going to lecture us on the geology and geomorphology of Prince Edward and Marion Islands.'

'He gave himself a quick work-out on my taxi driver.'

I saw a new Linn then. She didn't smile, but said very seriously, 'It's not as bad as the jargon makes it sound. Prince Edward and Marion are receiving a great deal of attention from scientists these days because of their position in the broad framework of the earth's history. Both islands are very young in time from a geological point of view, and they are terribly important for an understanding of the theory of continental drift and of the way the ocean floor is spreading. And because they are so young, whatever life is there has arrived comparatively recently and the way it's established itself under such tough conditions fascinates the experts. So these islands are just as interesting to scientists as the one which was born off the coast of Iceland a few years ago – Surtsey.'

'I'll view the place with new eyes when I see it next week,' I said.

'Don't be put off when I say lectures, John,' she went on. 'The experts will conduct us round the islands and talk about their subject in the field. It's not going to be a series of dry-as-dust lectures. It's a *living* tour, don't you see?'

'If you can get ashore in the first place. It's not as easy as all that, Linn.'

'We'll make out, I know we will,' she replied confidently. 'You'll do everything you can to make it a success. Because of my father.'

Not only because of your father, Linn, I thought as I looked at her.

She said, 'On our way down to Prince Edward we're going to have the services of one of the greatest living experts on marine birds – Doctor Kebble. He's from the Percy Fitzpatrick Institute of African Ornithology, here in Cape Town. How long do you reckon we're going to take to get to Prince Edward? Six days?'

'Yes, but you've got to take into account that I'm not

making the usual direct course south-east from the Cape to the island.'

'Aren't you? Why not?'

'Because of the buoy. Let me explain. We'll be crossing two distinct zones of the ocean as we go South. First we pass what's called the Sub-tropical Convergence, where the warm water and the particular life it supports ends. The second zone has as its boundary the Antarctic Convergence, which is where the cold north-flowing Antarctic surface water plunges beneath the warmer Sub-Antarctic water. Prince Edward is nearly forty-seven degrees South, almost on the Antarctic Convergence. This Convergence is the Great Divide of the Southern Ocean – it's a quite unmistakable boundary in the sea, something real and physical. Life changes dramatically from one side to the other. It's a marked boundary line but it's not always in the same place. Prince Edward usually lies about one hundred and sixty kilometres to the north of the divide but it has been known to reach the island on occasion . . .'

'And so, John?'

'Sorry. I'm beginning to sound like one of your guide-lecturers. What I was coming to was that the Weather Bureau wants its buoy and balloon launched at a spot much further to the west than Prince Edward itself – about fifteen hundred kilometres, but on the same parallel, in order to probe Convergence conditions. The idea is that it will drift eastwards in the general direction of Prince Edward at a speed of between a quarter and one knot an hour. When the buoy nears Prince Edward, the weather station next door on Marion will also monitor it, checking its readings against its own. The actual launch-point is almost due south of the Cape coast. That's where we head for first.'

The telephone rang. Linn stiffened. We both thought, but neither of us said, that this would be the hospital.

I said, 'I'll take it.'

I went over and stood holding the receiver, looking at her. A voice came over the wire, 'Is that the captain?'

'Captain here.'

'Hold on for the Director of the Weather Bureau.'

I put my hand over the instrument and said to Linn. 'Weather Bureau.'

Another voice came through. 'Is that Captain Prestrud?'

'No,' I replied. 'Captain Prestrud has been injured. He is in hospital. Shotton speaking. I've taken over.'

The Director's anxiety made the earpiece vibrate. What was going to happen? What about the cruise? And the launching of the buoy?

I quickly outlined the situation and added, 'You don't have to worry, sir. We'll sail on schedule. Tomorrow, Friday.'

'I'm very distressed to hear about Captain Prestrud,' said the Director but I could nonetheless sense the relief in his voice. 'I only rang to wish the *Quest* good luck.'

'Thank you, sir. One always needs luck in the ice.'

'I'll be in radio touch and give you the go-ahead on Monday at the exact time – ten hours GMT. You do realize the importance of the buoy and the balloon, don't you, Captain Shotton? There are a hundred and forty-five nations depending on you.'

'I do, sir. I'll launch Bokkie on time, whatever.'

I liked his laugh. 'Bokkie! So you know, eh?'

'If Smit is married, his wife has a rival.'

He laughed again. 'Keep in touch, eh? After you've set Bokkie on her way, make a signal personally to me, will you, Captain? We're one of the Regional Communication Hubs for this project and I must let the other stations know as soon as Bokkie is away.'

'You can count on that, sir. Four days from now.'

'I'm already counting in terms of hours, not days,' he replied. 'Good luck, Captain Shotton.'

I put down the phone.

'Four days from now!' echoed Linn. 'Our banquet's the night before – let's make it a double celebration.'

I stood by the phone looking down at her. 'I'm all mixed up about this banquet affair.'

'Didn't my father explain about it before he went to hospital?'

'No. He merely mentioned there was to be a big dinner. Lots of goodies and cases of wine came aboard, but I was much too busy getting the ship ready to ask what it was all about. I didn't realize how important it was to him until he made me promise when I saw him in hospital that it would go ahead as planned.'

'I wonder . . .'

'See here, Linn. Looking back on it now, I think your father was in even worse shape than I thought at the time. He made me promise the dinner would take place. It seemed to be linked with what he was trying to tell me about his war-time escape. I was crowded for time and couldn't press the question, but I doubt whether he would have been able to reply, even if I had.'

'It was very important to him,' she explained. 'It's been a Prestrud occasion for years. Every five years he and Captain Jacobsen hold this dinner to celebrate their escape from the German raider. Sunday's dinner was to have been the biggest occasion of them all because it would have been in the very area where the escape took place.'

'I see.'

'What's the matter, John? Why do you say it like that?'

I felt a little shiver in the spine. I was remembering the injured man's desperate attempts to marshal his facts. It was more than just a dinner he had been trying to get across. He'd wanted to tell me something relating to the *Quest*'s voyage. But he hadn't succeeded.

'I was thinking of something your father mentioned. One of the other catcher skippers – Torgersen – was murdered, wasn't he?'

'Yes. It was all a long time ago.'

'But we've got Captain Jacobsen with us on the *Quest* and we're going into the very area where all this war-time business occurred.'

She eyed me penetratingly. 'Yes. Captain Jacobsen and Mrs Jacobsen are both aboard. She's very possessive about him. He's got a slight heart condition and she insists that he should rest up after the long plane trip.'

'Linn, are you certain your father never told you what happened when the three of them escaped from the German raider?'

She shook her head emphatically. 'Never. He didn't like to talk about it. But I do know that after he and Captain Jacobsen had held one of their get-togethers he always seemed more comfortable and relaxed. They must have chinned over old times.'

'I don't quite follow how two seafaring men whose jobs

took them to the ends of the earth could settle on a firm date to meet every five years.'

'The answer is that it was very important to them both,' she replied. 'All I know is that they did keep their date faithfully.' She pointed to one of the photographs on the wall of the cabin. It represented a fjord, a timber house, and snow-covered trees. 'I remember them foregathering at our home once – no, it was twice.'

'It's difficult to think of you as Norwegian. I'd say English, if I were to meet you casually.'

'My mother was English. She was a schoolteacher on exchange in Norway. That's how they met. My father didn't marry till late in life. He'd spent all his younger years saving up to buy his own ship.'

'And your mother?'

'She was killed in a car accident on an ice-bound road about ten years ago. I was at school in London when it happened.' She made a slight gesture of impatience. 'We came to discuss passengers, remember? Not to talk about me. I'm sure there'll be a crowd to see them off when we sail. We'll have to make sure there aren't any stragglers left aboard.'

'I intend to sail early. Too early, I hope, for most people to come to the docks.'

'Too early for your wife to come and wave you goodbye?'

She was concentrating on the list in front of her as she spoke.

'My wife waved me goodbye a while back, Linn. From a divorce court.'

'I'm sorry, John.'

'You don't have to be. It was a low-profile emotion which couldn't stand the strain of my absences at sea. After a while she grew colder than the Southern Ocean itself. Nothing much was hurt except some vanity on my side.'

'That sounds very defensive, very modern. Like a punch-line from a TV drama.'

'Forget it. I'd much rather hear how you came to be involved in a way-out venture like this cruise.'

It was good to exchange her level voice for my brittle cynicism.

'Well, that old satin souvenir of the Tasmanian ball sparked it off, as I told you. Once the hunt was on, I spent a couple of years doing research in London, and then at the Scott Polar Research Institute in Cambridge. It was for my own interest. The cruise hadn't been thought of at that time. It didn't materialize till later when Dad and Orbit Travels got together. By then I'd accumulated a great deal of background. So it happened that both projects dovetailed very neatly.'

The idea flashed through my mind: if anyone would know about Dina's Island, she would. But before asking, I started off at a tangent.

'Linn, you know that the old clipper men used to steer a course for Australia via the Cape to get them there as quickly as possible – you've heard of a Great Circle Course?'

'Vaguely.'

'Time became a major factor on the Australian run during the great gold boom of the eighteen-fifties,' I explained. 'Until then the sailing ships followed a long slow route laid down by the Admiralty. Then a new route was pioneered on the basis of recommendations of a great wind expert of the day, a man called Maury. He urged captains to take their ships far south for the wind. It was also the shortest distance between the Cape and Australia – a Great Circle Course instead of the old Admiralty route to the north. It worked. It cut about a month off the time.'

She regarded me with interest. 'The way you talk makes me wonder whether you wouldn't like to sail that way too.'

I smiled. 'Sailing is a big love of mine. I've skippered and crewed a lot of yachts. None of them in that direction, unfortunately.'

'Unfortunately? After your warnings about Prince Edward?'

I dodged her question and went on: 'There was one snag about this wonderful new fast route to Australia – Prince Edward Island.'

'Just one little island?'

'Many fine ships went missing in the area. At first it was attributed to the bad weather. Then the real culprit showed up – Prince Edward. You see, the island lies right athwart the shortest and fastest route to Australia.'

'They could easily have steered past it.'

I laughed. 'In theory, yes. In practice, maybe. You'll be surprised to know that even today Prince Edward's exact position is not known – some on-the-spot calculations from

Marion have put it four miles east of where the charts show it, others a mile west, and still others a mile and a half south. What's really needed is a proper scientific astro-fix – if the weather ever cleared enough to make that possible. I don't believe any of my own calculations, either, when I'm approaching Prince Edward. I believe it when I see it.'

'Are there a lot of wrecks there?'

'The island got such a bad reputation that the old clipper-men coined a new name for it. They christened it Southtrap.'

'But everything has changed since the times you're talking about, John – navigation, everything.'

'Not quite. If you study the track-charts of round-the-world yachts sailing races you'll see how they skid around Prince Edward. On a couple of occasions the *Cutty Sark* shaved by when making some of the greatest runs of her career.'

'You're quite an authority on Prince Edward,' she commented.

I pulled myself back to the question from which I'd been side-tracked. 'Ever hear of Dina's Island, Linn?'

She looked surprised but replied without hesitation. 'Yes, I have. Strange you should ask. I got quite excited about it while I was researching at the Royal Geographical Society. In fact the follow-up took me to Holland.'

'Go on.'

'I dug around in the Algemeen Rijksarchief at The Hague – that's the marine archives where documents from the early Dutch days at the Cape are housed – and happened on something I thought was really quite remarkable. A century before the official discovery of Prince Edward by the French, the Dutch sent two ships from the Cape to Java. Captain Barent Ham was in command. He strayed south of the usual route to the Indies, and for once the weather was clear. Suddenly he sighted two islands ahead. He named them after his two ships? Maerseveen and Dina.'

'Dina!'

'Yes,' she went on. 'It's reasonably certain, after you've made the necessary navigational adjustments, what it was he'd found.'

I'd guessed by then, of course, but I waited for her to say it.

'Dina and Prince Edward are the same island,' she said.

CHAPTER SEVEN

The *Quest* sailed early next morning.

I had put to sea before breakfast, but the hour did not deter the crowd. It was like a mail-ship departure. Or like the *Titanic*, whispered a malign gremlin at the back of my mind as the *Quest* rounded the breakwater. I set course past Green Point, Sea Point and the terraced warren of seaside hotels, flats and houses spilling down the Cape Peninsula's western flank. Soon the warming sun would bring out tanned bathers like termites to the white beaches. The south-easter was blowing already, but it wasn't as noticeable as the slight tug at *Quest*'s keel of a weak current which the wind generates round Mouillé Point during the summer.

As a tug pulled the *Quest* clesar of her berth, the *Erebus-Terror* banner, which McKinley had forgotten to unfasten, ripped. Someone ashore snatched a piece for a souvenir; in a moment the idea spread like wildfire through the crowd. I saw the flashes of press cameras as people fought for fragments of the cloth. The incident left a nasty taste in my mouth. Wegger, who was with me on the bridge, stood watching with a face of iron.

I scanned the passengers lining the rail and was disappointed but not altogether surprised to see no sign of Linn. She had gone to the hospital the previous evening – alone, at her own wish – and had come back depressed and tired. Captain Prestrud had not yet recovered consciousness and his condition was as well as could be expected.

The *Quest* cleared Mouillé Point for the run parallel to the Peninsula. Lion's Head, Lion's Rump and Table Mountain itself, slightly obscured by early cloud, looked indescribably majestic against the back-lighting of the early sun. I reached for the bridge telegraph to ring down to the engine-room for more speed, and it was at that moment that I felt there was no more chance of turning back, even if I had wished to do so. The brass pointer of the telegraph, worn smooth by countless hands, was comforting to the touch, an assurance of many voyages safely accomplished. In the quadrant opposite were the words 'finished with engines'. What would the *Quest* have seen and done, I wondered, before I rang down for that . . .?

I snapped out of my introverted train of thought and jammed the pointer to 'full ahead'. The repeater swung round with a metallic rattle.

An hour later we were off Slangkop lighthouse, a landmark halfway down the Peninsula towards its extremity, the Cape of Good Hope. The funnel burbled in low, comfortable contralto. I picked up the phone to the engine-room.

'Chief? Everything okay down there?' I asked.

'Aye, Skipper, that it is.'

MacFie's Ayrshire accent was as soothing as the regular sound coming from the stack.

'No problems?'

'Not one. They don't make engines like these any more, laddie.'

'Good. Now listen, Chief, I want you to draw on the for'ard half-height fuel tanks first, but not the forepeak tank. I want that to stay full as long as possible while we're in the ice.'

'Aye, I'll do that, though I canna understand why.'

'I want her trimmed higher by the head,' I explained. 'She's riding too deep.'

'Then why not use the forepeak tank first?'

The reason had come to me the previous night as I checked the ship before going to my bunk. If I kept the forepeak tank full of its bunker fuel and the *Quest* tangled with dangerous ice, the bow plating would be the first to rip. That would spill the oil. I would then have some sort of defence against the sort of waves we would encounter in the Southern Ocean. It was a kind of built-in desperation precaution.

'It's a bit complicated, Chief,' I replied. 'I'll tell you later.'

'It must be, that's all I can say,' he grumbled.

I looked up from the phone into the eyes of Petersen, the third officer, who was sharing the morning watch with me. He looked more like a gangling schoolboy in uniform than a man; his cap made his fair hair curl over the nape of his neck. He did an abrupt eyes-front as if I'd caught him out at something and blushed guiltily. The previous night we had had an animated discussion about the stars Alpha Crux – brightest in the Southern Cross – Achenar and Antares and their respective merits for obtaining a star-fix of Prince Edward. Navigation was his strong point, and I sensed his hero-worship. I only wished his authority matched his navigation. A man like Jensen, the quartermaster at the wheel, would get away with anything if I wasn't there to back Petersen up.

Unnecessarily I growled at Jensen. 'Steer small, will you? There's a squall coming off the land.'

The squall was ripping down off the slopes of the beautiful mountain on the *Quest*'s port quarter. It appeared from the sea to follow the course of the magnificent scenic highway which clings to the coast over and beyond Chapman's Peak. This was a favourite trick of the south-easter as it freshened; it also told me that the wind would become worse after we had rounded Cape Point and lost the shelter of the land.

The *Quest* rolled against the thrust of the squall.

A voice said, 'I wonder if some of the passengers are already regretting their breakfast.'

It was Linn. I hadn't heard her come on to the bridge while I had been watching the squall.

'Hello, Linn.'

She smiled back at me. She looked as fresh as the morning. She was wearing a sleeveless turquoise-and-white striped dress, and a single gold brooch with a dolphin motif at her left shoulder.

I gestured at the Slangkop lighthouse coming abeam. It stands on a flat-topped hill which gives the place its name – Snake's Head. A village is snuggled at its foot.

'Any moment now their breakfasts are going to have a change of motion,' I said. 'This sort of wind usually abates a little about here but veers more south, which means that the *Quest* will begin to pitch in earnest.'

She drew me over to the port or landward side of the bridge.

'You know this coast pretty well, don't you, John? Are you a South African?'

'No. London born and bred. I first came south and saw

the Cape about ten years ago. Before that I'd been in the North Atlantic.'

'Look! What's that – there in the water off the rocks?'

'The sooner you get acquainted with that, the better,' I replied. 'That's kelp. You'll see more of it along this shore. And plenty round Prince Edward.'

'It's terribly exciting – isn't it? – getting an introduction to Prince Edward things so soon after we've sailed . . .'

Her enthusiasm was infectious. 'We can see better from the flying bridge,' I said. 'We'll go up there. Carry on, will you, Mr Petersen.'

'Aye – aye, sir,' he stammered.

We went up to the flying bridge. It was like a little steel island all to ourselves, with a well-deck separating it from the stack and superstructure aft. Dr Kebble, the bird man, with binoculars strung round his neck, was in a group aft gesticulating in the direction of some birds in flight.

'One thing I do know about birds,' I told Linn, 'and that is that Prince Edward has its very own bird. It's unique to the island, so I'm told. It's called the Pilot Bird.'

She was amused. 'Move up to the top of the class, Captain.'

She gazed excitedly at the splendid shoreline and I caught her mood.

'If you want a further reminder of Prince Edward,' I said, 'there's Albatross Rock a little further on.'

She turned to me. The new light off the water was faceted green-blue in her fine eyes.

'It's so wonderful, John, to think I'm actually looking at a land that men dreamed of for two thousand years before it was ever discovered!'

'You're going too fast for me, Linn. Slow down, and give me a chance to catch up.'

'What I'm trying to say is that this is the point of Africa – the very southernmost tip of the continent of Africa that remained unknown and unexplored for so long. Ptolemy called it the Promontorium Prassum and nobody came here until thousands of years later when the Portuguese rounded . . .'

I didn't want to correct her geography but to kiss her mouth.

'Take it easy!' I grinned at her. 'If I'm going to learn about a place I've navigated scores of times then I want time to remember all these names that I've never heard before. The Cape of Good Hope may be all you say, but to this clottish sailor in front of you the very southernmost point of Africa is Cape Agulhas. I know that because it's going to be our departure landfall.'

'It's sweet of you to be so tolerant about my geography, John. Actually I do know about Agulhas but the Cape of Good Hope is *really* the place the great explorers were searching for – it's grand, it's dramatic, and Dias planted a cross on it to mark one of the greatest discoveries the world has ever known.'

'If all your lectures are going to be like this,' I said, 'I'll vacate the bridge when we get to Prince Edward and join the tourists.'

We both laughed. Then I said, 'You're seeing the Peninsula under the best possible conditions. It's a very different place in a south-westerly or north-westerly buster. Look at it with a sailor's eye and all you'll see is a great navigational hazard littered with wrecks. It's not for nothing it's called the Cape of Storms.'

'Cabo Tormentoso,' she said, rolling the phrase round her tongue as if she were sampling a fine wine.

I said lightly, 'These are the *Flying Dutchman* waters. Pity it's the wrong sort of day for you to sight him.'

'Have you ever seen him?' she asked, quite seriously.

'Never. I may be superstitious but I certainly don't suffer from hallucinations.'

'He was an actual person. Didn't you know that, John?'

'I thought it was purely a legend.'

'When I was researching in London I came across an article in a newspaper dating from the eighteen-eighties. It quoted a sailor whose great-grandfather claimed to have seen the real ship called the *Flying Dutchman* in Table Bay on her way to Java. There was quite a lot in the papers about it at the time because, when King George V was a midshipman, he actually sighted it off the Cape in 1881. So the legend was given a sort of royal sanction.'

'It's extraordinary, the things you know,' I said. 'What a strange girl you are.'

She continued as if she had not heard my interjection. 'Most people confuse the sea legend with the opera bit version of the story. The real Vanderdecken did in fact reach Cape waters when he returned from Java in his ship the *Flying Dutchman*, and he ran into a north-westerly gale which prevented him rounding Cape Point. So he cursed God and swore that if he had to beat into the gale until Doomsday he would make it, and the curse laid on him was that he should continue to beat around the Cape of Storms for all eternity.'

'As a sailor,' I commented, 'I can take the full measure of that curse.'

'It's not everyone who sights the *Flying Dutchman* who is doomed,' she went on. 'Only those who see her heave to and start to lower a boat.'

Her talk made me think of *Botany Bay*. 'Did you happen to see the windjammer which occupied the *Quest*'s berth immediately before us?'

Linn shook her head.

'She was a modern replica of a convict hell-ship,' I said. 'Wax-works show. Very realistic. She's on her way to Australia now. She would have beaten round Cape Point in the teeth of just such a south-easter.'

Linn pointed ahead to where, beyond the *Quest*'s dipping bows, the land ended in twin peaks.

'Which is Cape Maclear and which is Cape Point?' she asked.

'You know more about the place than I do.'

'They're only names in my head,' she replied. 'I know of them because it's somewhere about here that Dias planted his cross.' She put her hand over mine on the rail. 'This is sheer magic, John. Sheer magic.' She leaned her shoulder unself-consciously against me as she craned to see something under the bows.

'What is it, Linn?'

'Did you notice the *Quest*'s figurehead, John?'

'Of course. Thor throwing his hammer.'

'But you may not know that when a *Thor* ship is sold the original bronze figurehead is always removed and an imitation painted in its place.'

'I didn't know,' I said. 'I'm still learning from you.'

'Dad prevailed on the owners to let him keep the *Quest*'s original. So Thor throws his magic hammer and it comes back to the thrower fulfilling his wish. I'm having my wish today,

John. I'm seeing the sheer magic of the Cape.'

Magic in you too, Linn. Woman's magic.

My apprehension and unease about the *Quest*'s voyage began to fade a little. With Linn by my side it could turn into a bright adventure.

'I want to stand here and watch and watch while we round the Cape,' she went on. Her hand still lay on mine. 'Did you ever hear the expression, " to shoot the gulf"?'

'Never.'

'Funny how phrases die out. When Drake sailed into the Pacific from Cape Horn, sailors called it "shooting the gulf". For many years afterwards it meant breaking out into something quite new, a whole new world. I feel as if I'm doing that now. Shooting the gulf. Just like Drake.'

'These are Drake waters too. Right under *Quest*'s keel at this moment.'

'I know. He called it "the fairest Cape in the whole circumference of the earth".'

Our moment was killed by a discreet cough behind us. It was Persson, the radio operator.

He said formally, 'Personal to you, sir. Mr Wegger was with me when it came in. He said he'd keep an eye on things in the radio shack while I found you.'

Even as I took the signal slip I wondered why in hell Wegger should have been concerning himself with the radio. But it was only a momentary thought. The contents of the message obliterated this and everything else.

It read:

> *Captain Prestrud died 08h30 this morning. Police taken possession body pending post-mortem and inquest. Norwegian consul Cape Town informed. Groote Schuur Hospital.*

The shock of it made me pull my rank. 'My compliments to Mr Wegger, Persson. Tell him that his duties do not include being stand-by radio operator.'

I saw the light which had been in Linn's eyes dim at my tone. As she turned away from Persson's startled embarrassment I guessed what she was thinking of me – a smoothie with women but a bastard who rode his crew and made a show of it to impress.

I went on roughly, 'Get going, your job's not on deck watching the scenery.'

'Aye, aye, sir.' He scuttled off.

'Linn.' I felt some of the sandpaper still in my voice.

'Yes, John?' She was cool and poised – until she saw something was amiss.

I held out the signal slip. 'I think you'd prefer to read this for yourself.'

I was already making calculations for the *Quest*'s return to Table Bay; automatically I had noted the ship's position. The mouth of the Klaasjagers River was slightly ahead and the land became more rugged and unfrequented; it is a nature reserve.

Linn read the signal. The colour rose and went from her face. She stared at the slip, but her eyes were unfocused. When she raised them they looked as if they had been weighted behind like a doll's.

She said in a small, strangled voice, 'Thank you, John. I think I'll go below to my father's – to your cabin.'

'I'll see you down . . .'

She shook her head and went quickly down the short steel ladder. As I followed more slowly I noticed Wegger striding away from the radio shack as if he were heading for his quarters. He could hardly have missed seeing me but he walked on without giving me a glance. When I reached the bridge I could sense the effect of the message I had sent to Wegger by the tight silence among the men. Jensen at the wheel was making a study of the compass; Petersen was standing almost to attention, just where an officer of the watch should stand.

'I'll take the deck, Mr Petersen,' I said.

'Aye, aye, sir.'

I went to the telegraph and rang, 'Half Ahead.' No point in carrying on at her present speed. The *Quest* would only have to retrace her course when we turned back, as we surely would, once Linn had recovered sufficiently from the shock.

The *Quest*'s heartbeat slowed. She pitched more as the way fell off her. The splendid panorama out to port became meaningless to me. It had been a brief moment, mine and Linn's, and we would remember it. Life always kicks you in the balls when you aren't looking, an old bo'sun I sailed with used to say. It seemed as if he hadn't been so wrong, after all.

Quest coasted on, waiting for Linn's word to about-face. Now that the cruise was finished, I realized how keenly disappointed I was. For all my doubts and unease I'd wanted to challenge those wild seas, wanted to put the *Quest*'s nose first into the south-easter building up beyond Cape Point, and then to face the Brave West Winds. Above all, I'd wanted to get to Southtrap. The nickname for Prince Edward was in itself a challenge. I must ask Linn, I thought, who was the Prince Edward Captain Cook had named it after. But with this thought came a fresh thrust of disappointment. It didn't matter now.

'Sir!'

There was nothing deferential about the word. It was curt, imperative, explosive.

I swung round. Wegger was standing at the rear of the bridge. There was about him that air of truculence and intensity which had marked him on the dockside. Only now it was hardly concealed.

For a moment I thought it was my reprimand which had got him on the raw. But only for a moment.

'The ship's slowing – why?' he demanded.

I replied tautly. 'Mr Wegger. When I give an order aboard my ship I don't go around broadcasting explanations. The ship's slowing because I ordered it.'

I could feel the vibrations rippling from Petersen and Jensen behind me. But Wegger was completely unaffected by my tone.

'Are we going back because of Captain Prestrud?'

My look was meant for an up-and-downer to put him in his place. It stopped at his left jacket pocket. It was heavy and sagging, the way a pocket sags when you carry a gun.

'Miss Prestrud is naturally shocked,' I retorted levelly. 'She has gone below.'

He took a step towards me in that same uncontrolled way as he had done ashore. If I had to hit him, it would have to be hard and once only – before he could get the Luger.

'The ship can't turn back now,' he said. 'We've got the drifter buoy ...'

'I am well aware of the implications, Mr Wegger, and of our commitments to the Global Research Programme.'

An icebreaker would have come up short on the ice in my

60

voice. Wegger didn't.

'You've slowed the ship before you know what she intends to do . . .'

It was lucky for him that the bridge phone rang. Petersen answered and held it out to me as if it might bite.

'John?' said Linn. 'Can you come down to the cabin, please?'

She might have been calling from the South Pole, she sounded so far away.

I pushed past Wegger and went down to her.

Linn was sitting at the desk on the swing-chair. Her eyes looked dark, very different from how they had looked out on deck only a little while before.

I said gently, 'Linn?'

She responded with only a faint tremor in her voice. 'An inquest can take a long time, can't it, John?'

'It can, Linn. The police have to carry out their investigations first. Suspects, and all that. Then there are all the legal processes which have to be put in motion.'

She looked at me squarely. 'And the medical.'

'A post-mortem can be a long and tricky business when you've got the implications of . . .' I couldn't say it. I had liked Captain Prestrud too much.

'*Quest* could be at Kerguelen before . . . before – ' she hesitated a little – 'before they finished that side of things.'

'It might be even further. We may well reach New Zealand in time for you to fly back for the official enquiry.'

'I hadn't pictured things as clearly as that yet.'

'*Quest* belongs to you now, Linn. The decision whether or not the cruise goes on is yours.'

She shook her head. The action loosened tears which hung on her cheek.

'You have a stake in *Quest*, too, John. Not a material share maybe, but nonetheless very real.'

This woman would read and understand me better than any of the others had done, I found myself thinking. Including the one I had married. Or those who had provided me with bed-comforts. Because she understood the Southern Ocean with her heart.

'Thank you, Linn. I won't forget that,' I answered lamely.

She got up, paced across the cabin, and then swung round

and faced me. Her words came with a rush, 'For my part, the cruise goes on.'

'That's for my part too, Linn.'

She came back to the desk and slumped in the chair as if the effort of making the decision had exhausted her. 'I'll have to tell Captain Jacobsen. He was Dad's dearest friend.'

I went to the phone next to her. As I picked up the instrument, I put my lips for a moment against her hair. She didn't look up, but brushed a hand across her eyes.

'Bridge,' I said. When the connection was made I continued, 'Mr Petersen, full ahead, if you please. Same course. And is Mr Wegger still there?'

'Yes – I mean, aye, aye, sir.'

'Tell him to come to my cabin.'

'Very good, Captain – I mean, sir.'

It scarcely seemed a moment before Wegger entered. I stood next to Linn's chair. The controlled intensity of the man seemed to radiate around him like a ship's electrical field in the sea. It was as if he were balancing on the balls of his feet, ready for anything.

I dropped the formal 'mister' in addressing him, now that no other member of the crew was about.

'Wegger,' I said, 'you had no right to be doing anything in the radio shack. Signals – especially those marked personal – are for my eyes only.'

'I told you before that I knew about radio. I'm interested in the *Quest*'s equipment. I was only looking around.' Then he added with a note in his voice I didn't care for: 'And I don't like being bawled out, especially in front of a woman.'

'Miss Prestrud happens to be the new owner of the *Quest*.'

'Is that supposed to make a difference?'

I kept my cool. 'Miss Prestrud has decided to proceed with the cruise in spite of her father's death.'

The ugly lightning flashed in his pale eyes. And, like real lightning, it seemed to bring an instant relaxing of tension in the big body clad in nondescript uniform.

'Good.' His left hand went to his pocket and unconsciously smoothed it as if wanting – now – to conceal the gun. He took a grip on himself and said formally to Linn, 'My condolences, Miss Prestrud. I am sure your father would have wished us to go on.'

'You happened to be a party to a confidential signal, Wegger,' I told him. 'It's to remain confidential, do you understand? We don't want a shadow over the trip, for the sake of the passengers.'

He replied readily, too readily, 'Of course, sir.'

'I intend to carry on with my lectures and the tour part of it as if nothing had happened,' Linn added. 'That's the way we want it.'

I didn't miss the way she said 'we'.

Wegger's whole bearing appeared to have changed abruptly. He said in the half-servile way which had grated on me when he had asked me about the job, 'I'm sorry I was a bit sharp on the bridge, sir. You see, this voyage is very important to me and if it had been called off . . .' He let it hang for a moment and then added, as if his words needed further explanation: 'When you've been out of a job for a long time a berth like this means everything. If there's anything I can do – in my watch off if necessary . . .'

'Thanks,' I replied. 'I'll keep that in mind.' What I had in mind, though, was that I would like to frisk him and see whether his Luger was loaded.

As he left, I felt the engines picking up their running speed. Linn wasn't with me when the *Quest* rounded the twin peaks and the majestic cliffs of Cape Point and dug her bows deep into the swells of the freshening gale. She missed the sight that she had dreamed of, that mariners ever since Ptolemy had dreamed of. Later in the afternoon, however, she came up on to the bridge and stood silent, watching as the low, hummocky spit of gale-blasted land that is the extremity of the continent of Africa hove into view and then began to disappear astern. I made Cape Agulhas my departure-point along the 20th parallel which intersects it.

The *Quest* headed South, and there was no more land between us and the Pole.

CHAPTER EIGHT

I let the special ten-year-old Cape brandy trickle slowly out
of the screw-stoppered bottle into my glass. It was after dinner
that same evening after we had left Africa. Captain Prestrud's
cabin – my cabin, I kept telling myself, the man was dead – was
hot and stuffy. I had taken off my uniform jacket, my collar
was loose. At last I was alone and had a chance to think.

I stopped the brandy at three fingers, and added only a
little water so as not to dilute its superb bouquet. I dropped
one cube of ice thoughtfully into the drink, then another. A
random thought crossed my mind, triggered off by the sight
of ice. Where we were going, the fish have their own in-built
anti-freeze. I sipped and the brandy warmed my blood. I sat
down, sipped again. I wanted to be alone, and yet I did not
want to be alone. I looked idly round Captain Prestrud's
pictures on the walls, including the fjord scene of Linn's home.
They would have to come down. That went also for the pre-
served tip of a killer whale's fin which hung like a stiff
leather triangle over the desk.

I was restive. I moved towards the desk and fingered the
fin. The phone rang.

'Wegger here, sir. Sorry to disturb you off duty.'

'No hassle. What's your problem?'

'Those cases of explosive charges for blasting a way through
the kelp for the boats when we land . . . I'd like your permission to re-stow 'em.'

'Aren't they safe enough where they are?'

'They're in Number Three hold, sir. I've been down checking. They're stowed above the shaft tunnel, aft the engine-
room. It's pretty warm down there tonight. There's the heat
from the engine-room and this hot wind. I'd like to bring the
cases up to Number Two 'tween decks, where the ventila-
tion's better. It's also easier to get at them there.'

I was to remember that comment later. At the time I en-
dorsed the suggestion. If the hold were anything like as hot
as my cabin – which had an open porthole – Wegger's was a
sound idea.

'Carry on, Mr Wegger.'

Since the incident earlier in the day over the radio signal Wegger had proved himself a professional. Already the crew was functioning as a team, although I didn't care for his slave-driving methods. This was the second idea that Wegger had had for negotiating the kelp, which blocks Prince Edward like a floating reef. Before the ship had said goodbye to Cape Agulhas he had proposed that we sharpen the leading edges of the propeller on the boat we would be using – weather allowing – to land the shore parties. The sharp edges would serve as a kind of rotary knife to hack a way through the barrier. Kelp is especially thick off the landing-place at Cave Bay, in places up to 50 metres wide. Trying to row through its strangling fronds is for the birds. The idea was to blow a path through the kelp first with small charges of explosive and then negotiate it by means of the boat.

I put down the phone and reached for my drink. There was a knock at the door.

'Come in!'

It was Linn. Her black pants and champagne-coloured tunic made her look slimmer than before. At dinner she had squired the VIPs to the captain's table – my table. The Jacobsens did not put in an appearance. However, captain's tables are not my scene. I had been grateful, for once, to have McKinley around.

Now the tell-tale marks of her grief were skilfully masked by eye-shadow.

She said, 'I'm suffocating. It felt as if the walls of my cabin were closing in on me. Does it mean anything in particular, this frightful sogginess in the air?'

'It goes hand-in-hand with the south-easter. And the Agulhas Bank is one of the worst areas in the world for electrical storms.' I ushered her to a chair. 'A drink? – mine's brandy.'

'No brandy, thanks. Something short.'

'Vanderhum? Might as well keep it in the Cape family.'

'That will do fine.'

I fixed the drink and said, 'I'm glad you came, Linn. I was in a miscellaneous mood. I don't know where to start my thinking.'

She pulled out a coin from her pants pocket and laid it between us on the desk-top. It was a Krugerrand, the South African coin which contains exactly one fine ounce of gold.

I picked it up. It was warm – warm from her groin where her pocket was, a surge of my pulse told me.

I said lightly, 'Now you're compounding my confusion.'

She eyed me over the rim of her liqueur glass. 'When the old Norsemen set out on voyages into the unknown they buried a gold coin in the step of their mast to bring them good luck. Can you find a similar place for this?'

I couldn't see myself boring a hole into the *Quest*'s utilitarian mast – it was more a crane than a mast – and attempting to conceal the coin. At today's gold price it would be a healthy lucky dip for any crewman who might spot it.

Wegger and his boat were still in my mind. 'I'll tell you what I'll do – I'll salt it away in the mast of the launch we'll be using for the shore parties at Prince Edward.'

'You're not just fobbing me off? You're not laughing at me, John?'

She seemed very small, vulnerable and so alone. She looked into her glass and added: 'The voyage came unstuck right at the start – didn't it? – except for that little time on deck before the message came about Dad's death.'

So the bells had rung for her, too.

'A bad beginning can mean a good end,' I replied. 'There's no reason why the trip shouldn't go off smoothly from now on. We've got a good ship and a good crew. Everything's running like clockwork.'

'That's what you say, but do you really believe it, John?'

I side-stepped the question. 'I didn't see Captain Jacobsen at dinner. How did he take the news of your father's death?'

'Badly, I'm afraid. It was a traumatic occasion for both of us. I felt I had to be the one to break it to him.'

'You don't evade your responsibilities, Linn.'

'Mrs Jacobsen wasn't pleased – I think my news could have aggravated that heart condition of his.'

'What did he say when you told him?'

' "Now there's no point in going on" – something like that.'

'Anything else?'

'Why do you ask, John?'

'I can't get your father's last words out of my mind. Or rather, not so much his words, as what he was trying to say but couldn't. I'm quite sure he wanted to explain something about that war-time business. And Jacobsen was one of the three captains who escaped.'

Linn put down her glass. 'When you meet Captain Jacobsen you'll find he's not the talkative kind. In fact, he's pretty dour and reserved. After he said that about no point going on he just sat and stared for a long time. Then he muttered something that sounded like, "It's not far from where it all happened – the position for launching the weather buoy. About a day and a half's steaming." '

'What was he driving at, Linn?'

'I don't know. After that his face went purplish, and then very white. Mrs Jacobsen rushed for his heart pills and shooed me out.'

I poured myself another brandy. 'Does it strike you, Linn, that Jacobsen is now the last skipper alive of the three who were involved in that war-time escape? The other two – your father and a man called Torgersen – are both dead.'

She answered so softly I could scarcely hear. 'Murdered.'

'It doesn't make sense,' I went on. 'There's a gap of about thirty years between the two deaths. If they really are linked, and someone is bent on taking revenge . . .'

'But why, John? In God's name, why? My father never did anything wrong . . .'

I recalled the dying man's words about doing something which seemed right at the time. I looked at Linn's strained face and decided not to mention it. My mind went on to Captain Prestrud's final words.

'Linn, you were telling me Dina's Island is Prince Edward . . .'

'It was never actually called Dina's Island. The name figures on some eighteenth-century charts, that's all. Captain Cook's name for it, Prince Edward, has always been the one in general use.'

'Which adds to the puzzle, Linn. Your father's last words to me were, "Stay away from Dina's Island." '

She stared at me. 'Are you sure you heard right?'

'Quite sure. He said that very clearly. But why should he, when the whole purpose of this cruise – and apparently a life-time ambition of his own – was to get to Dina's Island, in other words, Prince Edward? And why should he call it by a name which it took you ages to unearth in the archives? How did he know the name? It doesn't add up, Linn.'

She stood up. 'Let's go on deck and get some air. These walls are beginning to close in too.'

Once we had got clear of the shelter of the lifeboat deck I took her arm to steer her towards the stern. Our eyes were not yet fully adjusted to the darkness. I kept close to the rail to avoid a newly-painted red patch on the deck.

'What's that, John?' she asked.

'They're supposed to be markings for a deck quoits court, but in fact they have an ulterior purpose.'

The outline on the deck was like a miniature helicopter landing-pad.

'I don't like the colour of *Quest*,' I told her. 'White's all right for a fine-weather cruise. Nice and yachty, like in the magazines. But it's too near the colour of ice. If this ship ran into trouble down South she'd be mighty hard to spot by air search. I'm hedging my safety bets – this red patch and the *Quest*'s red lifeboats combined would be visible from a search plane twenty kilometres away.'

She shivered and was silent.

We went aft. At the rail by the jackstaff above the stern a bare-footed man in crumpled running shorts and towel singlet was getting ready to throw something overboard. It looked like a hooped butterfly net with a bottle wedged in its end, and it had a weight attached.

He said, without preliminary, 'We're travelling much too fast for me to collect anything, really. But I go on hoping.' He pitched the thing untidily over the side and gestured at the water.

'That's what I'm after.'

Little globes of luminosity were passing along the ship's side beneath the water. The *Quest* appeared to be skimming on ballbearings of warm light.

'Nothing very unusual, but they never fail to thrill me – jelly-fish.'

He straightened up and laughed. A stray wisp of hair couldn't hide his receding hairline.

'They say all oceanographers are nuts. Or is it ocean-ologists? I never know. Maybe I am. But you can't live in the presence of great mysteries without some of them rubbing off on you. I'm Toby Trimen.'

He tugged at the dip-net and gave a small whoop. 'Got him!'

Deftly he swung the net clear of the ship's side and manoeuvred it upright. Then he rummaged inside the muslin-like material and towing bridles and untied the tapes that held a collecting-jar in position at its rear, and showed us the bottle containing the sea-creature. It looked like a beautiful pale pink toadstool, except that it had trailing tentacles. It was all aglow.

'*Noctiluca* – light of the night,' Toby Trimen said. 'Poor thing! He's still trying to get orientated after what I've done to him.'

Linn smiled at his enthusiasm. 'Did he tell you that?'

Toby made a gesture which took in the whole sea as far as the South Pole. His eyes were as limpid as new ice.

'It's not sea or ice or creatures but a wonderful – an enormous wonderland,' he said. 'It's so full of wonders that it makes me breathless. Look, our jelly-fish is getting orientated. He's got the most wonderful built-in gadget inside him to tell which way up he is. Just like a plane's blind-flying instruments – would you believe it?'

He saw from our polite amusement that we didn't. He plucked the jelly-fish delicately out of the bottle and continued, 'Inside this umbrella, which is his top, is his self-righting gear. When he tilts, there's a small ball which rolls around inside and touches nerves which automatically stabilize him. It's a miracle in itself. If you were an atheist, you'd be cured if you knew just half of the master-plan there is among the creatures in these seas.'

He put the jelly-fish back in the bottle and held up his hands like a showman. They were all aglow from handling the creature. Then he bent down and scrawled '*Quest*' on the deck with the luminous slime, straightened up again, and grinned at us.

'D'you see the jelly-fish's trailing tentacles? At the base of each one there's a group of cells which is sensitive to light. If I once start on the mysteries of phosphorescence you'll . . . you'll . . .' He was at a loss for words. 'It's what scientists don't know about it that's even more wonderful still. The photophores – those are the light-giving mechanisms on sea creatures – are so engineered, so perfectly planned . . .' He shook his head like a diver coming up from a deep dive. 'It's a miracle. They've found out that the light's produced by a substance called luciferin plus oxygen reacting in the company of an enzyme named luciferase . . .'

He laughed back his own exuberance. 'See why they say we oceanographers are nuts? Why, even the krill are packed with wonders. They're those tiny creatures which are the basic diet of whales. Their sex-life is the most delicate and lovely thing I know – the male has a special very complex little hand complete with minute fingers, and with this he takes a little flask of sperm to the female during courtship . . .' He turned away, as if he realized he was over-reaching himself, and pitched the jelly-fish carefully into the sea.

Then he resumed in a much more matter-of-fact voice. 'With conditions like these tonight, we could get a superb display of phosphorescence. But it seems to need a sort of trigger to set the whole sea alight. If you suddenly switch on a ship's radar, for instance, it's enough to do it. No one knows why it does, but it does.'

Linn said, with a twitch of her lips, 'Why don't you ask the captain to switch it on then?'

'I wish I could.'

'He's standing in front of you.'

'You're kidding!' he replied. 'If I'd known . . .'

'Don't panic,' I assured him. 'I don't eat passengers. The radar should start working any time now. We're approaching the tanker lanes and if there's anything that needs watching with radar, human eyes, direction-finders, the lot, it's supertankers. They'll mow you down without batting an eyelid . . .'

Suddenly the sea switched on as if my words had liberated light. The whitecaps of the day's gale became vivid lantern-bearers of the night, rippling, foaming, recurving in fantastic shapes. The churning screw threw up a wide wake of what looked like a billion Bunsen-burners of blue-green flame. The water which burst from the *Quest*'s sharp cutwater was softer in colour than bursting napalm, harsher than phosphorous. All the waters to the horizon were a welter of living and moving light.

Toby Trimen's recital of the scientific names of the creatures

staging this fabulous display sounded like an incantation:
'*Ceratium! Peridinium! Noctiluca!*'

Linn whispered to me, as if speaking louder would destroy
the magic, 'John – have you ever seen anything like this
before?'

I found myself whispering back. 'Once. Further South. Not
anything as spectacular as this, though.'

'It's fabulous . . . it's . . . there are no words . . .'

It was I, however, who was at a loss for words at what
followed. As we stood entranced, there was a series of loud
clicks: the *Quest*'s masts, derricks, wire stays, the oval of the
stack, the extremities of the deck-houses and bridge, the radar
and D/F aerials all lighted up, each a flaming point of light.
The clicking reverberated like a chorus of ten thousand
beetles.

I wheeled round to face Linn and Toby Trimen. Linn's fine
hair was surrounded by the sort of golden halo you see on old
frescoes in Italy; the fire crackled off the oceanographer's
auburn top-knot and contrasted with the jelly-fish's luminous
slime on his hands. Then there came striding towards us the
figure of Miss Auchinleck, who had materialized out of the
blackness of the stern. She looked like a devil with a flaming
poniard in her mouth: the discharge spat off the end of her
cigarillo-holder.

The sight of her brought me back to earth.

'John! . . . what's happening?' gasped Linn.

I answered a little unsteadily, as the unburning flames
enveloped the ship. 'St Elmo's Fire! I've only heard about it
– never seen it. It's caused by the build-up of electricity . . .
it's discharging from every point of the ship . . .'

Toby Trimen began to laugh; he looked like a fire-eater
breathing out little bursts of blue-green.

I went on, 'What's happened is that the *Quest* has become
the conductor for a big electrical build-up in the atmosphere
– that's why it was so oppressive all evening. It's a natural
phenomenon – no need to be scared. It looks bad, but it won't
last . . .'

'But that noise, John!'

It sounded like foil being crumpled by a thousand hands.
'That's the sound of the discharge. I believe it's harmless.

71

But I'm worried about the radio and other instruments. It could damage them . . .'

Persson came sprinting along the deck, trailing fire like a jet's afterburner.

'Sir! Sir! What's happening! The radio's gone – it nearly burst my eardrums – everything's blown –'

I repeated my explanation and added quickly, 'It'll pass. There's nothing to be done until it does.'

The *Quest* was a fiery ship slicing through a burning sea; the firmament above our heads was black, except where Orion's belt cut it like a sword. Toby Trimen held up a hand in astonishment – it pulsed flame from the tip of each finger and thumb.

I told them, 'St Elmo's Fire is believed to bring a ship bad luck. At any rate the U-boat aces of the last war thought so. One of the greatest of them – Kretschmer – found his U-boat enveloped in St Elmo's Fire just before it was sunk.'

'I think they were wrong, John,' said Linn in a strange, subdued voice. 'Look at that.'

She gestured astern of the ship. Holding position effortlessly above the jackstaff was a Wandering Albatross. He was the biggest I have ever seen. He must have measured four metres from wing-tip to wing-tip. As he came into the ship's field of discharge, the individual feathers of his great wings stood out clearly demarcated. Each one became a tiny muzzle of soft flame which he aimed at us.

Linn took my arm and held me to her, so that I felt the softness of her breast against my upper arm.

'It looks – holy!' she burst out.

The great bird lifted slightly as an updraught from the stack eddied in his direction. For a moment he hung there, the silent and luminous ambassador of the Southern Ocean.

Then everything went black.

The St Elmo's Fire had shut off as swiftly and dramatically as it had come. My eyes were still dazzled and I couldn't see the length of the *Quest*'s deck.

Then, as my eyes accustomed themselves to the change, I saw that the sea still flamed – a softer glow, a gentle feminine thing alongside the harshness of St Elmo.

The *Quest* drove on into the blue-green ocean with its

million lances and bickers of light. After a while this, too, began to fade, not suddenly but slowly, as the ship drew clear of the phosphorescent patch. Then finally we were in the night again.

CHAPTER NINE

'It's just a mess, sir.' Persson, the radio operator, handed me the RTT signal. 'I can't make head or tail of it.'

A mess the radio-teletype slip was. Anything further from a weather report would have been hard to imagine. There was a garbled string of disconnected letters and figures.

He stabbed the slip with his finger. 'ZRS – that's about all I can make out – that's Marion Island's call-sign.'

We were on the *Quest*'s bridge the next morning, Saturday. It was shortly after seven o'clock. What I had wanted was Marion's weather report at 6.45 a.m. as well as the first mainland Weather Bureau forecast at seven. The previous night I had ordered all the ship's clocks to be switched to GMT. This was because the buoy launch was scheduled for 10h00 GMT on Monday.

'Looks like an ionospheric storm to me,' I remarked. 'That means a radio black-out, if it's bad.'

'I've never sailed this way before, sir,' replied Persson. 'I haven't any experience of them. But after last night . . .'

'The St Elmo's Fire was purely a local phenomenon,' I assured him. 'An ionospheric storm is something very different. Sunspots. This is a year of maximum sunspot activity. We must expect trouble.'

'It was bad enough last night, sir. All the instruments went for a burton. I worked halfway through the night getting 'em right again.'

'They're all okay, then?'

'The radar's still flukey – I've nothing to test it out on. No ships or land.'

'That's the way it is in these waters, Persson, no ships, no land.'

We had run clear of the Agulhas Bank during the night. The *Quest*'s jerky motion in the short, savage seas of the Bank had given way to a long see-sawing up-and-under motion as she felt Antarctica's first great swells under her. Judging from the deserted decks and empty corridors of the ship, the members of the cruise found little to choose between the two types of motion.

'No signals coming direct from the mainland?' I asked Persson.

'No, sir,' he replied gloomily. 'They're more confused than Marion's signals – if that's possible.'

'What's this grouping – ZRP?'

'That's the SANAE station on Dronning Maud Land, on the mainland of Antarctica itself,' he answered. 'I was fiddling around trying to raise something or someone. There's sometimes a relay via Mawson, the Australian ice station.'

I made a mental note to check the *Quest*'s magnetic compass. A magnetic storm can affect a compass to the extent of a couple of degrees. I would also have to check her gyro. She was equipped with the old type of gravity-controlled instrument which is inclined to wander when a ship is far South, and I didn't want any inaccuracies due to gyro error at the buoy's launch-point, still less in the vicinity of Prince Edward's dangerous approaches.

'There's nothing we can do but hope,' I told Persson. 'When's the next signal scheduled from Marion?'

'At half-past nine, sir.'

'My bet is that it will still be just as bad, Persson. Keep trying, though.'

'Aye, aye, sir.'

Even as I gave the order I knew I was kidding myself. I was well aware that what the weather might or might not be doing at Marion, over a thousand kilometres to the east, was as immaterial to the state of the *Quest*'s immediate weather as would be a forecast from Gough Island, a thousand kilometres in the opposite direction, to the west. The *Quest* was completely on her own. It might be snowing on Prince Edward now, while the *Quest* swung through blue seas, a clear blue sky and a cool breeze.

Suddenly I became aware of a commotion at the rear of the bridge. MacFie, the chief engineer, rushed up. His face
74

was angry and flushed and for a moment I suspected he might have been having a liquid breakfast.

'What the hell . . .?'

'You'd better come below,' he snapped at me. He shredded a piece of oily waste between his powerful fingers. 'You've got a mutiny on your hands.'

'What the devil are you talking about, Chief?'

He glanced round the bridge. All eyes were on him. He had the sense not to blurt out anything further. He jerked his head. I followed. We had got only as far as the bridge companionway when he started again.

'It's that bluidy ghost. And they're Irish. Bluidy Irish. They say they won't go on watch and the Norwegians are with 'em . . .'

'Pull yourself together, man! Talk sense!'

MacFie halted suddenly on the steel steps so that I was almost on top of him before I could stop myself. Close contact with MacFie meant a smell of oil, grease and an overlay of sweat.

'It began with O'Byrne,' he growled. 'Then Reilly came into the act. He's a sea-lawyer, a trouble-maker, if ever there was one, blast him! Now the two Irish greasers have been joined by two Norwegian motormen. They're all great pals. They're saying they won't stand watch. How the hell am I supposed to run the ship . . .'

'What *happened*, Chief?'

'You'd better read 'em the riot act. Or lay the bluidy ghost.'

'MacFie!' I called. The note in my voice brought him up short. 'Come back here. I want an explanation, a proper one. Make it official.'

'Goddamned Irish greasers!' he muttered to himself. Then he said, 'It was like this, sir. O'Byrne and Reilly were on the stint after midnight. O'Byrne went to his locker . . .'

I broke in sharply. 'How much Tullamore Dew did O'Byrne bring aboard, Chief?'

MacFie said drily, with a cynical smile, 'I haven't run an engine-room all these years without learning a few tricks. If O'Byrne had any booze left, it wasn't much. I searched the place myself when we sailed. No, he'd stashed away some supper and was wanting a bite in the early hours.'

'And so?'

'His locker had been broken open. His plate of chow was gone.'

'This sounds to me like a storm in a teacup. Or in a dinnerplate. Surely you're capable of settling a little thing like this yourself, Chief.'

He bridled under my tone. 'I've settled better men than O'Byrne and Reilly before now. But they're all in, and standing together. The whole ruddy watch. Even the electrician.'

'Go on.'

'O'Byrne wasn't too upset, I might say, when he missed his food. He went and told his chum Reilly. Reilly handed over his duties for a moment to O'Byrne and went to look. He came back and said he'd seen a ghost between the deep tank and the shaft tunnel. It's dark down there.'

'Carrying O'Byrne's supper?'

MacFie eyed me grimly. 'No. A sub-machine gun.'

'Rubbish, Chief.'

'That's what I said. But he spread it around among the rest of 'em and now they're on his side.'

I thought quickly. 'I'll have this out with Reilly myself. Chief, what have you heard about Captain Prestrud?'

He appeared surprised. 'He's in hospital. Got hurt. That's why you've taken over.'

'You didn't hear anything more on the engine-room grapevine?'

'Is there more?'

'Yes, but keep your mouth shut. I thought Reilly might have heard something and his Celtic temperament had embroidered it into a ghost story. Captain Prestrud died yesterday morning.'

'I'm truly sorry,' MacFie replied slowly. 'He was a great gentleman.'

'The passengers don't know this either,' I added. 'Miss Prestrud and I decided to go ahead with the cruise as if nothing had happened.'

'I'm certain Reilly and O'Byrne don't know,' MacFie said. 'If it had been Captain Prestrud's ghost, it wouldn't have acted that way anyhow.'

'What d'you mean, Chief?'

'Reilly said the ghost held the gun on him, down there next to the shaft tunnel. It backed away and vanished, he said.'

'Anything else?'

'Reilly keeps saying what big hands it had. The automatic was half-hidden in them.'

Reilly stuck to his story when I confronted him in the engine-room. The little group of sullen strikers were gathered in a corner like guilty schoolboys. Except that they were frightened. Reilly was scared and his fear had infected the others.

'Listen, Reilly,' I told him. 'If I search the ship myself, will that satisfy you?'

Fear also made him truculent and impertinent. 'I know what that means. In half an hour you'll come back and feed us a load of crap that you didn't find a thing. You'll never have moved out of your cabin.'

I wanted to take a swing at him, ugly little runt though he was.

'You'll come along with me, Reilly. If you want to piss yourself, do it before we start.'

It was the sort of talk the others understood. They laughed jeeringly. Reilly realized he was losing his grip. MacFie grunted satisfaction.

'I'll come – but only if you have a gun,' answered Reilly. '*He* had a gun. One of those automatics with a skeleton butt. I've seen 'em back home.'

'Belfast, I'll bet,' I retorted. 'You didn't by any chance have to get out quick to save your skin, did you, Reilly?'

The others were siding with me now. O'Byrne said mockingly, 'Go along with you now, Paddy boy. Show the big man you aren't scared.'

Reilly turned on him angrily. 'It was your friggin' grub he pinched. Now I've got to friggin' well go and hunt him down.'

My mind was busy while I kept the exchange going. The only gun I knew of in the ship was Wegger's Luger. Wegger had the dogwatch; he'd be asleep now. I had no intention of going cap in hand to wake him and beg his gun just because a sea-lawyer of a greaser had claimed to have seen a ghost.

I said to MacFie, 'Give me a spanner, Chief. A hefty one.'
I addressed Reilly. 'If that's not enough for you, you can stay.
Coming?'

The tool MacFie handed me was big enough to drive a hole
through the *Quest*'s plating.

Reilly asked, 'Now?'

'Yes. Now.'

He said in a whining tone, 'Ghosts don't walk around in
daylight. And he had a *gun*.'

I laughed derisively. 'Come on, Chief. Get back to work,
you others. Reilly can have a break until I come back and
report to him on the incidence of the supernatural.'

They didn't know what that meant, nor did I intend them
to. They started to grin and break up. Reilly hung back unde-
cidedly.

I started my search with the shaft tunnel. It was dark and
dank in the bilges, and noisy from the engines and the propeller shaft. MacFie held a torch. Bent double, we worked our
way along the tunnel in the direction of the stern. My foot
slipped on something. I thought it was a dead rat. MacFie
directed his flashlight beam on it.

I eyed the pulped thing under my shoe and called above
the noise to MacFie, 'This is the first ghost I know that eats
cold boiled potato.'

MacFie replied thoughtfully, 'So Reilly did see someone,
after all.'

I gripped the spanner tighter. 'Let's get on.'

We completed our search of the shaft tunnel. There was
nothing.

Number 3 and 4 holds, abaft the stack, were likewise
empty.

We went for'ard and cased the forecastle, where the crew
lived.

Nothing.

Number One hold was nearest to the foc's'le. When we had
been through it without result, only Number 2 hold and the
'tween decks were still unaccounted for.

We found ourselves in Number 2 hold among cases, pack-
ages, and all the miscellaneous things which go to make up a
ship's cargo.

MacFie shone his flashlight on his watch. 'I must be getting back. Wait till I get my hands on Reilly. I'll trim his arse-feathers all right!'

'Quiet!' I snapped. 'Out with that light! There's someone coming!'

There was a pad-pad of bare feet from the direction of the deep-fuel tank which separated the hold from the engine-room. MacFie and I shrank back against the nearest case, clear of the gangway which had been left open between the cargo.

He was coming at a trot, breathing hard. I took a tight hold of the chunk of spanner. As he came opposite our hiding-place, MacFie threw the beam and I launched myself.

I had raised the spanner to half-brain him.

I stopped in mid-stroke.

It was Wegger.

He had the Luger in his left hand.

He had the gun by the barrel, with the butt extended, like a club. You can't fire a Luger like that.

He dodged aside as quick as a boxer side-stepping a blow, and swung to meet me. He raised the butt with a quick, deadly motion.

Then he, too, stopped.

'Sir! Are you all right? I heard there'd been a mutiny . . .'

He was panting hard, like a man who has run up half a dozen ship's ladders. He was dressed in a peculiar rig, washed-out jeans and a karate-type blouse.

'Put that bloody gun away!' I snapped to hide my own taut-ness. 'It might go off and hurt someone.'

Wegger seemed to become suddenly conscious that he was swinging a lethal weapon.

'It isn't loaded – I prefer to use it this way – I mean, there wasn't time to load it . . .'

There was a cold excitement about the man which vibrated through the hold. His chest rose and fell with his quick breathing.

'Listen,' I went on. 'There's no need for panic. Or to flash a gun all round the ship.'

'Did you find anyone?' he demanded.

'You should have been in your cabin asleep,' I retorted.

'How the hell did you hear about this mutiny business?'

He ignored my question. 'Did you find anyone?' he repeated.

MacFie interrupted. 'We've searched the bluidy ship and wasted the skipper's time and mine just because some sonofabitch Irishman . . .'

'Chief,' I said, 'now that I've got an armed escort you can get back and kick Reilly up the backside. Mr Wegger and I will finish off the search just as a formality.'

'There's nothing I would like better,' replied Wegger, with a strange note in his voice.

'We'll take a quick look-round here and then finish with the 'tween decks aft where the drifter buoy and the instruments are,' I went on. 'If anyone's been acting suspiciously the met. men and the scientists are bound to have spotted it.'

MacFie turned to go. I returned the big spanner to him and said, 'That's too big a weapon to use on one small Irishman, Chief.'

He snorted with disgust and went.

Number 4 'tween decks, the scientists' preserve, was over the stern. I opened the door ahead of Wegger and went in. It was a big, bare space, well lighted.

A remarkable sight met our eyes.

Holdgate, the volcanologist who was sharing with the three met. men, was lying on a wooden board the shape of a coffin lid. Next to him was the shroud-like shape of the plasticized nylon drogue. This was to be attached to the bottom of the buoy to stabilize its drift. Holdgate's arms and legs were fastened to the board with straps and buckles.

'Now!' called Smit, the senior weatherman. He gave his knuckles a crack as a preliminary. Then the three grabbed the board by Holdgate's head.

'Transmit!'

Holdgate sucked his teeth in an ineffectual kind of whistle. The three up-ended the board so that Holdgate stood almost upright.

'Buoy away!'

Holdgate gave another whistle.

Smit said, 'Okay, boys. That's it. Just like a real burial at sea. All we need is the captain . . .'

'He's here.'

I couldn't warm to the harmless horseplay – you can't once you've done the real thing. The three lowered the plank to the deck and began to loose the straps in a self-conscious way.

'We were having a run-down for the launch on Monday,' Smit apologized. 'The carpenter fixed us this plank.'

I stood silent and eyed them. Accompanied by Wegger, tough and bare-chested, we must have looked as if we meant business.

Smit laughed uncomfortably and cracked his knuckles.

'Why not practise with the buoy itself instead of a man?' I asked.

Bokkie was lashed to a couple of eyebolts on the floor nearby.

Smit crossed to the orange-headed drifter and ran his hand affectionately down its centre tubing.

'We can't risk this PVC tubing – it's the weak point about Bokkie. I'd rather have had fibre-glass but it couldn't be moulded in time.'

Holdgate had regained his feet and his dignity. 'I offered to deputize for Bokkie,' he said.

'Are you telling me there are weak points in a buoy which is going to hit some of the wildest weather in the world in the West Wind Drift?' I said to Smit.

Smit rushed to his own and Bokkie's defence with a spate of technical talk.

'She's not weak for that. It's okay when she's floating. But she isn't meant to be stood up and extra weight put on the long body. We're re-testing every component again now. We scrapped the French barometers because they drifted too much. The British type are fine, except that they eat current, don't they, Pete?'

Pete, a bull-necked young man with a growing-time of only two days on his beard since he embarked, said in a deep voice, 'Bokkie's now got one of the new Yank-model barometers. They cost less, use less power.'

Smit stroked Bokkie's lower limb, inside which was the power pack. 'These batteries have got to last a year. A whole year!'

T-shirt Jannie broke in. 'I remade the antenna myself before we started off. The old one was up to maggots . . .'

'Wait,' I interrupted. 'There's something I want to ask you

about the buoy. But first of all, did any of you see anyone suspicious around here this morning?'

'There was an old bag with a cigarette-holder,' answered Jannie. 'She was suspicious of everything. Mostly of us. Wanted us to promise we wouldn't photograph the penguins or something.'

'Or something,' echoed Smit.

'Good,' I replied. 'That's that, then. Now, about the buoy.'

Smit was like a skua hen defending a chick. 'What about the buoy?'

'The radio's gone sour on us. I reckon we're running into a full-scale radio black-out. Ionospheric storm.'

'So what?'

Holdgate wandered away disinterestedly to his own instruments.

'Well, won't that affect Bokkie?' I asked. 'What about the automatic signals to the satellite?'

'It makes no difference,' replied Smit. 'It's a line-of-sight transmission.'

'I don't follow.'

He regarded me as if I'd been a spastic case. 'The Tiros N satellite was fired into polar orbit specially for the Global Atmospheric Research Programme. Tiros will make four passes a day over the area where Bokkie and the balloon operate after we've set 'em going on Monday. Clear?'

I nodded and he went on. 'Tiros is equipped with what we call a Random Access Monitoring System – RAMS for short. It picks up the signals from the buoy and the balloon.'

'*All* the buoys and balloons,' Jannie corrected him. 'It's a global-scale experiment. Bokkie's only a part of it. But a very important part. The Southern Ocean's a tough proposition, as you know. That's why it's so important that nothing should stop us launching the buoy on Monday morning . . .'

'Ten sharp, GMT,' Smit added.

'On the dot,' echoed bull-neck Pete.

'You still haven't answered my question,' I persisted. 'As I see it, the whole project could misfire if the ionospheric storm goes on. In my experience they usually last four or five days. That means Monday may be blacked out. Also, I don't understand how the satellite can distinguish whether it's Bokkie or our balloon signalling when there are others scattered about the oceans of the world.'

Wegger shifted his feet. Duty forced him to stay and listen.

'Each buoy or balloon transmits signals with a specific frequency at short intervals,' Smit explained. 'The series of signals in each transmission is the method of identifying the buoy or balloon as well as giving the various readings of pressure, temperature and so on. The transmission consists first of a ten-bit data word used for barometric pressure, word two is an optional parameter, and word three must be eight bits showing surface water temperature . . .'

I cut in. 'Skip it. I simply don't know what you're talking about, man. Just tell me in one-syllable words why the radio black-out won't affect signals from the buoy to the satellite.'

He thought for a moment, wrestling with the problem of getting down to my kindergarten level.

Finally he said, 'This is how it goes. The buoy is floating in the ocean – right? The satellite appears over the curve of the horizon – four times a day it does that. Right? As soon as it does, it picks up the buoy's signals because the buoy and the satellite are now *seeing* each other – line of sight, it's called. Right? The process is not like ordinary short-wave radio signals which bounce off the high layer of the upper atmosphere. It's more like pointing a gun – while the buoy and the satellite are in sight of one another, the signals get through. It's like your ship's radio-telephone – you could speak on the R/T to another ship during a full-scale black-out providing you were close enough.'

'Are you telling me that, in spite of the radio black-out, I could have a ship-to-ship conversation on the R/T? It's a new one on me. I'd like to have tried it, but it so happens that there's never been another ship around on such occasions.'

'Of course it would depend on the distance between the ships.'

'How far would that be?'

'It's not easy to estimate – an outside limit of four hundred to five hundred kilometres, I'd say. Of course the quality of voice would deteriorate considerably, but it might still be hearable. Other factors come into it too, like the strength of the signals.'

T-shirt Jannie added, 'As the satellite orbits the earth, it picks up masses of information from all the other buoys and balloons. This is recorded on magnetic tape, and then – it's really very smart – the satellite "dumps" all the information to the receiving station at the National Center for Atmospheric Research at Boulder, in the United States. Boy, you should see their computer! It digests all the information, and works out every buoy's exact position . . .'

'It sounds like black magic,' I interrupted. 'I wish it were as easy for me to calculate my ship's position. How does it work?'

'When the satellite approaches Bokkie or leaves her behind, the frequency of the signals varies all the time,' he explained. 'From these varying frequencies the exact position can be computed. And it really is exact – down to less than half a kilometre in a very wide ocean.'

I said, 'I'm beginning to get the measure of Bokkie's importance in the chain.'

Smit said, 'We've checked and re-checked the electronics package. We'll re-check finally tomorrow, just to make sure. But it's all systems go for Monday morning.'

I could sense that Wegger was growing more restive, but I persisted with my questions. 'I can see that the whole project is a miracle of planning but what if something goes wrong? What happens, say, if Bokkie's transmitter packs up when she's been only a few days on her own?'

Smit frowned. 'It can't – it mustn't. If the data parameters show something wrong . . .'

'One-syllable words please!'

He grinned. 'If Bokkie suddenly starts giving information on sea temperature or barometric pressure which is haywire, an alert goes out. Likewise, if her rate of drift went wild . . .'

'How could anyone know? Anything can happen in these seas.'

'No, it can't, Captain. The buoys which were set adrift last year as a pilot experiment showed that the fastest drift speed we can expect from a buoy is about one knot. The biggest distance she will cover is slightly under fifty nautical miles a day. An alert would go out if it was suddenly much different from that. We can pinpoint Bokkie's position precisely four times a day, like I said.'

'Who alerts who?'

'Boulder would contact the Regional Telecommunication

Hub involved – that's South Africa. Then the wires would hum!'

'The same thing applies to the balloon,' added T-shirt Jannie. 'We know the balloon will travel like smoke in the Westerlies. But if she suddenly started slowing before she reached her ceiling of twenty-five kilometres above the earth, we'd want to know why. Boulder would sound the alert. Come over here.'

He led me to the balloon. The envelope was spread out on the deck for checking like a huge parachute. At its base was a tiny aluminium box.

This was Jannie's scene. 'Bokkie's a marvel, but this instrument package is . . . is . . .' He indicated the box. 'Feel it.'

I weighed it in my hand. It was the size of a miniaturized transistor radio. 'It's incredible,' I said.

'Weighs about half a kilogram,' he told me. 'It's the sort of thing the Yanks use in their space probes. This isn't one of those zero pressure balloons the French and us are using for research in the stratosphere. They're huge and carry a scientific payload of about thirty kilograms. Their data is telemetred to earth in the fifteen MHz frequency and picked up in Réunion and Pretoria by special tracking stations. This is a little beauty which can be launched from a ship without special apparatus.'

Smit joined us. 'This Global Experiment is the biggest thing that's ever been undertaken weatherwise – there'll be detailed observation made for the first time of the entire atmosphere of the world and the surface of the Seven Seas.'

'Including the Southern Ocean,' I added.

'They singled out the Southern Ocean specially,' said Smit.

Holdgate said from his corner, 'The way you lot go on, you'd think that meteorology was the only science in the world. Why, if we knew more about Prince Edward geologically we'd open up a new chapter in the history of the earth. It's one of the most important places for understanding the composition of the earth's upper mantle and the theory of continental drift and ocean floor spreading. The island's practically unexplored. The only work done was for a few days about ten years ago . . .'

I broke in. 'You may never get ashore, Doctor Holdgate – let me warn you before you start raising your hopes. The

85

Quest could lie off Cave Bay for a month without the opportunity.'

He brushed my cautions aside. 'Do you know the big cave?'

I sensed Wegger tighten up. His boredom during the discussion of the Bokkie project had vanished. He was staring keenly at Holdgate.

'No,' I replied. 'Or rather, I've only seen it through binoculars from about half a mile out to sea. The anchorage is very tricky and I couldn't get close. There's also a barrier of kelp between the anchorage and the cave. It didn't look much from the sea – just a huge hole in the cliffs about four metres in diameter, big rocks, no beach and some wiry-looking tussock grass here and there.'

'My theory is that the cave is a lava tunnel which goes right under the island,' said Holdgate in his lecturing manner. 'If it is, it's the only one so far as we know which belongs to the older period of volcanic activity on the island. When the volcano erupted originally it must have been like a blast furnace under the island and the gas pressure must have been colossal to blow out . . . anyway, I intend to explore the cave and find out.'

Wegger's voice sounded thick. 'You're wasting your time. There's nothing there. The cave stops after a short distance.'

Holdgate looked mulish. 'You're wrong. My information is that the cave goes deep, very deep. That's what the geologists reckoned who managed a few days on the island in the sixties. Anyway, how do you know anything about it?'

Wegger's damaged right talon plucked at his karate-type blouse. 'I've been there,' he replied harshly. 'Years ago. Before your scientific pals. There's nothing except a few old dates scratched on the walls by survivors of ships who sheltered in the cave.'

The two of them seemed to be generating enough heat to re-kindle the fires of Prince Edward's dozen extinct volcanoes.

'Now get this clear,' I snapped at both of them. 'I don't give a damn whether Prince Edward's cave is or isn't the most fascinating place on the face of the earth, or whether it does or doesn't go under the island. But I'm not going to risk my ship for anyone's scientific hobby-horse – understood? I'm the person who's going to make the decision whether parties go ashore or not – whether it's to explore volcanoes, or look at the birds or any other bloody natural wonder. It'll depend entirely on the weather and on how I and I alone interpret the danger factor.'

The echoes of my broadside were still snarling in the 'tween decks beams that night when I was called to the scientists' sanctuary. The top-like head of the buoy glowed in the beam of my flashlight. Next to it was the shroud-like drogue, and the balloon with its aluminium instrument package.

Holdgate was there, too, lying strapped to the burial board.

This time he wasn't play-acting.

He had a knife in his throat.

CHAPTER TEN

The scrimshawed ivory handle stood out like an obscene white fang below the left point of his chin. His half-open jaw rested on one of its notches. The blade itself was lost in the ginger growth of his beard.

I knelt to examine him. The torch reflected a glimmer of unfocused eyes. Before I put my hand against his heart I knew he was dead. His skin was cool and clammy. He had been dead some time.

I directed the beam into his eyes, then at the knife again. There was surprisingly little blood. On the side away from me the knife handle was engraved. I scanned it more closely. The outline was unmistakable. It was a killer whale. The killer whale is the Southern Ocean's most feared and relentless killer.

'Petersen!'

It was Petersen who had burst into my cabin a few minutes before – it already seemed like hours – and had stood swaying in the doorway. His face had been blanched and his eyes wide with horror. He had been violently, cruelly sick. I had grabbed hold of him and forced the rest of my nightcap brandy down his throat while he had hung, incoherent and half-fainting, in my grip. He had finally coughed out Holdgate's name and pointed aft. I had left him hanging over a chair and sprinted for the stern, telling him to follow. As I had cleared the superstructure, the cold wind had made me gasp.

'Petersen!'

He wasn't there. I straightened up and swung the flashlight round to find the light switches. Then I thought better of it. The murderer might be lurking somewhere. Even if he were not, to put the lights on would be to attract anyone who might be around. My first instinct was to bar anyone from seeing what lay there on the burial board.

I groped for the door. As I got there, the chilling implications of murder hit me: locks, fingerprints, door handles, keys, clues.

There was a sound on deck outside. I fell back, waited. I snapped the beam suddenly on to the face of the man in the doorway.

It was Petersen. He was swaying. I thought he was about to pass out again.

'Come in!' I ordered.

'Is . . . is . . .?' He coughed.

I kept the torch off Holdgate and snapped, 'He's dead. There's nothing we can do about that. But there's lots we can do about finding out who did it.' I found the switches. 'Listen, Petersen, before I put on these lights, get a grip of yourself. You're a ship's officer. Keep your eyes skinned. The killer could be around. No one is to know about this business – understood?'

'I understand.' His answer came from very far away.

I used my handkerchief to grip the key in case of fingerprints. We were still in darkness. Then I remembered something.

'Was this door open or shut when you found him?'

'That's why I came and looked in,' whispered Petersen. 'The door was slatting in the wind. So I came to see and . . .' In the dimness I could see that he was clamping his teeth into his knuckles to steady his jaw.

'I know what you saw – I've seen it close,' I replied, deliberately roughly. 'It's Holdgate, the volcanologist. He's dead. He's been murdered. That's a knife in his throat. Now I'm going to switch on the lights.'

I did. The place was empty.

Shock had already drawn older lines in Petersen's schoolboy face. He'd be older by years before the night was out.

I wrapped up the key and put it in my pocket. I went over to the body.

How, I asked myself, had Holdgate allowed himself first to be strapped to the board and then murdered? Smit, T-shirt Jannie and the bull-necked man named Pete weren't murderers. They'd all been having fun together when they had strapped Holdgate down that morning. Yet only they and Holdgate had keys to the place. They'd be the first I'd have to question.

Who could possibly have wanted to kill harmless Holdgate, and why?

My mind raced to the sharp exchange between Holdgate and Wegger in the morning. It had been very heated, but nevertheless you don't murder a man because you disagree about whether or not a cave is a lava tunnel. I pulled myself up. What I was thinking implicated Wegger. But then was there anyone on board who wasn't implicated? I asked myself grimly. Even Petersen. You're going crazy, I told myself roughly, without bothering to turn and see what Petersen was doing. Anyway, Wegger had been on watch on the bridge. The unknown who had threatened Reilly in the tunnel shaft?

I tried to defuse my exploding thoughts. I'd be suspecting Linn next if I went on like this.

I rounded on Petersen. He was shaking, partly from shock, and partly, I realized, because the night had turned very cold. He was concentrating his gaze on Bokkie and the balloon.

I checked my watch. 10.45. Time, too, had become a clue.

'I want you to do two things, Petersen – quick,' I said. 'Three, if keeping your mouth shut is included.'

He wouldn't face my way. I positioned myself where he wouldn't have to look in the direction of the body.

'Aye, aye, sir.'

'First, get up to the bridge and tell Mr Wegger I want him here – at the double. Say to bring his gun with him – loaded.'

My words didn't seem to penetrate. 'He's – got – a – gun?'

'You heard me.' Shock demands shock treatment. 'Pull yourself together, man! A gun. Loaded. Is that clear?'

'Yes – I mean, aye, aye, sir.'

'Second, I want you to rout out the TV cameraman who

came aboard with the tourists – I don't remember his name. He's doubling up in one of the new cabins next to us here, not the old ones amidships.'

'Which cabin?' asked Petersen.

'How in hell should I know? Look on the purser's list. It'll be on his noticeboard. Whoever his cabin mate is, keep him out of it. Tell him I want him with a camera and flash equipment.' I jerked my head in the direction of the body.

Petersen hung back.

'Well, what is it?' I demanded.

He said in a rush, 'Someone murdered him – I mean, he could still be lurking about. If you're left alone he might . . . might . . .'

'I hadn't given it a thought,' I replied. 'Thanks all the same for your concern. I don't think whoever did it will risk a second attack.'

I became still more aware of how cold it was. 'Drop into my cabin and bring me a sweater also, will you? And have yourself a shot more brandy at the same time. Captain's orders.'

He managed the beginnings of a wan smile. I locked the door behind him, still safeguarding the key with my handkerchief.

I felt quite impersonal about the grotesque object strapped to the board. It seemed to have nothing at all to do with the young-old-maidish fuddy-duddy I had known as Holdgate. He was the most unlikely knife-death victim possible. What did I know of his background?

I shivered in the icy air. My mind baulked at the jump ahead of it: murder, with a thousand complications. When Nelson's gunners at Trafalgar were stunned by the thunder of a thousand broadsides their minds shied away from thoughts of victory and took refuge in the trivialities of battle. In the same way my mind leapt to the tiny events of the day which had intervened between the time I had last spoken to Holdgate and now, when he would never speak again. A day of trivialities, of splendid trivialities. Linn and I had stood on deck and watched the dolphins, 'the swallows of the sea'. They had dived and swooped and performed their graceful arabesques both in the air and in the blue water alongside the *Quest*. The ship was still in blue water – the blue water of the Subtropical Convergence, Toby Trimen had told us. Linn and I had followed – as had most of the tourists – the 'swallows' with delight. Toby had also identified two types for us: the customary Southern white-sided dolphin and the dusky dolphin. He had taught us how to distinguish the two – the common type by its dark area behind the flipper, by its blunter head and broader dorsal fin.

Sea-birds, too, had convoyed the *Quest*. Dr Kebble had talked – one couldn't call such informality a lecture – about Prince Edward's very own bird, the Pilot Bird. White as an angel, it is unique to the island.

Then, in the afternoon, I had seen ahead a long grey-black line blocking the southern horizon. It had risen, the closer the ship approached, like a tangible physical barrier in the ship's path. It marked the end of the Sub-tropical Convergence, where the warm seas ended – the end of the dolphins, the Portuguese men-o'-war, the blue water, the yachting weather.

I had pointed the bank out to Linn and warned her of the storms which lay beyond it. It seemed to me now that that funereal range of fog was symbolic of the storm I had run into with Holdgate's death.

With that thought, my mind snapped back to the scientists' sanctuary and the grim reality confronting me. Holdgate's was the second death involving the *Quest*. Captain Prestrud had been pistol-whipped to death. Holdgate – struck by a sudden suspicion I went over to the body and looked at his throat. I was right. He hadn't been strapped to the board conscious. He had been half-strangled first. There was a hideous bruise round his windpipe. Someone – and it must have been a powerful man – had choked him senseless from behind, strapped him to the plank, and then thrust the knife home. It had been as calculated as a farmer butchering a sheep.

Why?

Who?

Like the *Quest* late that afternoon, I had crossed into stormy waters. The sea had turned a cold green at evening – in these high latitudes the twilight never seems to end – and ahead of us was the bank of fog, nearer now, and as dark in the approaching night as the thoughts at present in my mind.

I had cut the *Quest*'s speed to half, a night-ice precaution.

Deaf, for the radio black-out was total, and blind except for the uncertain radar, the ship had begun to pitch heavily as she felt her way South. I had doubled the look-outs and put the searchlight squad on the alert.

Before we plunged into the fog-bank I had spotted a single patch of white far out on the starboard bow. For a moment I had thought it was a growler or a bergy bit. When I put my glasses on it, however, it turned out to be the white snout of a Southern right whale dolphin. Then it was lost in the green-black water.

I was brought back sharply to Holdgate's murder by a rap at the door of metal against metal. I remembered to hold the key in my handkerchief when I opened it. It was Wegger. He had used the Luger as a knocker.

I indicated the body. 'What do you make of that, Number One?'

He came in. I watched him closely. From now on, everyone was under suspicion.

He stopped, raised the Luger muzzle to his lips, and blew into it. The low whistle it gave was a macabre sound, a death-watch sound.

His face had its iron-hard look in it. All expression was expunged from his eyes.

'Is he dead?' he asked.

'Yes.'

The *Quest* gave a deep roll as the south-westerly run of the sea lifted her keel. Holdgate's head rolled with it. First it went leftwards. On the return roll it only got halfway. The weight of the knife kept it pinned left.

Wegger went over to the corpse. Before I could stop him, he had reached down and tested the knife with his hand.

'It's firm – into his neck vertebrae, I'd say.'

'Take your bloody hands off that knife!' I rapped out. 'What in hell d'you think you're doing?'

He swung round on me and appeared to go into a half-crouch, as if ready to jump me. Then I realized that he'd stooped to the body. His eyes were burning in the shadow of his cap-peak.

When he spoke his voice was completely at odds with the rest of him. It was like that first time on the dockside when I suspected him of sucking up to me.

'I'm sorry, sir. I never gave it a thought. I only wanted to see . . .'

Handling the knife was the sort of thoughtless action one could take in the stress of the moment. Outwardly, he'd shown no nerve-reaction to the sight of the body. But I'd learned already that Wegger was more complex than he appeared on the surface.

'Forget it,' I retorted brusquely. 'Where's Petersen?'

'Petersen asked me to give you this.' Wegger handed me my thick off-white sweater with a fisherman's collar. 'He's cleaning up the mess he made in your cabin.'

'What did he tell you?'

'Nothing – except that you wanted me urgently, and there was a dead man.'

'No one else hear?'

'No,' Wegger answered. 'But you can't keep anything like this dark for long. It'll be all over the ship by morning.'

He was right, of course.

'What are you going to do about him?'

That was the hurdle my mind had jibbed at a little while back. What I decided about Holdgate would also determine the fate of the *Quest*'s cruise. Linn had come to me to make her decision after her father's death; now, deep down, I wanted to be with her when I made mine over Holdgate. It was a captain's decision – and there are times when a captain can be more alone than an albatross riding the West Wind Drift.

'I sent Petersen to wake the TV cameraman and bring his flash gear,' I replied obliquely. 'I want the body photographed as I found it.'

'I thought Petersen found it,' he remarked in an odd voice.

'A manner of speaking. He called me immediately.'

Wegger went on. 'How do you know that, sir? I mean, with murder one has to look at every aspect.'

'Petersen was in no state to do anything but what he did,' I answered. 'It was purely a reflex action. He called me. I sent him for you.'

'You didn't question him?' he persisted. 'I mean, did he see anyone around? In here, perhaps?'

It didn't need Wegger's remarks to tell me that I had to be suspicious of Petersen, and of his apparent concern for my safety.

'He was in no shape to be cross-questioned,' I said. 'That will come.'

'Have you searched the place, sir? The murderer could still be close by.'

'The place is as bare as a nude show,' I replied. 'Try the body, if you care to. He's been dead some time, I'd guess.'

'Good.'

'What the devil do you mean, good?'

He patted the Luger and said levelly, 'I mean, then we don't have to start fine-combing the ship.'

'I've done that once today – with you and MacFie.'

Wegger gave a slight shrug. 'How long would you estimate he's been dead?'

'An hour – two hours, maybe. I can't say. I'm not a doctor. He's scarcely warm.'

'That would make it after I'd taken over the bridge at eight,' he said.

Was he talking his way into an alibi? There wasn't any need. The bridge men could prove or disprove anything he said. If I could not trust even my own first officer . . . I jerked my thoughts together. I wasn't a detective. My function was the safety of the ship.

And all those who travel in her.

The way Holdgate's head rolled from side to side reminded me that there was at least one person whom I had failed.

The thought goaded me. 'What's keeping Petersen, for Chrissake?'

Wegger remained collected. 'He was very ashamed of what he did to your cabin.'

'Blast my cabin. I want the photographer.'

'He said he wouldn't be long.'

A silence fell between us. But the ship wasn't silent. The creaks a vessel gives when the seas start to work up and tax her fabric were all around. The *Quest* was flexing her sea muscles after their flaccid stay in port, although the swells weren't really anything yet. A squall with a spatter of rain brought new noises from seams and beams. If the wind veered south-west from its present quarter, which was west with a touch of north in it, those squalls would throw themselves at the *Quest* with relentless savagery, armed with hail, ice and snow and the knock-down punch of a Force 10 gale.

There was a ragged clatter against the door. Petersen knocking. Wegger jerked round, more nervously than his outward appearance would have led me to expect.

I held the door before admitting Petersen and the photographer. The latter's hair was tousled and he wore a leather jacket with a fur collar, shortie pyjama pants and furry ankle-length slippers.

I addressed him. 'Before you come in, I must warn you that there's something very unpleasant in here. That's why I sent for you. It's an emergency and I require pictures for the record. What's your name?'

'Brunton. John Brunton.'

His brown eyes were bright and alive with no trace of sleep in them.

'I was a press photographer before I went ecological,' he replied. 'I once saw a stiff they'd found in a river. He'd been there two weeks. He'd been strangled with a length of barbed wire. That cured my stomach for keeps.'

'This isn't all that bad.'

I let them in. Petersen still kept his eyes averted.

Brunton's eyes – like those of Miss Auchinleck's penguins – seemed to work independently on either side of his head. One took in the body, and the other the rest of the scientific gear. They appeared to be assessing camera angles and the situation all at once.

'I want pictures for the record and the police,' I told him. 'I'll also require a sworn statement from you later.'

'Any particular angle?'

'If you've done police work you'll know better than I do.' Brunton licked the connection of his electric flash, plugged it in, and got to work. The place sparkled with quick flashes.

He half-knelt, half-crouched by the corpse and called back to me, 'Close-ups of the knife too?'

Wegger said unnecessarily, 'It's very hard in – right through his neck, I'd say.'

Brunton rolled the eye not focusing the viewfinder at me. The glance was a mixture of query and surprise.

My mind was already leaping on ahead – post-mortem, court

processes, being put through the hoop by some smart-alec lawyer. Brunton's questions smacked home a pressing problem which I'd thrust to the back of my mind. What did I intend to do with the body? Take it back to land? Bury it at sea?

The thought rattled me and I retorted, 'He didn't put it there himself. The whole lot of us on this ship are going to be put through the mill of a murder hearing. There'll be thousands of questions asked.'

Brunton pushed his lens within inches of the dead face.

'Odd sort of design on the knife,' he said.

'Killer whale,' I replied.

Brunton went on working the trigger. 'Could narrow the field of suspects considerably. Not everyone packs a weapon like that.'

I hadn't thought of that one – yet.

'What about his hands?' asked Brunton.

'What about them?'

'Want me to take 'em close-up also?'

'Why?'

'Right one's clenched. You may want to open the fingers.'

Petersen made a gurgling noise and walked over to the opposite side. Wegger stood watching, completely expressionless.

'I'll log that fact later,' I said. 'Will you help me, Number One?'

Wegger started, as if his thoughts had been elsewhere. 'Of course.'

He used his left hand – his sound working hand, his gunhand – to assist me. We prised open the fingers. The palm was empty.

Brunton's flash blinded me. Then, for the first time, I felt a surge of nausea. The muscles that had contracted those fingers had done so from the agony of the knife taking his life.

'Now a couple of general shots of the environment.' Brunton rose and began shooting again. When he had finished, he remarked, 'That should tell the story.'

'It's a story I don't want told to anyone,' I said. 'That's not a request but an order. In a situation like this the captain is the law. He has unlimited authority. I could even put you in irons if I wanted to.'

Brunton replied with a peculiar half-grin, 'I believe you would, too.'

'Thanks,' I said. 'I wasn't meaning to pull my rank, but it's a good thing to know where you stand. This is a serious situation.'

'I'll say. I'll keep this roll of film safer than fine gold. Ten million dollars' worth.'

It was as if an electric shock had passed through Wegger. The muscles of his neck corded and bulged and his hand went to his gun pocket as if it had a life of its own.

Brunton's keen eye didn't miss it. 'Have I said something wrong?'

Wegger laughed it off, not very convincingly. 'That's a lot of gold to compare it to.'

Brunton eyed him for a long moment. Then he said to me, 'If you don't want me for anything more, I'll be getting back to bed. With these shorties I'll land myself a severe dose of Antarctic testicle.'

'Thanks,' I said. 'I'll see you tomorrow.'

When he had gone, I said to Wegger, 'We'll lock the body in the sick-bay. We'll leave him strapped. This plank is the best thing to carry him on anyway. Petersen, go and find a blanket, will you?'

Petersen was only too glad to leave.

Wegger asked, 'Burial at sea?'

That was going too fast for me. I fobbed off the question. 'He's halfway prepared already.'

'We'd better unstrap his arms,' Wegger went on. 'Easier later for sewing him into canvas. Rigor mortis and all that.'

I didn't like Wegger's tacit assumption of what would be done. I felt he was subtly pressuring me.

'Leave him how he is,' I ordered. 'I'll decide all that later.'

When Petersen returned with a couple of blankets, it was Wegger and I who carried the deadweight board after we had covered and wrapped the body. Petersen led, with instructions not to use my torch in the unlighted section between the stern and amidships deck-houses. I didn't want any stray passengers to witness our passage. Perhaps my caution was a mistake. Shortly after leaving the locked door behind us Wegger tripped on something on deck. The body's weight transferred to his damaged right hand. I did a quick snatch to save the board from falling. I sensed him fumbling near the head for a moment or two to find a grip. Then he regained his balance.

We hurried from the deck into the lighted corridor where the luxury accommodation was situated. The sick-bay was at its forward end. I glanced at Number 3 as we hastened past. Linn's cabin.

The key was in the sick-bay door. I locked it and pocketed the key after we had stowed Holdgate safely inside.

I dismissed Wegger and Petersen. 'See you on the bridge. I take over at midnight.'

'I'll stand your watch if you like, sir,' suggested Wegger. 'I won't sleep much anyway.'

No more would I, I thought grimly. 'Thanks,' I said, 'but it won't be necessary.'

The more I saw of Wegger, the less I understood the man. There had been times during the photographing of the body when he'd been all screwed up with tension. Now he seemed completely relaxed, in spite of what he said about not sleeping. But Petersen was different. If I hadn't thought it bad for his morale I would have ordered him to bed. He looked ghastly.

When they had gone I made my way to my cabin. I sat down at the desk and started to frame a radio signal. I didn't get far. How do you convey in a few crisp sentences that a man has been murdered? I didn't address it either. To whom? The police? The port authorities? The Weather Bureau? I crumpled the paper and tossed it into the wastepaper basket. The *Quest*'s radio wasn't working anyway because of the radio black-out, but I'd have to try to get through to someone.

I hurried to Persson's cabin in the officers' quarters and hammered on his door. I would have to tell him the truth. A radio operator is to a captain as his own thoughts. Persson answered, full of sleep and surprise.

'See here,' I told him. 'There's been an emergency. Can you raise Cape Town on the radio?'

He shook his head. 'No. Reception's been getting worse all day, the further South we go. It was hopeless when I packed up a few hours ago. No sferics, even.'

I recalled Smit's remarks about the black-out. I didn't want to try and teach Persson his job. On the other hand if I put an expert like Smit on his back it would only cause friction.

'Can I come in?' I asked. 'What I have to say is confidential.'

'Sorry, sir. I must be half-asleep still.'

I went in. The cabin was warm and smelt of cigarettes and the indefinable odour of male-aloneness. A pin-up whose breasts ballooned close to the pillow hung above his bunk.

'What are sferics?'

'Bits and pieces of noises, sir. They used to be called static. They don't mean anything. Or, rather, they do if . . .'

I cut him short. 'You mean the radio's stone dead?'

'Yes, sir. Both receiving and transmitting. I've heard about this sort of thing but never experienced it.'

'What about the radio-telephone?'

'It's got no range at all, sir. I couldn't reach the mainland that way.'

I glanced at the door to make sure we could not be overheard. 'Listen, Persson. A man was killed aboard tonight. I've got to get a signal out somehow.'

He said quietly, as if only a part of him were listening while the rest was wrestling with the insoluble technical problem, 'I see, sir. Then the R/T's our only hope. Maybe . . .'

'Yes?'

'The US Navy works the KC-4 USV station from McMurdo at certain times as a ham station for direct voice talks with the men's relatives back home. It's a powerful transmission. Maybe – only maybe – I could patch a signal from us into it.'

'What would that mean, if you did?'

'It would mean someone talking from America to a guy in McMurdo would get the message. Or vice versa.'

'Where – I mean, what station in the United States?'

'An ordinary telephone, sir. That's the way it works.'

'I don't follow the ins and outs of this, but if you think you can establish contact with the outside world, go ahead right away,' I replied. 'If you can't, I want you to stand a round-the-clock radio watch until you do. Got that?'

'I'll be up in the radio shack in about five minutes.'

'Good. If you make a contact, let me know at once. I'll be on the bridge after midnight. In my cabin until then.'

I went from Persson direct to the engine-room. As I clattered down the ladder into the oil-warm comfort and racket of the place, MacFie's assistant started up in astonishment from a nudey magazine and a cup of coffee. A captain doesn't usually pay social calls to the engine-room in the middle of the night.

'I want to see Reilly,' I told him. 'He's on duty?'

The man pointed. His attitude asked, 'More trouble?' but he didn't speak.

Reilly was dripping oil out of an outsize oil-can with the fixed zombie-like look machine-men develop in the presence of continual noise. His brown overall was open to a stained singlet. It was as warm down here as all that.

I tapped him on the shoulder. He started as if he'd been shot. I gestured to a corner away from the other men. Not that they could have overheard with all that noise going on.

When we were there, I said, 'Reilly, I want you to tell me something.'

His eyes were bitter under their pale lashes. 'I said all I had to say to the Chief. You can't get anything more out of me.'

I wasn't in the mood for this prima donna stuff. 'That business is finished.'

'Then why come and try to twist my arm?'

I bit back my retort. 'Reilly – what did the ghost look like? The one who held the gun on you?'

'There wasn't a ghost. You searched the ship. You said there wasn't.'

I went on, jumping the credibility gap, 'You said he was big.'

'Aye, his hands were big. He was a *big* man.'

'A man, not a ghost?'

Reilly looked shiftier, if that were possible. 'You searched the ship. You said there wasn't.'

Next he'll be talking leprechauns, I told myself savagely. I hid my fury as best I could.

'Bigger than – Mr Wegger, say?'

'I dunno who Mr Wegger is.'

'Than me, then?'

'Aye, bigger.'

'His hands – was there anything wrong with either of them?'

He looked stupid. 'Naw. Big hands, that's all. *Very* big. The gun looked small.'

'You're sure it was a machine-pistol? Not a Luger?'

'I seen plenty of machine-pistols. In Belfast, like I said. You shot all over me for saying it, remember?'

Reilly would store up grievances all his life like a computer. A computer never forgets.

'What about his fingers? Did he have all his fingers?'

'His hand were big like I said.'

'For Chrissake – his *fingers*?'

He replied sullenly, 'It was dark down there. I dunno.'

I had to steel myself to say, 'Thanks, Reilly. That's all I want to know.'

He watched me suspiciously as I rejoined MacFie's assistant.

'Can you spare a couple of cups of coffee?'

'Sure, a pleasure.'

He went over to the sort of cubby-hole you find in all engine-rooms, where there is a spout of steam, a tin of coffee and condensed milk and some off-white mugs. He brought two back. They looked good.

'Thanks,' I said. 'I'll return the cups.'

He nodded. He, like the rest of the engine-room crew, was wary of my visit.

I retraced my steps to my cabin, balancing the cups against the roll and pitch of the ship. I put the bottle of brandy under my arm and headed in the direction of the sick-bay.

I stopped at Number 3.

I put down one cup in order to leave me a free hand to knock on Linn's door. My pulses raced. I didn't give myself time to think. I knocked sharply.

Again.

I was about to knock a third time when the door opened and Linn stood blinking at me in the light of the corridor. She had on a blue quilted dressing-gown, and her eyes looked soft and sleepy.

'John . . .!' Her eyes went from the cup in my hand to the brandy bottle under my arm. The misty expression vanished from her eyes and gave way to coolness. And to disappointment. Brandy – the crude Panzer spearhead of a midnight assignation.

Then she saw what was in my face, and her expression changed again.

'John! What's wrong? What's happened?'

I picked up the second steaming cup from the floor. 'You may need this when I tell you. The brandy's there for medicinal reasons.'

'Come in. It's perishing out here.'

I moved into the cabin. She was fumbling for the light switch, so that we were very close. She was all woman-sleep and warmth.

I said a little unsteadily, 'You'd better take the bottle before I let it fall.'

She had the light on now. She eased the bottle out from between my arm and my side.

I scarcely heard her whisper, it was so soft. 'Sorry. I should have known you better than that.'

'Thank you, Linn.' I put her cup down. She sat on her bunk and I took the chair that stood at a small desk. 'That's genuine engine-room brew,' I said, 'guaranteed to keep the patient awake.'

She eyed me. 'You haven't been asleep, John.'

I took a drink of coffee and filled the space up with brandy. 'I'm afraid I've some bad news, Linn,' I said.

I could see the skin round her cheekbones tighten as she waited to hear.

'There's no point in beating about the bush. Doctor Holdgate, the volcanologist, was murdered tonight.'

She reached for her cup, slopped it unsteadily, and put it down again without tasting.

She said slowly, 'I can't believe it. That's what people always say, isn't it? I can't believe it. But I suppose I must try to believe it.'

She managed her coffee cup this time. She held it out to me before drinking. 'A medicinal measure from the bottle, please. I feel as if I'd been kicked in the stomach.'

She leaned towards me. The weight of her breasts pushed the lapel of her gown partly aside. She'd been sleeping in the nude. Her pyjamas lay on her bunk among the blankets she had thrown back.

'Go on.'

My thoughts yawed like a ship with a bugged gyro. I replied, 'Young Petersen was doing his rounds when he saw Holdgate's door open. He went in and found him with a knife in his throat. He called me. Holdgate had been dead for some time.'

'It's incredible! Holdgate!'

'Yes, Holdgate – bumbling, inconsequential Holdgate,' I answered.

'He wouldn't have hurt a fly.'

'That's what I thought.' I recounted the night's events: my discovery of the body, the photographic record, and, finally, the radio black-out and the very faint hope that Persson had of transmitting a signal. I left Reilly out of it. I let her think my visit to the engine-room was to fetch our coffee.

Then I asked, 'What do you know about Holdgate's background?'

She seemed grateful to steer away from the details of the killing. 'Not much. I think he must have had quite a brilliant academic record. I seem to remember from his application to join the cruise that he'd been a lecturer at the Australian National University at Canberra and had been given some big geological award by the Rijksmuseum in Holland.'

'Where was he from?'

'British-born, I think.'

'I don't mean that. Where did he come from to join the ship?'

'Geological Survey, Pretoria. He was an expert on palaeo-magnetism. That's why the rocks at Prince Edward fascinated him so. There's very little work being done on them.'

'No cause of murder in any of that,' I said. 'Married?'

'No. Confirmed bachelor type, I'd say.'

I poured a trickle more brandy into my coffee. 'Linn,' I went on, 'whoever killed Holdgate for whatever reason is not really my affair – that's a police job. What does concern me greatly, however, is that at this moment there's a killer loose in the ship. And because of that, the fate of the *Quest*'s voyage is at stake.'

She shivered. It wasn't cold in her cabin. It was snug. Some-where there was a lingering trace of the perfume she'd worn when we'd danced together earlier in the evening. I tried to think whether I had seen Holdgate at the dance. Probably not. He wasn't the sort to socialize with tourists. Perhaps his absence had been the cause of his downfall, being alone with his work when everyone else had been enjoying themselves.

'Explain please, John.'

'This voyage is jinxed. There've been two killings.'

'I can scarcely credit it, even now.'

'Your father was killed,' I went on. 'He was savagely beaten to death. Now Holdgate. His death was just as brutal, in its way. There's a connection between the two.'

'What possible connection could my father have had with Doctor Holdgate? They never even knew each other.'

I answered slowly, 'Linn, my mind feels like those fancy modern navigational systems they call SINS – ships inertial navigational system. They're marvels – providing your initial fix is spot-on. That's what I am lacking now – a reference point from which to begin.'

'And failing that?'

I looked at her squarely. She looked very lovely. Because of the crisis, we had already moved closer to each other and I knew instinctively that she was glad I had turned to her.

'It's nearly midnight,' I said. 'The *Quest* is now just over the halfway mark to the launching-point for the buoy. I could put the ship about and land Holdgate's body in Cape Town on Monday, at roughly the same time the launching is scheduled. Then I could turn the whole matter over to the authorities.'

She looked away and found an imaginary thread on her quilted sleeve.

'And then?'

'I would have discharged my responsibility as captain.'

'But not your conscience, John.'

'On the other hand, I could carry on. I could bury Holdgate at sea tomorrow. In that event, the case against the killer might break down for lack of evidence. Both police and medical evidence. There would be no body, no clues. It would all be at the bottom of the sea.'

'There must be a doctor somewhere, John!'

'There is. In the Crozet Islands. That's about two days' steaming east of Prince Edward, as you know.'

'You'd do that?'

'I couldn't keep a body on board that long.'

'What . . . what . . . have you done with . . . it . . . him?'

I gestured with my head. 'In the sick-bay. Just up the corridor.'

She started to her feet. 'John – it's all a nightmare! It's too horrible to think about . . . !'

I reached out to her and she came fiercely to me for a moment. Her lips were hard against mine. Then she pulled away.

'We mustn't, John! I don't want you this way if it's just because . . . because . . .'

'Because what, Linn?'

'People who are under threat are driven into one another's arms – like in a bombing raid – and then when the danger's gone they find they have nothing left for each other.'

She moved away and stood between the edge of her bunk and the door of the built-in clothes cabinet. Her head was held back in her characteristic way.

'Do you think I regard this danger as big as that?'

In answer, she spread her arms wide across the corner where she stood so that I could see the deep cleavage of her breasts.

I went to her. Her tongue was warm and soft and seeking against my palate.

Light years passed.

It was she who ended it, breathless, sobbing, pulling her elbows down over her breasts like a boxer covering up from an attack which could have only one outcome.

'Now's not the time, my darling! I need you, I want you, but we've got this horror to attend to . . .'

I found my voice. 'Sometime?'

'Any other time you want, my darling. You don't have to have an excuse to bring coffee next time.'

A roll of the ship brought us together again. We let the sweet electricity flow between us until both of us had sense enough left to throw the trip-switch.

We found our previous places and our half-cold coffee. As I looked into her green-grey eyes, I felt I was talking on two levels – outwardly about Holdgate and inwardly in a silent exchange about ourselves.

I tried to marshal my thoughts. 'Listen, Linn. I believe the key to both murders lies in what your father tried to tell me in hospital. I can't forget those words of his – stay away from Dina's Island. It was like a command. I can't help feeling it was tied up with what he did in the war when he escaped the

German raider. But it was all so disconnected and rambling.'

'We're right back to where we started, John.'

'Not quite. We have Captain Jacobsen aboard. I'm going to interview him in the morning. There's a lot I want to ask him.'

'Mrs Jacobsen's a big obstacle. She's very protective about him and his heart condition.'

'Maybe. But Jacobsen is the only one left of those three catcher skippers who escaped. Both the others died violently. I've got to know more about the circumstances because of what's happening now, right here aboard this ship.'

'But Holdgate can't possibly have had anything to do with them.'

'I said earlier I felt like that fancy navigational device,' I replied. 'I still do. A feature of the instrument is that it accumulates errors and gradually and imperceptibly one strays further from the original true position.'

'So whether or not you carry on with the cruise depends on what Captain Jacobsen says?'

I finished my laced coffee and lit a cigarette. I needed both.

'I also intend to show Captain Jacobsen the knife that killed Holdgate. That killer whale on it has some significance.'

'John, this is a Norwegian ship. Dad recruited the crew from whalermen he'd known in his whaling days. That knife could belong to any of them. *What do you intend to do, John?*'

Her face was very strained now.

I still temporized. 'You're the owner of the *Quest*, Linn. Don't forget that.'

'But you're the captain, John.'

I stood up and looked down at her. 'Linn, when I knocked at your door, I hadn't finally decided. As you say, it's my decision, and my decision alone. If I call off the cruise it would be a deathblow to a large part of one of the most ambitious international scientific projects ever planned. Maybe the project is big enough to outweigh the death of one man, even of two men. I wouldn't know about that. I only know that by pushing on I am somehow honouring the memory of a man whom I respected and liked beyond anyone I have met in my life. This cruise was his dream.' I leaned down and kissed her gently. 'And also the dream of someone I love.'

She held me, until at last I looked at my watch and said,

'I'm overdue on the bridge already.'

'Do you have to go, my darling?' she whispered.

My mind was already racing to the cold hard realities beyond her closed door. Tomorrow's burial at sea. All the questions to be asked and to be answered. Captain Jacobsen.

I kissed her again in reply. She said, 'I'm going to dress. No point in trying to go to sleep.'

'When you're up, use the day cabin if you like. You can reach me on the bridge any time you want.'

I shut her door behind me. But I hadn't yet finished with the corridor. There was something I wanted to check in the sick-bay. I wanted to examine the knife in Holdgate's throat more closely in case I couldn't risk Captain Jacobsen's health by showing him the body.

I took the sick-bay key from my pocket where I had put it after Wegger, Petersen and I had stowed the body inside.

I rolled back Holdgate's blanket. I need not have been concerned for Captain Jacobsen.

The knife was gone.

CHAPTER ELEVEN

My thoughts spun like the circular fan that cleared the bridge window of fog condensation and of the vicious spatters of rain brought by every squall. It was after midnight and I was on watch on the port side of the bridge, trying to see through the cleared space. Two of the nine bridge windows had the fan-like device for keeping vision clear. Mine was the second from the port side. There was a similar window to starboard.

I could not penetrate the murk ahead. The fo'c'sle deck and bow searchlight were an amorphous blur. Mentally, I was equally blind – in the fog of unanswerable questions, surmises and doubts which Holdgate's death had pitched at me. I had no recollection of making my way from the body in the sick-bay to the bridge. I might have been suffering from that strange loss of memory which hits men in mid-winter deep in the ice towards the South Pole.

I crossed impatiently to the window on the starboard side of the bridge, as if that would help. In spite of the fan it was as fogged as the one I had left. The wind rattled a loose pane – this was the windward side and taking its force. I felt confined and restricted, as out of touch with the elements as the ship's models in bottles which the travel agency had distributed among the passengers as a publicity gimmick.

Inside the steel-and-glass capsule of the bridge each man was at his station and all was in order – the big wooden wheel, the instruments, the clicking log, the silent Kelvin Hughes echosounder, the pulse of diesels, the brass clock on the bulkhead with its hands at ten minutes past midnight. I felt trapped, insulated from reality. I wanted the icy wind on my face; I wanted to watch it mow the tops off the white-capped swells racing in from the south-west as they became visible close to the *Quest*'s side. I needed its lash to shake loose from deep within me solutions which were at that moment out of reach.

I made up my mind suddenly. 'I'm going up aloft for a moment,' I told Jensen at the wheel.

I secured my weatherproof and made my way up to the exposed flying bridge above.

As I reached it, I gasped and ducked at the icy punch of a fresh rain-squall. I abandoned the windward side for the lee. Then, almost at once, the rain stopped and the *Quest* broke out of the patch of fog. I saw that the smother overhead was not a deep overcast but a ragged conglomeration of cloud, whipping and plunging eastwards. I saw a star briefly; without the cloud the night would have been aglow with the magic light of the Antarctic summer. That magic had been strong enough to have been in Captain Prestrud's mind when he had been dying.

The first I knew that Linn was with me was when she took my arm. I hadn't heard her come. The frame of her dark woollen cap emphasized the fine bones of her face.

She said, 'It's your world up here, isn't it, John?'

'We've just crossed into the Westerlies. They're trying to prove they're Westerlies but they're not succeeding yet. This capful of wind is nothing to what is to come.'

The *Quest* lifted her bows high and then plunged deep. A burst of spray drenched the figurehead and searchlight platform.

'The Roaring Forties,' she said.

'Aye, Linn. But you're wrong if you think they blow steady all the time. They don't. They work themselves into a frenzy, blow their heads off, then slacken. Then the process begins all over again.'

She laughed. 'How much is slacken, sailor?'

I grinned at her. I wished I could see more of her face.

'See those seas? Something's holding them down. They're being damped. They're not doing their best – or worst.'

'Why not, John?'

'Ice. There's ice ahead. Big ice. A lot of ice.'

'Then why isn't the searchlight on?' she asked.

'The ice is still quite a way off, I'd say. I don't smell it. This wind hasn't got ice on its breath – yet. It's a raw, primitive, exciting, frightening smell, Linn. The weather people showed me a satellite photo before we left. They reckoned the ice was farther north in the Southern Ocean than it usually is in January.'

'How close are we, according to the photo?'

'I don't believe everything I see on a satellite photo. The experts often get mixed up and interpret a white cloud-cover as ice. I prefer to trust my own senses.'

'You love this Southern Ocean, don't you, John?'

I ran my fingers inside her cap and tucked in a strand of hair which had blown loose.

'I'm my own man down here, Linn,' I replied. 'The place throws you back on what you really are – look at the *Quest* now, at this moment. The radio's out. The gyro's also affected by the ionospheric storm, and so is the compass. We're practically down to man himself – man against the elements. Your own resources, your own ingenuity, against an enemy which never lets up. Both sides play rough. It's the way I like it.'

I was looking at her. Her face suddenly became clearer, lighter. Her eyes, too, defined themselves in the darkness of their sockets.

'John!' she exclaimed. 'The sun's rising!'

She pointed. There was a glow, like dawn, low on the horizon ahead.

'The sun doesn't rise in the South, Linn. Nor in the middle of the night.'

'Then what . . .'

It was not the rose of the sun's dawn. It was palest mother-of-pearl, faintly green.

'It's making amends for bugging our radio and instruments,' I told her. 'It's the aurora.'

A great arc, stretching from horizon to horizon, began to emerge in place of the glow. It was greenish-yellow, a rainbow of single, not multiple colour. We could see the cloud-wrack spinning against it like ragged patches of batik-work.

'John – look!'

The single band of the rainbow began to dissolve into a series of rays whose points reached upwards into the firmament itself. Meanwhile the entire arc moved above the southern horizon – ever upwards. Next, like a scene-shift whose stage was the world, another arc materialized from under the horizon and followed the first up into the sky. It was like a procession of lightning-kings.

The topmost peaks of the pale greenish-yellow rays became tipped with purple, blue and red. As the first arc reached a point overhead, a third arc heaved over the horizon, while the middle rainbow dissolved into steepled rays.

Then the uppermost arc burst into a corona like a gigantic napalm explosion. Whirling, spinning, interweaving, blending, its colours were red, blue, purple and orange. It was a tapestry which occupied the whole sky, from the zenith to the southern horizon.

'John! . . . John! . . . John!'

The strange light from the firmamental draperies played across her upturned face, making it indescribably lovely.

Then the aurora died suddenly, like a brief burst of breathless love-making that would be remembered always.

Linn said very quietly, 'I see now what the Southern Ocean holds for you, John. It's not only its challenge. It's also the most beautiful place in the world.'

The soaring glories of the aurora meant less than nothing to Persson. Linn and I left the flying bridge and went together to the radio shack.

'Any luck?' I asked him.

'Dead. Stone dead,' he replied gloomily. 'Not a murmur. Not even a distorted voice, let alone a distorted signal. There must be a million amps circulating in the upper atmosphere to do things like this to reception.'

'This is the Year of the Unquiet Sun,' I told him. 'Isn't there supposed to be an eleven-year cycle of sunspot activity?'

'Then I guess we're right in the middle of it,' he said.

He picked up the voice microphone with its heavy stand and stared at it. Then he stared at the typewriter on the low side desk; then at the main table bearing the transmitter and a metal box containing signals filed in loose plastic envelopes. He might have been willing the whole set-up to react.

'Keep at it,' I told him. 'There was a similar big black-out some years ago during a Presidential election. The Yanks at McMurdo nearly went crazy. No one knew for days who'd been elected.'

He began his muezzin-like chant with *Quest*'s call sign. 'F-L-O-E . . . calling all ships and shore stations . . . F-L-O-E . . . F-L-O-E . . .'

Linn and I left him to it, and went down to the day cabin. I turned off the main overhead light, leaving only the desk lamp. The place was warm and inviting.

Linn's face looked very tired.

'Wouldn't you be better off in your cabin?' I asked.

'It's no good,' she said. 'I can't possibly sleep. There's too much going on inside me.'

I kissed her. 'Me, too. But I have the advantage that I can work mine off in running the ship.'

'You've been away from the bridge a long time.'

'I know. I'll get back. I'll come down here now and then and if you want me in the meantime just pick up the phone.'

When she hadn't rung an hour later, I went back to the cabin. She was curled up fast asleep on a worn leather couch with her cap for a pillow. Her knees were drawn up and her hands tucked between them for warmth.

I went quickly to my own cabin and brought back a rug made out of penguin skins which had been given me by a seaman whose life I had saved one night in a Southern Ocean storm. I put it over her and she did not wake.

I was making my way back to the bridge when I met Wegger. He was fully dressed and was carrying a tin plate and a mug.

'Raiding the galley,' he said jocularly. 'I said I wouldn't sleep. Everything in order?'

There was an odd air of levity about the man. At 1.30 in the morning humour is hard to take. I wondered whether he

111

had been drinking, but couldn't smell any sign of it.

'Why shouldn't it be?' I retorted.

'Well, we've just had a murder. What time is the burial service? I expect you want all the officers to be present.'

The fact that the *Quest* was holding course was enough to make my intentions about burial clear. All the same, I didn't care for the way he was usurping my prerogatives.

I said briefly, 'I've put Persson on round-the-clock non-stop radio watch. I'll decide about the burial when I get a signal out.'

He still seemed amused. 'Did you see the aurora?'

'Yes. I don't think I've ever witnessed a finer.'

'Persson doesn't stand a hope in hell,' he said. 'The further South we go, the worse it will become. We're now into the northernmost reaches of the auroras. They usually stretch in a great ellipse about three thousand kilometres long starting from the South Pole. The field shifts from west to east as the summer wears on, and then back again.'

'You seem to know a hell of a lot about it, Wegger.'

'Radio is my subject. Always has been. I know what a blackout means down in this part of the world.'

'Maybe you can suggest something to Persson? I've told him to try with the radio-telephone.'

Wegger replied – a little contemptuously, it seemed to me, 'Have you withdrawn your ban on me and the radio, then?'

I repeated, 'Any suggestions?'

'The R/T simply hasn't got the range. These seas are empty. Persson's wasting his breath.'

I knew in my heart that I had put Persson on merely to salve my conscience. I realized as well as Wegger did what an Antarctic black-out meant.

'Persson will keep trying,' I retorted. 'Thanks for your help.'

He went off in the direction of the galley. It seemed to me that the plate and mug had a jaunty clatter to them.

The horizon was already lighter when I got to the bridge. Given a clear dawn, one can see by 3 a.m. in these high latitudes. I rang for more speed. The *Quest*'s motion became quicker, and an occasional dollop of sea came aboard.

After a while we ran into a fresh patch of squalls and more fog. The night reverted to pitch-black under heavy overcast, and I reduced speed. It was a routine procedure which was to go on until morning.

My mind swung as erratically over the problem of Holdgate as does a compass needle when a ship gets close to Prince Edward Island. Scientists have yet to account for it. Nor could I account for Holdgate. I did not fancy the idea of putting possible suspects through the hoop. Yet it was something I had to do, and I began trying to compile a short list in my mind. It was obvious that since Smit, T-shirt Jannie and Pete had the only keys to the scientists' work-place they must come first. Besides, they had play-acted with Holdgate alive on the burial-board. It seemed to me that all three of them were very unlikely suspects, but I had to begin somewhere . . .

Captain Jacobsen!

All my free-wheeling suspicions suddenly came into abrupt focus. What did I know of Jacobsen? I hadn't even clapped eyes on the man. He hadn't been in to meals. He had always stayed in his cabin because – according to his wife – of his heart condition. Only Linn, as far as I knew, had spoken to him.

Jacobsen, as I had reminded Linn, was now the sole survivor of the three catcher skippers who had been involved in the war-time adventure with the German raider. And that adventure had been so significant that Captain Prestrud had tried to tell me about it with his dying breath.

I decided to interrogate Jacobsen with an eye to the mystery surrounding Holdgate's death, but I would still see the three met. men first. It was very likely that their interview would be purely a formality.

At the very moment when my mind was breaking into greater clarity the *Quest* broke out of the fog-bank, and it became remarkably light.

I rang for full speed ahead.

That killer-whale knife.

Captain Jacobsen was a whalerman. He might know something about it. I checked myself. As if Jacobsen would admit to knowing anything about such a knife if he were in any way incriminated in Holdgate's death! The kicker was that there was no way in which Jacobsen or anyone else could have removed the knife from Holdgate's throat from inside the locked sick-bay. There was only one key, and it had been in my pocket. I had been with the body all the time from the moment Wegger and I had lifted it on the board. I knew how tired I was becoming when my mind latched on the question – could the knife have been dislodged and was it, in fact, still with the body hidden in the blanket? I hadn't searched for it. I had worked on the assumption that, as Wegger had stated, the blade had been lodged firmly in Holdgate's neck vertebrae. But was that so? After all, I had only Wegger's word for it. No one else had touched the knife.

My thoughts turned to my coming interview with Jacobsen, and I asked myself again and again what possible connection Holdgate could have had with the war-time adventure. He'd only have been a young child at the time. And how was I going to talk my way past Mrs Jacobsen? Was the heart condition genuine? Or only an excuse for keeping him hidden?

I decided I would announce Holdgate's death to the ship early over the loudspeaker system, but that I would not mention foul play. I would leave everyone to think it had been a sudden tragedy. If I could establish radio contact with the outside world I would call off the burial. It would take place about mid-morning, before the seas became too heavy to risk stopping the ship.

Yet another squall and a new blanket of fog doused the ship in darkness again. The *Quest* slowed.

McKinley came on watch at 4 a.m. He was heavy-eyed but clean-shaven and smelt of after-shave and fresh deodorant. I took him aside and briefed him about Holdgate.

He examined his nails and said, 'I hope it doesn't upset some of the passengers.' He didn't specify which.

I checked again, via the intercom, with Persson. Nothing. When I enquired, he said that Wegger hadn't been near the radio.

When finally the daylight held, I sent for Frank Gretland, the ship's carpenter. He came, half-asleep. He left, wide awake, after I had shown him what was in the sick-bay. I told him I wanted Holdgate sewn into a length of canvas with a couple of anchor-links at his feet to take him deep. I didn't want the body sucked into the screw once the *Quest* started on her way again.

I went to the day cabin. I opened the door quietly. Linn was still asleep.

I stood by the couch. She looked about sixteen, except that there was a small in-drawn line at the right-hand corner of her mouth and a faint purplish-blue in the delicate flesh of her eyelids. I paused for a moment before rousing her, conscious of how I would look to her when she woke, with the whiteness of sea salt on my overnight beard and on the shoulders of my dark pea-jacket.

Her fingers plucked convulsively at the edge of the penguin-rug and her eyes came open. They were on me, but unfocused. The recognition came into them and she reached out a hand to me.

'Hello, John.'

I wanted to have her say that a thousand times, to hear her sleep-soaked voice linger over my name.

'Hello, darling.'

I put my hands under her armpits and lifted her into a sitting position.

She looked at me but it was plain that her thoughts were turned inward.

'I was dreaming,' she said. 'I dreamed I was a penguin and was being chased round and round an ice-floe by a savage bird with a knife for a beak.'

'You'd better consult Miss Auchinleck about it,' I replied lightly. 'You're guaranteed protection if you're a penguin.'

She kept on looking at me. I was to remember that look.

She went on, as if the dream were enacting itself still, 'You were on another floe nearby. There was a cold green sea between us. I couldn't reach you in time.'

'That comes of sleeping in a penguin-skin.'

She smiled. 'It's yours, of course? I didn't even hear you come.' She lifted her lips to mine. 'You taste of salt and salt and salt. I don't suppose you've had a wink of sleep.'

'I've been thinking.'

'I feel ashamed of myself. You could have thought out aloud to me, if I'd managed to stay awake.'

In my mind I said, Not my terrible knife-thoughts, Linn darling. I'd kill anyone with my bare hands who touched her.

115

Aloud I said, 'I'm going to have a chat with Captain Jacobsen this morning after I've buried poor Holdgate.'

'You don't think he did it, of all people?'

'He might have done it. He might have had the opportunity – or the motive, for all I know. But he certainly didn't have the opportunity to remove the murder weapon.'

She sat up straight, every trace of sleep gone, and echoed my last words.

I told her what I had discovered in the sick-bay, and she looked stunned. 'The whole thing grows more and more incredible!'

'Listen, Linn,' I went on. 'I told you earlier I was lacking a reference-point to start off from. I'm beginning to wonder now whether that reference-point might lie further back than we think.'

'What do you mean, John?'

I said slowly, 'I want Captain Jacobsen to tell me exactly what happened during or after his escape with your father and Torgersen from the German raider. Everything. What the three of them did that made your father feel guilty when he realized he was dying. Why he begged me to stay away from Prince Edward – from Dina's Island.'

She stood up and straightened her jersey so that her breasts and nipples swelled against the wool.

'In spite of not knowing, you're still pressing on.'

'I feel rather as if I were being programmed by an invisible computer into taking my actions,' I replied. 'Each step seems so right, so inevitable. I wonder where it's all leading. I can't even send a radio signal to consult authority.'

'You didn't engineer the radio black-out, John.'

'No, but it's a vital factor, nevertheless. It could have been anticipated by someone with sufficient opportunism.'

She came close to me. She smelt dry and sweet, an overtone of slept-in wool. 'You've had a rough night, John,' she said. 'Things can look very distorted after nights like that.'

I smiled at her concern. 'I've had lots of nights without sleep at sea. One sleepless night doesn't matter much.'

'May I come and attend the burial this morning?'

'I had hoped you'd be with me.'

'Will everyone be there?'

'Everyone will know. Whether they'll come is another

matter. There's something far more awesome about a burial at sea than one on land.'

'It's a frightening thought that the murderer could be there watching it all.'

'I've thought of that, too. There might even be a give-away.'

'John, what hideous things we're talking about – burial, murder, knives!'

I drew her against me. 'Why do you think I don't sleep?'

She said decisively, and I loved her the more for it, 'Do you want me to be at your interview with Captain Jacobsen?'

'Not at first. Later, perhaps. It depends how it goes.'

'You'll have to get past Mrs Jacobsen.'

'I intend to. She may be part of his cover.'

'You must find out, John.'

'Again, I intend to.'

'You'll be careful, won't you, my darling? I could not bear anything to happen . . .'

'For your sake, Linn dearest, I won't let it.'

She kissed me and said, 'I'm off to bath and change now. I want to be ready in time for your announcement over the public address.' She consulted her watch. 'When's it to be?'

'When I've changed too – in about half an hour.'

'It all sounds so normal,' she said, 'but it isn't. It's horrible. It's all shadows and horrors and unknown things. Like in my dream. And I'm frightened. Like in my dream too.'

She went. I took the penguin-skin rug and folded it slowly, feeling the warmth of her body spill out of it.

Then I, too, left the cabin and made for my quarters.

CHAPTER TWELVE

'. . . We therefore commit his body to the deep . . .'

I looked up from the service-book and nodded to the sea-men at the rail.

They cast loose the lashings from the canvas thing on the board and started to up-end it over the *Quest*'s starboard quarter.

'. . . looking for the resurrection of the body, when the Sea shall give up her dead . . .'

One of the men slipped on the thin coating of hail which covered the deck as his shoulder came under the body. In the brief moment of absolute silence before he regained his balance I heard the hail rattle against the canvas. I heard, too, the faint whirr of Brunton's camera as he knelt on the deck recording the ceremony.

The thin rain was icy cold. The body hung in balance on the fulcrum of the rail. The ship's officers – Wegger, McKinley and Petersen – stood in a group facing it, their backs to the wind. I faced it, cap under my arm. Linn was next to me, the big hood of her soft brown-and-white Icelandic jacket half-hiding her face as the wind blew it against her cheeks. They were as white as the white woollen lining of the hood and the wide cuffs of the dolman sleeves. The three weathermen – Smit, T-shirt Jannie and Pete – grouped themselves behind Linn. After their stunned reaction earlier when I had confronted them with the news of Holdgate's death, I had given up the idea of even formally interrogating them.

For one mad, brief moment while the body hung in suspense I wondered if I shouldn't still call the whole thing off. In less than a second all Holdgate's secrets would be for ever beyond recovery in the black-green water which creamed against the *Quest*'s quarter now that the way was off the ship.

Who had done it?

My glance went to the officers. Wegger's face was a mask. He appeared impervious to the bitter cold. McKinley, next senior, was shivering. Petersen looked as if he were about to pass out again. To keep his mind occupied I had ordered him beforehand to take an exact fix of the burial-spot. With the heavy overcast sweeping almost at mast-level, it was an impossible assignment. But he had seemed grateful for the order, and his sextant was on the deck behind him.

Now the seamen got it right. The board went up, and Holdgate's passage was marked only by a small additional patch of white amidst the white foam under the stern.

I put on my cap and saluted. The others did the same.

'Mr Wegger,' I said formally, 'get the ship under way again, will you? I don't like the way her head's falling off in this wind.'

'Aye, aye, sir.'

Petersen picked up his sextant. He looked miserably at the sky and then at the sullen sea. McKinley's eyes were on someone in the group by the opposite rail. His hand went up to his head, flicking the water clear of his collar.

'Gretland,' I called to the carpenter who had headed the burial party, 'get that board back inside, will you? Mr Smit here will show you where to stow it.'

Like Petersen, the met. man appeared grateful to have something to occupy himself with. 'It's okay,' he replied. 'Jannie and Pete and I can manage it. We don't need any help.'

'Good,' I said. 'Don't let anything happen to that board – we'll be needing it in just twenty-four hours from now to launch the buoy.'

T-shirt Jannie said, 'I didn't ever expect to have this sort of curtain-raiser with it. Holdgate was a good type . . .'

I didn't want a display of sentiment. To probe Holdgate's murder I'd have to put aside human sympathy and act like a cold-blooded machine, if the necessity arose.

I replied tersely, 'Check all your gear, will you? Whoever got in and killed him could have smashed up something. That goes for Holdgate's instruments as well.'

'We'll check all right, you can be damn sure of that,' answered Smit.

There was a flurry at the stern. The *Quest*'s screw had started to bite. It felt reassuring, normal and familiar.

'Coming, Linn?' I asked.

We headed for the forward superstructure along the windward side of the deck so as to avoid the passengers opposite.

I nodded towards the south-west quarter. 'There's an old saying for a gale down this way – long foretold, long last. Launching the buoy tomorrow could be tricky if the weather breaks the way I think it will.'

The high white polo collar of the jersey she wore under her jacket reached right up to her chin. A broad belt of rectangles – a typical Icelandic pattern – was knitted into the fabric down the front. The white colour was a perfect foil for her pale gold hair.

She said suddenly, 'Are you going to see Captain Jacobsen now, John?'

'In a few moments.'

'How did you get past Mrs Jacobsen?'

I laughed a little ruefully. 'When I knocked at their cabin door I was confronted by a squat square person in a leather coat. I thought for a moment that it was the Captain.'

'She's pretty formidable, isn't she?' said Linn.

'I thought she'd throw me with a judo hold, or mule-kick me in the chest. But she just said flatly, "You're not going to see my husband." A lioness guarding her cub had nothing on her. You know, Linn, for one dreadful moment I found myself wondering whether she could have done it herself.'

Linn paused and eyed me. I wished at that moment I were alone with her in the *Quest*, in a wide, wide sea, without a thousand problems riding on my back.

'I think she'd be quite capable of such a thing if his well-being were involved,' she answered quietly. 'But is it?'

'I mean to find out shortly.' I glanced at my watch. 'He's due in my cabin in ten minutes.'

'With or without Mrs Jacobsen?'

'Without.'

'I don't know how you contrived it, John.'

'When she refused, I said, "I'm the captain." Captain Jacobsen was in the lounge section of their suite and he must have overheard. My luck was in. He emerged of his own accord. Being a sailor, he knew the significance of a visit from the captain. The rest was easy.'

It wasn't easy, though, when Captain Jacobsen knocked at my cabin door a little later – not to start with, anyway.

The first thing I did when I opened the door was to judge whether he tallied with Reilly's description. His hands were certainly big but his frame was more square and stocky than big. He'd gone to seed and his belly pushed his sea-cut jacket tight. If he really had a heart complaint, then he would have been better at sea, I reckoned, keeping himself trim instead of being cosseted by a domestic dragon.

I closed the door behind him. I wondered whether a man-to-man approach mightn't pay off.

'A drink, Captain?'

It did. He grinned like a schoolboy playing truant. 'My wife won't like it, and the sun's not over the yardarm yet as you British say – schnapps.'

I poured two small glasses. I had warmed to him even before I felt the warmth of the fiery liquid down my throat.

'You didn't come to the burial service,' I remarked.

His eyes were bleached to pale blue from gazing too long at horizonless oceans.

'I wanted to, but my wife said the strain would be bad for my heart. I've buried quite a few men at sea in my time.'

'Then you know what it's all about.'

'Aye. It's worse in a small ship like a catcher when you know everyone personally, even if you are the skipper.'

I said, watching closely for his reaction, 'This man was killed. Murdered.'

He held out his glass for more schnapps. His hand was quite steady. He sat like a judge considering his verdict. It was a ponderous silence.

Then he said, 'That makes the captain's position very difficult. Your position.'

'It does.'

'Why should you want to talk to me about it?'

I saw the opening I had been looking for. 'Because Captain Prestrud was also murdered.'

The glass fell from his hand and spilled some of its contents on him before reaching the carpet. He made no attempt to recover it. He gaped at me and his face became grey-blue mottled. He began to frisk his pockets.

I held out a pack of cigarettes.

'My pills – I should have a pill with news like this,' he replied thickly.

I retrieved his glass, which had not smashed. 'Another drink will do you more good.'

I pressed it upon him, together with the smoke. He lit up and inhaled deeply. 'This, too, is *verboten*. But the hell with that.'

Then he eyed me steadily. 'Is this true what you say about my old friend, Captain Prestrud?'

'Yes. He was pistol-whipped to death. The accident story was a blind so as not to upset the passengers.'

He sank the schnapps. 'His daughter told me . . .'

'I know what she told you. Why I asked you to come here now is to find out whether there is any connection between Captain Prestrud's death and Doctor Holdgate's.'

'Doctor Holdgate – I never heard the name.'

I believed him. I sketched in Holdgate's background – what I knew of it – quickly.

'It makes no sense, Captain Shotton,' he replied.

'It would make less sense to me if Captain Prestrud hadn't confessed something to me shortly before his death.'

I could have been mistaken, but there seemed to be a spurt of fear in his eyes. Of caution, certainly.

'What did he say?'

'It is what he left unsaid, Captain Jacobsen. I believe you can fill it in for me.'

'I don't understand what you are driving at.'

'Listen. What I want to know is what happened in these waters during the war. The incident took place very close to here. The German raider *HK-33*, which was also called the *Pinguin*, captured the entire Norwegian whaling fleet. You were there, Captain.'

'As you say, I was there.'

'Captain Prestrud was there also.'

'Aye, he was there.'

'A few hours before he died, Captain Prestrud started to tell me about it.'

'There's very little to tell. It was about the same time of the year – mid-January of 1941. Captain Krüder was the raider captain. He was a very clever man. We catchers were all grouped about the factory ships. He surprised us in the middle of the night. There was no fighting. Three of us – Prestrud, Torgersen and I – managed to escape. That's all.'

I poured myself another drink. 'That's laconic enough to be a Royal Navy despatch, Captain Jacobsen.'

'You think I'm lying.'

'I didn't say that. Your account is remarkable for its brevity. But it's the bits and pieces that are important to me.'

'Such as?'

'You escaped, you three. Fair enough. Where did you go?'

'To Cape Town. It was the nearest friendly port.'

'You're going much too fast, Captain Jacobsen. You three gave the raider the slip – how?'

'We bluffed our way past. We didn't stop when Krüder signalled us to stop. We knew he was a humane man and wouldn't fire. He didn't.'

This checked with Captain Prestrud's account to me.

Then I fired my first broadside.

'What about the torpedo?'

He put down his glass and stared at me. 'The torpedo?'

If you can bluff a man at poker, you can bluff him at interrogation. Your hand can be empty. Mine was.

'You were at great pains, you and Torgersen, to guard Prestrud's flanks in order to get the torpedo safely away.'

I didn't care for the throaty way he coughed. Perhaps his wife was right about his heart.

'It was a trick, a *ruse-de-guerre*, it was legitimate,' he answered thickly. 'Krüder used a Norwegian radio operator – a quisling – to bluff us. Fair's fair. War makes things like that legitimate.'

'I'll come to that quisling in a moment,' I went on. 'Let's stick to that torpedo. What were you doing with a torpedo? None of you were warships. You couldn't have fired it if you'd wanted to.'

He smiled, and I knew I'd come unstuck somewhere. 'I think I could manage another schnapps,' he said, holding out his glass.

I poured it and he went on, 'We brought the torpedo with us from Norway. It was a German one. A souvenir, you could call it.'

'A torpedo – for a souvenir!'

He smiled again. 'Prestrud and Torgersen and I were all on the factory ship *Pelagos* in port at Narvik when the Germans attacked. That assault brought Norway to her knees.'

'Go on. This was all before my time.'

He became more animated, as if the memory of the action had given him a shot in the arm, a stimulant even more effective than the schnapps.

'You must have heard about it. The Royal Navy was superb in action during the First Battle of Narvik. One of your destroyer captains won a Victoria Cross.'

'Sorry. My history doesn't run to that.'

'Well, the Germans grabbed the port of Narvik. There was a whole squadron of their destroyers. Then the British broke in through the fjord in the snow and the mist – very brave, very daring. There was shooting, shooting, shooting. Every warship fired torpedoes. The harbour was full of torpedoes.

It was all darkness and confusion and we snatched one before we escaped with the factory ship. A piece of cake, as you say, in all the smoke and shooting and snowstorms.'

'*You – took – a live – torpedo – as – a – souvenir?*'

'Yes. It was floating around near a quay.'

I sat and stared at him.

'You don't believe me?'

'I most certainly don't believe you. No one would be crazy enough to risk a torpedo with a live warhead which was liable to go up at any moment.'

He laughed. 'You're smart and you're tough but you're not very old and you don't know everything. I'll tell you. The Germans were using magnetic pistols to trigger the warheads. Narvik is very far north. In high latitudes the pistols were affected by the magnetic field. It would be just the same very far South. They failed to explode. It was safe enough.'

'Okay, I'll buy it,' I retorted. 'And subsequently this souvenir was valuable enough to you and Prestrud and Torgersen to risk your chances of escape by taking it along with you.'

He chuckled, and I realized I wasn't getting anywhere. 'Yes, we valued that torpedo a lot, Prestrud and Torgersen and I.'

I struggled to regain the advantage I knew I'd lost, but at what point in our exchange I did not know.

'Listen,' I resumed. 'When Captain Prestrud spoke to me for the last time he was definitely feeling guilty about something. Guilty enough to want to get it off his chest to a comparative stranger. It was something to do with your escape. What was it?'

Jacobsen froze. He said heavily, 'There was nothing for us to feel guilty about.'

'Torgersen knocked down the quisling radio operator – did he kill him? Or did you and Captain Prestrud?' I pressed him. 'He mentioned having done something which was justified at the time. If that means killing a man in war-time . . .'

'No one killed him,' broke in Captain Jacobsen. 'He was only stunned. We took him along with us. That's all.'

He clammed up completely, and I began to be afraid that he would actually walk out.

I took a shot in the dark. 'Torgersen got killed later.'

'Aye,' retorted Jacobsen savagely. 'We ought to have killed that quisling Rolf Solberg at the time. Torgersen and I wanted to but Prestrud had a soft heart. We let him live. And thirty years ago today he killed Torgersen. It was after the first of our get-togethers.'

'Yes, Captain Jacobsen?' I said encouragingly.

'We three decided that after the war we would foregather once every five years on the anniversary of our escape from the German raider. The first celebration was held in our home port, Sandefjord.'

I gestured at the picture on the panelling that Linn had pointed out to me. Jacobsen nodded. 'That's the place. But our gathering was before Prestrud married and had a home. We celebrated it as comrades-in-arms should. Next day Torgersen was found in his hotel stabbed to death. I think Rolf Solberg must have been temporarily insane when he did it. He left clues everywhere. The police had no difficulty in tracking him down.'

Apparently unrelated circuits in my brain started to make contact.

'You say he was stabbed to death. What sort of knife?'

He thought a while and then replied, 'I don't think the police ever found the murder weapon. I can't remember it on exhibit in court when he was tried.'

'It wasn't a knife with a carved handle and a killer whale engraved on it?' I asked.

'No. I'm quite sure now. There was no knife exhibited at his trial.'

'You were at Solberg's trial, of course?'

'Prestrud and I were key witnesses. Solberg was sent to prison for life. He's probably still there.'

I fired my next question, 'What did you and the other two skippers actually do to the unfortunate Solberg?'

Jacobsen gave a half-roar, half-grunt, like an elephant seal. 'Unfortunate! We ought to've killed him! I said so then and I say so now! He got what he deserved.'

'What was that, Captain Jacobsen?'

He shrugged. 'It all happened a long time ago. There's no point dredging it up now.'

The man's silences were as solid as he was. I tried another tack.

'See here, Captain Jacobsen. Captain Prestrud tried desperately to tell me something, but he didn't make it. But he did warn me with all the strength he had left to stay away from Prince Edward Island.'

Questioning Jacobsen was like sounding unknown waters with a hand lead-line. You never knew when you would strike a shoal or deep water.

'He was my good friend and comrade for many, many years. It was a good thing he told you that.'

'*Why*, Captain Jacobsen? *Why?*'

He remained unresponsive and withdrawn.

I threw out a fresh probe. 'But in spite of that warning, this ship is bound for Prince Edward Island. And for tonight Captain Prestrud had planned another anniversary celebration of your escape – a very special one – thirty years to the day, as you said yourself. What is it about Prince Edward Island that meant so much to both of you?'

He replied sullenly, 'There's nothing there any more. Nothing!'

'Any more?' I pressed him. 'Any more? What *was* there, then?'

'Nothing.' But he was lying. He got to his feet.

I went quickly to the chart cabinet. He turned to see what I was doing, so that he faced away from the door.

It opened. Wegger took a step in. I looked up. 'Yes . . .?'

He wasn't looking at me but in Captain Jacobsen's direction. Without replying, he turned on his heel and was gone, banging the door shut behind him.

I was too preoccupied to worry about Wegger at this moment. I found the general chart showing the Sub-Antarctic islands. Jacobsen joined me at the table and I deliberately kept the chart flat while I stabbed it with my finger.

'Where did all this take place?'

'Here. Quite close to Prince Edward Island.'

'Ah!'

I let the printed lettering at the top unroll itself into his line of vision. '*Teddy. Atlantis-Pinguin-Sibirien. January 14th 1941.*'

He stared at it, shaken. 'Where did you get this?'

'It belonged to Captain Prestrud.'

He read the words aloud, ' "*Teddy. Atlantis-Pinguin-Sibirien.*" These are all forgotten things from a long-forgotten past.'

'Maybe. But I'd still like to know about them. *Teddy* is the name of a ship, I know that much. And *Pinguin* was the raider which captured the whaling fleet.'

'Aye,' he agreed. 'Aye. The *Teddy* was a tanker, so it seemed . . .'

'So it seemed?'

'She sailed with us – eleven catchers and the factory ship *Pelagos* from Narvik after the battle. Outwardly *Teddy* was a tanker. But underneath . . .' He shrugged. 'It doesn't matter any more if I tell you. She was the flagship of the Free Norwegian Navy. She was fitted with gun positions and everything for a warship. Solberg – the bastard!'

'What did he have to do with *Teddy*?'

'He'd been her radio operator before the war. He knew she was a warship. When he went over to the Germans, he gave her away. The German Naval High Command was on the look-out for her. She was captured by the raider *Atlantis* in the Indian Ocean when she was on her way to protect the whaling fleet in Antarctica. *Teddy* was carrying the overall master-plan for the Free Norwegian Navy, and the details of the whaling fleet's rendezvous-point near Prince Edward. *Atlantis* seized the lot. As if that wasn't enough, Solberg also turned the *Pinguin* on to our fleet by chatting in Norwegian over the R/T and pretending to be another big factory ship called the *Harpon* which was due to join us from South Georgia.'

'*Sibirien* – what does that mean?'

'It was the code-name for the whaling fleet's Antarctic rendezvous-point. *Sibirien* – Siberia – cold. It was a large area of sea divided into grids in order to fix an exact rendezvous.'

'What area did *Sibirien* cover?'

'It was a big rectangular stretch with Bouvet as western terminal and Prince Edward as eastern.'

'So it all comes back to Prince Edward Island, doesn't it?' I said.

Not that that threw any light on Holdgate's death, I added to myself. Why a volcanologist whose only interest in Prince Edward was its rocks should have been brutally stabbed to death all this time after the events Captain Jacobsen was speaking of was incomprehensible.

Jacobsen was breathing quickly and shallowly. I realized

that he had reached the limit of what he would answer. So I switched to another tack.

'There's something else I want to discuss with you – or rather Captain Prestrud's daughter and I both want to discuss it with you,' I said. 'It's about tonight's celebration dinner.'

'I do not wish to celebrate anything tonight,' he replied. 'These are old wounds you have re-opened.'

I picked up the phone and while I was waiting to get through to Linn, I said to him, 'I didn't open them, Captain Jacobsen. It was someone else who did. Someone on board my ship at this moment, and I'd give my left arm to know who he is.'

He eyed me keenly. 'I don't like the way you've handled this affair, but I think we are on the same side. I'm beginning to like you better now, Captain.'

Linn answered at the other end and saved me from the awkwardness of having to reply.

'Linn,' I asked, 'can you come to my cabin, please? Captain Jacobsen is here.'

'I'll be right down.'

She shook hands formally with Captain Jacobsen, and then came and stood next to me.

He surveyed the two of us. Either he was shrewder than I had thought or else our feelings were more obvious than either of us was aware of.

'So,' he smiled. 'That's the way of it, is it?' He gave me a warmer glance than any we had exchanged during the interview. He said to Linn, 'I am happy for the daughter of my old comrade-in-arms. You have made a good choice in this man.'

Linn answered quickly, to cover her confusion. 'I thought we were going to discuss the celebration dinner.'

Jacobsen said, still smiling, 'Before you came in, Linn, I told the captain I was in no mood to celebrate, but I feel different now. Everyone else will think we are celebrating the anniversary of a war-time escape but we three, we'll be thinking of your future.'

She touched his arm with spontaneous warmth.

'Thanks, Captain Jacobsen, you've done me good. I needed cheering up. All the passengers are standing around in little groups talking in hushed tones, and the whole ship is drenched in gloom. This weather isn't exactly helping matters, either.'

'I was afraid it would be like this,' I said.

Linn said, 'I thought it might help to cheer things up a bit if we staged an exhibition of the drifter buoy and the balloon and the various instruments in the main lounge this afternoon. Everyone's curious about them, and about the launching tomorrow.'

'How did the met. boys react?' I asked.

'Jumped at it,' she replied. 'They've been checking and rechecking everything until they're seeing double. They'd welcome a break.'

'Right,' I said. 'Follow it up with a good dinner and plenty of wine and it'll be just what the doctor ordered.'

Captain Jacobsen broke in. 'When your father and I used to get together, Linn, one of us always made a speech. I'm the only one of the three left, so I will make tonight's speech.'

I felt uneasy at the suggestion. 'No skeletons out of the past, please, Captain Jacobsen.'

He grinned and shook his head. 'We'll forget all that – and we'll forget what's been happening aboard this ship – for a few hours anyway. As I said just now, it's what I'll be celebrating in my heart – that's what matters.'

His enthusiasm fired Linn. She said, 'I'll find some volunteers and we'll decorate the dining-room this afternoon.'

'I saw some cases of *Kaapse Vonkel* coming aboard just before we sailed,' I said. 'Cape Sparkle. Genuine Cape champagne. I'm told it's good stuff.'

Jacobsen rubbed his hands. 'When a man talks like that, the party's halfway to success.'

He looked years younger. I hoped the afternoon in close proximity to his wet-nurse wouldn't kill his mood.

'That's fixed them,' I said. 'Linn, will you make arrangements with the cook? He'll need both his assistants – aspirant cooks as he calls them. His English isn't all that hot. You'd better stick to Norwegian when you're dealing with Klausen.'

'There's no knowing what he'll serve if I don't.' She smiled.

Jacobsen was getting up to go. At the back of my mind was something else I'd wanted to ask him. I remembered it as he reached the door. 'Wait a minute, Captain Jacobsen. There's just one more thing.'

I went to the safe and took out the leather-framed picture

of the beautiful, strange-looking woman.

Jacobsen studied it intently, without lifting his eyes. An expression of tenderness came over his face; there might have been nostalgia there too, but there was no trace of his light-hearted mood of a few moments before.

When he did not speak, I asked, 'Do you know who she is?'

Jacobsen snapped the case shut and returned the picture to me. 'No one will ever know her,' he said, and left the cabin.

His emotion remained after he had gone, invisible and yet there, like a radio-active cloud from a nuclear satellite which has burned itself up on re-entering the earth's atmosphere. Dangerous, too, when fall-out begins.

Linn said thoughtfully, 'John, there's an awful lot of things I still don't understand about this cruise.'

I locked the picture away. You can't be more puzzled than I am. Even after talking to Captain Jacobsen.'

She came close and held the lapels of my jacket. 'But there's one thing I can see perfectly plainly – you're dead on your feet, John. You need sleep, and I intend to see you get some – now.'

I threw her a mock salute. 'Aye, aye, Captain Linn.'

She looked at the time. 'I'll have a tray of lunch sent in to you here right away. When you've eaten you're to go straight to your cabin and sleep.'

I knew she was right. I could feel the stresses catching up on me. Ahead of me was the dinner celebration followed by a night of what I believed would be piloting the ship through the first ice-fields.

'If I sleep, it'll be in here,' I told her. 'With one eye open, next to the phone.'

She didn't argue, but kissed me and went away.

I must have been in poorer shape than I thought. I did not hear the lunch tray arrive but I was roused by the imperative ringing of the phone. I swung myself off the couch. I was wide awake as soon as my feet hit the floor. Automatically I noted two things – first, that it was half-dark and that the ship's motion was increasing; second, that I had been covered by the penguin-skin rug.

I snatched the phone from its cradle. 'Captain here.'

'Sir! It's Persson! Come quickly! It's a Mayday!'

CHAPTER THIRTEEN

I wrenched open the door. As I did so, something fell from the outer handle where it had been balanced. I snatched it up. It was a long envelope addressed to me.

I thrust it into my pocket and raced to the radio shack.

As I threw open Persson's door I was struck by a wash of sound. Sferics came screaming in over the volume-up loud-speaker, hissing like a steam locomotive. The sound grew, then ebbed.

'Repeat! Repeat!'

Persson was sitting with his elbows on the desk juggling with the clumsy microphone like a rock star bewitching a teenage audience. His jaw was dark with unshaven beard and his short hair was uncombed.

A fresh burst of hissing filled the room. Then a tiny hard core of voice became audible.

'Mayday!' it whispered. 'Mayday! May . . .'

'Goddammit!' exploded Persson. 'Just got him, then it goes!' He beat at the microphone. 'Repeat! Receiving your May-day. Repeat! Repeat! What ship is that . . .?'

'Mayday,' it whimpered. 'Mayday. Mayday. Mayday.'

'Repeat!'

The voice brightened like a sight of salvation. 'Do you hear me? Mayday! Mayday!'

Another long surge of sound broke over the reefs of inter-ference.

'Don't lose him!' I snapped at Persson. 'Where is he? Is he close?'

'He could be anywhere – I can't get a D/F bearing on that sort of transmission,' he answered. He said coaxingly into the microphone, 'I hear you, Mayday. Repeat, I hear you. What ship is that?'

'Position,' I broke in. 'Give his position!'

'. . . Bay. Mayday . . .'

'Did you hear Bay or Day?' I demanded.

'Bay. B for Bertie. Sure.' Persson replied.

Then the voice, as disembodied as if it came from a microphone in the throat of an albatross a thousand kilometres away, said, 'Full-rigged ship *Botany Bay*. Repeat, *Botany Bay*. Collision . . .'

'*Botany Bay*!' I echoed. 'That was the horror ship in Cape Town! She was on her way to Australia!'

'Got him!' Persson's voice vibrated. '*Botany Bay* – I hear you!'

'Position!' I repeated. 'He was starting to give it.'

'No.' Persson shook his head. '*Botany Bay* said collision, not position.'

'In these waters?' I asked incredulously. 'There's not another ship to collide with!'

There was another long burst of sferics. We only caught the last few words '. . . collision with ice . . .'

'Iceberg!' I echoed. 'My oath, she hit an iceberg!'

Persson said, '*Botany Bay* – repeat your message about collision . . .' To me he added: 'Did he say iceberg? I only heard ice.'

'She must have collided with an iceberg – it's all it could be down here,' I answered. 'We must get a bearing on her – we must!'

Persson fiddled with the dials. Hissing noises cascaded over everything.

Then he observed, 'She's just about on the limit of reception range.'

I recalled what Smit had told me. 'Four hundred kilometres? Or less?'

'Less, I'd say. But I don't know. I can't place him . . .'

Again came the tiny thread of human voice. '*Botany Bay*. This is the master of the *Botany Bay* speaking. Tom Kearnay. Mayday. Do you hear me?'

'I hear you, *Botany Bay*,' replied Persson. 'Keep talking. Cruise ship *Quest* here.'

He was manipulating the reception dials and the remote-control for the D/F aerial alternately. But one D/F bearing is not enough: to fix a vessel's position there must be at least two intersecting, and ideally three or more. Persson had the radar going too. The sweeping beam showed nothing.

'Give me the mike,' I ordered Persson. '*Botany Bay*! This

is Captain John Shotton, cruise ship *Quest*, speaking. Reply!
Reply!'

Persson and I strained for the response. It came, fragmentary, but still a reply. 'I hear you, *Quest*.'

'State your position,' I said. 'We can scarcely hear you. Do
you understand? Position!'

It was hopeless. Somewhere in the remote background I
could distinguish Kearnay's voice, repeating, repeating. What
t was was the waves' guess.

I cut in on him. 'Shotton here again. Hold it, Kearnay.
Listen carefully. I reckon you're at the extreme range of
voice radio. That makes you within four hundred kilometres.
We heard the word ice. Collision with ice. Ice means you're
outh of me. I'm heading due south along the twentieth
parallel. Twenty degrees east. Approximately forty-four and a
half degrees south. Your position, please!'

I half-heard the answer but Persson's more finely attuned
ear caught it and he grinned triumphantly. 'Approximately
forty-seven degrees south, eighteen east.'

'Roger, Kearnay,' I said into the microphone. 'Position
heard. Approximately forty-seven south, eighteen east.'

'. . . sinking . . .' the voice wavered on.

'What's that?' I asked. 'Sinking? Are you sinking?'

The reply was incomprehensible. I handed the microphone
o Persson. 'Keep at it,' I told him.

My mind raced. Angles, distances, calculations. I could
hardly credit *Botany Bay*'s position. If the windjammer was
where Kearnay said she was, she certainly was way off course
between the Cape and Australia. A mental picture flashed
n front of me of the Southern Ocean chart. Kearnay's
position put the windjammer about 280 kilometres distant
rom the *Quest*, slightly off to the south-west. What about the
buoy launch? A new set of time-distance calculations flooded
my mind. Could the *Quest* afford to go to the rescue of the
sailing ship if we were to launch the buoy on schedule?

I saw in my mind's eye the relative positions of the two
ships and the buoy's launching-point. They formed a triangle.
Botany Bay was about 110 kilometres west of the launching-
point, the *Quest* about 280 kilometres north-east of her. But
would the *Quest*'s engines stand up to the hammering I'd

133

have to hand out in order to make it? Equally problematica
would the hull stand up to the kind of sea that was buildin
up? I'd have to put the *Quest* at full belt through a sea whic
I now knew via Kearnay was dangerous with ice. One touc
and the *Quest*'s thin hull would rip open like a sardine-can . .

Yet I couldn't leave a shipful of men to die. Risking th
rescue would mean a hell of a squeeze between distance an
time. I reckoned I could get to *Botany Bay* in ten hours. I
would be then four in the morning – light enough to carr
out a rescue. From *Botany Bay* to the launching-point, an
other four hours, give or take some. That left two hours fo
the operation of saving the windjammer crew. I could jus
make it – if everything worked out according to plan.

Persson broke in on my thoughts. 'He's fast to the ice, sir
He says he's fast to the ice!'

'Fast!' I exclaimed. 'What the hell does he mean? He can'
be *fast* to ice in these waters! The pack's still thousands o
kilometres further South.'

'He said *fast*,' reiterated Persson. 'I'm sure, sir.'

'Keep at him – find out what's happened!'

Again the sferics hissed like a gale. It was that compariso
which brought home to me why *Botany Bay* had landed u
where she was and not well to the east en route to Australia
I'd been thinking like a steamship man. If Kearnay had saile
in a south-easterly gale from the Cape as the *Quest* had don
he would have followed the course of any true deep-water
man in sail: he would have stood away boldly to the south
west,. apparently *away* from Australia, in order to get we
south. There he would pick up the powerful westerlies t
enable him to run his easting down to his destination an
more than make up lost time. It made sense. *Botany Ba*
could be where she was, with reason.

Persson said, 'I heard something about damage, sir. Bo
split, or something like that.'

My mind was on windjammers. 'You're sure he didn't sa
bowsprit?'

'Could be either,' Persson replied.

'More likely to have been bowsprit,' I went on. 'If h
tangled with ice, *Botany Bay*'s bowsprit would have bought
first.'

I glanced up at the big brass-faced clock on the shack's wa

Five minutes past six.

I borrowed the microphone from Persson. 'Kearnay – Shotton here. If you have to abandon ship, keep your boats together as near your present position as you can. I estimate I am now two hundred and eighty metres north-east of you. My ETA to be up with you is about four a.m. I'll use my searchlight, but it'll probably be light enough to see. Start burning distress flares from o-three-hundred-hours onwards – a pair of red every ten minutes. Got that? Confirm, if you can.'

I could scarcely wait while Persson tried to filter out *Botany Bay*'s reply. Once or twice we thought we could distinguish the voice, but that was all.

I used the microphone again. 'Conserve your batteries, Kearnay. I'm making all possible speed. Contact *Quest* again every hour on the hour. Maybe we'll hear you better as we get closer. If you abandon ship, keep your key down until she sinks, will you? We'll be monitoring you all the time.'

I returned the instrument to Persson. 'Let me know any developments, will you? I'll be on the bridge . . .'

Then I remembered the banquet. I added, 'Between seven and nine I'll be in the saloon at dinner.'

'Aye, aye, sir.'

I headed for the bridge. Wegger was there. I said briefly to him as I hurried to the engine-room telegraph, 'I'll take the deck, Mr Wegger. Emergency. There's a Mayday out.'

I felt the thin electric thrill run through the men on watch. I pushed the telegraph over to 'full ahead'. At the same time as I reached for the intercom to MacFie I ordered the helmsman, 'New course. Steer south-west by south.'

'South-west by south it is, sir.'

I hadn't had time to calculate an exact course; the sailing-ship notation was good enough temporarily.

The intercom came alive. 'MacFie here.'

'Mac,' I said, aware that every ear on the bridge was strained to listen, 'I want everything those bloody engines of yours have got.'

The reply was slow and caustic. 'I've just seen the pointer go full ahead, laddie. Do you want to shake the screw out of her in this sea?'

'Sorry, Mac. I've just had a Mayday signal. A windjammer.

135

She's tangled with the ice ahead. We've got to get to her, quick. Those engines of yours . . .'

'They're good, but they're old, never forget.'

'Can you get sixteen knots out of them – or more?'

'I can get sixteen knots out of anything – for a while.'

'For ten, twelve hours?'

'That's quite a while, as whiles go.'

'Mac, I need every horse you can coax out of them. No one can do it except you.'

'Aye, butter my backside while you blow my engines.'

'Listen, Mac. Those windjammer lads are really in trouble. I've got to get to them – quick. And you're the man to do it.'

'Feel that?' – I hadn't noticed the increased vibration. 'All of fifty-six hundred horse-power. That's all these bluidy engines are meant to do. But I'll see what else I can manage. Don't blame me if they don't last.'

'They will, Mac, they will. Give them the gun.'

The *Quest* steadied on her new course. She gave a deep plunge as the run of the sea caught the bow and threw water all over the searchlight platform.

I turned from the phone. 'Mr Wegger . . .' I began. I stopped when I saw Wegger's face. He looked as if he had absorbed a right cross to the jaw. The expression was remote, the eyes were distant. At the same time, paradoxically, the face seemed to be filled with the intensity which had puzzled me before on several occasions. But now it looked as if there were a savage pressure behind that tension, as if it would explode at any moment. His damaged hand flexed and contracted as if by reflex.

My first thought was that he was afraid of the emergency.

I hoped the others hadn't noticed. I went close to him and hissed, 'Pull yourself together, man! Snap out of it!'

The moment his eyes came back into focus, I knew I was wrong. I drew back. I had never seen such naked hatred in anyone's face.

'Mr Wegger,' I said formally, 'have the searchlight team take up station immediately. I want lifelines rigged for'ard so that they can hang on when she takes it green. Double the look-outs – put four in the crow's nest. I want any floating object reported to me immediately. Understood? Tell 'em to keep their eyes skinned. There's ice ahead.'

He didn't react.

'Is that clear, Mr Wegger?'

There was another moment's hesitation, and then he asked thickly, 'You say a windjammer's in trouble?'

'Yes. The picture's pretty confused but it seems she's tangled with the ice. She's damaged – could be sinking.'

His Adam's apple jumped up and down as he swallowed. Finally he got a proper grip on his voice. 'How bad is the damage?'

I kept talking in order to defuse whatever crisis had boiled up inside him.

'It sounded as if the skipper said "bow split" but I'd guess it was "bowsprit", being a windjammer.'

'The situation's not critical, then? She's still afloat?'

'For how long is another matter. We can only find out when we get closer and hear what she's saying – if her batteries last.'

He asked, with a strange inflexion in his voice, 'You know a lot about sailing-ships, don't you?'

'Yes. But at the moment that doesn't matter. I want the searchlight men . . .'

'You could sail one like *Botany Bay*?' Wegger persisted.

I eyed him curiously. 'Yes, I suppose I could. But the need won't arise. She's got a perfectly good skipper and crew.'

The *Quest* gave a deep plunge, then rolled so far over to port with a corkscrewing motion that had her loading derricks been rigged outboard she would have put them under. Both Wegger and I tottered a couple of paces across the bridge.

'Get those lifelines rigged in the bows – quick,' I ordered Wegger. 'If anyone goes overboard in this sea we'll never find him again.'

Wegger stood for a moment, as if considering my order.

'Mr Wegger!'

'Aye, aye, sir!'

He moved quickly to the rear of the bridge, as if he had suddenly made up his mind about something. At the head of the companionway he almost collided with Linn.

'What's happening?' she asked me. 'I was in the galley – half the crockery's smashed . . .'

'There's been a Mayday call . . .' I outlined the situation briefly, explaining how little I knew about the extent of the windjammer's damage.

'You're going to her rescue?' she asked when I had finished.

'Of course.'

'You're cutting it very fine if you're going to launch the drifter buoy on schedule, John.'

'I know. And it worries me. But when I think of a sailing-ship in the conditions which must lie ahead . . .'

'You'll abandon her once you've rescued the crew, will you?'

'I may have to.'

'You sound as if there is some doubt.'

'If there is any chance, I'll try and save her.'

'What! And endanger the launch?'

'Linn, I don't know what the conditions are like. But I do know that sailing-ships are as rare as fine gold in this day and age. I won't let her go unless I'm forced to.'

I picked up the crow's-nest phone. 'Captain here. Have the extra look-outs come on duty yet?'

The man sounded surprised. 'Not yet, sir. I don't know anything about it.'

'Hasn't Mr Wegger been in touch with you?'

'No, sir.'

I put down the instrument. A doubt nagged at my mind. Could I trust Wegger in a crisis?

'John,' asked Linn. 'Does this mean the banquet's off?'

I checked the bridge clock. 'We can't call it off now but it will have to come second.'

The *Quest* gave another one of her lurches.

'Nobody will be able to keep their food off their laps if this goes on,' she added.

What she said made sense. I also realized that by pushing the ship before I had lifelines rigged I might precipitate a delaying man-overboard tragedy.

I used the phone again. 'Searchlight crew? Captain here. Put Mr Wegger on the line, will you?'

'Mr Wegger, sir? Mr Wegger isn't here.'

'You mean . . .?' I stopped myself in time from giving away an officer. 'Haven't you had my new orders?'

'Only standing orders, sir, nothing new. Searchlight team to stand by in the foc's'le.'

'You mean you aren't manning the damn thing at this moment?'

'We've had no orders, sir. There's a lot of water coming over the bows.'

I choked back a command to send the men out on to the platform at the double. The ice was still hours away. But Wegger – where the hell was he? It was his job to get the crow's nest and searchlight manned immediately I ordered him.

'Keep on stand-by for the moment,' I told the man. 'Mr Wegger will be along shortly with my orders.'

I put down the phone unnecessarily hard. Linn's eyes followed me.

'Something wrong, John?'

'Could be,' I answered briefly. 'Look, Linn, I've been doing a quick think about the banquet. If I keep the ship at this speed, it will kill the whole occasion. And it *is* an event, and I promised your father it would go ahead. At this stage *Botany Bay*'s position is guesswork. There's no point in smashing up the banquet and possibly the ship as well at this early stage. I'll reduce speed for an hour or two to give the banquet a steady platform.'

'I'm glad, John. My father would have been, too.'

The bridge phone rang. 'Persson here, sir. I thought you should know. There's something on the radar. Small target. Not clear.'

'What range, Persson? What do you make of it?'

'Twenty kilometres, sir. The image isn't very solid. I'd guess it was hail clutter, maybe rain. I can't say. I can't clarify the image on this set.'

'It's not a ship?'

'Definitely not, sir.'

'Ice?'

'I doubt it, sir. There's too much speckle. But ice can be tricky. I can't be sure.'

'I'll be along shortly to see for myself. Keep me posted, will you?'

'Aye, aye, sir.'

'And – Persson, have you seen Mr Wegger?'

'No, sir. He's not been here.'

'Thank you.'

My anger blazed against the man. Where the devil was he? The first officer is the kingpin of a ship, and now that the

139

Quest was facing a crisis the kingpin was missing.

I rattled the phone. 'Give me Mr Wegger's cabin.'

'No need. I'm here.'

Wegger stalked on to the bridge. I noticed immediately that he wasn't wearing weatherproofing and that his uniform was dry. He was breathing fast, like the time MacFie and I had surprised him in the hold.

I dropped my voice so that the others on the bridge would not hear. 'You will report to me in my cabin in ten minutes.'

He seemed amused, insolently amused.

I added in my normal tone, 'The searchlight isn't manned yet. Nor is the crow's nest.'

He stood swinging on his toes for a moment, and then took a step – the same type of menacing step I'd seen before – towards me. Then he checked himself.

'I know. I was checking the motor-launch for the rescue.'

It was an obvious lie. His dry uniform was proof of that.

'Who told you to check the motor-launch?' I snapped. 'Who said anything about using the boat for the rescue?'

'Of course we'll use the motor-launch,' he replied truculently. 'How else will we get them off?'

'Any rescue arrangements are my affair – get that clear,' I said tautly. 'How we do it is for me to decide.'

He shrugged a shoulder. I was at a complete loss to understand his attitude. It didn't help my anger.

I repeated, in as controlled a voice as I could muster, 'I'll see you in ten minutes in my day cabin. Meanwhile, get on with the business of running the ship.'

The ugly lightning flashed in his eyes, but his mouth retained its half-sneer. 'You can rely on me to run this ship. You can be damn sure of that.'

CHAPTER FOURTEEN

The celebration banquet that evening was shadowed for me by Wegger's exhibition of bloody-mindedness. I couldn't get the man out of my mind as I sat at the head table in the fine teak-and-maple-panelled saloon facing the guests. There was a full turn-out of passengers – Linn had been right when she said they needed something to take their minds off the tragedy of Holdgate. She had provided it in full measure. There was a gala atmosphere and the place buzzed with animated conversation. Overhead two big brass lamps swung in rhythm with the *Quest*'s long rise and fall.

The saloon, which was unusual in running athwartships the whole breadth of the ship, was decorated. Streamers were suspended overhead. Klausen, the cook, had excelled himself and provided a culinary masterpiece. It stood on the heavy carved sideboard at my back – red crayfish pincers clasped fish delicacies of all kinds round a centre-piece consisting of a whole fish about a metre long.

My captain's table formed the crosspiece of a T with the other table. Linn, wearing a severely cut white dress with a cowled collar, sat on my left; next to her were the three weathermen, looking uncomfortable in suits. On my right was McKinley, the master of ceremonies. It would be his function, now that the dinner was heading for its climax fuelled by liberal glasses of *Kaapse Vonkel*, to call on me to propose Captain Jacobsen's toast. That done, Captain Jacobsen would make his speech. He was in high spirits: Mrs Jacobsen appeared to have let him off the leash. McKinley was chatting up his fancy, the dark-haired Barbara, whom he had managed to seat at the junction of the two tables.

Behind me, to my right, a door led aft to the main lounge and bar; the forward entrance to the saloon, which I faced, was through a pair of swing-doors whose upper sections were diamonds of coloured glass. Miss Auchinleck sat nearest the swing-doors. She wore a feathery pink rig which made her look like a down-graded punk-rock star.

Linn caught my glance and whispered, 'I think she's almost enjoying not being a penguin.'

For all her apparent amusement, I knew that she was as worried as I was about Wegger. He had not shown up in my cabin as ordered, and I had gone to the bridge ready for anything. When I demanded to know where he was, the helmsman pointed to the bows. Amidst the bursting spray Wegger in oilskins was rigging the lifelines. No one was assisting him. As I watched, a sea came over green and threw him to the limit of his securing rope. It was a kind of crazy do-as-you-dare professionalism which partly defused my anger. Whatever his shortcomings, he was a fine sailor.

I gave the order to reduce speed, left the bridge and Wegger to his task, and came on to the dinner. That didn't mean I was any nearer peace of mind. I still wanted to sort it out with him. Also on my mind was the fact that there had been nothing from *Botany Bay* at the first scheduled signal hour. Persson remained glued to his post.

McKinley broke in on my thoughts. 'Looks as if everyone's about ready, sir. Shall I go ahead?'

'Carry on, Mr McKinley.'

McKinley stood up, rapped the table with a spoon. The chatter died down.

He was suave, easy. 'Ladies and gentlemen, we now come to the highlight of the evening. As you all know, the occasion is to celebrate the war-time escape by our distinguished guest, Captain Jacobsen, from a German raider in these very waters . . .'

The passengers couldn't have cared less what they were celebrating. It was a good party, that was all.

'. . . and I call upon Captain Shotton to propose the toast of our guest of honour . . .'

I got to my feet, my mind blank. My only resolve was not to make a heavy-handed, tedious speech. Still, it was a party and the captain was expected to rise to the occasion.

I half-turned in the direction of Captain Jacobsen on my right. As I did so a slight movement of the door – almost directly behind Jacobsen – caught my eye. Then the door was quickly pulled shut.

I lifted my glass and gave the traditional Scandinavian toast – '*Skoal*!'

That wasn't enough from me; I racked my brains for something else to say. Why not rattle off all the other names I knew for toast in other languages to get a laugh?

'*Skoal!*' I repeated. '*Slainthe!* Good health! *Gesundheit! Alla salute!* . . .'

The crowd began to laugh and got to its feet.

I went on, 'Bottoms up! *Nazdar! Lyia sos! Kenkeh!*'

The passengers started chanting after me, lifting their glasses and thumping the table. Captain Jacobsen looked as if he'd come into a million dollars. Mrs Jacobsen was bobbing with gratification.

He rose to reply. 'My friends – you have made for me a happy occasion out of something which was an unhappy occasion. War is an unhappy thing . . .'

I had been watching him closely, wondering how his heart would stand up to the strain.

Then I saw the knife stand out in his neck.

It had a scrimshawed handle.

Jacobsen's voice rattled on the last word. His left hand plucked at his neck. Then he pitched forward with a crash of broken glass and crockery.

Wegger materialized inside the doorway behind me. He was at a half-crouch. His left hand was at full stretch. It held the Luger. His right talon, which had hurled the knife, was gripping a grenade. He was snatching at the firing-pin with his teeth.

Simultaneously, the double door at the far end of the saloon burst open. Two men fanned out, one right, the other left. A Scorpion machine-pistol was half-concealed in the huge hams of one. The moment I spotted him I knew this was Reilly's tunnel man. He was as wide as a hatchway and probably the biggest man I have ever seen. Two grenades dangled at his groin like giant misplaced testicles. The other gunman had a frame which looked as if it had been plaited from steel rope ending in a bristly topknot. It would have taken 30 seconds for the crossfire from their automatic weapons to have wiped out the whole company.

I leapt to my feet, wheeling. 'Wegger, you bastard . . .!'

A frightening, inhuman sound cut the stunned silence. It came from Mrs Jacobsen.

She threw herself at Wegger, who was only a pace or two away.

He must have been expecting it, because he waited until she got up to him. Then he swept the Luger barrel across her eyes and head. The force of the blow threw her against the panelling. She slid to the floor, scrabbling at the woodwork.

'Keep still!' shouted Wegger. 'Keep still, everyone! Everyone keep to their seats!'

Linn started up to help Mrs Jacobsen. Wegger put the Luger on her.

143

'Linn! Do as he says!' I rapped out.

'She's hurt . . .!'

'Get back! He's mad!'

She shrank uncertainly back into her chair.

I heard, rather than saw, Miss Auchinleck's protest to the big man at the other end of the table. A whale might as well have attacked a harpoon gun. He struck her in the face with the back of a great paw. She tottered and lay down like a piece of crumpled spun popcorn a child has discarded in the gutter.

Wegger turned the Luger on me. In a flash I knew now where he'd been when he had been missing from the bridge. He'd been laying the hijacking on the line, mustering his bully-boys, whom he must have smuggled aboard in Cape Town. There had been a near-miss in the hold when I had searched the ship, and when I had planned to turn back after hearing of Captain Prestrud's death. The whole operation had been carefully planned. The reason for his puzzling tensions was now as clear as day.

His pistol barrel was trembling. Now was my moment if I were to achieve anything before he steadied down to business.

I snatched up a table knife, ducked behind McKinley, and launched myself at him. The knife went hard against the steel of the gun. The crash of the shot deafened me. At the same moment the saloon was filled with sound as one of the other hijackers opened up with his Scorpion over the heads of the crowd. Ricochets whined and ripped the panelling.

In the split second when my knife struck the Luger, I knew that I had lost. The thrust had been meant for his heart. He had parried it by reflex.

He acted with great speed. I was still coming up to barrel my head in his solar plexus when the clubbed Luger struck at my head. I snicked my head aside. It caught my shoulder instead. It felt as if I had stopped the *Quest*'s bow at full ahead. I dropped to one knee with the agony of it, cringing for the shot.

But Wegger held his fire. He pulled back, panting.

'Ullmann! Bravold!' he shouted. 'Hold it! Hold it! We've got 'em!'

There was a thin high hysterical scream as incongruous as

Mrs Jacobsen's animal keening. It came from McKinley's Barbara.

'Shut up!' snarled Wegger at McKinley. 'Shut her up, or I will!'

He rounded on me. 'Up!' he ordered. 'Back – over there against the wall! Away from me! All of you here – move! Keep your hands high!'

Smit, the met. team leader, started to growl something and drag his feet.

'Forget it!' I told him under my breath. 'It's too late. We've lost. Forget it!'

The top table guests lined up against the panelling. The rest of the passengers sat transfixed in their chairs. McKinley was trying to quieten Barbara, who was still sobbing loudly.

'Ullmann!' called Wegger. The huge man moved cautiously round the port side of the saloon towards us, stepping over the pink bundle which was Miss Auchinleck. He kept open a field of fire for himself and Bravold. His skin was blotchy and his hair pale, almost white. His place was behind a harpoon gun. If the harpoon missed, he could always throw the gun.

Wegger jumped on to my chair, watching every move. I think any of the trio would have shot a mouse had it moved.

The fiery pain in my shoulder shot up into my neck like a tracer bullet.

'Wegger!' I managed to say. 'Stop this damn nonsense! You must be crazy . . .!'

'Stow that crap!' he retorted. 'You'll take orders from me from now on, all of you, d'ye hear!'

'Wegger,' I said, 'I'll see you tried for murder. I'll make sure the law gets you. There are thirty eye-witnesses here.'

He jumped off the chair and took a step towards me.

'Law!' He made it sound as if it should be a four-letter word, and not three. 'Law! Take a look at the law from now on, will you!'

He gestured at Ullmann and Bravold. They were in a position to cut everyone down with a burst.

'So you killed Holdgate too,' I said. 'With the same knife. You've killed two men.'

'Holdgate got in my way,' he said. 'That's why he had to be killed.'

I glanced round the saloon hoping someone would support me in my threats to bring Wegger to justice, but the rest of the room seemed in shock. The faces were unresponsive. Ullmann and Bravold stood like human pillboxes with the barrels of their automatics jutting out from flesh instead of casemates.

Linn said in a wobbly voice to Wegger, 'Doesn't human life mean anything to you?'

The muscles in Wegger's face twitched and tightened as if they had been manipulated by wires from behind. His voice rose.

'Human life meant nothing to them! Nothing, I tell you! My life! My life, do you hear! The three of them – Jacobsen, Torgersen and Prestrud! It meant nothing to them!'

'My father – Torgersen! Jacobsen! You killed them all!'

Wegger continued to shout. 'Yes! I killed them all! The last of the bastards tonight – on the anniversary. They were celebrating what they did to me, d'ye hear! Don't give me that crap about human life! They took *my* life! They didn't think I'd come back and take theirs!'

'Talk sense, Wegger,' I cut in. 'Nothing can justify what you've done!'

'My father!' went on Linn in a strangled voice. 'You pistol-whipped him until he died!'

I put my sound arm round her. She didn't sob; the convulsions I felt were dry spasms of shock.

'Listen, Wegger . . .'

'They took my life!' he mouthed. 'What do you know of how it feels to have your life run out, day by day, week by week, month by month, fighting with the birds and the elephant seals for stinking scraps that would make you puke, living on Kerguelen cabbage and birds' eggs, the skuas coming at your eyes all the time!'

'When and where was all this?' I demanded.

'Where else?' he said wildly. 'Prince Edward Island! They called it Dina's Island after they'd seen her lying there – and they left me with her! They sailed away and left me marooned – alone, alone – Jesus! Alone and knowing no one would ever come and rescue me. I got so that I used to sit and talk to her – she lay there on her back looking up at me and

146

smiling and when I tried to kiss her the ice came between us. I wanted to make love to her, but she was cold, she was ice! They left me on Prince Edward and sailed away!'

The realization hit me as I pieced together his story from what I already knew.

'So you were *Pinguin*'s radio operator, Wegger!'

'Of course. I homed her in on the whaling fleet – we took the lot, eleven catchers and two factory ships, without a shot.'

'You led one of the boarding parties – the one which boarded Prestrud's group,' I continued.

He seemed to be reliving the past so intensely that he was almost oblivious of the present.

'I was too confident,' he said. 'I thought the show was over. But Prestrud was a very brave man. I went ahead of the German boarders – I called to Prestrud in Norwegian. They said afterwards I was a quisling. It wasn't so. My mother was German. I was on the Germans' side because it was in my blood.'

'And then?' I asked.

'The three of them grabbed me. They knocked me out. They must have had a pre-arranged escape plan. They must have cast off from the factory ship right under Krüder's nose. When I came round, we were miles away. I don't know how long I was out. They were safe, because they hove to. The other two skippers came aboard Prestrud's ship. Torgersen and Jacobsen were for killing me out of hand, but Prestrud said no. Maybe he wanted to turn me in as a prisoner-of-war. They accused him of having a soft heart.' Wegger's voice cracked. 'Soft heart! Does a man with a soft heart maroon a fellow human on the most god-forsaken island on the face of the earth and leave him there to rot to death? That's what they did, those three, instead of shooting me. They went to Prince Edward. They put me ashore – there, right by the big cave. Eight months! Eight months of living hell! Only the birds and the seals and the cold! I didn't believe it when the British cruiser came. She lay off and fired her guns. The sound echoed in the big cave – I thought at first the dead volcano was coming alive again. I went outside and I saw the ship . . .'

'What was her name, Wegger?'

'*Neptune* – HMS *Neptune*, one of the big cruisers from the Cape,' he babbled. 'I can see her still. I just stood and looked and . . . and . . .'

He looked as if he would break down any moment. Then he resumed.

'She fired her guns a second time and I lit some kelp I'd dried at the mouth of the cave. She saw my signal. She sent a boat. They were searching the remote islands for U-boat bases, they told me later. When I waded out waist-deep to the boat, the officer said, "What a zombie!" I wasn't human any more. Then he asked, "Any kit, chum?" Kit! Kit – on Prince Edward Island! I just said, "Get me out of here, get me out!" I don't remember much after that. I even forgot my name.'

'You were Rolf Solberg in those days,' I reminded him.

His eyes hardened and he said flatly, 'I changed my name after I came out of prison. They gave me a lifer for killing Torgersen. Twenty-three years behind bars. But it was better than eight months on Prince Edward.'

So I had been right about my first impression of Wegger. There had been a prison-like subservience in his manner which had puzzled me at the time, but which I now understood.

Calculations machine-gunned through my brain. The skippers' first anniversary gathering had been thirty years ago to the day. The actual escape had been in 1941. For Torgersen's murder Wegger had served a term of twenty-three years: that left seven still unaccounted for. If his revenge lust had been as violent as it appeared, why hadn't he gone after Prestrud and Jacobsen immediately on his release from gaol? Why wait until the *Quest* was ready to sail to Prince Edward? Why . . .? I looked at Wegger's face. It wasn't the question to ask of a madman with a gun in his hand and two of his strong-arm boys at call with machine-pistols in their paws.

'Is this really happening?' cried Linn. 'Aren't we all in a nightmare?'

Wegger got a hold of himself. 'I was in a nightmare, I was being tortured! I sat on a rock at the cave entrance where the killer whales came close in. That's where I carved a handle for the knife. The knife I was going to use on them for what they'd done to me. It was an elephant seal's fang I used. The killer whales gave me the idea for the picture.' He indicated Jacobsen's body. 'I used it, as I said I would.'

'You bastard, Wegger!' I burst out. 'You vicious, murdering bastard!'

That seemed to bring him right back into the present. 'No more of that, Shotton! I'm the captain now!'

'What do you think you're going to do with a ship and a load of passengers into the bargain – kill us all?' I went on. 'How far do you think you'll get when the radio black-out's over? You won't be coming out of prison next time, Wegger.'

'That's my problem, isn't it?' he sneered.

Our exchange was interrupted by Persson pushing open the door through which Wegger had burst. When he saw Wegger's Luger on him he stopped dead as if he'd been hit by a bullet.

Then he looked at me and exclaimed, 'Sir!' as if he could not believe what he had seen.

'Watch out, Persson! Don't do anything silly. The ship's been hijacked. These men are killers.'

'Hijacked!'

'You'll report to me from now on,' Wegger said tersely. 'I've taken over. No signals are to be sent without my express permission. Try any funny business and you know what to expect.' He gestured with the pistol.

Persson, however, still addressed me. '*Botany Bay* came through on the hour, sir. I could just hear. She's still afloat. Seems the danger . . .'

'Persson!' snapped Wegger. 'Anything you've got to say, say it to me.'

Persson looked uncomfortably from me to Wegger. I eyed Wegger's face and knew that *Botany Bay*'s crew was doomed. He'd never burden himself with another shipful of potential hangers. He'd simply leave them to die.

'Wegger!' I said. 'She's a windjammer – she's damaged. *Quest* is her only hope!'

He didn't answer me but said to Persson, 'Get back to the radio shack – direct. No blabbing to any of the crew about this . . .' he indicated the saloon. 'Understood?'

Persson replied uncertainly. 'Understood – sir. But do I keep touch with the windjammer?'

'Stick to the arrangement – for the present,' replied Wegger. 'Now – get out!'

He went.

'I want you in the day cabin,' Wegger said to me. 'I hav
something more to say to you.'

'No!' exclaimed Linn. '*I* have something to say to *you*
You killed my father . . .'

'Keep back!' he ordered as Linn moved towards him
'Don't tempt me to finish off all the Prestruds!'

I restrained her. 'Linn! Don't!'

'I'm not having you shot in secret by this maniac!' sh
burst out. '*I* am the owner of this ship. I've more right tha
anyone to know what is going on . . .'

'Ullmann!' ordered Wegger. 'Keep this woman here – b
force, if necessary. You, Shotton, march!'

In a flash, Linn sprinted past him through the door whic
Persson had left open. Ullmann swung the Scorpion b
Wegger was blocking his aim.

Then Linn was through. The door crashed shut.

'Move, you!' Wegger jammed the Luger into the small
my back. 'After her! Okay, Ullmann, I'll attend to this. Kee
the others here. Move, damn you!'

CHAPTER FIFTEEN

I obeyed – fast. I took a minute to reach the day cabin, whic
was situated a deck lower.

Wegger jostled me in.

Linn stood defiantly at her father's desk. Her head wa
thrown back. She hadn't had the time to use the desk phon
if that had been her intention.

Wegger kicked the door shut and waved me to join he

'That was a very stupid thing to do, Miss Prestrud,' h
remarked. 'Next time you might not be so lucky.'

'I'm not afraid of cheap threats,' she retorted.

'Shotton – get on that phone to the bridge,' Wegger sa
brusquely. 'Full speed ahead.'

I feared again for *Botany Bay* when I asked, 'Course?'

'Same course.'

Petersen answered my call. There was nothing about h

reaction to indicate that he knew anything of what had taken place in the saloon.

'Mr Petersen,' I said. 'Full ahead, please.'

'Aye, aye, sir.'

I put down the instrument. 'Wegger,' I said. 'You won't get away with this. Where do you think you're going to run to in Antarctica? There aren't any ports. There's nowhere to hole up . . .'

He seemed amused. 'I know. You don't have to tell me.'

There was still something else imperative that I had to know.

'What about the buoy launch tomorrow?'

'The hell with the launch,' he rejoined. 'I couldn't care less about the bloody GARP programme or whatever its name is.'

He had played me an ace with this reply. 'Fine. No launch then. No satellite trackings. No buoy or balloon positions. When that happens, a general alert will go out. The world weather spotlight is on this ship. After ten o'clock tomorrow morning the *Quest* will be the most sought-after ship in the Seven Seas.'

'You could be right,' he answered to my astonishment. I hadn't any idea how his mind was working; we were on different wave-lengths.

Linn interrupted, 'This was my father's ship. It's mine now. I'll use it any way I can to see you answer for what you did to him and the others.'

The lightning blazed in Wegger's eyes. 'They were bastards, all three of them. They got what they deserved.'

'You know as well as I do that the radio black-out won't last more than another couple of days,' I persisted. 'As soon as we're missed the search will be on. The Weather Bureau knows our expected daily position precisely.'

Linn added, 'We're also due to land the three met. men on Marion Island. The radio station there will be monitoring us round the clock from the launch-time tomorrow.'

Wegger said, completely out of the blue, 'I need people around me with guts. Shotton, how would you lose a ship in these parts if you had to? This ship in particular?'

The question and his changed tone took me wholly aback. 'The question's purely academic as far as I am concerned.'

He eyed me. 'I wonder.'

'What are you driving at, Wegger?'

'Nothing can get round the fact that you've killed four men,' Linn said hotly.

'I wonder,' he repeated.

'Say what's in your mind, Wegger,' I told him. 'You didn't bring us here to listen to riddles.'

'I would rather have discussed it with you alone, Shotton,' he answered. 'But the girl's thrust herself on us. If that's the way she wants it, fine. It means she'll have to pay the price also, if necessary.'

'You can't scare me,' rejoined Linn. 'I'm ready to pay any price to see you brought to book.'

'Fine words,' he sneered. 'Words are cheap. Deeds could be worth ten million dollars.'

'I don't know what you're talking about,' she replied.

'Your father did,' retorted Wegger. 'That's what this cruise is all about.'

It was Linn's turn to look puzzled. 'Ten million dollars? This cruise? I don't know what you mean.'

Wegger looked penetratingly from her to me. 'What did Prestrud and Jacobsen tell you about the capture of the whaling fleet?' he demanded.

'Little enough,' I answered truthfully. 'Captain Prestrud gave me his account when he was dying. It was incoherent. Jacobsen filled me out, but he became cagey when it came to Prince Edward Island and the details of the escape.'

Wegger said in a carefully controlled voice, 'The capture of the whaling fleet took place in January 1941 but the story goes back a lot further than that. Goebbels' propaganda blew up the capture until every angle was sucked dry. It was a great single-handed feat all the same, and Krüder was the man to carry it out. The bag was eleven catchers and two factory ships filled with whale oil. We –' I did not miss his use of 'we' for the Nazis – 'were desperately short of oil at that time. Krüder was a hero in Germany. He was awarded the Iron Cross.'

He began to speak rapidly. 'The whaling fleet was important enough for the German Naval High Command to position the pocket battleship, *Admiral Scheer*, only six hundred miles from Krüder as a back-up if needed. In the event she wasn't, as you know.'

I interrupted him. 'Krüder knew the whaling fleet's rendezvous. You were responsible, Wegger. You sold your own country's secret warship, the *Teddy*, down the river.'

'It was war,' he shrugged. 'What does that matter now?'

'What does it matter now?' I echoed.

Linn sat down at the desk. The vibration of the *Quest*'s engines at full revolution-plus rattled the fitments.

'You gave me a shock when you pulled out *Teddy*'s chart,' said Wegger. 'However, it only told me what I already knew, that Prestrud was not on a pleasure cruise to Prince Edward Island.'

'It was my father's dream,' Linn said vehemently. 'He talked about it for years. He saved and bought his own ship especially to go to Prince Edward.'

'So would I have, if I hadn't been in gaol,' he retorted. 'So would I, for the sake of ten million dollars.'

'Go on,' I said, watching all the time for an opportunity to jump him.

'I was one of three radio operators in *Pinguin*,' he went on. 'I handled the confidential signals from OKM – German Naval High Command – to Krüder. Would it surprise you to know that the whaling fleet was only the raider's secondary objective? That the pocket battleship had sealed orders to stand by because . . . because . . .'

He stumbled, as if he couldn't bear to part with the secret.

Then he said, 'I will tell you. When Germany attacked Poland at the beginning of the war the Free City of Danzig, which was the real reason for the Allies' intervention – they had guaranteed its status – sent its entire gold holding to the United States for safe-keeping. It was in gold ingots – ten million dollars' worth. That was what *Pinguin* and the *Admiral Scheer* were after, not the whaling fleet.'

His disclosure had Linn sitting bolt upright in her chair.

'The Danzig authorities consigned it via Narvik,' he went on. 'The gold was in Narvik when we Nazis attacked the port. The Norwegians escaped with it in their whaling fleet. That is why OKM despatched Krüder into the Antarctic after the fleet, and into the bargain was willing to risk a pocket battleship. At that time Germany was desperately short of foreign exchange in the form of gold. Ten million dollars of it would have been a godsend.'

'How do you know all this, Wegger?'

'I saw it,' he answered simply. 'I lived with it for eight months. In the great cave on Prince Edward. Gold ingots. Ten million in gold. In a torpedo casing.'

'A torpedo casing!'

'Prestrud, Torgersen and Jacobsen took the torpedo with them when they escaped,' he continued in a strained voice. 'They were very daring. Prestrud towed the torpedo clean past Krüder. Jacobsen and Torgersen shielded his flanks with their catchers so that the raider wouldn't spot it. I heard them talking about it when I came round and they had got clear.'

Linn and I stared at him.

He went on matter-of-factly, 'The Free Norwegians had hidden the gold in a German torpedo casing during the attack on Narvik – no one would have looked twice at a stray torpedo casing in all the confusion. They had it rigged in the slip of one of the factory ships. All they had to do was to knock out a shackle and it slid into the water of its own accord. That's how Prestrud got it and towed it away. The plan had all been carefully worked out beforehand. It worked – except for me.'

'You're imagining things, Wegger,' I said. 'Prince Edward must have blown your mind. If those three skippers had wanted to stash the gold away the last thing they would have done was to have left you there with their secret.'

'They meant me to die!' he burst out. 'They meant me to die, don't you understand! They never thought I'd survive and be rescued! It was cleaner than shooting me!'

'So you told the British cruiser about the gold and everyone lived happily ever after!' I retorted derisively.

'The cruiser's boat never landed – I told you that!' He started to shout. Then he got a grip of himself and said more quietly, 'The gold is still there. On Prince Edward. In the great cave. Deep. That's why I had to stop Holdgate. No one has ever been deep inside it, except me. That's the reason why Prestrud organized this cruise. It was a cover. He intended to lift the gold – my gold, you hear! My gold! I lived with it, nearly went out of my mind watching over it, month after month . . .'

'There was no such thought in my father's mind,' Linn said

coldly. 'I *know*. If there had been any truth in this yarn of yours he would have gone straight to the authorities and told them. He was that sort of man. He wouldn't have wanted it for himself.'

Wegger laughed harshly, sceptically. 'Every man has his price – ten million dollars!'

'Wegger,' I said, 'I think we all need a drink.'

He waved me to the cabinet with the Luger and stepped well back to keep it aimed on me. 'Right. But no tricks, Shotton.'

'There's no gun hidden amongst the bottles,' I said sarcastically.

I poured three brandies and handed them round. Wegger wouldn't let me come close. He made me put his drink on the desk where I couldn't reach him.

He took a long pull at it and then said breathily, 'Shotton, we can do a deal. If you will take this ship to Prince Edward and lift the gold, I'll cut you in to the tune of one million dollars. In gold bars. No questions asked.'

'In a ship that the whole world's looking for? Be your age, Wegger.'

'It's easy,' he went on quickly. 'You don't have to do anything but agree. We can go ahead with launching the buoy after we've rescued *Botany Bay*'s crew. Everything will then be according to schedule and no suspicions roused. Then we can push on to Prince Edward. We'll use the motor-launch to transport the gold from the cave to the *Quest*. Then we'll go on to Mauritius . . .'

'Mauritius? That's a new one.'

'Yes, Mauritius,' he went on excitedly. 'See here – since the island became independent it's become the fag-end for things the rest of the world doesn't consider respectable. Black market gold, for instance. Gold – no questions asked.'

I shrugged.

'I tell you, it's true!' His voice rose. 'Mauritius is the Indian Ocean terminal of the gold-smuggling pipeline. The centre is Dubai, in the Persian Gulf. Dubai will handle any amount of hot gold. The dhows take it to India, Hong Kong, anywhere. At a premium.'

I allowed a little false admiration to creep into my reply

155

in order to extract more from him.

'You seem to have done your homework pretty well, Wegger.'

'Listen, Shotton, you don't have to get involved. You only have to stay not involved – get me? Your ship has been hijacked. The guns are on you. You only have to string along with me and not interfere.'

I sensed Linn's tension.

'For a million dollars? What rake-off do those two thugs with machine-pistols get?'

'A million each,' he replied, too readily. 'It's share and share alike.'

'And you get the lion's share.'

'I've taken the risks. It's my plan.'

'You want me to sail the *Quest* to Mauritius once the gold's aboard – for what reason? Everybody aboard knows the hijacking score. It won't wash.'

'You could have developed engine trouble – any sort of eyewash. Even that you're sailing under threat of death if you don't go.'

'And in Mauritius I simply allow you to climb overboard with your load of gold and disappear? What do you take me for?'

'You don't have to go into port if you don't want to,' he explained. 'You drop Ullmann and Bravold and me off out at sea in the motor-launch once we're within reach of Mauritius. We'd disappear. Your nose would be clean. You could go ahead then and report the hijacking like an innocent victim. You'd have a million dollars – in that safe there behind you.'

I kept stringing him along. 'It could be feasible.'

'John!' Linn's protest was agonized. 'John! You wouldn't . . .!'

'Let him finish. How would you expect to get away with it?' I asked Wegger further.

'I know whom to contact. Ten million in solid gold can buy anything.'

'Less three,' I said. 'Remember – one million for me, one for Ullmann, one for Bravold.'

He stood considering me for a long moment. Then he dropped the Luger's muzzle. 'You'll go along with me then, Shotton?'

'John!' exclaimed Linn. 'John!'

I said deliberately, 'Wegger, you can go and stick yourself and your plan and your million dollars up the *Quest*'s sewerage outlets. I'll turn you in, whatever.'

The gun came up again and he pointed it at my head.

'You fool, Shotton! You blundering, do-gooder fool! It could have been so easy for you. You know too much now. The girl too. Your usefulness ends once we've lifted the gold at Prince Edward. Don't say I didn't give you the chance!'

Linn put her arm hard in mine. It was worth more than ten million dollars.

I said with more bravado than I felt, 'If this story of yours is true, Captain Prestrud would – as Linn says – have turned the gold over to the proper authorities years ago.'

'Proper authorities – bullshit!' he exploded. 'Whose gold is it anyway? It wasn't Prestrud's any more than it was mine to begin with! And where is the Free City of Danzig today? It doesn't even exist. The Russians swallowed it up when they took over Poland. It was ten million dollars' worth of gold floating around without an owner. Prestrud meant to lift it, I tell you! That's what this cruise is all about! *Erebus* and *Terror*! My oath! What a cover story! And everyone fell for it, except me, who knew! Why do you think he was so keen on having Jacobsen come along? They were both in it, up to the hawsehole! Now you're playing along because you think you'll get his daughter! You won't, I say! You won't live to see the end of this bloody *Erebus-Terror* cruise, I promise you that!'

'Think, Wegger,' I snapped. 'I'll grant you the gold story just for the sake of the argument. So Prestrud and Jacobsen waited all those years just so that Prestrud could save up and buy a ship and fake a cruise when there was ten million dollars for the taking ...'

'He needed a ship!' Wegger was losing control over his voice. 'They needed a ship to do it! They wouldn't share their secret ...'

'Ten million dollars – belonging to no one in particular.' I went on sarcastically. 'They could have bought a dozen ships after the war for that! There were plenty of enterprising gentlemen around at the time who would have been only too willing to *give* them a ship. For that matter, why the hell didn't you try for it?'

'I was in gaol – I told you.'

'You've been out of gaol for years,' I rejoined. 'You've had plenty of time yourself. Why didn't you try for a ship without waiting until the *Quest* came along?'

His voice was sour with anger and frustration. 'The whaling went bust in the Southern Ocean after the mid-sixties. The catchers didn't go South any more.'

'You could have picked up a laid-up catcher for a song in Cape Town or Durban any time during the past decade.'

'You've never been in gaol,' he got out. 'You've never . . .'

'Never killed a man, Wegger?'

I thought he was going to come at me with the Luger. He'd reversed it almost involuntarily in his grip and had it by the barrel. I decided to dodge and try a swing at him with the brandy bottle if he did.

But instead he said threateningly, 'There are still a couple of things I need you for, Shotton. But I warn you, try anything on, you or the girl . . .'

As if to reinforce his threat, he strode across to the desk and plucked the phone out by its wire and threw it down. Then he went to the door and jammed the key savagely into the outer lock.

'I'll come back for you when I've tidied up in the saloon. Then you'll come with me to the bridge and tell 'em I've taken over. That we're headed for . . .'

'There's no place to hide down here, Wegger – remember that.'

'No?' he replied with a sneer. 'I'll teach you how to hide a ship in the Southern Ocean.'

CHAPTER SIXTEEN

Captain Jacobsen's letter lay on the cabin desk between Linn and myself like a testimony from the other side of the grave.

I had discovered the long envelope in my uniform pocket shortly after Wegger had left. I had removed my jacket at Linn's insistence in order to try and get my bruised shoulder comfortable and for her to examine it. The letter was the one I had picked up on my way to the Mayday call.

The big scrawling handwriting read:

Dear Captain Shotton,

You were right in suspecting my story about the torpedo which Prestrud, Torgersen and I towed away under the Germans' noses. After our conversation today I realized that I am now the only one left who knows the truth and why we did what we did. I am writing this before tonight's celebration dinner in the hope that you will see me in a somewhat different light, and believe that what we did was right at the time. You were also Captain Prestrud's good friend – there is no need for me to repeat how happy I am about Linn and you. It is part of the reason for this letter.

Our torpedo contained ten million dollars' worth of gold bars which were in transit from the Free City of Danzig to the United States via Narvik. That is what made that torpedo so precious to us! After our escape, we hid the gold in the great cave on Prince Edward Island. We also left the quisling, Rolf Solberg, behind on the island. I still say – but no matter, it all happened long ago. Solberg was rescued by a British cruiser – you know how he returned to murder our companion Torgersen. Solberg did not mention the gold at his trial. I also want to confess that it was the intention of the three of us, Torgersen, Prestrud and I, to recover the gold after the war. However, when we learned that the island had been visited by a British cruiser we suspected that the gold might have been found and that our private expedition would be a waste of time. So it proved.

Prestrud approached the Tripartite Commission consisting of official representatives of Britain, France and the United States which handled war-time property seized by the Western Allies and was informed that ten million dollars' worth of Danzig gold was indeed in its safe keeping. The Commission also informed us that the Royal Navy had retrieved the gold, but gave no details, and refused to do so when we enquired subsequently. The Commission also informed us that the gold had been in transit via the port of

Bergen; this was obviously a mistake since we knew that it was Narvik. But what does all this matter now? Of course the information put a stop to our expedition to Prince Edward Island, and the tragedy of Torgersen cast a lifelong shadow over us.

Now that I have told you the true story, I will enjoy tonight's occasion with an easy mind for the first time in many years.

> *Your good friend,*
> *Axel Jacobsen.*

'I was sure there was nothing underhand about this cruise!' Linn exclaimed. 'This proves it.'

'Linn,' I said, 'Wegger's out of his senses. His long stay on Prince Edward must have unhinged his mind. We're in the hands of a madman and a killer who will stop at nothing to get back to where he believes the gold hoard is still hidden.'

'It terrifies me to think what will happen when he finds the cave empty, John.'

'He obviously suffered hallucinations,' I added. 'Look at his story of the girl on Prince Edward he wanted to make love to. That isn't the product of a sane mind.'

'Sort of wish projection until it became real, you mean?'

'More or less.'

'What are you going to do now, John?'

'My first concern is for *Botany Bay*. I don't want to do anything which may make Wegger abandon them. In fact, I'm at a complete loss to understand why he's still carrying on. It only complicates his position.'

'Those two thugs with their automatics wouldn't stop at anything,' Linn shuddered. 'John, please be careful, for my sake!'

'I will, Linn, I promise you.'

The key rattled in the lock and the door was thrown open. Wegger stood well back, Luger at the ready. With him was Ullmann. There was enough hardware between the two of them to strafe a destroyer.

Wegger nodded to the huge man. 'Okay. I want to talk to them. Shut that door and keep guard, see? If you hear anything odd, come in at the double.'

'That I'll do,' Ullmann replied in a voice that was surprisingly light, considering his size.

Wegger shut the door. 'The ship is completely in our hands. There is no resistance.'

'That sounds like a stock terrorist bulletin,' I scoffed.

'Don't try and be funny, Shotton. It doesn't pay, in your position.'

'Does the bridge know what has happened?' I asked.

'Not yet. That's what I've come about. I'm giving you a last chance to reconsider, Shotton. You can make it very easy for yourself if you don't obstruct me. You can run the ship as if nothing had happened. Go along with me – and you pick up a million dollars.'

'Wegger,' I replied, 'the boot's on the other foot. It is I who am giving you a chance to reconsider.'

His eyes blanked and two thin, savage, white lines leapt into the furrows of his face, from jaw to cheekbone.

'What are you trying to say?'

'See here,' I answered. 'New information has come into my hands. If you think there's gold on Prince Edward, you're chasing shadows.'

His voice sounded like ice grating. 'You're lying, Shotton. How could you get any new information, locked in here without a phone?'

I pulled out Jacobsen's letter and read: '. . . Prestrud approached the Tripartite Commission consisting of official representatives of Britain, France and the United States which handled war-time property seized by the Western Allies and was informed that ten million dollars' worth of Danzig gold was indeed in its safe keeping. The Commission also informed us that the Royal Navy had retrieved the gold . . .'

He snatched the letter from me and shouted, 'You liar! You've concocted this! You're trying to con me!'

The door burst open and Ullmann poured in. He smelt of bilges and of Ullmann. He trained the Scorpion on Linn and myself. As far as his whale-like face could register any emotion at all, it was surprise.

'Get out, you stupid fool!' ordered Wegger.

'You called . . .'

'Get out!'

Ullmann retreated, bewildered, with the machine-pistol at the ready.

F   161

'Jacobsen wrote that letter a few hours before you killed him,' I stated. 'Read it all for yourself. There's no gold on Prince Edward. You were out of your mind at the time, Wegger. The Royal Navy found it and turned it over to where it rightly belonged.'

He plucked at the letter, turning it round and round. 'Jacobsen never wrote this – why should he?' he demanded. 'You – you and the girl – you made it up. You're trying to put me off and lift the gold for yourselves!'

'Pull yourself together, Wegger. Or Solberg, whatever your name is. If you hadn't half-killed Jacobsen's wife you could get her to confirm his handwriting. Jacobsen and I had a discussion this morning. He realized I didn't believe his story. Subsequently he wrote me that. I found it at the door when the Mayday signal came in.'

'The gold is there!' Wegger's voice rattled like an engine running at plus-maximum revs. 'I've seen it! I've lived with it! It's in Credit Danzig ingots – small bars, like slabs of chocolate. *It is there*, I tell you! The cruiser never sent anyone ashore! They took me aboard. When I told them the island was deserted they sailed away! They sailed away, I tell you!'

'Wegger,' I interrupted his outburst, 'you weren't in your right mind. You had a nervous breakdown, a mental blackout. You don't remember. There's a proper medical term for it . . .'

'Goddammit, I remember every smallest detail!' He thumped the desk and kicked the smashed telephone aside. 'I *know*! I was there!'

'Wegger,' I persisted, 'you've killed four men. You spent a life sentence in prison for one murder. Do you want to spend the rest of it inside too?'

He leaned with one hand on the desk and raised his pistol.

'Don't say that – not to *me*, Shotton! Do you know how it felt after all these years to have a deck under me again, to *feel* the wind? And the first smell of the ice? I died a thousand times in prison, Shotton. Nothing, but nothing, will ever put me inside again. Not you, nor anyone else!'

I believed him. He'd use the Luger on himself first.

'What do you intend to do when you find the gold gone, Wegger? You can't put the clock back. You can't bring Holdgate and Captain Prestrud and Jacobsen to life again.'

162

Linn said, 'At your trial they should have taken your mental state into account . . .'

'Don't try and soft-soap me, you little bitch! You and Shotton, you've put your heads together and are trying to con me! You're trying to say I'm mad, talk me out of it, that the gold isn't there. It *is*, I tell you, it *is*! We're going there. I'll show you it is! Ullmann! Ullmann!'

The thug came in. 'We're going to the bridge – now,' Wegger told him.

'And the girl?' the big man asked.

'There's nothing she can do.' He addressed Linn. 'Keep to your cabin, if you don't want to get hurt, see? That's what the other passengers are doing.'

She glanced at me. She held her head back. She looked very fine and brave.

'I'll be all right, Linn.'

She held my eyes for a moment. They said everything I wanted to know. Then she stalked out.

For a moment Wegger stood undecided with Jacobsen's letter in his hand. Then he crumpled it into his pocket.

'March!' he ordered. 'The bridge!'

The bridge was a haven of peace compared to the below-decks ferment. The news obviously hadn't reached it. Jensen, the quartermaster, was at the wheel. Petersen had the watch. The only noise was of the revolving scanners clearing the spray and rain from the bridge windows and the murmur of the log. The hands of the bridge clock stood at almost nine. In the bows, the blue-white beam of the searchlight cut a traverse on blowing whitecaps and dark menacing troughs.

Petersen came half to attention when he saw me, then his jaw sagged at the sight of Wegger's gun. Before he could say anything, Ullmann moved swiftly ahead of the binnacle and pointed his machine-pistol. Jensen let go of the wheel and started back, almost colliding with Wegger close to me.

'Get back!' snapped Wegger. 'Don't let her head fall off, you bloody fool! You won't get hurt unless you try anything on!'

Jensen stood there gaping.

'Jensen!' I ordered. 'Do as he says.'

The *Quest* started to plunge; the spokes spun. I jumped forward and grabbed the wheel.

'Sir . . .!' whimpered Petersen. 'Sir . . .!'

I shoved Jensen into position and put the spokes into his hands again.

'Pull yourself together!' I told him. 'You'll get us all killed if you don't.' I indicated the gunmen. 'The ship's been hijacked. These men have taken over. You'll take your orders from them from now on.'

'Petersen!' snapped Wegger. 'That's it, the way Shotton says. Understood?'

Petersen looked almost as numb as when he had seen Holdgate on the plank.

'Yes . . . I mean, aye, aye, sir. But why . . .?'

'You don't have to know,' replied Wegger. 'Do your job and you won't get hurt.'

Petersen looked appealingly at me.

I simply said formally, 'Carry on, Mr Petersen.'

'Shotton,' said Wegger, 'get on to the engine-room. Tell MacFie.'

MacFie himself answered my intercom call.

'Chief,' I said, 'how are your engines standing up?'

'So far so good,' he replied. 'But I don't like the way the screw's racing. The shaft . . .'

'Mac,' I cut in, 'we both owe Reilly an apology. His ghost in the tunnel is for real.'

I heard Mac's long-suffering sigh. 'Laddie, I know you and the passengers had a ball tonight. Now forget about ghosts and go and sleep it off.'

I went on, eyeing Ullmann, 'Reilly was right about the Scorpion too. It looks very small in his hands. He's got it held on me at this moment.'

'Laddie . . .'

'He looks and smells as if he's been living in the bilges,' I added. Ullmann's face remained impassive to the crack.

Suddenly MacFie's tone changed. A new, anxious note came into it.

'You don't sound drunk. What are you saying, skipper?'

'The ship's been hijacked, Chief. Wegger's taken over. He's here on the bridge in company with our bilge ghost. He's also pointing a gun at my head – a Luger.'

Wegger said harshly, 'Cut out the bull, d'ye hear? Tell him to carry on as usual if he doesn't want to get shot.'

I had held the phone clear of my head to catch Wegger's words.

'You heard, Mac.'

His Scots accent thickened. 'I heard! Hijacked! Wegger! I'll be stuffed with a goose-necked spanner!'

'Chief,' I added, 'you've got the message. Take it from there, will you?'

'Aye, but . . .'

Persson hurried on to the bridge. He made a great effort to appear controlled but his eyes couldn't stay off the stubby barrel of the Scorpion.

He addressed me. 'Signal from *Botany Bay*, sir. Will you take it, or will . . .?' He indicated Wegger.

'We'll both come,' Wegger answered. 'I want to keep an eye on the radio, too.'

'It's still only the R/T operating,' Persson added.

'What does *Botany Bay* say, Persson?' I asked.

'Reception's still very bad, sir. Only a word or two here and there.'

It was worse than he had led us to believe. In the radio shack I tried the microphone. '*Botany Bay*! Cruise ship *Quest* here. Reply, reply!'

I missed the answer but Persson was smarter. 'It's Kearnay, sir.'

'Kearnay,' I asked, 'are you still afloat?'

'Fast,' wavered the disembodied voice. '. . . no longer afloat . . . nipped . . .'

'How the hell can you no longer be afloat and signal me?'

'Fast . . . fast . . . list of fifteen degrees . . .' The rest of it was lost.

'Your message not understood,' I replied. 'What do you mean, nipped? You aren't in pack-ice! Repeat, please!'

I strained to catch the reply. It was hopeless.

'Kearnay!' I said. 'You're wasting your batteries and your breath. In another couple of hours we'll be that much closer. Signal me at midnight, on the hour exactly, will you?' I didn't look at Wegger for confirmation before I added: 'Meanwhile, I am proceeding to your position at all possible speed.'

A reply came back. It could have been 'aye' or 'ice'.

I returned the microphone to Persson. There was a tight

pause. Then I said, 'Wegger, we'll have to work on the chart. There's nothing here at the moment.'

'Report at midnight,' Wegger told Persson.

Wegger and I went through to the chart-room. He was watchful and alert, and gave me no opportunity to jump him. But a moment later he gave himself away. I spread open *Teddy*'s chart of the Southern Ocean. *Botany Bay*'s position was only a tiny cross in a vast expanse.

I pointed to it and went into technicalities. 'That's as near as I can place the windjammer at this stage. It's about one hundred and ten kilometres west of the spot where the buoy should be launched. What's your onward course to Prince Edward Island from there?'

He stood there staring uncertainly at the chart without replying. For a moment I thought he was working on the intricacies of a Great Circle course. Then my brain gave a print-out quicker than any computer – Wegger didn't know what he was doing! This was why he needed me. He could handle a course only if he were told where to sail! He didn't know how to work out a complicated one! It flashed through my mind that during the past few days I'd never seen him busy alone with the navigation of this ship – he'd always had Petersen or McKinley with him. My thoughts raced still further back, to our first interview. There hadn't been time before the *Quest* sailed for me to verify his certificates. I'd taken them at their face value. Now I realized that they had been faked. Twenty-three years in gaol – that didn't give him much chance, especially at his age, to obtain a master's certificate.

'Wegger,' I said tersely, 'you can't kid me. You're bogus. You don't know what the hell I'm talking about!'

He put the chart table between us. His face was a tight mask. He lifted the Luger until I could see its blue rifling level with my eyes.

'If I didn't need you, Shotton, I would kill you.'

I believed him.

'You'll sail this ship where I tell you,' he went on, his voice full of menace. 'If I so much as suspect you're fooling me . . .'

I realized how close to the limit he was. I said steadily, 'Fair enough. Let's assume that *Botany Bay* is more or less where we anticipate. I then head *Quest* for the buoy's launching-point . . .'

He laughed, and I didn't care for it any more than I had for his threat.

'You're very casual and very clever about it – the buoy's launching-point,' he mimicked me. 'What do you take me for, you fool? You don't get me going anywhere near there.'

'Wegger! The launch is the most important thing . . .'

'Stow it!' he retorted. 'Don't try that on! Do you think I intend to give my position away? The one point in the whole of this ocean –' he swept his hand across the chart – 'that's known, fixed, timed? The radio's been out for two, three days. No one knows where the *Quest* is. No one will ever know. She could be anywhere! You could search until you were blue in the face and the chances of finding a ship without anything to go by would be as remote as spotting a penguin's egg from the air at the South Pole!'

For his purposes, he was right. It made me more puzzled than ever why he should press on to *Botany Bay*. I decided that the less I said about the windjammer, the better.

I shrugged. 'Once the buoy and the balloon don't report via the satellite, the alert will go out. Then it's only a matter of time before they track down the *Quest*.'

'Only a matter of time!' he echoed. 'There'll be enough time to lift the gold and get clear.'

The gloves were off in earnest now. We were on our way. Wegger's way.

The *Quest* was on her way, too. When Wegger and I reached the bridge it was blowing a near-gale. The bow searchlight probably made the sea look even worse. The waves were heaping up in endless succession as far as the blue-white beam penetrated. White foam appeared in long streaks coming straight at the *Quest*. She was butting and lunging headlong at the rollers and throwing up clouds of spray; rising with a thrilling buoyancy which proved her to be the thoroughbred she was. But nevertheless we could not go on pitting her at full speed much longer into those hills of water rolling in from the south-west without something giving.

I went to a cleared window. The searchlight picked out an onrushing, foam-crested wall ahead. There was no escaping it. The *Quest* put her bows down. Then – up, up, up. Tons of water poured over the bow. The wind caught the burst and hurtled it back against the bridge windows. The ship rolled to port, staggered, lifted. It was probably the acute angle which threw the searchlight beam further ahead than normal.

The white thing hung in our path at the summit of the next hill of water, poised like an ungainly surfer.

I knew in an instant what it was.

I knew also we would hit it.

I spun from the window.

'Get that wheel down!' I yelled at the startled helmsman. 'Down! Hard aport! Hard, man!'

He didn't react; or perhaps time had stopped for me.

I threw myself at the wheel. I knocked his hands off the spokes, spun them, wincing at the shaft of pain in my hurt shoulder.

'Ice! Ice dead ahead! Hold on! We can't miss it!'

I held the wheel hard down, shifted head-on to face the menace out for'ard. The bridge phone rang. Wegger took the call.

'Crow's nest!' I heard the man's anguished voice vibrate in the earpi ce clean across the bridge. 'Ice right ahead!'

It felt to me that *Quest* wasn't answering her rudder. Her head scarcely seemed to have moved. The searchlight held the ice – it was a big growler – and kept on it like a stage spotlight. It hung poised at the top of the massive wall of water. Then *Quest*'s bow seemed to shift a fraction. That meant the collision might be a glancing one. But it would still take the bow plating and rip the whole length of her starboard beam . . .

The ship's head went down deep into the trough. She'd had the maximum bite the rudder would give. As the stern lifted, the rudder would grip less. The searchlight still held the growler. Finer, now, to starboard – the bow was swinging! Her head was swinging! But would it be enough . . .?

Quest barrelled into the roller. The searchlight blanked opaque. Water broke and roared. Where was the growler? For a fearful moment I thought it would fall bodily on the foc's'le deck.

The wave punched the swinging bow like an uppercut to the jaw. No man-made force could have done what that huge wave did. It slammed *Quest*'s bow aside. The searchlight beam held the growler like a bomber trapped in a night raid. The white menace cartwheeled.

Quest's bow slewed to port. Sweat poured off my hands on to the spokes. For a moment the growler hung suspended in the beam's maximum traverse. It was whiter than the white foam. Then it slid, yawed. *Quest* swerved aside.

It missed; it vanished into the night behind.

I still held on to the wheel. My legs felt as if they wouldn't hold me. Then I shifted the helm back amidships. When I handed over I scarcely recognized my own voice.

'Steady as she goes,' I told the white-faced helmsman. 'Keep her south-west by south!'

Then I rang the engine-room pointer down to three-quarter speed.

Wegger was still clutching the crow's-nest phone unseeingly in his damaged hand. The gun hung loose in the other at his side. His face was a grim mask of fear.

I relieved him of the phone. 'Crow's nest!' I said. 'That's the first of 'em – there are plenty more ahead. Keep your eyes skinned if you don't want an ice-bath tonight.'

The man's voice replied, 'I thought we'd bought it, that time.'

The *Quest* plunged on into the mounting storm.

By midnight, the scheduled time of *Botany Bay*'s signal, the *Quest*'s bridge and superstructure were streaked with long streamers of spindrift. It collected round the pulpit rail of the crow's nest like clotted cream. When it became thick enough, it blew clear in great dollops which smashed against the bridge windows like snowballs bursting. I had the look-outs replaced every hour. An hour was about all they could take in the freezing wind. The searchlight shifts were even shorter – forty minutes. The drenched and frozen crews were fed coffee laced with rum when they were relieved.

The hands of the bridge clock were on midnight when Persson reported.

'*Botany Bay*, sir.' He did not address either Wegger or me directly, which satisfied protocol.

I looked my question at Wegger without speaking.

'Take it – I'll stay here,' he said. 'Report to me as soon as you've spoken to Kearnay. Ullmann, watch him.'

I went with Persson. The wind ripped and pummelled the ship. He opened the radio shack door for me.

'Linn!'

'John!' She came forward and kissed me. She smiled but her eyes looked tired and drawn. She was wearing her heavy Icelandic sweater and dark pants. 'I've brought you some coffee.'

'MacFie's own special?'

'Yes. I didn't want to bring it to the bridge. If I'd mentioned Wegger, MacFie would have put poison in *his*, for sure.'

She tried again to smile. Then she said with a rush, 'I couldn't stay in my cabin as he ordered – you see, I heard them carrying Captain Jacobsen . . .'

'Where did they put him?' I asked gently.

She shuddered. 'In the sick-bay. Just like Holdgate. It's become a mortuary, for me.'

'And Mrs Jacobsen?'

'She's still unconscious.'

'*Botany Bay*, sir,' interrupted Persson.

Reception was hardly better than it had been earlier.

'Kearnay! This is Captain Shotton!'

I caught only isolated, out-of-context fragments. '. . . bowsprit . . . ice . . .'

Persson whispered to me, 'She should be much clearer than she is, sir. Those batteries are packing up fast.'

'Kearnay,' I said, 'hold it. Save what power you've got for later. Just answer briefly. Are you still afloat?'

The reply was just audible. 'Not afloat . . . on the ice . . .'

'The ship!' I repeated. 'Is she afloat or has she sunk?'

I caught a word of the reply clearly and Persson and Linn both nodded confirmation as I repeated it.

'Iceport.'

The rest was lost in a surge of sferics.

'The weather, Kearnay – what's your weather?'

Persson strained and repeated the fragmentary answer. 'Calm in here. Outside . . .'

'Outside?' I echoed. 'Outside where, Kearney?'

The answer was as faint and indistinct as a dying man's whisper.

'Kearnay. Listen. I reckon I'm ninety, maybe one hundred and ten kilometres north-east of you. I'm using a searchlight. Watch out for it. Start firing those flares from three o'clock onwards. I'll be up with you thereabouts, depending on the weather.'

It was, in fact, nearer four o'clock when the phone from the crow's nest cut through the long tense silence on the bridge.

I snatched it up.

It was the look-out. 'Distress flares, sir! Fine on the starboard bow!'

CHAPTER SEVENTEEN

'Bearing? Distance?' I snapped.

'Bearing two-two-zero, distance approximately fifteen kilometres.'

'Good. Keep a sharp look-out. Keep me informed.'

'Aye, aye, sir.'

I touched the mouthpiece down for a moment, lifted it after the cut-off. I glanced at Wegger. There was no sign of the exhaustion which I had hoped would dull his vigilance. His stubble-coated face seemed to tauten and become youthful at the news from the look-out.

'Bo'sun?' I enquired. 'Rescue team to emergency stations midships. Everyone to wear survival kit – parkas, overpants, rubber thermal boots, gloves. I want scrambling nets rigged both port and starboard sides below the lifeboat-deck.'

'Hands to emergency stations – aye, aye, sir.'

Wegger still wasn't interfering. However, *Botany Bay* was in sight and that was what mattered – for the moment.

I made another call. 'Persson? *Botany Bay*'s in sight. See what you can manage with the R/T, will you? Tell him we've sighted his flares. I'm going up aloft to assess the situation for myself.'

I worked the engine-room pointer to 'slow ahead'.

Then I said briefly to Wegger, 'I'll be on the flying bridge.'

He nodded to Ullmann without speaking. He uncurled himself from a high stool on which he'd spent most of the night like a sleepless tiger. I was uneasy. The entire rescue procedure was too normal, as if they hadn't hijacked the ship at all. McKinley was on watch. He looked like a playboy deprived

171

of his playthings.

I caught my breath as I swung on to the outer companion-way with Ullmann behind. The wind was backing west from the north-west. As it did so the snow squalls would come, just as surely as the north-wester had brought the rain. It shoved a frozen fist into my face and icy fingers lanced through the gaps in my parka hood and blew the nylon securing cords against my mouth. The flying bridge's deck was slippery with accumulated spume; below me the winches, hatches and rigging were all white, like a snowstorm.

I tried to forget Ullmann's presence and my glance sought the south-west quadrant where the look-out had seen the flares. The light had an out-of-this-world quality, as unreal and insubstantial as a dream. It wasn't Captain Prestrud's blue mystical light. It was like seeing things through a stage curtain of grey. The horizon and sky were like a vast inverted bowl which was lighted round the rim where it met the ocean; overhead it was almost black from the overcast, plus a curious touch of blue depth. The eastern rim of the sky-bowl was light with the new sun, but the south-west was lighter – a wide band of strange, hard, white light which illuminated ten degrees from the horizon upwards into the overcast. Ice blink! That was ice ahead!

At first I couldn't distinguish anything against the line of white which might be a ship.

I found my Bausch and Lomb G-15 sunglasses which, with their Eskimo slit-goggle principle, improve light-shadow discrimination.

Immediately a row of table-topped objects like castle battlements showed up against the flat white line.

Icebergs!

The crow's nest must have seen me on the flying bridge. The man called through a megaphone.

'Icebergs, sir. Five – no, six . . .'

I cupped my hands and shouted back, 'Where's the wind-jammer?'

'No ship in sight, sir. Nothing on the bearing of the rockets.'

Had *Botany Bay* indeed sunk? How then could she be signalling? The rockets were too big for boat flares.

The *Quest* rattled and vibrated as the way fell off her. She was dipping and sliding into the deep troughs and then lifting with a protesting groaning. She wasn't throwing water all over herself as she'd done during the night. Her well-modelled bow lifted over all but the biggest rollers now that she had slowed down.

Three red rockets rose against the white horizon like stripes across a top secret file. I trained my binoculars on the spot.

The masts and spars which would be a windjammer's tracery against the backdrop were missing. There was nothing.

I shouted to the crow's nest, 'Where is that ship?'

'No ship, sir. Those rockets came from an iceberg.'

I headed for the radio shack. Persson held up his hand for silence when I entered.

'*Botany Bay* says, "I can't see you from inside,"' he reported.

'Inside! What the devil is he talking about? Why is the R/T so faint – we're within a few kilometres of her.'

I took the microphone impatiently. 'Kearnay! Shotton here. I've sighted your rockets. But where in hell are you? Is your ship afloat?'

'. . . inside an iceberg,' said Kearnay's remote voice. '. . . Fast . . . on the ice . . . not afloat . . .'

'For crying in a bucket!' I rejoined. 'You're *inside* an iceberg?'

'. . . Iceport . . . watch out for grease ice . . .'

I passed the instrument back to Persson. 'One of us is nuts. I'm going in close to that berg to find out what the position is. If *Botany Bay* makes sense, call me. I'll be on the bridge.'

When I got there with my gun-toting shadow Wegger said, 'What's the delay, Shotton?'

I didn't care for his tense, hectoring tone. 'There's no ship. It's as simple as that.'

'Don't give me that sort of double-talk,' he snapped. 'I saw the rockets myself.'

'The flares came from an iceberg,' I replied.

'*There has got to be a ship!* Do you hear! *There has got to be a ship!*'

As if in answer, another trio of rockets fanned upwards from one of the bergs near the windward edge of the line. The bergs looked like old-time men-o'-war formed up in battle line ahead. The red flares cast an unearthly glow over the

173

steely turquoise hue of the ice. It wasn't the usual plaster-of-Paris colour of the flat-top which is common to Antarctica: I could distinguish an irregular outline against the skyline, which meant that the berg was old and weathered. We were still too far away to make out detail.

It also showed me something which made me reach for the engine-room intercom. Despite the swell, the sea in the vicinity of the berg had an odd matt appearance – it was thick and soupy.

'Mac,' I said, 'we're running into grease ice. Watch those engine suction strainers. I don't want 'em fouled.'

'I'll watch 'em all the way,' Mac replied.

The *Quest* tiptoed through the turgid sea towards the group of bergs. Small lumps of ice thumped against her hull.

I kept my binoculars on the rocket-berg. From our angle of approach, the lee or port side of it consisted of a weathered pinnacle fronted by two lower flat-topped pieces of ice each a couple of hundred metres long. It was impossible to tell whether or not they were attached to the main berg. The right-hand slope of the peak fell away sharply. Because of shadow (it was on the side away from the sun) I could not make out detail at water-level. The extreme windward bulk of the berg consisted of a solid flat-top at least 300 metres long and 30 high.

Where was Botany Bay?

I noted as I cased the mass with my glasses that the shadow cast by the peak against the massive upright section moved. The berg was swinging. That meant the wind was slowly revolving it.

Then the berg swung further in the *Quest*'s direction and everything became clear.

Between the left-hand peak and the right-hand buttress was an enormous archway through the solid ice. Open water lay beyond.

I realized immediately where *Botany Bay* was. She *was* inside! In an iceport, a calm sheltered embayment with ice of the berg all round and a gateway to it via the majestic archway.

That is what Kearnay had meant.

I tried Persson's intercom. 'What does the windjammer say?'

'Her batteries must be dead,' he replied.

'Tell her . . .' I began but Wegger snatched the instrument from my hand.

'Tell *Botany Bay* nothing – understand?' he snapped.

'Fine,' I said. 'Run the bloody show yourself, Wegger, if that's the way you want it.'

He responded by shouting to the rescue team sheltering in the lee of the *Quest*'s bulwarks.

'Clear away the motor-launch!'

A single rocket – green this time – soared from somewhere inside the iceport.

'She's inside – but where, I don't know,' I pointed out to Wegger.

'I'm going to look – and you're coming, too. Ullmann, you also. Call Bravold to replace you.'

Ullmann went, passing his Scorpion to Wegger, who stood against the bridge windows and regarded us.

'See here,' he told the others on the bridge, 'don't get any ideas of seizing the ship while I'm away. Bravold is a very impatient man. There's nothing he likes to hear more than the sound of automatic fire. His own.'

I wondered afresh at Wegger's concern for the windjammer. There was a great deal in his mind that I didn't understand.

'Motor-launch cleared away, sir!' came a shout from the seamen in their orange lifejackets.

I focused my glasses again on the arch. Stretched across the entrance like the arm of a breakwater was a low line of what looked like small pieces of ice coagulated together. If that line were as unnegotiable as it appeared from a distance, nothing could save *Botany Bay*. She was completely boxed in.

Bravold came on to the bridge. He was as thin as Ullmann was broad but his face appeared more intelligent. He must have been asleep somewhere, but his eyes were alert. Like Ullmann's, they had an awful blankness of emotion. In addition to his machine-pistol his belt was strung with five grenades.

'Warn the passengers over the public address system to keep off the decks,' Wegger told him. 'Shoot anyone who disobeys – right?'

Bravold's eyes travelled round the bridge. McKinley dropped his glance. There was a line of sweat on his upper lip.

'Right.'

'Shotton, Ullmann – come!'

The three of us made our way to the lifeboat deck. The motor-launch, a 25-footer with auxiliary sail and decked-in bow and stern, hung in the falls.

'In,' Wegger ordered me.

'How many men are coming?' I asked.

'None. Three's a crowd. Let go of those falls!'

The men seemed only too eager to get away from the gun muzzles. The launch reached the water.

'Fend her off!' said Wegger. 'You're not the captain any more, Shotton. Get going!'

I fired the engine and took the tiller. The mast, unshipped, lay the length of the craft. My eye went to its step in the bottom of the boat, which was where I had hidden Linn's golden coin. It looked as if we would need a lot more than Viking's luck to beat Wegger.

We headed for the iceberg over roller-coaster waves, weaving and dodging between the smaller ice clutter. My approach was roundabout in order to avoid the spit across the entranceway. When we came closer, I could see that it did not extend right across: there was open water both under and beyond the arch.

The whole majesty of Antarctica was in its frozen architecture. The arch was fronted by a double portico on the left side towering almost as high as the main structure itself. There was a deep cleft between it and the great main solid buttress on the right. The passage led through and under a soaring bridge which ended in a triangular roof like a huge hall. Calm open water was beyond.

What lay inside there was anyone's guess.

Wegger was for'ard gazing at the stupendous natural wonder. Ullmann didn't take his eyes or the Scorpion off me.

I called to Wegger, 'What now?'

'Take her in! I'll con her.'

I throttled back slightly as we passed under the ice-bridge. The wind cut off and we were in a haven. And a death-trap.

Why, I saw.

The sight ahead looked like an old print from the days of sail.

Threequarters of a kilometre away a windjammer with bluff bows and bulging sides lay canted over against an ice-cliff across ice-blue water. She looked like a bygone East Indiaman. She was full-rigged, and her sails were harbour-stowed. Her stern was half towards us. It was a great square-cut affair with big windows and quarter galleries. Gingerbread work flowered gold against dark blue, the colours bright despite the grey light. She must have been about 45 metres long with a beam of nine. The steeve or angle of her bowsprit was very sharp against the ice and I could see heavy chain guys holding it in position. The bowsprit was not fashioned to form a harmonious whole with the bow; there was a tiny platform under it, for'ard of which was a figurehead. Ice coated her footropes, sheets and stays.

Wegger swung round. 'She's afloat! She's afloat, d'you hear!'

I throttled back to a crawl and indicated a solid shelf of ice which locked *Botany Bay* to the cliff.

'No. She's fast. She's trapped.'

'Get on over there!' he ordered. 'Get on! We'll move her out of here!'

CHAPTER EIGHTEEN

The sound of the launch's engine brought figures rushing on to *Botany Bay*'s deck. They started to wave frantically.

I picked a cautious way through the soupy water and as we neared I saw that the windjammer was listed over in a tumble of small, broken blocks of ice. She lay on her starboard beam with warps out. The port anchor, the one facing open water, was cockbilled at the cathead like a last vain attempt to claw her way free of the icy fist which had closed round her.

Wegger said to Ullmann, 'Put that gun away – for the moment.' He shoved his own pistol into his pocket but kept his hand on it.

Two men broke away from the stranded vessel and came

177

ploughing across the ice-blocks to the water's edge.

'Stand off at speaking distance,' Wegger warned me. 'No going close.'

The motor-launch reached the ice edge before the men. I held her off a couple of boats' lengths away – it was a natural jetty. I couldn't judge how thick the ice was; it groaned when we ranged close.

Small haloes of steam from their panting enveloped the two men's heads when they reached the water's edge.

'Ahoy!' yelled the taller. He was fair-haired, with a non-descript beard. He wore a shabby peaked cap. 'Ahoy! What the hell! Come close! Let me grab your hand!'

'Keep off!' Wegger growled at me.

'I'm Shotton,' I called back. 'You must be Kearnay. Glad to see you.'

He was grinning and gesticulating. 'Aye. This is my second string, Geoff Biggs. That was a great effort, Captain Shotton!' Then he repeated, 'Bring your boat in. It's safe enough. I should know.'

When I still did not approach, he looked puzzled and went on, '*Botany Bay* isn't a yellowjack case, Captain. Come on in!'

I replied as evenly as I could, 'Looks as if you've got problems.'

'Problems – my bloody oath!' he exclaimed. 'I never thought I'd see another ship again – where is she, Captain?'

'Lying off outside. It's pretty snug in here. The weather's getting worse out there.'

'A couple of trips will do for all of us,' Kearnay went on. 'We're only fourteen all told.'

'What happened?' Wegger asked. 'Is *Botany Bay* damaged?'

'Throw us a line,' said Biggs. 'I'll hold her fast. Then we can talk.'

'We're quite comfortable where we are,' replied Wegger.

Kearnay looked startled. 'Who's the captain – you or . . .?' He nodded in my direction. His open face was as uncom-plicated as a trade wind.

To paper over the situation, I called, 'Listen, Kearnay – how did all this happen?'

He looked taken aback by our cool reception but he ex-plained slowly, eyeing us all the time in a puzzled way.

'Five, no six, days ago *Botany Bay* smacked into a growler

at night. We couldn't see a thing. She took it for'ard, under the starboard cathead. Carried away the anchor and lower bowsprit guys. I think the fore topmast stay caught it some-how too – anyway, it's weakened the fore topgallant mast. It's a wonder it's standing up to its present strain.' He indicated the vessel's tilted masts.

'How did you get into this place?' demanded Wegger.

Kearnay's glance again travelled from Wegger to me. His growing puzzlement at Wegger's assumption of authority was clear.

'She was leaking for'ard,' he went on. 'There was a lot of water coming in. It seemed worse than it was, maybe, and it was blowing great guns. So I decided to warp her fast to an iceberg and try and fix the leak before she went to the bottom.'

'It's been done before,' I said.

He threw me an appreciative glance. 'To begin with, the berg gave me a lee where the water was smooth enough to work. Then, when I got close, I saw through the arch that there was an iceport inside. It seemed safe enough at the time.'

'As one sailor to another, that was quite something to do in a windjammer,' I remarked.

He laughed self-consciously. 'She's an old bitch and she sails like a teatray, but I'll be sorry to abandon her.'

'I want to see for myself whether that will be necessary.' Wegger interrupted.

'You can have her,' Biggs added. 'She'll never get out of this trap.'

'How did you come to be nipped by the ice?' I asked. 'That's what I don't understand.'

'The leak wasn't too bad, actually, we found,' Kearnay went on. 'We frapped a sail round the hole as an emergency patch. We were all dead on our feet and in need of a night's rest. So I warped her fast to the ice-cliff. There must have been a bummock or underwater shelf under the ship which was attached to the main ice. The place was also full of grease ice as well as some bergy bits. When we woke up in the morning the whole lot had banked up against the ship and frozen solid. But we were still okay and I could have got her free. Then there was one hell of a crash – the berg must have

calved on the seaward side and she tilted. That brought the
bummock up under *Botany Bay*'s keel. She went over on her
side – she would have gone further except that the yardarms
propped her up against the cliff. There she is. That's the
story.'

'The hull's still sound, though?' Wegger demanded.

'Sound as a bell. She's built of teak – teak decks even. They
slip like hell in a seaway. I keep the lifelines permanently
rigged.'

'We'll come and examine her for ourselves,' said Wegger.

Kearnay replied, still watching me as if he could not understand why Wegger should be spokesman, 'Come, by all means.
But there's not a chance of getting her out.'

'We'll see,' Wegger answered. He turned from Kearnay to
me. 'Stand away until we're out of earshot.'

I gunned the engine.

'Hey!' yelled Kearnay. 'What's up? Where are you off to?
You can't leave us!'

Wegger gestured impatiently. 'Back in a moment or two.'

As we withdrew I saw men start to climb *Botany Bay*'s
rigging. They must have been as puzzled as Kearnay and
Biggs were.

'Get back to the *Quest*,' Wegger ordered Ullmann, 'and
bring that case of explosives we have for the kelp at Prince
Edward.'

Ullmann exhibited a flicker of animation at the word explosives. 'Will do.'

'You, Shotton, come with me. We're going to blast that
windjammer free with the kelp charges.'

I shrugged. I knew a beset ship when I saw one. Better
ships than an ungainly replica showboat had been pinched to
crumbling timber in the Southern Ocean.

The blue veins in Wegger's face darkened with fury at
my reaction. He drew Ullmann aside and whispered something I couldn't catch. It was obviously something to do with
me and whatever it was, it pleased Ullmann.

'Take the boat alongside now,' Wegger instructed me. 'And
remember, Shotton, I've got a gun in my pocket.'

At the ice edge Kearnay and Biggs caught our rope and I
jumped ashore. Kearnay pump-handled me but nevertheless
he eyed me searchingly. With the other man, Biggs, my hand

might have been a buntline in a gale, the way he gripped it.

'Ullmann is returning to the ship for help,' Wegger announced briefly.

Kearnay's handshake for Wegger didn't emulate Stanley's for Livingstone. The hijacker's aura was as frigid as the Pole of Relative Inaccessibility.

We started towards the windjammer. Kearnay fell into step alongside me, with Biggs on my other side. Wegger was behind. The ice shelf had a brittle, shiny crust between the broken mass of blocks. From the shuga – the spongy white lumps of ice which floated greasily off the ice edge – and the tumble of accumulated blocks I could deduce by hindsight the tragedy which had overtaken *Botany Bay*. She had been in clear water of low salinity when she had originally entered the iceport; the switch in the wind had brought with it a sudden freeze-up which had solidified her haven into a death-trap. There was no knowing how long that freeze would last. The berg might drift east in high latitudes for another six months and never relax its fist round the sailing-ship.

Kearnay broke the awkward silence as we stumbled towards the ship which lay like an old-timer beached for careening. The port ratlines below the maintop were full of men waving and shouting.

'I told the crew to keep aboard until Geoff and I found out from you what the score was,' he explained. 'I didn't want to raise their hopes unnecessarily.'

Biggs added, 'Every man jack of 'em's there – even a couple of frostbite cases.'

As we approached the stern, under its elaborately carved quarter galleries, the men burst into spontaneous cheering. Hands reached down and helped us aboard. The ordeal still apparent in their taut faces exploded into relief in the form of a flurry of back-slapping and hand-shaking.

Wegger barely gave it time to work itself out before he made his way carefully across the tilting deck to the starboard rail of the quarterdeck to examine the windjammer's side. The ship lay at a 15-degree angle to the ice-cliff with her fore royal topmast yard against it. I estimated the cliff to be about 35 metres high – higher than the top of the vessel's main royal mast. Between the ship's side and the ice-cliff – a distance of about 10 metres – the sea had frozen and locked her in. There was no way of knowing how thick the ice was which supported her. But it had been strong enough to have lifted the windjammer's 600 tons clear of the water.

Kearnay called out to the chattering crew, 'Stay on the port side, lads – keep as much weight there as we can.'

Then he showed me the foremast. 'See that? She's leaning all her weight on that parrel of the topsail yard – I reckon it's bent already and could go at any moment. Those top-mast shrouds and backstays must be as tight as a fiddler's bitch. See the strain they're taking?' He grinned apologetically. 'Sorry. You don't know what I'm talking about.'

'On the contrary,' I replied. 'I've sailed everything except a square-rigger.'

'Good. Then we're on the same beam.'

I risked a glance at Wegger, who seemed preoccupied. I eyed Kearnay keenly and hoped he got my message.

'We're on the same beam, Kearnay.'

He followed my eyes and looked puzzled. But he went on about the ship.

'I'll have to do something about that rigging before she'd take a blow – that is, if she ever sees the open sea again. I won't be happy until I've checked the rudder also. Come and look at this.'

He led me along the slippery deck to the big double wheel and indicated the base of the binnacle.

The dark teak of the deck had been inlaid with a segment of wood of lighter colour.

It was the shape of a coffin.

In my surprise, I forgot all about Wegger for a moment.

'This wheel's a killer – it was in the original *Botany Bay*,' Kearney explained. 'That's an *in memoriam* notice in wood. The helm works off a tiller below decks . . .'

'A tiller!'

He grinned. 'Aye, a great hunk of wood. I've got kicking tackles rigged on it, but let a beam sea strike the ship and it throws the helmsman across the deck as if he didn't exist. It takes four men to hold her in a quartering sea.'

Wegger interrupted us harshly, pointing overside, 'We'll drill a row of holes for charges along the length of her side – how thick's her timber, Kearnay?'

182

Kearnay bridled at his tone but replied levelly, 'Four inches, mainly. Six in places. The knees of the beams below-decks look like whole trees.'

'I'll use ten-kilogram charges,' Wegger went on. 'We'll fuse 'em for simultaneous firing. They'll crack the ice in a line along her keel. When the ice gives, the weight of the ship will do the rest.'

'That's fine – as far as it goes,' I said. 'But the main cause of the trouble seems to be the underwater ice shelf, the bummock. You won't blast that loose.'

'Don't start creating difficulties,' he snapped back. 'My plan will work, I say!'

It took me everything I had to hold myself back. Nor did it escape Kearnay. He gave Wegger and myself a long, contemplative look.

Then he went quickly to the poop rail.

'Men!' he called to the crew on the main deck. 'Aft here, all of you. I want to say something to you.'

'There's nothing to discuss,' Wegger retorted. 'I've sent for explosives and a couple of augurs to drill holes in the ice, and that's that.'

Kearnay didn't turn at his truculent tone, but I saw the red flush of anger mount in his neck.

'I happen to be the skipper of this outfit, and on my ship what I say goes.'

The men filing aft must have heard his rejoinder because there was an air of expectancy about them. They congregated on the port side, the side canted highest away from the ice-cliff, because of the weight-balance factor. Geoff Biggs headed the crew, standing at the foot of the ladder leading to the break of the poop.

At that moment I saw my chance.

On Kearnay's left, within reach of his hand, was a row of belaying-pins in a rail.

The belaying-pin – a length of iron round which rope is cleated home to make it secure – was the favourite weapon of tough old skippers who held on to their sails when their crews thought the world was falling on top of them when running their easting down.

There were fourteen able-bodied gale-hardened men in a

183

group within feet of one man with a pocketed pistol. I'd get Wegger before his hand even reached his gun. One quick rush would do it.

I edged forward towards the belaying-pins as if to hear better what Kearnay was saying.

Kearnay slapped the palms of his hands down on the rail. He rounded on Wegger and myself, talking to the crew as well as to us.

'Men – there's a scheme here to blow *Botany Bay* free of the ice. I'm all for it, and I know you will be. But there's something I have to understand. At the moment I don't.' He addressed Wegger and me. 'You say you are the captain, Shotton. But it seems to me that Wegger gives the orders.'

A hush settled over the men. I didn't have to look at Wegger. I could feel his vibrations. I wondered for how long he would be able to hold himself in.

I moved forward quickly, then leapt. I shouted, as I snatched a heavy belaying-pin from the rail, 'Wegger hijacked my ship! He's a maniac . . .!'

I swung at Wegger. His gun-hand was moving – fast.

I'd overlooked the state of the deck. The teak was as treacherous as the ice which coated it.

My feet spun from under me as I struck at Wegger. I hit the deck with a bone-thumping crash. The wind was kicked out of me.

Time seemed to go into slow motion as I watched what followed.

Kearnay was lightning-quick, a man used to taking snap decisions in conditions which would mean life or death to his ship.

He grabbed a belaying-pin and went for Wegger.

I found breath to jerk out to Kearnay, 'He's got a gun!'

Kearnay was almost on him when two shots rang out. The momentum of the downward blow he had aimed at Wegger's head carried him onwards, but the two 9mm man-stoppers had done their work. There was no power left in his blow. The glancing impact as Wegger dodged knocked the pin from his paralysed muscles. The belaying-pin ..nd his head struck the deck at the same moment with a crack. He cartwheeled over into the starboard scuppers.

I tried to raise my head. 'Get down!' I yelled feebly at

the men. 'Down, all of you, for your lives!'

But Biggs came bounding up the four-step ladder shouting an oath.

Wegger steadied, shot him between the eyes.

The body spun, recoiled into the men crowding up behind him. They broke.

Wegger held a striking crouch, feet splayed, Luger levelled, deadly as a mamba.

I saw two of the crew crawl on hands and knees to try and shelter behind a brace-winch at the foot of the mizzen mast. There was no other shelter between it and a cabin skylight across an open stretch of deck.

'Stop!' Wegger ordered. 'Anyone who moves gets it! Stay where you are! All of you!'

Suddenly there was nothing but the silence. A fine cascade of ice crystals and frozen snow, dislodged by the concussion of the shots, filtered down from the mizzen yard like a delicate shroud. A straining piece of ice groaned under *Botany Bay*'s keel. There was a light patter on the deck from Biggs's body. A last reflex of a signet-ring finger beat a faint tattoo on the planking. Then it, too, stopped.

'Shotton!' snarled Wegger. 'Up! On to your feet! Get up!'

I rose slowly, still breathless, wondering how soon the bullet would come.

'I ought to kill you!' Wegger went on. 'This is the second time I've been near it. It's only because you're useful to me . . .'

'Go ahead!' I retorted. 'Take your own bloody ship to Prince Edward Island!'

'Shut up!' He glanced at the men holding frozen attitudes about the deck. 'Keep your mouth shut!'

Then he shouted at the crew. 'Everyone get below! And keep below!' He moved the Luger threateningly in an arc across the main deck.

The men near the winch got to their feet. They were frightened, sullen. One of them pointed at Biggs.

'What about him? You can't leave him like that.'

'He'll stay there until I say move him,' snapped back Wegger. 'Get below, all of you, and keep out of my sight!'

The men filed away. They were a young lot, all in their early twenties.

When the deck was clear, Wegger came upright from his shooting stance. He kept the gun on me.

'Here!' he indicated a stretch of quarterdeck for'ard of the wheel and binnacle. 'Keep clear of the gear and rigging. And that belaying-pin rail.'

I took up the position as ordered.

'It's a pity Kearnay made me shoot him,' he said. 'He'd have served my purpose and I could have got rid of you.'

'You wouldn't have sold Kearnay that gold yarn any more than me,' I answered.

'It doesn't matter a damn to me what you believe,' he said. 'All that matters is to get to Prince Edward and collect it. And that's what I'm going to do.'

I checked the time. It was shortly before six o'clock.

'You've got four more hours of freedom, Wegger,' I said. 'The buoy launching is due at ten. After that the *Quest* is a marked ship. They'll hunt the seas for her. They'll find her, all right. And you too. You've killed men here and aboard the *Quest* in front of enough witnesses to convict you a dozen times over.'

'It's a pity about Kearnay,' he remarked thoughtfully. 'Maybe I should only have winged him. I've got to have someone who can handle a sailing ship.'

'Biggs could too,' I replied.

'He had his chance. He came at me,' Wegger retorted. That ugly look was coming back into his face at the recollection of the rush at the quarterdeck as he justified the shooting to himself. Wegger couldn't help himself. He'd kill – regardless.

'Wegger,' I said, 'all this is getting us nowhere. If you have anything to say to me, say it.'

'Don't come the heavy captain over me! Shut up and listen!'

'I'm listening.'

He said breathily, as if the words were being forced out of him under pressure, 'I told you I'd show you how to hide a ship in the Southern Ocean. And that's what I'm going to do.'

I showed him my watch. 'You can still make it to the buoy's launching-point if you hurry. Four hours and you could be there. First we rescue this crew in two trips with the motor-launch . . .'

'Stow it, Shotton. Don't tell me what to do. Get this absol-

utely clear, there is not going to be any buoy launch. Next
. . .' he leaned forward towards me and made little chops at
the air with the Luger '. . . you're taking this ship to Prince
Edward Island.'

'*This ship?*'

'This windjammer, this ship, *Botany Bay*.'

'It's impossible!'

'You and Ullmann and Bravold and me – we're going to
Prince Edward in *Botany Bay*.'

I simply stared at him.

'I realized all along it would be pretty risky using the *Quest*,
but I had no choice,' he said. 'But the minute *Botany Bay*'s
Mayday signal came in, I had my answer.'

'Go on.'

'What's one unknown windjammer compared to a vessel
which the eyes of a hundred and forty-five nations are on?'
he asked rhetorically. 'No one but the *Quest* heard her
Mayday call. If she doesn't turn up in Australia, so what?
There'll be very few questions. She'll be dismissed as a
cranky replica of a cranky old windjammer. She won't be
considered worth searching for. There'll be no follow-up
when she's posted overdue. She'll be lucky if she rates a
paragraph or two in the newspapers. So you and I and
Bravold and Ullmann will take *Botany Bay* to Prince Edward,
lift the gold, and sail on to Mauritius. My plan goes ahead
as scheduled.'

A new fear swept over me. What did he intend to do with
the *Quest*? He'd not mentioned Linn either.

'And *Quest*?'

I didn't like the way he laughed. 'You'll see. You'll see for
yourself in good time.'

I kept my feelings hidden. 'Your plan is fine and dandy
except for one thing.' I waved a hand at the ice locking in
Botany Bay. 'You talk as if you had a ship to sail. You
haven't. You'll never get *Botany Bay* out of this.'

He pointed the gun between my eyes, grinning like a death-
mask.

'*You* will, Shotton. You will, if you have to spill your guts
on the deck doing it. You'll see why.'

I did, half an hour later when Ullmann returned, bringing
Linn with him.

I recognized her as soon as she stepped on to the ice shelf from the motor-launch by her brown-and-white coat and hood.

When she came close to *Botany Bay*'s side I saw she was walking stiffly and holding her head awkwardly.

I hurried to help her aboard. She stood on the ice, unspeaking, looking up at me, strained and white-faced, her head at a strange, stiff angle.

'Linn! What . . .!'

Wegger was laughing. He called down to Ullmann, who had unmasked the Scorpion after Wegger had shouted a go-ahead to him.

'Show him, Ullmann! Show him why he'll do everything to get *Botany Bay* free.'

Ullmann went to Linn and wrenched down her hood. Her lovely hair was pale gold against the whiteness of the ice.

But it wasn't her hair my eyes were riveted on.

A grenade was tied against her neck.

CHAPTER NINETEEN

'Heave short!'

Ten men at the hand-operated capstan on *Botany Bay*'s foc's'le-head bent their backs to the capstan bars. Their boots beat a treadmill pattern on the deck, a pattern which had been repeated time and again during the past two hours. They were sweating even in the icy cold. The sheep-stink from their heavy sweaters was rank and raw.

The clumsy old-fashioned anchor with its big flukes and long shaft rose to the end of the foreyard like a corpse on a hangman's gibbet. As it reached its extremity, a man watching at the rail called to me.

'Up and down, sir!'

'Hold it!' I ordered the exhausted men. I was waiting until the anchor steadied. It weighed a couple of tons; this was the tenth and – I hoped – last time I would have to order the sullen, resentful men to put their backs into the heavy task.

Two hours had passed since Ullmann had come aboard

with Linn as a hostage. Wegger wasn't bluffing. He had her standing in full view on the quarterdeck while he kept guard. Ullmann was up for'ard with me and the crew. His Scorpion was over us like an evil dream. I knew how much the men had been shaken by the sight of Linn with that grim talisman of death fixed to her neck. They had seen for themselves over Kearnay and Biggs what Wegger was capable of. Although their muscles were groaning, they kept going. I could only hope against hope now that my own plan would work.

When I saw the two small drills which Ullmann had brought from the *Quest* to bore holes in the ice for the explosive charges I knew Wegger's plan was useless. The augurs had a diameter of about 50 millimetres or two inches and were a metre long. It was sending a boy on a man's errand to expect toys like that to make holes to accommodate charges of ten kilograms.

I told Wegger so.

His only reply had been to fix me with his cold stare and indicate Linn.

It was hopeless to try and get past him.

The cockbilled anchor – the one I had spotted at the cathead when we had first approached the windjammer – had given me my idea. I had decided to use its weight with a length of heavy steel bar fixed into the crosspiece as a kind of jumper drill. The anchor had been run out at the ship's lower yardarms on the ice-cliff side, hoisted, and then let fall. The device had worked. We were now drilling the final hole.

But would the blast free *Botany Bay*?

I put the thought from me. That still figure on the quarter-deck drove me afresh.

'Up and down, sir!' The man repeated. We had adapted sailing-ship parlance to cope with the situation. 'Up and down' meant that the length of cable running through the blocks on the yardarm was now equal to the distance the anchor had to fall to hit the ice.

'Stand clear! Secure the pawls!'

The men at the capstan stood back. I took a hammer and knocked out the anchor shackle. I jumped clear to avoid the wire's backlash.

The anchor plunged from the yardarm with a crash. Splinters of ice shot up as the steel dug deep.

Now it was the turn of the explosives.

'Break that anchor out – handsomely, men!'

One of the young men spat on his hands and asked me as he passed.

'Will it work, sir? How thick is the ice?'

That was exactly what I did not know, how thick the ice was which locked *Botany Bay* fast.

I tried to sound confident. 'We'll have the ship back in her natural element before the day's much older.'

'Heave!' – the men renewed their effort to secure the anchor.

Explosion seismology.

The phrase sprang ready-made into my mind. It seemed to come from deep in my subconscious; probably it was from some forgotten piece I'd read or heard, concerning the way scientists had calculated the depth of the ice-cap covering the Antarctic continent. They had fired small charges of explosive in holes drilled in the ice and measured the time taken for the echo to rebound from the bedrock thousands of feet below. Knowing the speed at which sound travels in ice, they were able to establish how thick the ice-cap was.

Using the same principle, I intended now to probe the underwater ice shelf which held up *Botany Bay*. The thought of it brought a knot into my stomach – what if I should fail? How extensive was it? All I had gathered from Kearnay was that the berg itself had tilted and the underwater shelf had lifted *Botany Bay* bodily as it did so. Loose ice afloat in the iceport had also consolidated, making the trap complete.

Would ten charges of ten kilograms each be enough?

First, before the actual freeing attempt, I intended by a crude imitation of the scientists' method to try and determine the thickness of the underwater shelf.

I stalked past Wegger in my preoccupation.

'Where are you off to, Shotton?'

'It's my show, isn't it?'

'It's her neck,' he retorted.

I found one of the augurs on the quarter-deck. Linn was standing, remote and strained, at the binnacle. The only concession Wegger had made was to remove the icy metal of the grenade from against her skin. It was now lashed to her shoulder.

'Bo'sun!' I called. 'Lend a hand here, will you?'

I explained quickly and tensely that I wanted three holes drilled in the ice with the augur. Wegger held the Luger on me when I requested small charges of explosive weighing only half a kilogram each and gave them only on the assurance I wouldn't ignite them myself.

The bo'sun and I went ashore. It didn't take very long to drill three holes each a foot deep, one at the stern, one amidships, and the third under the bow.

I tamped the charges home and lit a short length of fuse for each. Ullmann had joined Wegger; two gun barrels followed every movement I made.

'I'm going below-decks,' I told the man. 'Fire these charges at three-minute intervals. Take cover behind the bulwarks when you do so. They're only small charges but they'll throw up splinters.'

I ordered the rest of the crew to stand clear, explained to Wegger what I was about and went below. He eyed me speculatively but did not interfere.

I hurried below. The only light in the dark interior was a dim kerosene lamp which hung from a beam.

A figure behind bars reached hands at me, his face contorted.

I stopped with an oath. I had quite forgotten *Botany Bay*'s cavalcade of horrors.

This was a tableau of the dreaded 'tiger's den' – and it looked it. Behind the bars was the waxwork figure of a man, stripped to the waist. A great weal from the cat-o'-nine-tails oozed make-believe blood. The first figure which had caught my attention supplicated through the bars like a caged wild animal.

I spared the tableau a passing glance and hurried on. These were only waxworks. The living horrors walked the deck above.

At the ship's side I put my ear against the teak planking. The subsequent crash of the charge nearly deafened me. I had forgotten in my tense state that ice is such a good conductor of sound that you can hear a man speak through it at a distance of 100 metres.

Apart from an odd creak or two, the test told me nothing. There was three minutes to go to the next shot.

191

I took the oil lamp from its gimbals, and made my way down a central gangway amidships, specially built to show the displays of convict imprisonment on either hand. I began to sympathize with the Cape Town taxi driver's hysterical girl.

The second explosion followed. This time I kept my ear a short distance from the planking. Even so, there was a marked difference. The concussion reverberated, heavy and thudding, unlike the first smacking whiplash. Its message was plain – here the ice was solid.

The third shot, which I tracked in the ship's bluff bow, was the lightest of the three. What the tests had established was that the ice was thickest under *Botany Bay*'s keel amidships, and thinnest in the bow and stern. She could well have been balanced with the underwater shelf acting as a fulcrum.

I returned to the deck past Wegger who had stood guard in the central gangway.

'Well?' he demanded when we reached the deck.

I avoided looking in Linn's direction.

'I don't rightly know,' I replied. I didn't, in point of fact.

'Get on with the job and stop fooling around,' he rapped out.

For the actual release attempt itself I took the final ten-kilogram charge and climbed overside under the gun muzzles to position it. I had laid the other charges previously while the crew took breathers at the capstan. I tamped it home with a length of spar. I measured an identical length of fuse to the other nine.

Now for the acid test.

'Hands to charges!' I called. One man per charge in order to have a simultaneous blast. The fuses were long enough to give everyone ample time to shelter below.

I raised my hand.

'Ready, men? Right! Light fuses!'

The matches went down.

'Everyone below!'

Wegger, Ullmann, Linn and I sheltered together near the chamber of horrors tableau. The crew kept to themselves.

We waited.

My watch said nearly nine o'clock. In the interval before the explosions were due I wondered about Smit and the other

two weathermen. There was no way now that the launch
could take place on schedule at ten o'clock 110 kilometres distant.

Then the hull kicked, kicked again. Even I wasn't expecting the size of the explosion. It was like a ragged broadside,
the charges exploding irregularly within seconds. There was
a heavy thump nearby as part of a waxwork display col-
lapsed, and a rattle of ice falling on the main deck, followed
by the heavier sound of a block or spar which had been dislodged from the rigging.

From under our feet came a grinding, rending, tearing
sound. *Botany Bay* might have been dragging across a reef.
It lasted only seconds.

Then everything went quiet.

The deck remained at its previous list.

Botany Bay was still fast.

I had failed.

I threw a desperate glance at Linn. The light was too dim to
see what was in her eyes. Equally desperate was my rush of
thought to try and jump our watch-dogs. Wegger, Ullmann –
either one of them would get me even if I managed to grab
the other's gun. I wouldn't stand a chance.

My voice sounded as harsh as the grinding ice.

'Let's get up on deck and see.'

Wegger fell back a pace or two and whispered something to
Ullmann. The nerves at the base of my stomach were stretched
to breaking-point.

We emerged on deck. The charges didn't seem to have done
much beyond dig a few man-sized holes. The force of the explosions had dissipated mainly upwards and the main and
topgallant yards were all askew as a result, like a slovenly
crew's work.

The only thing that I registered in my numb dismay was
that the wind had changed. Also, the berg had slewed further
and the wind was now filtering through the entranceway and
was stirring the protected water of the iceport.

I had to have time! Time to think, time to work out something else before the two started on Linn.

I said the first thing that sprang to mind. 'I'm going up
aloft – I want to inspect the ice from high up . . .'

Before Wegger could reply I swung myself into the lower

G

port shrouds. The ratlines to the maintop seemed to stretch upwards never-endingly. The ship in its ice cradle remained rock-steady.

I went up hand-over-hand to the maintop. Then up to the top-mast shrouds. Then on to the cross-trees. It was only when I was nearly up the topgallant shrouds that I got a grip on myself and slowed down – to think.

I felt the slender spar give a shudder. I threw one arm about the topgallant backstay to steady myself. My heart leapt. Was the hull, now looking like a toy more than 25 metres below me, starting to loosen? Or was it simply the over-strained mast starting to give at last?

Was it wind?

I climbed higher up the mast above the level of the iceberg's summit. The south-wester smacked me in the face.

My view was down, deckwards. The ice was green-white round the stern and bow and opaque amidships. That bore out what my elementary 'seismic charges' had indicated – thin ice there.

Next, I looked up, seawards. My eyes filled with moisture from the wind and I ducked down to avoid it. I caught a distant glimpse of the *Quest* standing off, pitching and rolling.

I tried again. My first incredulous thought was that somehow our iceberg had doubled its size, for almost on top of it was a second iceberg. Breakers climbed high up its side, exploding soundlessly in a welter of white. The second berg's tabular top was big enough to land a helicopter squadron on.

It was heading for us with a kind of slow malevolent purpose like an old-time battleship going in to break the enemy's line but holding its fire until it was alongside the enemy.

I realized what would happen when the two bergs collided. I cocked a knee in the ratlines and locked both my arms round the backstay to prevent myself being shaken off.

'Stand by under for your lives!' I yelled at the deck.

Almost at once the inevitable happened.

Tens of thousands of tons of ice, propelled by a 30-knot wind, swung and struck the buttress next to me.

I ducked. Impact and thunder came almost simultaneously. The concussion was stunning enough to be heard half across the Southern Ocean.

My topgallant mast whipped like a fishing-rod taking a strike.

The mast lashed towards the ice-cliff. I thought I would be pitched headlong against it despite my hold. Its supporting shrouds and stays made an agonized groaning, straining noise. The ropes tautened, tautened, tautened. How far to breaking-point? I could detect stretch – and I blessed the rigger who had used manila instead of wire.

Then the two bergs rebounded.

The mast whipped again, this time in the opposite direction. From the hull came the most dreaded of all sounds to a sailor's ear – a sound like timbers being torn apart.

But it wasn't *Botany Bay*'s timbers.

It was the ice.

The ice immediately round the ship's sides started to break off. Loose blocks porpoised to the surface. Next, it seemed to me, the underwater shelf rose and took the ship under her lee beam and lifted her bodily – the collision had snapped off the shelf from the parent berg and it was rising to the surface, pushing the ship with it.

Under its thrust, *Botany Bay*'s first movement was still further over to starboard, the iceberg side. I clung on. Any moment I feared the mast would shatter at the cross-trees and pitch me to death. Then the dizzy pendulum stopped short. The mast reversed its traverse. It rotated away to the lee beam in a long sickening arc. But it was a swing whose pivot was water, not ice!

'She's free! She's loose!' I shouted – but I couldn't hear my own voice above the uproar.

All round the ship the ice cracked, exploded and shattered in long cracks radiating from the hull. The noise was louder than gunfire. On the quarterdeck I spotted Linn, Wegger and Ullmann all hanging on to the big double wheel. On the main deck men with their feet sliding under them hung on for dear life to any rope they could find.

All round the sea boiled. The ship was half-lifted, half-pushed sideways. Then she went over until her port life-boats touched the ice-cluttered sea.

I hung on like a fly on the ceiling.

Would she ever come upright?

She did, swinging almost lazily on to an even keel.

I knew that I had to get her clear at once. At any moment there could be a second collision between the two icebergs. It would drive the jagged pieces of ice floating round the vessel like battering-rams through her timbers.

I threw a final look seawards. Floes of smashed ice were scattered all round the great berg, and the sea boiled and broke. The tens of thousands of tons of table-top was rocking slightly in the aftermath of the collision. That alone showed how stupendous it had been.

I took the quickest – and most dangerous – route to the deck. I went down, boots and hands, via the backstay. It took only seconds.

My mind had formulated its plan when I had felt the wind up aloft in the rigging. Down here it was still no more than a catspaw, not enough to power her big lower sails but strong enough aloft for her uppermost sails.

'Hands to the braces!' I shouted. 'Break out the main and fore royals! Slap it about, men! All hands!'

They went automatically to their stations like a stunned gun crew after a near miss by a shell. They reacted like automatons, too.

The yards came round. Four men – two would have done – shinned aloft and broke out the small topmost sails.

Collecting the drifting motor-launch on the way, *Botany Bay* clawed her way with nerve-shattering slowness through the ice, bumping and thumping, until we were at last in the safe open water of the iceport.

CHAPTER TWENTY

'Back the main royals!'

Tired as they were, the crew were twice the men they had been a short while before, and they went willingly to the braces. *Botany Bay* had put the danger astern and was easing through the open water of the iceport.

At my order, Wegger came to where I was standing at the wheel, his face dark.

'What are you playing at, Shotton?'

The yards came round. The backed sail acted as a brake. *Botany Bay* slowed to a standstill as the way fell off her.

I ignored his question and asked the bo'sun, whose name was Clem Bent, at the helm, 'How does she feel?'

He spun the spokes first to port and then to starboard.

'A bit stiff, sir, but okay.'

'Good. Hold her steady.'

I turned on Wegger. 'Get that grenade off Miss Prestrud and I'll tell you.'

His face clouded still further. 'Try anything on me . . .'

'Wegger! I've just snatched your bloody ship out of a death-trap. I did my part. Now do yours.'

He gestured to Ullmann, who cautiously passed him the machine-pistol so that he could loosen the grenade.

I started forward angrily as Ullmann took Linn roughly by the shoulder but Wegger exclaimed warningly, 'Keep away from that grenade, Shotton!'

When the grenade was free, I went to Linn and held her for a moment. I couldn't have cared whether or not a hundred hijackers were near.

She was trembling and she whispered, 'Thank God for you, my darling.'

'You were wonderful, Linn,' I replied.

Then I walked slowly back to Wegger.

'Listen,' I told him. 'Now's your time to reconsider, if you still intend to go ahead with that idea of yours about taking this ship to Prince Edward. She sailed in here, but she won't sail out. It's impossible to negotiate that entrance under sail – it's dead into the teeth of the wind. Also, the ship's damaged. She's got a leak in her bow. I don't know what other underwater damage she may have suffered in the ice.'

'We'll tow her out with the motor-launch,' Wegger replied. 'Don't try and blow up the damage. Kearnay himself said the leak wasn't bad.'

'A leaking ship is a leaking ship in the Westerlies – anything could happen.'

'Forget it. We go to Prince Edward, leak or no leak.'

I felt as trapped as *Botany Bay* in the ice. I said non-committally, 'I'll get the sail off her then if we're going to tow.'

197

'Not so fast,' replied Wegger. 'We've got some busines first with the *Quest*.' Both he and Ullmann laughed. 'We've also got to collect Bravold. You and the girl can use the opportunity to pick up your things.'

'Her things!' I echoed. 'What do you mean? Linn's no coming in this old sieve . . .!'

'John!' exclaimed Linn. 'I go where you go. Prince Edward Island or no Prince Edward Island, leak or no leak.'

'Too damn right,' sneered Wegger. 'She's coming – for my reasons, not hers, which don't count with me.'

'A sailing-ship is no place for a woman,' I protested. 'Es pecially one like this, Linn . . .'

'Do you think I'd leave her behind, knowing what she knows?' asked Wegger. 'She comes with us. That's final.

'Linn . . .' I started. But she stood there with her head held back, and I knew in my heart that I'd rather have her with me, Wegger or no Wegger.

'Right,' I conceded. 'But we're in for a rough ride. The sooner we get over to the *Quest*, the better. The weather' working up.'

Just how much it had deteriorated since we had first mad our way into the iceport was apparent once the motor-launch carrying Wegger, Ullmann, Linn and myself cleared the en trance and left the protected water behind. The launch started to pitch and toss and the *Quest*, nearer the ice than she should have been for safety, rose, corkscrewed and plunged. I wa now concerned about how *Botany Bay* would fare once she stuck her nose outside. I was also deeply anxious about Linn She sat silent, looking ahead. I admired her pluck in wanting to come but not her wisdom.

I checked my time as we cleared the arch.

Ten o'clock.

The buoy's launching-time.

I wondered how Smith, T-shirt Jannie and Pete would take missing it. Or the rest of the watching weather world.

Then suddenly the scheme to beat Wegger dropped tailor made into my mind.

It was so simple, so neat, that I almost laughed.

To carry it out, though, I would need another person's help Linn's help. They'd be guarding me all the time when w reached the *Quest*; I'd never escape their vigilance. But Linn could. It would need only a few minutes . . .

I shifted from the stern thwart and moved alongside Linn, who was amidships. Wegger frowned and Ullmann kept ready. I put my arm round her, as if to resolve our constraint over her attitude about *Botany Bay*.

I whispered, 'Into the bows. Quick! I want to tell you something!'

She gave me a startled, puzzled look, but did as I said.

In the bow I steadied myself by a grab-handle and said softly, 'Linn, I've got it! When we reach *Quest* I want you to go straight to the scientists' place and find Smit. Tell him to set the balloon's instrument package in operation . . .'

'But we've missed the launching-point, John! *Quest* is over a hundred kilometres from it!'

'I know, I know,' I responded urgently. 'Listen. The package is a tiny thing – it weighs about half a kilogram. Get him to set it working – right? Then take it yourself. Put it inside your parka . . .'

'Me? Take it?'

I threw an anxious glance astern. Both Ullmann and Wegger were watching us keenly but they couldn't hear what we said.

'It won't take a moment to unhitch it from the balloon's envelope,' I rushed on. 'Don't you see – explain all this to Smit – all the weather stations will be on the look-out for the balloon to track it across the sky. We'll start it operating. The GARP stations will pick up the transmissions via the satellite. But it won't be doing 30 or 40 knots on the wind as it should be, it'll be travelling a mere six or seven because we'll have it with us in *Botany Bay*. The experts will realize at once that something is wrong and an alert will go out. From the satellite's readings they'll be able to pinpoint the transmitter's position exactly – and with it, *Botany Bay*'s position. Got it?'

She pressed my hand. 'Wonderful, John, wonderful!'

'Careful,' I warned her. 'Don't let those thugs suspect us. It's up to you, Linn.'

'I'll do it, John.'

'There's more,' I went on urgently. 'Tell Smit to set the buoy's transmitter in operation . . .'

'John! Quick! Explain! I don't follow!'

I dropped my voice as low as I could. 'The tracking

stations know that the buoy's maximum rate of drift is less than one knot an hour,' I hurried on. 'If the satellite is registering the buoy's speed as fifteen knots – the same as *Quest*'s – a similar alert will go out as for our balloon package, which we will have in *Botany Bay*. *Quest* won't be able to explain until the radio black-out's over, but the experts will be able to pinpoint her position exactly, just like *Botany Bay*'s. They'll realize that the two transmitters are being transported artificially.'

'What chance of using *Botany Bay*'s radio when the black-out's over?'

'Nil, I'm afraid. The batteries are finished. Wegger will smell a rat if I suggest anything there.'

'John! Watch out! He's coming!'

'Here!' Wegger rapped out. 'That's enough chattering, you two.'

The *Quest* was now almost on top of us. Wegger steered for the scrambling nets I had had rigged. McKinley was making a poor job of holding position. He had her half beam-on, and the seas were letting the ship know it. She looked like a ghost ship. Her decks were deserted. The only figures visible were on the bridge.

I seized a boat-hook and held the motor-launch fast once we had gained the lee of the hull.

'Up,' Wegger ordered Linn. 'Get to your cabin – and stay there. Be ready in fifteen minutes – we'll fetch you.'

I steadied her hand. She gripped me reassuringly in return and started up the wet, swaying side of the hull.

Wegger pocketed the Luger. He picked up the case containing the explosives and swung himself effortlessly into the scrambling net.

Linn had almost reached the top when a head looked over. It was Smit.

I saw my plan vanish like a puff of smoke. If Smit stayed and argued with Wegger . . .

'Captain Shotton!' he called in an agonized voice. 'Where have you been? We've missed Bokkie's launching-time!'

I watched Linn race for the top, her shoes slipping on the wet net. She realized the dangers as well as I did.

Wegger stopped, glanced up, gestured to Ullmann.

'Get back to your cabin!' he shouted at Smit. 'Get back! Inside!'

Linn had reached the rail now and was throwing a leg over. Ullmann lifted the Scorpion. He couldn't fire without hitting her.

'For Pete's sake, Smit, do as he says!' I yelled.

Ullmann's warning shot into the air rang out simultaneously. Smit's head vanished. Linn disappeared, too. Wegger hung on for a moment or two and then looked enquiringly down at Ullmann.

'He took the hint, the stupid sod,' Ullmann called. 'He's gone, skipper. It's okay.'

Wegger nodded and finished his ascent.

'Shotton!' he called. 'Up! Make the launch fast. Then up!'

I secured the boat by running a line through the meshes of the net. I went up. The deck was empty – there was no sign of Linn or Smit. I breathed an inward sigh of relief.

Then Ullmann joined us.

'March,' ordered Wegger. 'The bridge!'

Before entering, Wegger called, 'Bravold! Everything okay?'

'No problems,' came the answer.

Both McKinley and Petersen were on watch. McKinley hadn't shaved and there were heavy shadows round his eyes. His face was blotchy as if he had been roughed up. Petersen looked as guilty and inadequate as if he'd been responsible for the entire hijacking.

'McKinley,' said Wegger, 'I'm leaving the ship to you. I'm taking your captain with me.'

'*The ship to me?*'

'That's what I said. And look after her well, you miserable runt!'

McKinley stood gaping at Wegger and me. He seemed to have lost his voice. Wegger strode to the engine-room telegraph. He rammed the pointer over. It's metallic clatter was almost a protest in itself.

Wegger rang, 'Finished with engines.'

McKinley stuttered, 'Finished with engines – sir?'

Wegger ignored him. He said to Ullmann, 'You know what to do.'

Ullmann took two 10-kilogram ice-charges from the box,

hitched his machine-pistol over his arm, and went.

'Finished with engines!' Wegger repeated.

The realization of what he was up to hit me then. 'Wegger – you can't blow up her engines!'

I started forward. Bravold was very quick in covering me with his Scorpion.

'Do you think I'd leave this little rat to turn tail and race back to the Cape to tell them what's happened?' said Wegger.

'You can't leave everybody aboard to die in a helpless ship in the middle of the Southern Ocean!'

He grabbed me by my front, taking me by surprise.

'They left me to die, Shotton! The three of them – Prestrud, Jacobsen and Torgersen! But I didn't die! I lived!'

'It's calculated mass murder!'

'Shut up!' he snarled. 'It isn't. They've got a shipful of food and water. They're in the track of the West Wind Drift. Plenty of ships have broken down and drifted safely to Australia before now. If they could, the *Quest* can!'

'Wegger . . .!'

A short rat-tat-tat rang through the ship from the direction of the engine-room.

There was a short pause, then two more shots.

Wegger and Bravold eyed each other.

We waited. Minutes passed.

Then Wegger picked up the engine-room intercom. At that moment the *Quest* kicked as if the inside of her hull had been struck by a giant's hammer.

Wegger relaxed and put down the instrument.

We waited. Then Ullmann came in from the companionway. He was fiddling with the machine-pistol's magazine, reloading as he walked.

'Trouble?' asked Wegger.

'Some. A stupid clot tried to stop me. Old bastard. Said he loved his engines.' The big man spat on the deck. 'Said they were his life.' He shrugged. 'It *was* his life.'

'MacFie!' I breathed. 'You killed MacFie!'

Ullmann seemed cynically amused. 'There was another,' he told Wegger. 'Did you hear the second lot of shots?'

I died a thousand deaths for Linn before Ullmann continued.

'A young 'un. Red hair. He came at me like crazy. Yelled

something about a ghost in a tunnel. Maybe he was trying to protect the old guy.' He shrugged again. 'It doesn't matter. He got in the way.'

'Fine,' said Wegger. 'Now fix the radio. A grenade will do.'

'Wegger,' I said deliberately. 'You bastard – you unspeakable bastard!'

'The test will put some guts into McKinley – if he has any,' he retorted. 'They'll be found – in time. After we've been to Prince Edward.'

Ullmann went off, and shortly afterwards the crash of the explosion set every piece of steel on the bridge vibrating.

When he returned, Wegger told him, 'Go and get the girl while Shotton collects his things. Everyone to meet here in five minutes.'

Wegger himself guarded me while I found my sextant and other navigating instruments as well as a couple of charts. As I finished, he said, 'You could have had it very easy, you and the girl . . .'

My anxiety over Linn and our scheme was destroying me. I didn't respond to his gambit. I gathered up the penguin-skin rug – for her sake – but I couldn't stop myself from looking at my watch.

'What's up?' Wegger demanded. He was living on hair-trigger tenseness. Luger trigger.

'Weather,' I replied. It was half the truth, anyway. 'The sooner we get back to the windjammer with the present build-up, the easier I'll be in my mind.'

This answer didn't quite satisfy him and he said, 'Get out of here. Back to the bridge.'

Linn was already there when we arrived. She was standing apart from the others, a small crush-bag at her feet. Her green-grey eyes held steady on mine. I knew she had succeeded. The minute transmitter was hidden away in the folds of her parka.

'Search her!' snapped Wegger. 'Her and her dunnage.'

My mind froze as Ullmann went forward. No frisking hand could fail to detect that light-metal box.

Linn pushed her bag at him with a foot. He stooped, unzipped it.

My tongue felt as if it had been immobilized by the sort of

ice which had frozen *Botany Bay* solid. But ice is wet. There was no moisture at all in my mouth.

Ullmann's hands began to explore Linn's bag.

'Wegger,' I remarked, trying to sound casual, 'maybe you've been too busy killing innocent people to notice that this ship is slewing. The wind has got hold of her bows. She's coming round. Any minute now that lee for our launch won't be a lee any longer. The boat isn't moored – it's only secured to the scrambling net. It'll stove in against *Quest*'s hull any moment.'

Wegger looked startled and said, 'Belay that, Ullmann. There's no other gun in the ship anyway – I know. Get overside quick and fend off the launch. Bravold, guard these two. Come!'

They shot off. Linn knelt and re-zipped her bag slowly, her relief apparent in the careful way she bent so that the transmitter inside her parka would not be visible.

I took the bag. I faced McKinley briefly. Petersen was gagging as if he were about to be sick.

'Good luck,' I said.

He regarded me bleakly without speaking.

'Get moving!' ordered Bravold.

Wegger and Ullmann were already in the boat when we reached the rail. Linn went down before me, cautiously straddling the rail and carefully nursing the concealed transmitter. I followed with her bag. Bravold brought up the rear.

We cast off the launch and pulled clear of the ship. The *Quest* wallowed like a harpooned whale. The wind had started to gust more strongly from the south-west. We felt its bite afresh the moment we cleared the shelter of the ship's side. The iceberg boxing in *Botany Bay* was only a couple of kilometres away now. It was anyone's bet how soon the *Quest* and the berg would collide. The light also had changed: it was dark in the storm quadrant although the sun had a whiteness high towards its zenith.

Dollops of spray started to break aboard. I called to Wegger, 'Can't you go faster? We're running into trouble already.'

He speeded up and the launch shipped more icy water. Finally we got inside the shelter of the arch, and hurried across the protected water to *Botany Bay*, which was still stationary with her main royal aback.

The first thing I noticed on the quarterdeck was that the bodies of Kearnay and Biggs were missing.

'What happened to them?' I asked Clem Bent, the bo'sun, out of Wegger's hearing.

'We buried 'em decently while those bastards were away,' he replied. 'We didn't want him simply throwing them overboard.'

Wegger and Ullmann set to work in the bows making the tow fast to the motor-launch.

'All hands!' I shouted. 'Men! We're towing the ship out of here. Get those royals clewed up! Secure the anchor inboard. Hands stand by tops'l and topgallant braces.'

I said to Bent at the wheel, 'Maybe you'll want help at the helm when we get outside.'

'Aye,' he answered. 'She steers like a bitch and kicks like a mule.'

The tow was finally made fast and the motor-launch tugged the windjammer slowly across the quiet water. The calm didn't last long. Once we hit the waves rolling in through the entrance the launch's towing speed fell off sharply. I began to wonder whether it had even enough power to fetch *Botany Bay* through the entrance. With the waves' thrust and the tow falling slack and then jerking taut again our speed was down to about one knot. *Botany Bay* was still the cork in the bottle.

The launch edged through the arch into the open sea beyond. *Botany Bay* dragged at her heels. Would the cork get out of the bottle?

'Hold her!' I told the helmsman. 'She'll swing when the wind catches her . . .'

She did, even before she reached the open sea. The bluff bow offered maximum resistance to the wind; the wind took full advantage. It jerked her head round in spite of the motor-launch. I dared not risk setting sail. The starboard mainyard scraped the ice-cliff, bumped, scraped again. Pieces of ice rattled on the deck. In her situation the ice portico flanking the entrance had become a dead lee for the ship. One rag of canvas would have driven her against it.

Botany Bay rebounded from touching the ice; the tow snapped taut; she lurched forward again. Half the length of the ship was now through the neck of the bottle. But the wind was pushing her round, round once again towards the menacing portico.

I simply had to chance the forward momentum a sail would give. It was a question of checks and balances. Would the sail's forward thrust be enough to carry her to safety or would the simultaneous sideways tug throw her to destruction against the towering cliff?

I made my decision. 'Hands aloft!' I shouted. 'Double-reefed topsails! Get the sails on her!'

The fore tops'l broke out first. It only veered her head closer towards danger.

Then the main topsail also billowed like bubble-gum blown from a giant child's lips.

'Put your helm up! Helm hard up!'

The veins started in the steersman's face as he battled with the primitive gear.

The wind bit the sails; the deck canted to their power. Rollers broke over the deadly ice, hard on our beam. It was less than a ship's length away.

Slowly, jibbing like a thrashed horse, *Botany Bay* clawed her way.

Then she inched clear with a spurt of foam bursting on either side of her blunt bows and drenching the foc's'le.

'Swing that launch inboard!' I shouted. 'Use the crojack yard before it knocks a hole in the hull!'

Lines went down to the boat, which was now alongside after having cast off the tow. It was secured and hoisted aboard. Wegger and Ullmann, streaming sea-water, climbed out of it on to the quarterdeck where I was.

Botany Bay was drawing steadily away from the ice-trap which had so nearly destroyed her. The *Quest* tumbled, unmanageable, further out to sea.

I strode across to the binnacle housing the compass.

'Steer east by north,' I ordered.

Prince Edward Island!

CHAPTER TWENTY-ONE

The main force of the storm hit *Botany Bay* shortly after two o'clock that afternoon.

From the time the ship had broken free of the iceberg she had been running free under triple-reefed main and fore topsails with a strong quartering sea and gale. There was also a rag of trysail in the mizzen stays to try and help the steering. The wind had steadied into the south-west in a full gale. Handling a square-rigger was as unfamiliar to me as driving a veteran car for the first time. And this was at open throttle.

A tremendous sea was building up and I blessed *Botany Bay*'s square, heavy stern. The waves would race up astern and tower ready to burst and poop the ship. Then I would hang on, waiting for the inevitable explosion which would sweep the ship and everything on deck into oblivion. But it did not come. The heavy stern would lift and in a flash the ship would lurch into the trough. The sails would go slack as the wind was cut off by the depth of the rollers. Then she would rise to the next crest and the sails would crash like gunshots as the wind caught them anew. She would find her keel, tear away again with a shock which seemed to set every scrap of standing rigging thrumming. It was a process which repeated itself time and again. The wheel was kicking like a rodeo jumper; to help Bent I brought along a young man with shoulders like a blacksmith. Kearnay's lifelines were in full use.

At the start, Linn had been on deck with me and I had lent her my binoculars for a last look at the *Quest*.

'They're all coming out on deck!' she had told me.

'Heaven help them, Linn.'

'That applies to us too, John,' she replied gravely.

But we also had that space-probe-sized instrument now transmitting from under her weatherproof. And from the buoy aboard the *Quest*.

The thought of the transmitter and what could happen if Wegger by some mischance spotted it fuelled my tension. I had decided that the ship could spare me for a few minutes while I settled Linn below, out of view of the hijackers. I gave orders, gathered up Linn's bag, and we hurried below.

When we were out of sight of the deck Linn stopped. Her lips came hard against mine, against my cheeks, my eyes.

'Darling! Darling! Darling!'

I drew her to me. I detected the outline of the aluminium box inside her clothes.

She eyed me between tears and laughter. 'I'm pregnant with secrets, my love!'

'That transmitter frightens me, my love,' I said in a low voice. 'We've got to hide it somewhere else, quick. I die every time Wegger looks at you.'

We were in the central gangway dividing the various exhibits in their cubicles and to our right was a horrifying real 'coffin bath' exhibit which showed convicts being thrown into salt water after being flogged until they fell unconscious. Tough-faced warders were apparently trying to revive some unfortunate.

'Nothing for us there,' I said. 'We mustn't be seen searching around, Linn.'

'We can pretend we're looking for a sleeping place for me, John.'

The next exhibit depicted a man being flogged at the dreaded triangle or flogging-post; nearby a blacksmith was riveting a huge iron ball round a new convict while a long branding-iron was thrust into the palm of his hand to mark him for life with an arrow.

'I couldn't stay there, even though I know it's not real,' muttered Linn.

'No place to hide,' I said, going on to the following exhibit. A man was dismounting from his horse amid a clutter of handcuffs, leg-irons, necklets, pistols and manacles, and a notice above read: 'Captain Starlight, legendary bush-ranger.'

'John – look, the horse has a real saddle. The saddle-bags! Perfect for the transmitter!'

Linn reached for the zip on her parka. 'Wait.' I gave a searching look in every direction.

'Okay. That transmitter's dynamite.'

She pulled it out. It looked ludicrously small and inadequate.

'It's working?' I asked unnecessarily. 'Sure?'

'Smit set it operating and it stays so, he said, even if it falls into the sea. It's waterproof, among other marvels.'

We unbuckled the saddle-bags of Captain Starlight's horse and hid the transmitter inside.

'I feel as if the world is off my neck, Linn.'

The creaks and groans of the ship's timbers in the seaway were like a muted chorus of wronged convicts.

'I've got to get back on deck – use one of these cubicles for a cabin. Maybe there's a bed somewhere as part of an exhibit. Try and make yourself comfortable.'

'You've no place either, John.'

'Put me next door to you – horrors don't mean a thing if you're close.'

She smiled and said gently, 'There's only one penguin-rug – we'll have to share, my darling.' Then she kissed me. 'Look after yourself, up there.'

'Don't come on deck unless you have to – the seas aren't funny.'

They weren't then, when I kissed her goodbye. That had been a couple of hours ago. They were even less so now.

I was hanging on to the weather rigging, a captain's station. The feel of this ship was coming through the soles of my feet, just as a racing-driver steers by the feel of the seat of his pants. *Botany Bay* was starting to lie over more and more as the wind worked up, and even her return roll was stiffening against the thrust of her storm canvas.

I felt her go over – and watched fascinated and afraid while she lay over until her lee gunnel was almost level with the water as if she meant never to come up again. Then the dense streaks of foam which were the crests of the rollers toppled, tumbled over, exploded, and vomited across the main deck and a welter of water poured into the waist. It seemed that the old-design hull could never have enough life in it to throw off the tons of water. *Botany Bay* hung like that, paused, and then began the reverse roll to right herself, taking her time, as if sea and waves didn't matter. Back and back she went, against the drag of the tops'ls and power of the gale, until her main yardarm dipped into the wild seas on the opposite side.

Each time *Botany Bay* did it my heart came into my mouth;

yet right herself she did until I was forced to accept that this was her way of sailing. To anyone accustomed to a modern yacht's manners, *Botany Bay* was terrifying.

Now, however, she was close to the limit. I would have to reduce sail soon, free her of some of the leverage aloft.

I put the modern battery-operated megaphone to my mouth.

'All hands! All hands! Aloft and stow! Four reefs in the tops'ls!'

The men dodged out from behind the foc's'le head where they had been sheltering and watched their moment. Gripping the lifelines as the main deck flooded from a sea which burst inboard, they clumped clumsily across the deck in heavy boots and sou'westers to the protection of the life-nets I'd rigged below the weather shrouds. As she rolled to port again, up they went into the rigging with astonishing agility. They would have to fist the thrashing canvas into quiescence: *Botany Bay* had only single topsails, not the more modern double sails, and their bigger area meant twice the muscle-power.

One of the men scrambling up the main shrouds stopped, pointed, and shouted something at me. His words were snatched away by the wind. I followed the direction of his hand. There was nothing but an endless succession of racing hills of water. Then the stern lifted, which gave me a wider sight of the horizon.

I stood rooted at what I saw.

The approaching snow squall looked like a destroyer's smoke-screen laid across the face of the west. Reaching out fingers towards the labouring ship was a millrace of clouds scudding low almost to mast-height. The squall was still about five kilometres off and travelling like a bullet.

But ahead of it was the thing which froze my blood.

It was a monster comber with a long overhanging crest of dense white reaching for the ship like an outrider of the main body of water.

No ship's stern would ever rise to that.

Botany Bay was already squirming down a roller, away, as if she realized what was coming.

I whipped the megaphone to my lips. I gave one of the rarest orders at sea.

'Stand by for your lives!'

That killer rudder wouldn't take it either. No two men could hold its rebound, even with its special kicking tackles.

I turned the megaphone on Ullmann.

'Ullmann! Get to the wheel! Forget that bloody gun!'

He stood hesitating.

I must have sounded like one of the Furies riding the gale when I re-directed my words at him.

'Ullmann! Lend a hand! *Get to that wheel!* The whole ocean's coming up astern! Run, man, run!'

He must have been convinced by my urgency, for he went across the lurching deck to Wegger, passed the strap of his machine-pistol round his arm, and seized the for'ard spokes of the double wheel.

The young man with the blacksmith's shoulders glanced astern over his shoulder. Many a better man than he had been killed in the Southern Ocean doing that.

'Keep your eyes front!' I shouted above the wind's roar. 'Don't let her broach to! Keep her head steady!'

Then I knew I might still help the ship, if the men now in the rigging could manage in time.

'Set the main tops'l staysail!' I shouted through the mega-phone.

The small triangular sail, which would be high above the swamping effect of the waves as the ship fell into the trough, might just carry her forward enough to ride out the monster when it struck.

I didn't have time for anything else.

I threw a bight of rope round the shrouds, lashed myself fast. It was impossible to tell whether the substance which machine-gunned my face was snow, hail, rain, ice or spray. It was equally impossible to hear anything. The wind was hurling itself over the starboard quarter with a roaring, moaning sound which changed to a higher pitch when it struck the rigging. The wild seas smashing against the hull under-wrote the din.

Then the great roller struck.

One moment the main deck, poop and helm were visible, the next all I could make out were three masts sticking out of a cauldron of water. I was punched in the back, but the rope held. Water poured over me as if I had been a surfer who had come unstuck from his board. *Botany Bay* heeled

right over until the main hatch disappeared. The lee main
yardarm went deep into the sea.

I caught a glimpse of the young man with the blacksmith's
shoulders being thrown loose and against the for'ard part
of the double wheel. He spread-eagled his arms, looking like
one of the waxworks figures below stripped for flogging on a
grating. The killer wheel jerked again and he was flung head
over heels into the scuppers. The breaking wave took him
overboard. There was nothing I could do to save him. Ullmann's face was purple as the veins stood out as he attempted
with Bent to hold the ship from broaching to. The driving
spray was too thick even to see what was happening to the
men on the foc's'le head.

'Don't let her head come up!' I tried to yell above the
din to the helmsmen.

No human power would ever bring *Botany Bay* upright
again.

Her stern lifted, lifted, and the bow went down, down.

She tobogganed into the trough.

It cut off wind pressure from the reefed tops'ls holding her
listed as surely as if they'd blown clean out of their bolt-
ropes. From the rigging high above there was a clap like
thunder. The small tops'l staysail blew away like an errant
albatross's wing.

Then from the maelstrom on the main deck I saw the top
of the main hatch start to emerge; two lifeboats lashed to
it were gone. We'd secured the motor-launch aft the mainmast on skids; now I saw it break clear of the foam – intact.

Botany Bay was making a great fight for it. She possessed an
unsuspected buoyancy. The lee ports of the poop deck
clanged as hundreds of tons of water poured overboard.

Then I spotted the young helmsman. He was sprawled out
floating mizzen-yard high, within three metres of the deck. It
might as well have been three kilometres. His arms were
reaching out helplessly for safety and his mouth was wide.

Now *Botany Bay*'s mainyard emerged from the spume and
she came on to an even keel and started to give that long
majestic roll to recovery. The lee poop deck flooded again at
the movement and scooped up the young man out of the sea
as neatly as if it had been intended. He crawled across the
deck and locked his arms round the binnacle.

'Get back to the wheel!' I shouted. 'Back, man, we'll make it still!'

The ship lifted as she began her ascent to the crest, shaking her decks clear of hundreds of tons of water like a terrier shaking itself after a bath. Unknown objects washed astern and thumped against the break of the poop.

If *Botany Bay* managed to pull herself back to life again, there was only one course left open for me – to heave her to and ride out the storm and give her time to lick her wounds. For wounded she was, as I could feel by the lethargic drag under my feet, which meant that huge quantities of water had poured in below through smashed hatches and skylights. The patched-up leak in the bow had probably broken out afresh. Muscle-power alone would have to rid her bilges of the water – *Botany Bay* had no mechanical pumps.

Now *Botany Bay* was straining as she climbed wearily out of the trough. Miraculously, the masts were still in her. The foremast seemed askew to me. I saw men still clinging in the rigging where I'd sent them to reef the topsails.

I ripped off my securing rope and swung myself up to check astern. There couldn't be another wave like that. There was only a plunging, rolling, racing, raging mass of hillocks of water pursuing the injured ship.

I regained the deck and shouted, 'All hands! All hands! Stand by!'

Orders were a good thing for a stunned crew. It stopped them from thinking about the death they'd escaped.

I hadn't given a thought to Wegger. Now I found him beside me.

'Shotton! What are you doing now?'

I rounded on him. 'I'm going to heave her to. Put her under storm trysail and try and fix things. We're lucky to still be afloat and not upside down . . .'

He pulled the Luger from his weatherproofing. It seemed a ridiculous token of force after what the Southern Ocean had just thrown at us. Part nerves, part reaction made me laugh in his face.

'Don't play kids' games, Wegger. If you want to go on living, let me handle this!'

He aimed the gun at me.

'Get on!' he ordered. 'Get on, Shotton! To Prince Edward

Island! No heaving-to!'

'You're out of your mind, Wegger! The ship's sinking under us . . .'

A crewman, with water and fear all over his face, clawed hand-over-hand along the life-nets and shouted at me.

'Sir! Sir! Come quick! She's making water for'ard! The patch has come adrift from the hole in her bow – it's pouring in . . .'

He stopped when he became aware of Wegger's gun.

'Get on with it, man!' I said.

He indicated the foremast. I scarcely needed him to tell me, when I saw the way it was tottering.

'The bowsprit chain-guy's parted again, sir – like it did after we hit the growler – and the foremast's taking the strain. All the rigging's stretching. It'll go overboard any moment!'

'I'll come.' Before I did so, I addressed the trio of helmsmen. 'Try and keep her steady – if you want to save your skins!'

Bent nodded but his eyes remained concentrated aloft. He was too good a helmsman to take his eyes off the sails.

I made my way for'ard along the life-nets, clinging like a spider and watching my moment as the seas burst aboard. *Botany Bay* was sick, lurching now like a drunk across the tops and troughs instead of riding them.

There was a small group of men at the foremast weather rigging. One glance was enough. The topgallant mast was leaning leewards and whipping. Any moment it would go overboard. It must have been a prime spar to have taken all it had.

'Frap those backstays together!' I ordered. 'Slap it about, men! We'll take up the slack of the lanyards later, when the weather eases. If that mast goes, cut it adrift.'

These yachtsmen-deepwatermen certainly knew their job. They started in with no-nonsense swiftness and competency. Their lives depended on it.

The motion here in the bows was frightening. The blunt cutwater was never meant to cleave the waves but ride over them. Tumults of seething foam burst from it. Two men were trying to keep their footing in the life-nets rigged below the jib boom while they did something about the patch in the bow

One of them called to me, 'It's hopeless, sir! The water drives in every time she plunges. It needs to be stopped with tar . . .'

Because my mind was anxiously on Linn the answer clicked into my mind.

I'd melt down those waxworks figures in place of tar!

'Do your best – I've got an idea. I'm going below,' I replied. 'It could work.'

The second man had a frost-bitten face and a sense of humour. 'Make it work before we drown, sir!'

I gave him the thumbs-up sign and hurried below-decks via the entrance below the poop.

The scene that greeted me was the way I imagined an old-time warship's deck must have looked after it had been swept by a broadside. It looked like a scene from Dante's Inferno. Light came from a dim smoking oil lamp. Headless wax figures rolled, banged and thumped. The stage-props of the various tableaux swept around in utter disarray. There was water everywhere.

'Linn!' I called. 'Where are you? Are you all right?'

'John!'

I found her crouched in a cubicle. She had barricaded the entrance against the debris. She had clipped a couple of pairs of exhibition handcuffs on to a hook on the wall and was using them as grab-handles.

'John! What's happening? Are we sinking . . .?'

Briefly I explained my plan for the bow leak.

'We've got to find some way of melting the wax and dipping the sail into it,' I added.

'What about the bath – the one they used for the convicts?'

'You're a sailor's daughter, Linn!'

'I could help,' she hurried on. 'We'd have to make a fire under it, though.'

The thought of a naked fire in a wooden ship would have sent any old shipmaster to his grave.

'There are as many ways to sink a ship as to hang a cat,' I told her, thinking of the crisis on deck. 'You're wonderful. I'll send down a couple of men as soon as we've worked on the rigging.'

Then I asked, 'Where is the transmitter?'

I saw she'd taken the saddle for a pillow.

'Yes,' she smiled. 'It's not as close to me as my shirt, but it's near enough.'

'Good girl. Keep at it. We'll beat 'em yet.'

I kissed her lightly and hurried back on deck.

I life-lined along the rail to the men in the bows and gave them my orders. Then I returned to the quarterdeck.

Bent called to me from the wheel as soon as I mounted the ladder from the main deck.

'She's wild, sir. She's running away. We can't hold her – not even three of us.'

Their faces were glistening with sweat; the cords knotted Ullmann's powerful neck every time the wheel bucked.

'I'll try and get a scrap of flying jib on her – if we can fix the foremast,' I told Bent. 'That will make her more manageable.'

I switched my attention to the men who were making their way cautiously down the ratlines from the upper rigging.

'Goosewing the main tops'l,' I ordered them. 'Let go the fore tops'l halyards – the mast may give at any moment.'

For four days *Botany Bay* fled before the gale on that goosewing.

Four days.

For four days the hill-like ridges of water chased her stern, each threatening to wipe the ocean clean of the only man-made thing in all its turbulent vastnesses.

For four days the gale held unabated from the west. For four days it raged steadily, relentlessly. My tired mind computed its average speed at 55 knots. It may have been more; it certainly was not much less. I remembered that the record for the Prince Edward channel was 72 knots in a blow. I didn't want any records for *Botany Bay*.

For four days the crests of the waves – and often the body of the rollers – threw themselves over the ship's rail.

For four days Linn and her helpers melted down the waxworks, head by head, body by body, exhibit by exhibit, dipping the sails which were the precarious membrane between life and death into the wax until each was smashed into uselessness by the waves. Then a new sail would be impregnated, a new patch rigged, until it, too, went the way of the others. The naked fire was a calculated risk. Time and again the burning planks – they burned the partitions between the exhibits first, then every scrap of loose woodwork they could find – spilled from their makeshift gratings under the bath and had to be soused with fire-buckets before the long process began again from scratch.

But it was no lasting answer. The sea kept streaming in through the leak.

On the first day squads of men pumped the bilges reasonably dry in two hours of back-breaking donkey work. At that stage the crew was still relatively fresh.

On the second day the clanging of the pumps rang through the ship for five hours. *Botany Bay* lived again.

On the third day it took eight hours.

On the fourth we pumped all day. All the waxworks had been melted down and the sail patch was now all but useless. The men were exhausted, driving themselves to the pump handles like zombies. While they pumped, we floated. But the water was beating them, creeping slowly but inexorably up inside the hull.

Between stints of renewing the sail patch, Linn made food for the tiring crew. At first, while there was still wood for burning, she supplied them with hot coffee to supplement their chunks of bread-and-meat. Now the fuel was gone and sea water was starting to pollute the fresh water tanks. By next day I knew the water would be undrinkable.

For four days *Botany Bay* staggered goosewinged under a sky as unrelenting as the sea and wind. The overburden of cloud seemed never to rise much above the ship's royal yards. It was impossible to obtain a fix to establish our position. We could have been anywhere. Our only course was the gale's course.

For four nights and four days I had conned the ship from my post at the weather shrouds until my eyes and face were aflame with salt. Wegger, Ullmann and Bravold – one of them had always been on guard. Both Ullmann and Bravold had put their strength to the wheel. Without them, the game but exhausted Bent and the other pump-drunk crewmen would never have held the ship.

Now it was the dawn of the fifth day. I was at my station. I had staggered below to try and get some rest. Linn had taken

me under the penguin-skin rug and pillowed my head on hers
against Captain Starlight's saddle. Sometimes I had not known
whether those capsuled moments of bliss and warmth were
dreams or not, until some savage lurch of the ship would
jerk me awake while Linn held me in her arms. Then I
would kiss her, drag myself away, and stagger back to face
the remorseless enemy on the quarterdeck.

Now it was the dawn of the fifth day. I was at my station.
Jets of icy spray whipped into my face, scouring it down
to the blood like sunburn. The bloodshot faces of the three
men at the wheel were haggard in the binnacle's light. Bent
was there, trying to penetrate the blackness and catch a
glimpse of the goosewinged sail. A sail to steer her by, I
thought light-headedly – then I realized something was amiss.
It wasn't the deck under me, growing deader and deader. It
wasn't the wind. Something was happening, my stunned mind
registered.

The sound which had run through the ship for days like
an undertaker's hammer had gone silent.

The pumps had stopped.

I pulled myself together. Before I could put my mind to
this new problem, a figure loomed up alongside me. He was
gasping and his face was ghastly with fatigue.

'The water – it's beaten us, sir! Pumps are no longer drawing. Must be fouled up. She's had it.'

He stood swaying, passing the responsibility for the dying
ship on to my aching shoulders.

I asked as steadily as I could, 'How much water is in her?'

'It's right up to the waxworks deck, sir.'

'I'll come below.'

I felt my way. The swinging lantern seemed dimmer than
before. But its light was strong enough to show me enough.
The water was ankle-deep. Linn was there, dressed in weatherproofing and boots. She had the hood drawn over her hair
so that her face was in deep shadow. She had the penguin-skin
rug looped about her shoulders against the cold. Ashes from
the fire sloshed about. The chopped partitions and air of
desolation made it feel as if *Botany Bay* had already passed
beyond man's recall.

I put my arm round her and said to the man, 'Get for'ard.
There's nothing we can do here any more.' My sluggish mind

was already made up. *Botany Bay* stood one last chance, the slenderest of chances. 'Get half a dozen axes. I want the fittest men up on deck. Have them man the weather deadeye lanyards.'

The man stared at me uncomprehendingly. 'Quick,' I said, as if that word had any meaning any more. 'Quick as you all can.'

He went.

Linn said, 'This is the finish, isn't it, John?'

I couldn't see into the depths of her eyes in the smoky light.

'It could be, Linn.'

'I want you to know I love you, my darling.'

'These days have been a voyage to ourselves, my love. You've given me everything I've ever wanted.'

I took her close in my arms. Immediately I felt the hard outline of the transmitter under her parka.

I smiled wryly and shook my head. 'It was a good idea, Linn darling. It could have worked except . . .'

'For the Southern Ocean?'

The water round our ankles sloshed alarmingly. I kissed her and said, 'I don't know whether there'll be room in the motor-launch for us all. The other boats are all stove in. I may have to stay.'

'If I stay also, there'll be room for one more man in the launch,' she replied. 'That's the way I want it, my darling.'

'Then keep very close to me, Linn.'

We went on deck. Wegger and Bravold were there, both with Scorpions. They seemed more ridiculous than ever. Ullmann was at the wheel.

'She won't last another hour,' I told Wegger. 'We can try the motor-launch. But it won't take everybody.'

'Where is Prince Edward Island from here?' he demanded.

'You must be bloody mad to ask a question like that at a time like this.'

'I haven't thrown in the sponge,' he said thickly. 'I'll make it yet. What course?'

I laughed contemptuously. 'Try east. Just due east. You may finish up in Australia.'

I turned my back on him and picked up the megaphone. I couldn't make out the crew but I knew they must be huddled somewhere up for'ard.

'One of you get below,' I ordered. 'Put a drum of oil in the for'ard lavatory so that it spills out the hawse-hole. Understood?'

'He's gone, sir,' called back a voice from the darkness.

'Stand by to wear ship,' I said. 'Men, I'm going to try and bring her head to the sea. If we can stream a sea-anchor, we might still make it. The ship's stone dead. She mayn't come round. It's just an outside chance. If she hangs in stays, chop the fore and mainmast lanyards free and send the masts overside. Clear?'

'Clear, sir,' came the muffled reply.

I paused for a moment, hoping for a smoother patch to risk the fateful manoeuvre, which is difficult enough in a storm in any sailing-ship, let alone one which is sinking under your feet.

I saw a blue, phosphorescent glow – it seemed almost tangible – to starboard, the weather side.

'Hands to wear ship!'

I do not know whether anyone got as far as his station.

The wind switched direction without warning as if it had cannoned off a solid object.

Simultaneously with a frenzied shout, 'All aback forward!' I heard a crash overhead as the single sail blew from its bolt-ropes. The wheel gave a tremendous kick out of Ullmann's hands, and the ship broached to. There was another shattering crash and the foremast went overboard, followed by the main topgallant mast. Blocks, yards, rigging came showering down on deck. *Botany Bay* went over on her beam ends.

There was only one order now.

'Abandon ship!' I shouted. 'All hands to abandon ship!'

Out of the darkness of the bow came a hysterical scream. 'Ship right ahead!'

I, too, saw the outline of the ship. It was the same bluish phosphorescent colour I had noted before the masts went.

It was a ship, oddly foreshortened, taller than *Botany Bay* along its tall cutwater.

I recognized it as I saw it.

It was a ship – and a rock. A rock shaped like a ship.

Ship Rock.

Ship Rock is one of the deadly outliers of Prince Edward Island.

CHAPTER TWENTY-TWO

Botany Bay's fallen tophamper smashed and thumped against the hull. It was a better sea anchor than anything which I could have devised. It dragged the vessel's head round.

But it was too late.

It could not drag her clear of Ship Rock.

She lay beam-on for a long moment cowering away from the massive black basalt stack which rose above her. A whole ocean broke over the rail. I saw one damaged lifeboat lifted bodily and smashed to splinters on the deck.

The rope I'd used to fasten myself to the shrouds I threw round Linn so that we were lashed together.

Then *Botany Bay* struck.

The port beam and quarter took the blow. There was a rending, sickening crash as her timbers disintegrated.

The sea, rebounding on the return from the streaming black cliff which rose up like a skyscraper, burst over the full length of the ship.

One moment I was standing with Linn on the poop, the next I found myself against a cathead in the bow. The rope had snicked fast about it; Linn was with me still.

I pulled myself to my knees, grabbed her, and pointed. 'The jib-boom! Up! Quick! Before the next wave!'

The spar was still intact above the maelstrom sweeping aft along the main deck and poop. I half-dragged, half-hauled Linn with me until I felt the footropes under my boots. I caught a fleeting glimpse of a figure doubled up between the outer bobstay and footrope stirrups – whether he was alive or dead I could not tell.

Botany Bay was thrown again against the cliff, this time stern-first. The bowsprit jerked at the impact as if in agony. I saw a group of men round the motor-launch as the main deck lifted up. They seemed to be cutting it free of its skids. Then, above the general din, came the sound of shots.

There was no time to think of what was happening. The ship sheered, the jib-boom dug into the cliff, and broke off short abaft of where we were.

Linn and I were pitched into the surging water. The cold was paralysing. I felt the backwash start to draw me away from the cliff. I seemed to be caught in a spider's web of ropes, guys, chains, wires and blocks all washing and entangling themselves.

I knew that in seconds the undertow would sweep us away from Ship Rock and the icy sea would do the rest.

I held Linn under the arms and snatched at the nearest thing. It wasn't a rope; it was thick and slippery, the thickness of a man's calf. It was a frond of kelp anchored to Ship Rock.

I hauled us in, hand over hand.

'Linn – ride in on the next wave – that ledge – there!'

The kelp seemed to originate from a ragged shelf about five metres above us.

'Use your feet!' I called, spitting out mouthfuls of water. 'Don't let the water smash you against the rock!'

There was no time for more. The next roller – a huge sea – picked us and *Botany Bay* up together and threw us against the rock. At the same instant I heaved all my weight on to the kelp, scrambling, slipping, grasping, keeping hold of Linn.

I felt the horizontal shelf – no more than a metre wide – under my clawing fingers. The water started to fall back. If I didn't hang on, there would be no second chance.

I whipped the rope linking us over a spur-like projection on the shelf and at the same time gripped the kelp frond with my knees and ankles the way I had used *Botany Bay*'s backstay to slide down. The roller took another side-swipe at the dying ship on its return. We were left hanging like two flies against the streaming black cliff.

'John!' called Linn faintly. 'Let me go! Let me go! I can't make it any more!'

She was about a metre lower than I was, trying to find a finger-hold in the smooth rock.

'Linn! Listen! The rope's fast round a rock. I'm going to ease myself down on this piece of kelp. My weight will counter-balance you and pull you up. When you reach the shelf double-loop the rope round the projection. That'll hold it for me. Then haul yourself on to the ledge.'

'John, it's hopeless . . .'

'Do as I say! Quick – there's another breaker coming!'

I eased my grip on the kelp. The seesaw effect of my weight was immediate. Linn went on up past me, I went down.

'John!' It was Linn above. 'I've got it!'

I knew she had, the way the rope felt. I scrabbled and clawed my way up the smooth cliff on the lifeline. It could not have been more than a couple of metres; it felt like a thousand.

Then I was up and over on to the ledge.

I threw myself to shelter on the narrow projection just as the next roller poured over us. Half an hour of that kind of drenching and we'd simply fall off the ledge into the sea from cold.

I risked a glance over the edge. *Botany Bay* had turned broadside directly under me. The next breaker would give her the *coup de grâce*. Then I spotted Wegger in the motor-launch, poised over the tiller. He was alone. He was seaman enough, and cool enough, to wait for it: he was going to float the launch off its deck skids at the next wave – if he wasn't dashed to pieces by it. Two or three men were on deck, shouting and gesticulating at him. They made a rush at the boat and I heard the sound of more shots.

Then the mainmast crashed against the cliff level with our ledge. The topsail yard scraped along our rock.

I knew in a flash what to do.

I stood up, half-carried, half-led Linn, and swung myself on to the yard by some trailing buntlines and sheets.

That mainmast must go at any moment; it also must fall clear the only way Wegger could escape in the motor launch, namely, on the weather side.

The mast sheared, the ship shattered, and we toppled side-ways all in one movement. The mast broke in two places, one at deck level and the other at the topmast cap-stay, just above our heads. The main section struck the rock first with a bone-shattering jar and then rebounded seawards in a slow arc from the drag of its retaining tackle.

We hit the water. I heard the crackle of an engine.

The mast had fallen almost on top of Wegger.

He wrenched the tiller over but before the rudder could bite he was amongst the ropes and fallen rigging. And us.

223

I shot to my feet, balancing myself on the plunging yard like a circus act, while I hauled Linn up beside me.

Within half a dozen metres the motor-launch had tangled with some shrouds and backstays. Linn and I raced along the intervening space like trapeze artists. We toppled headlong into the boat.

My first thought was to remember how Wegger had gunned down the survivors on deck as they made for the launch.

I pulled myself off the bottom-boards. 'Wegger . . .!'

He was trying to back clear of the wreckage.

'She's fast for'ard!' he rapped out. 'Quick, man! Free her! The screw mustn't foul!'

I knew as well as he what would happen if it did. I un-hitched myself from Linn and darted forward. The bow was enmeshed in some of the main deck life-nets and part of the maintop shrouds. I grabbed some floating wreckage and prised it free.

'Hard astern!' I yelled at Wegger.

Wegger gunned the engine, went astern for a few moments, and then skilfully manoeuvred the launch to clear the wreck.

Suddenly Linn called, 'Stop! There's a man swimming – right here! A little to your right . . .'

There was only one person that huge frame could have been – Ullmann. He was swimming strongly towards us.

One moment he was there, the next his face shot out of the water as he screamed in agony.

I saw the great black fin dart between the launch and the swimmer like a running torpedo.

Killer whale.

Then Ullmann was gone.

Four other black fins raced past us to the pounding wreck.

'Wegger,' I shouted, clawing my way aft, 'make for the shore! They'll come for the boat once they've finished off the men in the water!'

He didn't seem to follow me.

'You're heading out to sea, man! Take her in – port, port, port!'

He jammed the tiller over so hard that I thought we were lost as the fragile craft rose high on the next roller and plunged. From the wave's crest I had a glimpse of iron-bound black cliffs.

Ship Rock is about 100 metres from the shore but it seemed only seconds before we were amongst the boiling water of the reefs which run out from the mainland cliffs, dissected and serrated by a million storms.

The launch struck, slewed, stuck.

There was only one thing for it. I jumped over the bow into the perishingly cold sea.

I went up to my armpits. I felt my boots on the ragged out-crops. I put a shoulder under the bow, trying to heave the boat to safety. But she slewed further, canted, then went almost clean over with a grinding, rending noise as her bottom was ripped out. My grip on the bow was torn loose but I hung on to a painter which I had looped round my wrist. I stumbled, fell, stumbled landward – to safety.

The next wave carried the launch on and deposited it on the reef. High, if not dry.

'Linn!'

She half-fell over the side to me. Together, with my arm supporting her, we lurched higher on to the rocks, out of reach of the waves.

In a moment or two Wegger threw himself down alongside us.

For five, maybe ten, minutes, we all lay there gasping, panting, gagging seawater. Fine spray spurted over us at every roller.

The numbness of my feet and fingers matched the numbness of my mind. It was the realization that I might allow myself to slip into unconsciousness that made me pull myself into a sitting position. First, I dragged off my waterlogged boots. Then I started massaging my fingers and slapping my arms.

The initial thing I became conscious of was the absence of wind. For days the gale had tormented me; now its force was broken by the cliff at the foot of which we lay. There was hardly any light beyond a curious grey undertone to everything. We had finished up in a kind of rocky gully, not big enough to be styled a cove. There was a sheltering arm between us and the sea. The motor-launch lay on the seaward side.

'Linn! Wake up!'

She was lying on her side, coughing and shaking.

I crawled to her, tugged off her boots and started to mas-

H

sage the circulation back into her feet.

She sat up, tried to smile, but a spasm of cold rocked her. Then she managed to say, 'We made it, darling.'

'Yes,' I answered. 'We made it. Just.'

'Where are we?'

I had taken Prince Edward so for granted from the moment I had sighted Ship Rock that I found it hard to realize she did not know.

'You don't know? Prince Edward Island.'

She gave a gasp of surprise and glanced at Wegger, who had not opened his eyes.

The words acted on him like a shot of adrenalin. He sat up and shook himself like a dog. His clothes were soaking and his face was stained with salt and fatigue. But he vibrated at the sound of the name.

'Ship Rock – that's what she struck, wasn't it, Shotton?'

'Yes. We're ashore almost at the northernmost point of the island. I'd guess Vaalkop is right at the back of us now.'

Wegger turned the name over on to his tongue, almost affectionately. 'Vaalkop! I know every inch of it.'

'What is Vaalkop?' asked Linn.

'It's an extinct volcano. These cliffs are part of its lava which once flowed into the sea. Ship Rock is the submerged heart of the crater.'

Wegger sprang up.

'Shotton! The launch! We've got to get it higher out of reach of the waves!'

I ignored him and continued massaging Linn's feet. 'That boat will never float again – didn't you hear the bottom go?'

He pulled out his Luger and held it on me. 'Shotton! You'll do as I say!'

'Forget that bloody gun!' I snapped. 'The boat's holed – don't you understand?'

'We'll fix her, we'll patch her, you and me, Shotton. We'll make it yet.'

I reached for my boots. 'We've made it, Wegger. We're ashore on Prince Edward Island – your destination. At the cost of how many lives?'

Linn moved and I noticed the tell-tale sag of the transmitter inside her wet parka. I put my hand on her knee to keep her still. I looked hard at her, trying to pass on my warning.

'Rest a bit, Linn. You've been through quite something. Get your breath back – do you understand?'

Then she did, and sank down again.

Wegger stood over us like a grey ghost in the half-light. His words competed against the roar of the breakers.

'We *will* fix the launch, do you hear? Then we'll lift the gold – some of it, at any rate. We'll still take it to Mauritius. It'll buy a ship, I'll return for the rest . . .'

'Wegger,' I replied, trying not to provoke him, 'we're roughly three thousand and seven hundred kilometres from Mauritius. To begin with, where will the fuel for the motor-launch come from? That distance in an open launch!'

'Don't try and thwart me, Shotton,' he blazed back. 'It's been done before. In the old days men used to come down here in small boats from Mauritius to hunt seal. It's an easy ride once you're clear of the Westerlies. We don't need fuel – she's got a sail and a mast. She isn't an open boat either – she's decked in for'ard and astern. She'll make it, I say.'

Linn put her icy hand on mine. Perhaps, like me, she was thinking of her good-luck coin in the step of the mast. Sailing to Mauritius after our escape from Ship Rock would certainly be over-stretching our luck.

'How do you intend to repair the launch with its bottom stove in without tools, a fire, a proper slip or anything else?' asked.

'Shut up!' he retorted. 'Shut up! We'll make a plan! You *will*, Shotton! Now get down to the boat!'

We dodged from behind the shelter of the cliff. The wind was indeed less. The launch was half-awash among the rocks. One look at it convinced me that we could never repair it at Prince Edward. It had a gaping hole about two metres long in the bottom. Two planks were completely stove in.

Wegger's plan seemed to lend him an energy which my exhausted muscles did not possess. He did most of the work in hauling up the dead boat clear of the waves and making it secure.

Afterwards we scrambled back to Linn across the razor-edged rocks. She was standing against the cliff out of reach

227

of the spray, stamping her feet and banging her arms to keep
her circulation going. Her face was pinched and blue.

I noted immediately that the transmitter's tell-tale bulge
was missing from her parka.

I was not to know then what the fateful consequences of
her action were to be.

'Wegger,' I said. 'We've got to get ourselves warm. We won't
see the day out otherwise.'

Although his teeth were chattering also, he seemed in high
spirits. He was swinging his head this way and that, like a
dog sniffing home after a long spell in kennels.

I found a sodden box of matches in a pocket.

'Maybe we'll get a little sun later,' he said. 'The wind's on
its way out.'

'Difficult to say – we're sheltered here,' I replied cautiously
but I felt nevertheless that his forecast was right.

We had come ashore on the tip of the flat western coastal
plain, at the foot of the extinct volcano appropriately named
Vaalkop (Greyhead). The island's western shore was guarded
by a row of stupendous and precipitous sea-cliffs, backed
inland by a kingly ridge called the Great Western Escarpment.
The wind which had been deflected off Vaalkop's sinister
pallid slopes had caught *Botany Bay* aback and brought about
her final destruction. I had often seen this coast, with its iron-
bound cliffs and black and cinnamon-tipped volcano cones
from the sea. I had never thought to know them more closely.

'As soon as it's proper light we'll get moving,' said Wegger.

My soggy mind missed the significance of his remark at
the time. I presumed the move would be further from the
gully to higher, safer ground.

'I'll try and get these matches dry,' I said to Linn. 'There's
a way of doing it, when there's no sun.'

I went to her and stroked the matches individually through
her hair. It was wet at the ends but drier towards the roots.
The novelty of the operation took her mind off herself. As I
went on, she looked deep into my eyes. I wanted to kiss away
the grim marks round them, get rid of the sootiness which
had accumulated on her face from the constant tending of
the fire aboard *Botany Bay*.

'I never thought my hair would be used for fire,' she remarked.

'This is only stage one,' I told her. 'The second is to find something to strike them on.'

When I had a dozen or so dry I said to Wegger, 'I'm going to try the launch for something to burn.'

'Don't touch the planks,' he warned. 'I'm coming too.'

We returned to the wreck. I found some half-dry cotton waste in the decked-in bow section. I also discovered a tin of instant coffee. Most of its contents had spilled – the lid was missing – but the glutinous mess was still good enough to provide something warm and stimulating. There was also a packet of biscuits, mashed to dough-like pulp.

Then I tapped a little fuel out of the tank, wetting the cotton waste with it. I shorted the battery and got a feeble spark. When I held a match to it, it ignited, and I set the cotton waste smouldering.

Back where Linn was waiting, I found fresh water filtering down the cliff. I blew up the cotton waste and in the end we each had some pulpy biscuit and a mouthful of lukewarm coffee. But coffee it was.

I was still drinking from the tin when Linn exclaimed, pointing seawards, 'John! There's a man out there!'

I missed him at first because my attention was on the black fins of the killer whales racing like a U-boat pack through the floating masts, spars and timbers of the wreck.

'There – up on Ship Rock!' Linn said.

It was lighter over the sea than below our cliffs. Then I spotted the figure high up – Heaven knows how he had got there – clinging to the face of the massive pillar.

'God help him, Linn – we can't.'

'John – we can't leave him!'

'It will be a mercy if he drops off soon,' I replied slowly. 'He's only prolonging his own agony. He'll never last, up there.'

She turned away in silent grief and hid her face in her hood.

CHAPTER TWENTY-THREE

The growing light – it was after six o'clock – revealed a grim, savage scene both out to sea and on land.

Vaalkop's 200-metre crater was out of sight immediately behind us, but nearby another splendid crater-topped pair of cones known as Moeder-en-Kind (Mother-and-Child) was visible. Between Vaalkop and this group was a sloping valley like the centre section of a gigantic saddle. Mist swirled about the double cones. This mist was the only soft thing about Prince Edward.

There are about ten other major craters on the island, which is only nine kilometres long and seven broad. I had often viewed these old volcanoes through binoculars from a safe distance out to sea. They rose in succession to the splendid 670-metre summit called Van Zinderen Bakker Peak in the middle of the island. The aggregation of these great red crater cones, the undertaker's black of the lava flows, the precipitous sea-cliffs, the princely escarpment and the coastal plain in the north and east with its emerald-green coves of weather-defying plants, all make Prince Edward's landscape as strange as a new planet. As I shifted to get a better view of the high scarp which backed Mother-and-Child towards the island's central dominating peak, an eddy brought to my nostrils the unique smell of Prince Edward – a lava-born odour, harsh, ammoniacal, raw and primitive.

'Get moving!' It was Wegger. He gestured impatiently up a slope between the rocks.

'Which way?' I asked.

'There's only one way,' he retorted. 'I should know. I used it for months looking for a ship to rescue me.'

'What do you mean, Wegger?'

'The cave, of course. We go along the coast between the sea and the cliffs. There!' He pointed eastwards.

'The cave's on the other side of the island!' I exclaimed. 'We're all done in. We're in no shape to walk there at the moment!'

I didn't like the way he answered. 'It's eight kilometres and a bit. I know every inch. That's the way we're going – now.'

'We'll never make it!'

'Get this clear, Shotton,' he said with menacing deliberation. 'You are still useful to me. I need you to help me load the gold. I need you to help me sail me to Mauritius.' He addressed Linn in the same hectoring tone. 'You're still useful too, in a small way. You can make food, help keep us going. But I warn you, don't try shamming or coming any feminine weaknesses over me. It won't work. Don't either of you try escaping either. There's nowhere to run to. I should know – God, I should know!'

The forces driving him clipped his words tight with tension.

'Don't think you can escape to Marion – you can't. The channel's a death-trap. Marion's twenty-two kilometres away – you may get a sight of it, if the sky clears. Most likely you won't. I sighted it only half a dozen times in all the months I was marooned here.'

'Wegger,' I said, 'we're lucky, damned lucky, to be alive at all at this moment. The best we can hope for is to survive. Forget that dream of yours about gold in the cave. There isn't any there. Jacobsen said so, and he must have known. The British lifted it years ago – it's in the vaults of the Federal Reserve Bank in America . . .'

He strode over and struck me across the face with the back of his talon-like hand. I grabbed it but he tore free and had the pistol on me with the other. I never saw it move, he was so quick.

'If the gold's gone, you're no use to me anyway,' he replied roughly. 'Neither you nor the girl. You both know too much. The trip to the cave will take us five, maybe six hours. At the end of it, depending on whether the gold is there or not, you'll know whether you're going on living. Now – march!'

'Come, Linn,' I said.

I helped her over the serrated teeth of the rocks. Slowly we climbed out to the cliff-top. Wegger followed, ordering us this way and that, until we had skirted Vaalkop's wedge-shaped crater high above us and were on a scarp about 50 metres high which followed the coastline for the next two kilometres. At that point it seemed to run dead against the seaward edge of the base on which stood the great central block of craters.

It was a wild scene. The valley between Vaalkop and Mother-and-Child, viewed from close-up as we were, was a series of deep gullies radiating inland and then mounting in a succession of transverse lava ridges to the top of the twin summits. The banded platforms between the lava blocks appeared filled with a cement-like covering of old lava ash. There did not seem to be an inch of level ground anywhere which was not cluttered with conelets, balls or blocks of broken lava. Higher still, where the surface rose towards the main central scarp, the plate-like layers were covered with balls of mosses and here and there patches of rough tussocky grass which looked like a porcupine's quills.

Where we were standing the surface was a collection of rounded chunks of black lava interspersed with irregular lumps which looked like pats of cow-dung, big spheroidal 'bombs' deeply embedded, and curiously-shaped pieces shaped like the fangs of an extinct sabre-toothed tiger. A light scattering of snow was melting between them, making our onward path slippery and dangerous.

Wegger came up to us. 'I'll lead.' He cast about the grim, lunar-like surface like a hound looking for a scent and then headed diagonally across the small platform on which we stood. His sea-boots slipped on the uneven ground; both Linn and I were wearing thermal boots, which were warmer, but softer. I wondered how long they would last over that terrain.

I took a last glance at Ship Rock. The survivor was still there. Linn wouldn't look.

When Wegger was out of earshot, Linn asked, 'Is that true about Marion, John?'

'Yes. I've heard of survivors wrecked on Prince Edward who had boats but waited a year for a day favourable enough to attempt the crossing.'

'Only twenty-two kilometres to safety!'

'Linn – it was the toughest luck to be blown ashore at Prince Edward. A slight shift of the gale and it would have been Marion. Then all this nightmare wouldn't have happened. If only I'd had an idea of *Botany Bay*'s position!'

'You couldn't have known, John. I only hope the transmitter is still working.'

'It's safe?'

'Right inside here.' She smiled and tapped the region of her left breast.

I tried to return the smile but it was a poor attempt. 'I fear for us when he finds the cave empty, my darling.'

'He's mad, isn't he?'

'Mad, mad, mad. Also, he's got a grenade and a gun.'

'Here!' shouted Wegger. 'Stop dragging your feet! Hurry! I've located my old path!'

We headed up the ridge, slowing down and slipping as we negotiated what looked like gigantic fossilized roots stretching from the summit of the hillock where Wegger waited. In fact they were lava tubes spreading down the loose slope.

When we joined Wegger we saw ahead a scene in strange contrast to the unending black lava. As far as the eye could see there was a mosaic of swamp, herb-field and formations of tussocky grassland between the scarp and the sea. It overlay, and was pierced by, outcrops of black and maroon-red lava. The astonishing greenness of some of the patches, mixed with darker browns and russets, gave the vista a colour as unreal as Wegger's own dream of gold.

It wasn't a dream when we reached it. It was a nightmare. Wegger led. I didn't realize we were into a swamp until I saw the crust of ice on either side of the narrow path Wegger was scouting. Ice-needles, squeezed out of the ground by freezing and topped with tiny pebbles, made the path resemble a fakir's bed. Our boots crunched and squelched. Wegger quickly forged ahead. We lost his path. In a miry place I selected what appeared to be a firm patch of peat. In a moment I was up to the waist in icy water.

It took twenty minutes for me to fight my way clear of the trap.

Twice more in the next two hours I went deep into unsuspected pits, once up to the armpits. Linn took four falls. Once she fell as she tried jumping from a slime-covered block of red lava projecting from the marsh.

It took two and a half hours for us to negotiate the hideous Slough of Despond.

Wegger remained well ahead. Eventually he waited for us to catch up where the nauseous herb-field ended and the onward route, barely 20 metres wide, led between a cliff-face and the sea.

233

I was half-supporting Linn. We were splashed with icy mud and soaking wet. Wegger himself looked little better.

'Wegger!' I gasped. 'Stop this nonsense! We can't go on Linn's finished . . .'

He laughed threateningly. 'If you leave her she'll die. I endured this sort of thing for months. You're only getting a taste. Get on! The going's hard underfoot now.'

'How far is the cave?' asked Linn.

'Three, maybe three and a half kilometres.'

When, four hours later, we reached the two great yellow bastions named the Golden Gate which top the cliff below which the great cave lies, I was a man walking in my sleep, a sleep of utter exhaustion. I supported Linn round the shoulders. For hours we had edged along sea-cliffs, rousing birds by the thousand; we had ploughed waist-deep through disgusting wallows where elephant seals had mated; we had passed through an Alice-in-Wonderland world on the island's north-eastern side – a green, marshy flat on which perched hundreds of wandering albatrosses, each on its own small pillar of solid lava. This weird scene was the stuff of hallucinations.

During our march we had watched the sky grow progressively clearer and the cones of peak after peak of extinct volcanoes and blow-holes emerge until they seemed to fill the whole horizon. Finally it was the sight of a familiar one which made me realize where exactly we were. It was distinguished by a great bare welt down one side like a half-healed knife-thrust. I recognized it as McAll Kop, one of the landmarks above Cave Bay from the sea.

Wegger stood waiting for us again.

'Down here!' He indicated a slope running down to the sea.

We half-staggered, half-fell down the path.

Then the great cave opened in front of us.

I got out of Wegger's way behind a hummock of stone at the cave's entrance and eased Linn down on a clump of tussock grass. Her eyes were half-closed and her mud-splashed face a deathly white. My own knees felt as if they couldn't carry me one step further. I lowered myself down next to her.

The cave entrance was about four metres high and about
the same across. Rough tussocky grass draped itself from
niches and ledges. There were a couple of elephant seals
on the rounded pebble beach near the water's edge. They paid
no attention to us. A group of penguins started inquisitively
towards us. There were heaps of driftwood everywhere.

I shut my eyes. I was jerked awake by Wegger's boot
against my ribs.

'Matches! Where are those matches of yours?'

I'd stashed them away in my parka hood along with the
rike, which had dried.

'Get up!' Wegger went on. There was about him that
savage intensity I'd noticed when I first ran into him on Cape
own's docks. That, and something more.

He eyed me as I hauled myself to my feet.

'I'm going to show you what ten million dollars' worth of
old looks like,' he said. 'We need some light.'

Using dry grass and driftwood we started a fire. One of the
ephant seals started roaring when it smelt smoke.

I went to Linn to help her to the blaze.

'Keep with me, John darling,' she whispered. 'I've got an
wful premonition that something's about to happen to me.'

At the time, I put it down to her exhausted state.

Together we warmed ourselves at the fire. I wouldn't have
xchanged those ten minutes of warmth for all Wegger's
ream-gold.

Wegger was restless and impatient, as if his inner forces
ere racing at dynamo speed. He stayed at the fire only for
out five minutes before going off to search around the beach.
e came back with a length of driftwood about a metre long.

'That's long enough for a torch,' he snapped. 'Shotton, bank
that fire. We're going into the cave.'

I tried to play for time, even at that final moment, hoping
find something to beat him.

'Wegger, the gold's been there for forty years. A few hours
on't make any difference. Let's get ourselves fit first . . .'

The ugly frost-smoke expression leapt into his eyes. He
mmed the piece of wood into the fire. 'Don't try and stop
e, I warn you, Shotton. We'll load the gold right here on the
ach when we've fixed the boat – it's the best landing-spot

235

on the island. I *know*!'

He plucked his makeshift torch from the flames.

'In!' he ordered. 'Into the cave! Keep ahead of me!'

He had the Luger covering us; the grenade was at his bel[...]

We entered the great cave. Daylight and the torch com[...] bined were strong enough to illuminate the first few metre[...] After that came darkness. The floor soon became ankl[...] deep in water. There were a couple of big overturned re[...] rusted sealers' pots lying forlornly amongst a litter of elepha[...] seal bones, oily stinking feathered messes, and a number [...] modern beer cans. The place smelt bad.

'The water comes from a spring on the other side,' sa[...] Wegger. 'It was my fresh water supply.'

I started to slow down, trying to think up further delayin[...] tactics, but Wegger was alert.

'Get on – straight ahead.'

Linn and I sloshed onwards. It was bitterly cold, the col[...] ness of a morgue.

The torch Wegger was holding threw dim shadows on th[...] smooth basalt roof. The pool ended. It became impossible [...] see ahead.

I stopped. 'Wegger,' I said, 'it's no use having the tor[...] behind us. If we don't have it here in the lead someone[...] going to trip and break a leg.'

I hoped he would come forward and hand me the torc[...] My nerves stretched while I waited. One swipe across his ey[...] with that blazing faggot and he wouldn't be able to see h[...] Luger or anything else . . .

He did start forward, and then changed his mind.

'Here, you,' he spoke to Linn. 'Come and get it. And do[...] block my line of fire to your man.'

She did as he said and passed me the torch.

We went deeper.

Deeper.

Deeper and further, further and deeper. I lost track of di[...] tance.

Then the cave began to narrow like a huge funnel. The[...] seemed to be cinders or lava ash underfoot but it was to[...] dark to tell. Now the ceiling heightened and the tunnel curve[...] and ended in a wall of rock.

I was in the lead with the torch held high.

A face – a woman's exquisite face – shone out of the murky shadows.

It was framed in a white shroud of ice.

There was no mistaking who it was. I had seen her before. In the photograph in Captain Prestrud's safe. In that split second of recognition I realized that the photograph had not been taken through glass but through ice. Here, in the great cave on Prince Edward.

Linn grabbed my arm. 'John! It's her! The woman in the photograph . . .!'

I thrust the torch higher still to see better. The smoky light showed the body propped up against the wall, coffined in a casing of ice. Cut into the rock over her head was a single word, 'Dina'.

'Dina!' I breathed. 'Dina! That's who it was! Dina's Island . . .!'

Wegger came level with us, stumbled, then snatched the burning wood out of my hand and went to the dead woman.

I scarcely recognized his voice. 'Dina!' he said brokenly. 'Dina! It's been a long, long time . . .'

I missed my moment. If I had jumped him then I would have saved Linn. As it was, both of us were so stunned at the sight of the dead woman that we simply went forward and stood with Wegger looking at her. It was so silent deep in the bowels of the dead volcano that I imagined I could hear our hearts beating.

The flaring wood showed the body dressed in a sealskin jerkin with a high mandarin collar. She had on a short sealskin skirt and knee-high boots which looked as if they had come out of the 18th century. The tops of the boots were worked with a flower motif tooled into the leather.

'Who is she?' Linn managed to ask. 'She's perfectly lovely.'

Wegger's voice seemed to have deserted him. He waved the torch at the name on the wall. Then he said, 'Dina. That's all I know. Dina. She might be anyone. Perhaps a buccaneer's girl. A shipwreck survivor – anyone. I used to come here and talk to her. She was my only friend.'

Not friend, Wegger. Lover. You were in love with a dead woman. You still are.

He went on, catching his breath. 'I never said goodbye, when the cruiser's boat came. I was afraid they wouldn't wait . . .'

He pushed the torch forward to bring the light nearer her face.

The grey thing which emerged from the shadows on the floor was, I thought for a split second, Dina's coffin. But a coffin doesn't have a grey rusted warhead and a lean battery-compartment attached. It was a torpedo.

This was the German torpedo Prestrud and his fellow-skippers had smuggled from under the Nazi raider's nose.

The raider's main target was next to it, stacked in a little pyramid.

Gold. Ten million dollars in gold.

There were hundreds of small ingots of it, shaped like chocolate bars. Each bar had a small oval stamped in the metal with the words 'Credit Danzig' and a group of four numerals.

'By all that's holy!' I burst out.

Wegger rounded on me, as if the shock of seeing the gold had jerked him back from Dina to hard reality.

'So I was lying, was I, Shotton? Imagining it all? I was a madman whose mind had become unstuck from being marooned alone for so long? An insane killer? I'm mad, am I?'

'It can't be real – it can't!' Linn exclaimed.

'It's real, all right,' retorted Wegger. 'You fool, Shotton, you stupid fool! You could have had a share if you'd listened!'

'At the price of all those lives? Never!' I replied. 'I'm going to see you pay for all those lives, Wegger!'

'You'll see to it, will you, you blabbermouth!' he sneered. 'Go ahead then, go ahead!'

Now was the moment to cut the ground from under his feet.

'It's time you knew the truth, Wegger,' I said. 'You haven't a hope. You won't get away with that gold. You think you've reached Prince Edward without anyone knowing. You haven't. Every movement of yours since you turned the *Quest* adrift has been monitored. The GARP watchers know exactly where we are at this very minute. They also know exactly where the *Quest* is.'

He went into a half-crouch, as if an electric shock had hit him.

'You're bluffing, Shotton! There's no way that could be true.'

'Smit set the buoy's transmitter operating when we left the *Quest*,' I went on. 'Four times a day, every time the satellite passes overhead, the GARP watchers can read off her position to the nearest half-kilometre. They will have homed a long-distance rescue plane on her days ago, and ships as well . . .'

Wegger's voice was deadly. 'All right. Let them rescue the *Quest*. No one aboard knows where we went in *Botany Bay*. All you say about GARP knowing where we are now is so much bull. You're bluffing. It can't be done.'

'It can, and was,' I answered. 'Tell him, Linn.'

'I brought the balloon's transmitter from the *Quest* with me,' Linn said. 'It's a tin thing. Smit set it operating. I've carried it around all the time. It's here, inside my clothes, now . . .'

I saw the muscles of his face jerk tight and his eyes go killer-blank.

He swung the Luger and shot Linn through the heart.

CHAPTER TWENTY-FOUR

Linn spun, reeled, and pitched headlong across the body of the dead woman.

It could have been the ear-splitting concussion of the shot in the confined space which helped crack the ice across Dina's face, or it could have been solely the force of Linn's fall. Whichever it was, the ice splintered across. The mouth pulled open. It gaped teeth. In a split second the frozen half-smile became a cadaver's rictus, a hideous death-grin.

Wegger gave a cry which was more animal than human.

I don't recall clearly either the shot or the cry.

The kill-lust exploded in my brain.

I had to kill Wegger with my own hands.

I drove at him.

I was on him when the second shot went off under my right armpit. I felt the hot sear of cordite. The bullet whanged off a wall. No bullet would have stopped me then.

My first blow into his solar plexus carried all the agony of Linn behind it. I summoned up from my fatigued muscles some reserve I could not guess at.

Wegger's head came forward as the breath went out of him. I couldn't get my right fist clear in time to follow up. I chopped him across the neck with my left.

I heard but did not see the gun go flying.

Wegger lurched past, staggered, and then swung to face me. His breath whistled in his throat. He was very quick, very game, very tough. That first blow must really have hurt him.

He ran in low, baulking me from getting a clean blow to his head. His shoulder took me like a Rugby tackle. At the same time he kneed me in the groin.

I found myself flat on my back, writhing in agony.

He hadn't enough breath left to finish me off. He stood for a moment, trying to suck air. When he came a moment later I was ready for him. Sea-boots first, he tried to kick my head. I grabbed his boot, concentrated all my strength, and up-ended him.

I came back on my feet. My vision was misted with pain and the smoky light.

Wegger's hands were plucking at the strings of his parka, trying to get at the grenade.

I threw myself on him, reaching for his throat. The lacing where his hood joined the body of his weatherproof jacket saved him. It kept my choking fingers from closing his windpipe. Somehow he managed to find power enough to double his knees up and kick me clear. Gravity seemed to triple my weight. I came down with a sickening thump.

Again his left hand, his fighting hand, went to his waist where the grenade was. It came out too quickly to have untied the bomb, although my sense of time was haywire.

It held the knife with the killer whale handle.

He hurled himself at me.

I mule-kicked him in the chest with my boots as he dived on me but I hadn't the power left to make the kick do what it should have done. It threw him off line only. Then we were both on the ground on all fours, facing one another like animals.

Wegger came back on his feet as agilely as a cat, towering

240

and circling, looking for the *coup de grâce*. He had all the advantages.

My boot knocked against something hard behind me. In a flash I realized what it was. I reached back, snatched up one of the gold ingots, locked it between both hands and jerked upright as Wegger plunged and struck at my throat with the knife.

The bar met his jaw and face in a kind of crude Liverpool Kiss. I heard the crunch of bone and teeth; simultaneously I felt a red-hot line of pain as the knife skidded across my neck and shoulder.

Wegger somersaulted back. I was on top of him as the knife reached out again for me, striking madly with the gold bar, insanely, out of control with the lust to kill, again and again until his knife-hand fell back tiredly and my blows seemed to be striking a skull filled with sawdust instead of bone.

I got up.

There was no sound, no movement, from Wegger. But the rock chamber was filled with my retching gasps, my whooping for breath. The singeing white-hot pain near my ear was nothing to the pain in my mind.

'Linn! Linn darling!'

There was no reply. She lay doubled over, arms outflung over the grinning corpse.

I have no clear recollection of my movements after that. All I knew was that I had one thought – to get her out! Get her out of this death-house! Get her to warmth! Get her to help!

And then, the over-riding thought, like the punch of the heavy bullet itself – she's dead, she's dead, she's beyond help!

The light of day on my eyes at the entrance to the tunnel brought me to my senses. I found myself carrying Linn over my right shoulder. The torch was in my left hand. Her arms were hanging and she was limp. I had no memory of testing to see whether she was breathing. My mind was as dark as the rock passage I had just left behind.

Get her to the fire! Get her warm! See where the bullet went in . . .

The fire was barely smouldering. I put Linn down on the rounded pebbles of the beach. I cast about, grabbing anything that looked dry enough to burn. The penguins near the water's edge started to squawk. Four elephant seals remained as dormant as giant hibernating slugs.

I returned with an armful of wood, threw it on the fire. The sight of Linn's face drove me. It was a hideous putty-blue. There was a trace of pink spume at the corner of her mouth. Her eyes were half-open, unseeing.

I couldn't spot any blood. But there wouldn't be yet, through all her thick clothing. The only sign of violence was a small tear from the Luger bullet above her left breast.

I darted to the cliffside and plucked and tore handfuls of the rough tussocky grass for a couch. I arranged it, then laid her gently on it. The fire began picking up.

I plucked at the strings of her parka to examine the wound. My fingers were so stiff and shaking that I could not untie them. I stopped, looking for something to cut with. Like an evil dream the thought came to me; I had no knife, nothing. Wegger had allowed us nothing.

Then I saw his own knife at my waistband. I had no recollection at all of putting it there.

The sight of it pulled me together. There was no point in senselessly slashing her clothing. If she were alive, she would need every scrap of protection she could get.

I took a big grip on myself and set my fingers to untying the parka. Underneath, her jersey was water-damp but unstained by blood. There was only that hideous marker on the left breast. At the sight of it, my hands seemed to lose co-ordination. I pulled at her sweater and my hand struck something hard, metallic. I managed to get her sweater up a little further.

Then I saw the tiny transmitter lodged in the strap of her brassiere. It had a ragged rent in its inner corner. Two long blue-red bullet welts radiated from it across and up her chest.

One, about six inches long, travelled vertically in the direction of her shoulder-blade.

The second, an ugly blue-black score, had laid open the flesh across her breastbone and then disappeared in an angry ragged hole on her right side. Blood was pouring from both wounds.

I leant down with racing pulses, plucked away the transmitter, and put my ear against her heart.

She was alive!

Then I realized with a stab or unbelievable relief what had happened: Wegger's heavy 9mm Parabellum slug had smashed into the transmitter and splintered. One ragged fragment had shot upwards, making the long superficial wound to her shoulder-blade; the other had ricocheted sideways into her right side, entering her chest against the swell of her breast. That was the dangerous wound.

For the first time I became aware of my own wound when I felt blood dripping from the vicinity of my ear and saw it splashing against her chest. I felt my neck cautiously. The tip of Wegger's knife had torn the lobe of my right ear and then travelled back as far as my hairline. It did not seem more than a flesh wound although it was throbbing painfully. I tried to staunch the blood with my handkerchief.

I sat like that on my haunches, looking into Linn's pain-filled face. Out of reaction, the muscles of my legs and arms started to kick uncontrollably and I began to shake all over like a case of DTs. I crouched close to the fire to warm myself, getting Linn too as near the heat as I could. Cold meant death; the cold would get into her wound and kill her.

I knew I had somehow to stop the bleeding. The flesh wound was pumping freely but it was the other – which was showing also signs of heavy bruising – which I feared. I wondered whether, from the pink froth at her lips, the fragment of bullet had entered her right lung. I tested her breathing. There was not the wheezing there would have been from a lung wound. Then, to my relief, I found that the froth was coming from a gash where she had bitten her lip in agony as the bullet had hit her.

I had nothing with which to tend or bandage her wounds. The only thing I had was my woollen shirt, which was wet. Stripping myself of it, drying and tearing it for makeshift bandages; drying my other clothes one by one and replacing Linn's with them so that she was warm and dry; and getting her own things themselves dry was an operation as freezingly breath-catching as diving into the sea itself. When it was all done and she was as comfortable as I could make her, I took stock of my situation.

The afternoon was far gone. The cave's entrance, which faced east, was now almost in full shadow. The penguin colony

had been swelled by other individuals which had swum up
to the beach. They stood chattering and making tentative
sallies towards the fire. The elephant seals were still quiescent
The wind had dropped and I was surprised to see that there
were no more whitecaps out to sea. It had the makings of a
rare calm evening.

It didn't need a doctor to tell me Linn was a hospital case
The fragment of bullet would have to be removed from her
chest. That meant an operating theatre. The nearest hospital
was over 2000 kilometres away, on the Cape mainland.

Had the GARP network heard our signals? If it had, how
could I communicate further? Marion Island had powerful
radio weather transmitters but I had no boat to get there. Nor
had the weather station a boat. The channel is so dangerous
that all boats are banned.

I ruled out Marion Island.

I found Linn's smashed transmitter. If it had worked previously, it did so no longer. Its intricate circuitry had been
wrecked by the bullet.

The only method I could visualize of getting Linn out was
by helicopter. A helicopter-carrying destroyer would take five
days to reach Prince Edward from its Cape base. How – if
the authorities were immediately made aware of her plight
– would I keep Linn alive until then?

She had to have food. I had to have food.

Previous Prince Edward Island survivors – including Wegger
– had kept themselves going on elephant seals: their meat
for sustenance, their blubber for fuel, their hides for boots
and even to patch boats. They were the readiest source of
food in addition to birds, birds' eggs and the native vegetable
Kerguelen cabbage.

I eyed the group of elephant seals on the beach in front of
me and made up my mind immediately. I'd never killed an
elephant seal, but I knew how it was done. I hurried to the
sleeping group and picked up a large stone. It was over in a
moment. I was glad that the brute hadn't opened his saucer-
like limpid eyes before the stone crashed home on his protrud-
ing snout. I dragged the carcase back to the fire and set to
work with Wegger's knife, first slicing off the thick layer of
blubber and setting it aside for burning.

Then I realized that I had nothing to cook with.

There was the litter of broken pots and tins inside the cave entrance. Most of the stuff was so rusty as to be useless. The big sealers' pots were designed for whole carcasses and moreover had holes rusted through them. I earmarked a couple of beer-cans for blubber lamps. I sloshed over to the spring to wash them out and have a drink of water myself. My foot touched something else solid in the water. It was a 15cm shell-case, brass, unrusted. British? German? I picked it out of the water – it would make an ideal cooking-vessel. There was no time to puzzle how it came there. I hurried back to the fire.

'John! John!'

Linn's eyes were conscious but they were glazed with pain. Her voice was so faint that for a moment I wondered whether I'd imagined her call.

I dropped the shell-case and went down on my knees by her couch.

She tried to lift herself and fell back as the agony of the wound gripped her.

'John! Darling! It's dark – where am I? It's warm – my chest – '

I took her shoulders and held her gently so that she would not attempt to move again. I leaned down and put my lips to hers.

'Everything's fine, Linn, my darling. You're going to be all right. There's nothing more to worry about.'

Her shock returned with her consciousness.

'He – he shot me – my chest . . .'

I stroked her hair and noticed that she was warmer than I had anticipated. I feared it might be feverishness.

'You've got a bullet in you – only part of a bullet, my darling. You're still on Prince Edward. I'll get you out safely.'

Fear started into her shadowed eyes. 'Where are we, John? *Where on Prince Edward?* Where is *he*?'

'We're at the cave entrance, Linn. Forget Wegger. He won't worry us any more.'

There was a note of despair in her whispered question. 'John – please – I don't understand – the shot, the gold, Dina . . .'

I sat and told her as the sun disappeared but the long light remained over the sea and on the golden bastions over our heads.

When I had done, she said, 'Did the bullet finish the transmitter, John?'

'Yes, Linn. I'm afraid so. It's useless now. But it saved your life.'

'So nobody knows where we are?'

I had tried earlier to talk myself out of that one; now Linn's urgency placed the problem squarely in front of me.

'The GARP communications set-up has had days and nights to plot our position and follow our course. I'm sure that the search is on at this moment. They'll come – soon, Linn.'

'You won't let them take me without you, my love, will you?'

'Never, Linn.'

The flames crackled, the remaining elephant seals started shifting and grunting, and the penguins moved closer, standing their distance like well-dressed undertakers' assistants.

After a while she said, 'I'm dying, aren't I, John?'

Her question sent the cold fear sweeping across my heart. I tried to sound reassuring.

'No, Linn. The bullet was a soft-nosed one. It splintered. I don't think the fragment is deep. If it were in your lung you wouldn't be able to breathe properly or speak. A doctor with a probe would have it out in no time.'

She moved and then cried out in pain. It was her answer.

Later, she seemed to sleep after I had fed her the unappetizing mixture I'd brewed in the shell-case. I had some myself. It tasted oily and fishy. You get used to it, Wegger had said. I was still in my Prince Edward Island apprenticeship.

Night came, the half-dark of the Antarctic summer night.

I built a second fire just inside the cave entrance where it was dry and laid another bed in shelter for Linn as well as one for myself next to it. She did not fully wake but squirmed in agony when I carried her to it. I tried cushioning her head in my arms but she could not get comfortable, so I went and sat guard on my own heap of bed-grass.

I must have slept, for it was darker when I woke. It felt like half an hour but it was, in fact, nearly four hours. I went to the water's edge for more wood. It was a night as beautiful as Captain Prestrud's dream. The same pale opalescent blue was on the water and over the sea. Far out, a white iceberg seemed to hang like a star in space.

It was also fine enough to be able to see the all-night electric lights of Marion's weather station if I went up to higher ground.

I checked Lin. She was still asleep, breathing faster and more shallowly.

I hurried up the landslide pathway from our beach to the flat plateau above the cave. From its southern extremity I could detect a luminescence in the sky where I knew Marion must lie. But my direct view was hidden by a highland on the shore facing the channel. I dared not go further and leave Linn.

I hurried back to her.

She opened her eyes when I approached.

Her voice was so far gone that I had to bend right down to hear.

'John darling – our time together was so short, wasn't it?'

'It was a lifetime to me, my dearest.'

She shut her eyes and tried to smile, but the pain twisted her mouth. She drew in her breath sharply.

'I want you to promise me something, John.'

'Anything, Linn.'

'I want you to bury me in the Southern Ocean, here at Prince Edward. I want you to conduct the service.'

'No need to talk like that, my darling. You'll pull through, never fear.'

'I know I'm dying.'

In my heart I dreaded she was right. Her fever had been growing all the time. Her pulse was fluttering like a bird and her breathing was worse.

She took my hand. I was appalled at how hot it was.

'I'll love you always, John.'

Her eyes closed and cut short my reply. She didn't speak again.

I sat with her hand in mine, staring into the fire. After a while my thoughts switched from Linn to the grim chamber of death at our backs – and the gold. How, I asked myself, could the authorities have remained in ignorance of the hoard and have informed the three skippers that it was in safe-keeping in the vaults of the Federal Bank in the United States? I turned over every aspect, thinking back to try and find the

247

answer. I tried to recall everything Captain Prestrud and Jacobsen had said in my attempt to throw light on the mystery.

Then I sat upright, wide awake, remembering something in Captain Jacobsen's letter to me. The Allied Commission had informed the skippers that the gold had been in transit via the port of Bergen. I racked my brains for his exact words – 'this was obviously a mistake since we knew that it was Narvik!'

Bergen! That was the key to the mystery! Bergen is 1000 kilometres from Narvik. The Free Norwegian fleet had seized the gold in Narvik and had made off to the Antarctic with it. Later it had been hidden in the great cave. Wegger had said that the British cruiser's boat had never landed, and I had seen for myself that the gold hoard had remained undisturbed. The fact that the Nazis had sent a raider and a pocket battleship to Antarctica proved that the gold had come from Narvik, not Bergen.

Yet the Allied Commission had ten million dollars in Danzig gold still in its safe-keeping. The only possible solution was that there had been two shipments of Danzig gold of equal size, one consignment via Narvik and the other via Bergen.

I reasoned further that such confusion could be due to the destruction of records during the Nazi *Blitzkrieg* on Poland and to wartime conditions in general. And, after all, the Allied Commission could point to a gold hoard of similar value in its own possession. Theirs, I knew now, was the Bergen shipment; the Narvik shipment still lay in a pyramid behind me in the darkness, guarded by the bodies of Wegger and the enigmatic Dina.

I must have fallen asleep from mental as well as physical exhaustion after working it out, for I was jerked awake by a roaring noise. As I surfaced I thought the sea had risen and was thundering on the beach.

But it wasn't in the sea.

It was in the air.

It was a plane.

The rocks themselves seemed to shake as it passed over the cave at zero feet.

I jumped up and stumbled to the water's edge but I was too late to see anything beyond a big double tail disappearing behind McAll Kop as it travelled northwards.

I could have wept. The look-outs aboard the plane must have concluded that the cave was deserted. I cursed myself for having fallen asleep.

The fire – surely an alert crew would have spotted the fire even though it had burned low?

I sprinted back to it, gathering more wood on my way. I deliberately chose some which was wet in order to make smoke.

I threw armfuls on to the embers and blew it up. The time was a little past seven o'clock. The sun was already showing in the east over the horizon – it looked like becoming that rarest of things, a fine day on Prince Edward.

The smoke started to swirl skywards. I hastily checked Linn. Her drawn face was dreadful in the new light but her pulse was still going. I could scarcely bear to hear her gasping for breath.

To signal the plane and make myself visible as well I would have to get myself on the plateau above the cave. I could hear the sound of its engines in the direction we had made our nightmare march. I guessed it was casing the coastline for survivors.

My eye fell on the smashed transmitter lying near the fire. The ruse had worked! I found myself taking the plane's arrival almost for granted. *It had worked!*

I blessed the bashed little box, snatched up a burning faggot and an armful of wood, and sprinted for the plateau. The sky was empty; there was no engine sound any more.

I tried to tell myself that the great central highland and its craters was enough to shut it off. I revolved a full circle, searching. I had no eyes for the noble sight of the Golden Gate, its twin bastions of yellow strata soaring from their base of grey lava, or for the palette of colours – greys, blacks, greens, yellows, blues, opals – which the sun had drawn from the grim little island.

Now the smoke from my new fire was also rising in the still air.

Then the plane came in unexpectedly from the south, from the Marion Island side.

The great heavy Shackleton maritime reconnaissance aircraft skimmed the seaward bluffs and came towards me, manoeuvring to pass at mast-level between two nearby craters. Slung under the plane's belly was a sea-rescue lifeboat; the nose bristled with radio and radar antennae.

It came so low over me that the thunder of the four big propellers and the blast from the open exhausts beat like a drum on my chest. Simultaneously, a small parachute exploded in the slipstream and came spiralling into the tussocky grass which fronted the Golden Gate's bastions.

The plane dodged between the craters and disappeared.

I sprinted to the parachute package. The canister was bigger than I had at first thought. It was marked, in bold letters on four sides, 'Emergency survival package. Open here'

I tore it open. There were blankets, tins of soup and food, matches, a solid-fuel stove, and what looked like medical supplies.

There was also a small walkie-talkie. There was a tag attached to it which read. 'To operate . . .'

I didn't need to be told how. I got it going and clapped the receiver to my ear.

The voice, unnaturally loud, was chanting in the way radio operators have. 'Shackleton S for Skua, Shackleton S for Skua! Do you hear me? I repeat, do you hear me? Reply, reply . . .'

I had to steady my voice out of its first husky wobble.

'I hear you, S for Skua, I hear you.'

The operator's excited voice called out, presumably in the aircraft's cockpit, 'I got him, skipper! I got him!'

I heard the roar of the aircraft's engines relayed over the instrument and a chatter of talk. Then a different voice. It was formal, tentative. I realized why. He could have been talking to a hijacker.

'Captain, aircraft S for Skua speaking. Please identify yourself.'

'John Shotton, captain, cruise ship *Quest*.'

The voice said something aside and I heard the surge of other voices. Maybe the crew were all crowding round him.

The pilot's voice came back to me, relaxed, but filled with wonderment.

'Shotton! You must be indestructible, fellah!'

Then it hardened. 'Where are the hijackers?'

'Dead.'

There was a long whistle. 'All of them?'

'Yes.'

'The ringleader too?'

'I killed him myself.'

The pilot's voice sounded incredulous. 'How?'

'With my hands.'

The voice came back in rapid-fire. 'Listen, Shotton, they
wanted me to load up the media boys in this crate when I
took off but I wouldn't, because we're practically sitting up
to the ears in fuel. If only those pen-pushing sons of bitches
knew the story they're missing . . .'

'See here,' I interrupted. 'Forget the news story. I've got an
emergency here. Life or death.'

The flier's voice levelled off. 'I'm making a circuit of the
land. I'll be over you again shortly. Keep talking. What
emergency?'

'I have a woman with a bullet in her. Linn Prestrud. She's
dying. I've got to get her out. She's bad. A hospital case.'

There was silence. I broke it anxiously. 'Are you still with
me, S for Skua? I repeat, I have an emergency case . . .'

None of the pilot's earlier excitement was audible in his
reply. In its flatness I could detect the anxieties of that eight-
hour maximum range flight from the Cape over the wildest
ocean in the world, the skilled astro-navigation to pinpoint
Prince Edward, the superb achievement of having found us.

'I hear you,' he said. 'You've got to realize, Shotton, that I
can't land. I can't fly her out. There are medical supplies in
the canister we dropped. I'll drop you more. Everything I
have.'

The big machine lumbered into sight again. This time it
turned and started to circle over the sea in range of Cave
Bay. Dead despair closed over my heart. The Shackleton
might have been a ship in outer space for all the good it
could do Linn.

I said equally flatly, 'Medical supplies by themselves are no
good. It's skilled attention she needs. A doctor. And a hospital. Immediately. She'll be dead by this evening.'

The pilot must have heard the desperation in my voice.
'See here, Shotton. I've also got a doctor on board and he
can give you advice what to do. He's got his kit with him.
I'll parachute that to you. There's also a destroyer on her
way here from the Cape – I passed her five hundred kilometres

251

out. She'll be here in a few days. She's carrying a helicopter
Don't despair. They'll get her out.'

I nerved myself to repeat, 'I want you to understand. She'
dying.'

The pilot cut in, more formally still, 'Captain Shotton, yo
understand the logistics of the situation I'm faced with. I'n
flying on the limit of my fuel. I left the Cape in a storm and
a gale has been chasing my tail for 2300 kilometres. I'v
got to fly into that headwind all the way home. I might ever
have to ditch this crate before I reach base if I go o
circling and using fuel as I am. I appreciate your position
I'm handing you over to Doctor Lawson. We'll do everythin
to help, but you must understand there is a limit.'

'I understand.' My voice was stone dead.

A new voice came over the walkie-talkie. 'Doctor Lawso
speaking.'

'Doctor,' I said, trying to control my words. 'She's dying
She's got a bullet in her chest . . .'

'Not so fast, Captain Shotton. I must have details, if I an
to help.'

'The bullet split in two . . .' I pulled my thoughts togethe
and outlined how Linn was wounded.

When I had finished, he said, 'Hold on. I'll come back t
you.'

The radio operator came through in his place. 'Captai
Shotton? The doctor is consulting with the captain. Th
skipper asked me to tell you we rescued your ship.'

'The *Quest*?'

'Sure. This is our second flight to the ice in four days. Th
ground crews have nicknamed the Shack Antarctic Archie
That cruise ship was quite a proposition. A destroyer went t
tow her in after we'd located her. But the skipper – a youn
guy called Petersen – did a wonderful job. He'd rigged a kin
of sail and was keeping her away from the icebergs . . .'

'Petersen wasn't the skipper,' I said. 'I left McKinley i
command.'

'McKinley hit his bunk and a bottle, so they told us,' h
replied. Then he added admiringly: 'That was quite a brair
wave of yours about the transmitters, Captain.'

I couldn't go on listening. The thought of that shattere
transmitter which had deflected the bullet from Linn's hea

was too agonizing.

My voice was hoarse. 'Listen! For Pete's sake – tell the doctor to come back! What the devil does he have to consult the pilot about! It's me he has to consult . . .'

The pilot's voice, rattled and uncompromising, came on. 'Captain Shotton, Doctor Lawson has been arguing with me. He says he intends to make a parachute jump to try and save Miss Prestrud . . .'

'Parachute jump!' It came out in a sort of croak.

'Yes. In my opinion it's plain suicide. He'll kill himself on this terrain. But he's determined to try. He's getting into harness right now. I'm prepared to give him one chance – only one run, do you understand? No dummy approaches. One – for real. I can't spare the fuel. Where's the best place here?'

My mind couldn't absorb the news. I replied dazedly. 'Where I'm standing – it's pretty soft, right here in front of the Golden Gate.'

The pilot's voice remained distant, matter-of-fact. 'My fuel's so low I also intend to jettison my lifeboat. That will reduce wind drag on the way home. It's equipped with survival gear, engine, sails. Is it any use to you?'

My mind leapt ahead. If the doctor could help Linn, I could use the lifeboat with its special equipment to get her across the channel to Marion with its met. station, communications, sick-bay, warmth, food . . .

'Yes, I have a use for it,' I answered tightly. 'Drop it in the water near the mouth of the cave. It will drift ashore of its own accord.'

'Roger. I'm coming in.'

I watched the big machine straighten, aim for the cave. The words of the dropping drill came over the walkie-talkie.

'Turning on target – running in – doors open – distributor set – all switches on – camera on.' There was a moment's pause. Then: 'Lifeboat going – now, now, now.'

I didn't need to hear the finale: 'Lifeboat gone – in target area' because the lifeboat dropped from the machine's belly like a whale calving, its parachute billowed, and it landed spot-on 50 metres from the cave's entrance.

The machine swung round to the channel approach.

Now.

The walkie-talkie went silent.

I watched with my heart in my mouth. The plane headed out over the channel, turned, started its run-in. It was higher than before. Then it was over me. I didn't see the parachute burst from the door opposite me. The plane was gone, the parachute hung in the air.

The pilot's aim had been as sure the second time as it had the first. The doctor dropped cleanly in the grass between the two massive bastions as if he'd jumped off the top of one of them.

I raced across to him. Together we unclipped the harness as he got up. He held a small case of instruments. He was young, sunburned. He had the grip of a weight-lifter and the eyes of a saint.

He didn't waste words. 'Where is she?'

I led him down to the cave and took him to Linn.

She was unconscious, muttering from the fever. We drew up the thick sweater and removed my rough bandages, which were caked with blood. The entire side of her right breast was purple and swollen.

The doctor ran his probe along the path the bullet had taken, then felt the ragged place where it had entered her chest.

He took his eyes from the wound and fixed me.

I looked the question I dared not ask.

'I think she might make it,' he said.

Geoffrey Jenkins

Geoffrey Jenkins writes of adventure on land and at sea in some of the most exciting thrillers ever written. 'Geoffrey Jenkins has the touch that creates villains and heroes—and even icy heroines—with a few vivid words.' *Liverpool Post* 'A style which combines the best of Nevil Shute and Ian Fleming.' *Books and Bookmen*

A BRIDGE OF MAGPIES 85p
A CLEFT OF STARS 70p
THE RIVER OF DIAMONDS 85p
THE WATERING PLACE OF
   GOOD PEACE 75p
A TWIST OF SAND 75p
HUNTER-KILLER 85p

Fontana Paperbacks

Fontana Paperbacks

Fontana is a leading paperback publisher of fiction and non-fiction, with authors ranging from Alistair MacLean, Agatha Christie and Desmond Bagley to Solzhenitsyn and Pasternak, from Gerald Durrell and Joy Adamson to the famous Modern Masters series.

In addition to a wide-ranging collection of internationally popular writers of fiction, Fontana also has an outstanding reputation for history, natural history, military history, psychology, psychiatry, politics, economics, religion and the social sciences.

All Fontana books are available at your bookshop or newsagent; or can be ordered direct. Just fill in the form and list the titles you want.

FONTANA BOOKS, Cash Sales Department, G.P.O. Box 29, Douglas, Isle of Man, British Isles. Please send purchase price, plus 8p per book. Customers outside the U.K. send purchase price, plus 10p per book. Cheque, postal or money order. No currency.

NAME (Block letters)

ADDRESS
